J.D. MOYER

THE GUARDIAN

This is a **FLAME TREE PRESS** book

Text copyright © 2019 J.D. Moyer

FLAME TREE PRESS
6 Melbray Mews, London, SW6 3NS, UK
flametreepress.com

Distribution and warehouse:
Baker & Taylor Publisher Services (BTPS)
30 Amberwood Parkway, Ashland, OH 44805
btpubservices.com

Publisher's Note: This is a work of fiction. Names, characters, places, and
incidents are a product of the author's imagination. Locales and public names
are sometimes used for atmospheric purposes. Any resemblance to actual
people, living or dead, or to businesses, companies, events, institutions, or
locales is completely coincidental.

Thanks to the Flame Tree Press team, including:
Taylor Bentley, Frances Bodiam, Federica Ciaravella, Don D'Auria,
Chris Herbert, Josie Karani, Molly Rosevear, Mike Spender,
Cat Taylor, Maria Tissot, Nick Wells, Gillian Whitaker.

The cover is created by Flame Tree Studio with
thanks to Nik Keevil and Shutterstock.com.
The font families used are Avenir and Bembo.

Flame Tree Press is an imprint of Flame Tree Publishing Ltd
flametreepublishing.com

A copy of the CIP data for this book is available from the British Library
and the Library of Congress.

HB ISBN: 978-1-78758-369-6
PB ISBN: 978-1-78758-367-2
ebook ISBN: 978-1-78758-370-2
Also available in FLAME TREE AUDIO

Printed in the US at Bookmasters, Ashland, Ohio

J.D. MOYER

THE GUARDIAN

FLAME TREE PRESS
London & New York

For Tesla Rose

PROLOGUE

10.08.02727, the Stanford

Penelope Townes watched Ingrid and Per Anders through the observation glass. Ingrid patiently pointed to the objects on the table, naming each one in the Happdal dialect – a tongue they called *Norse*. The language was similar to Old Norse but also contained elements of Corporate Age Norwegian, as well as the odd German or English word. Per Anders stared blankly as Ingrid identified a ball (*knöttur*), then a spoon (*sponn*), then an orange (*oransje*).

Per Anders, the Happdal villager, had arrived on the *Stanford* ringstation, transported from Earth via the 'mule' SSTO vehicle. Car-En Ganzorig had suggested that rehabilitating Per Anders from his mushroom spore brain infection could be a huge research opportunity. It was one thing to secretly observe the lives of the Happdal villagers, another to interview one directly. But even though the infection was eradicated, Per Anders was still incapable of speech.

Ingrid changed her approach. "*Munnr*," she said, pointing to her own mouth. The patient's eyes flickered with awareness, or maybe just hunger. "*Munnr*, mouth. Are you hungry, Per Anders?" Ingrid picked up the orange and offered it.

The patient took the fruit and bit into the peel, spilling juice down his chin and shirt. Ingrid winced. Per Anders chewed happily away, oblivious.

Penelope sighed. This was after two months of neuroregeneration therapy. She'd been more hopeful at first; Per Anders had made real strides in the early weeks, making direct eye contact and demonstrating a greater awareness of his surroundings. But his progress had stalled. Still, Ingrid doggedly worked with him every day, often twice a day.

Penelope dimmed the glass and brought up the latest report from Adrian Vanderplotz. The ex-Department Head was now Station Director of Advance Field Station One, a small research community on the western side of the Po Valley. Townes had to stop herself from calling it a *settlement* – even in her own mind. The research station had a boring, utilitarian name for a reason. If anyone on the Repop Council slipped and referred to AFS-1 as a settlement or village, there would be a political price to pay with the other ringstations – especially the *Liu Hui*.

She skipped the long list of supply requests. She'd approve what they needed; Svilsson or Polanski could deal with the fulfillment logistics. The interesting part of the report was the Kaldbrek field research. The village, just a few kilometers northeast of Happdal, was culturally in a different universe. Svein Haakonsson, the young jarl of Kaldbrek, was a cruel tyrant. This was in sharp contrast to the steady leadership of Arik Asgersson, Happdal's older, wiser chieftain. Car-En – the young anthropologist who had first studied Happdal up close – was lucky that she'd fallen in love with someone from Arik's clan.

Penelope skimmed the written reports from Rosen and De Laurentiis, the two field researchers assigned to Kaldbrek. The surveillance video was more engrossing. She was ten minutes into a spear-and-shield combat drill when Ingrid interrupted her.

"Sorry – should I come back later?"

"No, just reading the field research reports."

"How are Alexi and Aaron? Staying safe?"

"As safe as you can be when you're hiding in the woods spying on insane Vikings."

Ingrid smiled, but there was real concern in her eyes. Penelope shouldn't be so flippant – so far the researchers had gone undetected, but that could just be good luck.

Ingrid sat across from Penelope, brushing her bright orange curls away from her face. "I hope they're observing protocol. I think the security buffer should be increased, at least around Kaldbrek."

"I'll consider it," Penelope said, feeling prickly. It was none of Ingrid's business. She should stick to exotic languages and rehab with Per Anders.

"Any word on Car-En? How's she integrating?"

"Well enough. She doesn't get along with her mother-in-law, but everyone else in the village loves her."

"Elke, right? She's a tough one."

"Dangerous," Penelope said. "We finally obtained a sample for her.

Very low empathy rating – borderline psychopathy, at least genetically. She carries some fascinating wildstrains too – enhanced smell and vision, also eidetic memory and enhanced cognition."

"Car-En can handle her," said Ingrid, grinning.

Penelope didn't get it. If the *Stanford* had anything approaching a folk hero, it was Car-En Ganzorig. She'd been the department's star field researcher for years. Thousands had followed her Happdal field reports. Now that she'd 'gone native,' her popularity had only increased. Even level-headed academics like Ingrid were starstruck by Car-En.

"I hope so," Penelope said.

Penelope could admit to herself that she was jealous of Car-En, but at the same time she liked the anthropologist. Car-En's decision to stay in Happdal, in flagrant violation of Non-Interventionism, was disruptive, impulsive, and impudent. Still, Penelope didn't blame her. It made sense, in light of what had happened with Adrian, who'd tried to murder Car-En with her own bioskin. Car-En had disobeyed her advisor, triggering what could only be described as a temporary psychotic break. No wonder Car-En had chosen to remain on the planet's surface.

Car-En's choice certainly was convenient. If she had returned to the *Stanford* and pressed charges against Adrian, the department would have been embroiled in scandal for years. Heads would have rolled. Penelope herself might have survived, but it was better this way. Car-En got to play Viking with her new lover, Adrian had his pet project on Earth, and Penelope was now leading the anthropology department. In addition, she still held her spot on the Repop Council, second only to Kardosh. The last five years of Penelope Townes's career had exceeded everyone's expectations, especially her own.

"I'm exhausted. I think I'll get some rest," Ingrid said.

Penelope nodded. She believed her, but Ingrid didn't look tired – she looked young and radiant. Townes herself had her good days and her bad, gray days. She was getting to the age where she sometimes avoided her own reflection. Maybe Adrian Vanderplotz had the right idea – maintaining appearances with rejuvs. "You do that. Good work with Per Anders. Keep at it."

"Thanks. I will."

Ingrid left the room visibly energized. People thrived on positive feedback. She should remember to give praise more often.

Penelope lightened the glass and watched Per Anders. A young intern had wiped his face and was preparing to escort him back to his quarters. Per Anders looked at her directly. It was an illusion – there was no way he could see her. He was staring at his own reflection. The look in his eyes, dull and affectless, scared her. She could imagine him killing, casually, without remorse. The intern touched his arm and the patient shuffled to his feet, once again harmless. He wasn't dangerous, just dimwitted. The mycological spores that had eaten their way through his brain – *those* were dangerous.

Penelope walked home via park tube instead of descending to the Sub-1 tram. The lush ferns and the warm, humid air helped her relax. She couldn't stop thinking about Car-En. Would she survive, without a bioskin, without a kit, without her old friends and family? Car-En's parents – Shol and Marivic – they were still alive. How did they feel? Were they happy their daughter had fallen in love, or were they just sick with worry and grief? Maybe she should visit them, check in. Reassure them that the denizens of Happdal were good people.

But they already knew that. *Everyone* on the *Stanford* knew about Jarl Arik, his wife Elke, their sons Esper and Trond, their daughter Katja, and a few dozen other characters. Through the department's public feeds, the ringstation citizens followed the lives of the villagers like a serial drama.

Car-En had made them famous.

PART ONE
THE BELLOWS BOY
CHAPTER ONE

Tem's hands hurt, but he was used to the pain, and focused instead on the counting. His right hand, which pumped the bellows handle, hurt more than his left. He reached nine hundred; it was nearly time to switch. One thousand strokes for each arm. Ten thousand strokes total, and his shift would be done. Except today there were only two boys working the bellows, so he would not rest for long.

"Do you tire, Tem?" It was Hennik, idly wandering by. Hennik worked at the dairy, where they started at dawn but often finished early. Or maybe there were still cows and goats to be milked, and Hennik had slipped away, shirking his tasks. "You look tired," Hennik went on, "and your face has gone from brown to black from the soot, like a creature from the woods. A sneaky marten, or a runty black wolf cub." Hennik, blond with pale freckled skin, big and meaty-limbed, was twelve – three years older than Tem. Hennik was strong but slow; Tem could beat him in a foot race. Truthfully Tem did not mind being likened to a wolf. He was fast, and liked to think of himself as dangerous.

"What's it like, being the only boy with brown skin?" Hennik asked. "Do you try to scrub your face, to make it lighter?"

"I'm no different than you," said Tem, without breaking his count. *Nine hundred ten. Nine hundred eleven.*

"You *are* different," Hennik insisted. "Your mother came from the sky, and your skin is brown, like shit."

Tem held his anger back, as Father had taught him. "My father is from Happdal, and my grandfather is jarl. One day I'll be smith."

"No you won't," Hennik said. "You're too small."

"Farbror Trond said that if I keep pumping the bellows, my arms will grow from twigs into branches." *Nine hundred twenty. Nine hundred twenty-one.* His right arm burned and his hand ached.

"Trond isn't your real uncle," said Hennik, sneering. "And he won't make you smith. You'll never be strong like him, or like Jense. And Nine-Finger Pieter is already apprentice. He's next in line – not you."

"Don't you have something to do?" Tem asked. He looked away, trying to hide his irritation. Trond *was* his real uncle. Well, half-uncle at least. Hennik was an idiot.

"Not really," Hennik said.

"Then go away." *Nine hundred forty.* Or was it nine hundred thirty? His right hand was cramping.

"I'll go when I please," said Hennik. "I enjoy watching you work. You do look tired though. I'd offer to help, if I liked you. But I don't. I don't like you at all."

Tem knew as much, and didn't care. He turned away, pretending that Hennik didn't exist, whispering the numbers under his breath. *Nine hundred forty, for sure this time. Nine hundred forty-one.*

At nine hundred fifty, Tem heard the sound of water. Hennik was pissing against the side of the smithy, only a few feet away from the bellows station. A brown puddle was forming in the dirt, dribbling toward Tem. It was close enough to smell. Hennik shook himself off and retied his trousers, smirking.

Nine hundred fifty-five. Hennik was walking away. Esper, Tem's father, told him to always count to ten when he was angry. Count to ten and cool off. Very well – he would take his father's advice. He reached nine hundred sixty. Only forty more strokes and he could give his right arm a break.

Trond isn't your real uncle.

He ran silently, like a wolf. Tomas, the other bellows boy, saw Tem and shouted to warn Hennik, but by then Tem was mid-leap. The impact landed both boys in the dirt. Somehow Hennik wound up on top. The larger boy held Tem by the throat and hit him in the face with his free hand. Tem lifted his hands to protect his face, but Hennik punched his stomach, then his groin, shifting his attacks to whatever body part Tem left unguarded. Tem struggled to breathe. He couldn't cry out. He hurt everywhere.

Suddenly the pain stopped. Hennik was no longer on top of him. Tem could once again breathe freely, and Hennik was running away. A large hand grabbed his arm and he was lifted to his feet. His grandfather, Jense, loomed over him. The old smith was as big as a tree, and smelled like smoke and metal. Comforting smells.

"Why did you stop pumping the bellows?"

Tem stared up at his grandfather, mute. Jense Baldrsson was Farbror Trond's father; his uncle and grandfather worked side by side in the smithy. Farfar Jense looked at him expectantly. It would do no good to explain. It might, if he had a true excuse. His grandfather was stern but not unfair. But the truth was that *Tem* had started the fight. He had allowed himself to be provoked.

"Godsteel needs air, boy. We depend on you. Are you all right?"

Tem wasn't all right. His nose was bleeding, his stomach hurt, and a deep ache was spreading from his groin. He felt as if he might cry, or vomit, or both. But he nodded. "Then back to work." Gently, Jense wiped the blood from Tem's upper lip. "You'll be fine. Hennik is a little turd. You want me to talk to his father?"

Tem shook his head. Jense grinned and patted Tem on the back. "Good – you'll take care of it yourself. But right now we need air."

Tem nodded and tenderly jogged back to the bellows station. He managed to hold back his tears until his grandfather was back inside the smithy. Even as he cried, he grabbed the bellows handle with his left hand and began the new count.

At home, he told Mother about the fight, but left out most of what Hennik had said. She washed his face and put ointment on a long scratch on his cheek that he hadn't noticed. She pressed softly on each of his ribs, asking where it hurt. She said that nothing seemed broken. When he clutched his groin in pain she made him show her. His penis and ball-sack were bruised blue and green from Hennik's pummeling. She clenched her jaw when she saw that.

Dinner was stew: deer meat, potatoes, onions, and herbs. Tem ate three bowlfuls, as did Father, praising the meal in a way that seemed overly enthusiastic. Mother ate little and said even less. Tem asked if he could go play by the river; it was late summer and there was plenty of light left in the day. Mother said no; Tem should rest. Up in the loft he practiced his letters in the notebook Tante Katja had given him. He could hear his parents talking in hushed voices. Father's voice was calm. Mother's voice started calm but then changed to a tone that worried Tem. Father no longer sounded quite so calm. They spoke for a long time. Whatever they decided, it seemed as if Mother had won.

★   ★   ★

In the morning he checked his injuries. His penis looked bad – greenish-yellow instead of green and blue – but it hurt less. His ribs only hurt when he took a deep breath. He dressed and climbed down to the main room. Mother had made porridge and bacon for breakfast. Father was already gone for the day.

"How are you feeling?" Mother asked. Her voice sounded normal again. Mother's skin was light brown. Tem's was lighter, more tan than brown. His skin tone was not even the darkest of the village children; he was paler than ruddy Tomas, for one. But he looked different, both his features and his small frame.

"Good," he said. It was the truth. He didn't care about Hennik. Not all the children were rotten to him – only a few. Hennik was wrong in thinking that Tem would never become a smith. When Farfar Jense put down the hammer and Nine-Finger Pieter became smith, then Tem would be chosen as apprentice. He wasn't the strongest bellows boy, but he was the quickest study. He would learn the Five Secrets of Godsteel. He would forge a sword so fine that smiths would speak Tem's name for generations, and study his work. Just like they did of Stian, first smith of Happdal, and Stian's apprentice, Jakob the Bold. And after him Kai, and then Baldr. Baldr, fourth smith of Happdal, had taught the Five Secrets to Jense, and Jense had taught them to Trond (though Trond said that Jense had taken a long time to reveal the fifth – for years Trond had thought there were only *four* secrets). Farbror Trond would teach them to Tem. Or Nine-Finger Pieter would. Or perhaps both of them.

"Where did your mind go?" Mother asked. "You looked very far away just now."

"Did Father ever want to be a smith?" asked Tem.

"No. I don't think so. But I didn't know him when he was a boy. You should ask him yourself."

"I will."

Mother served him a bowl of steaming porridge with three fat slices of bacon placed across the top of the bowl, like a bridge. He thanked her and ate in silence, using the bacon as a spoon to scoop up the porridge. A delicious spoon.

"Would you like to meet your grandmother and grandfather one day?"

Tem looked up. He had two grandfathers and one grandmother, and knew them all well. Farfar Arik, Esper's father, was jarl of Happdal. And Esper's mother, Farmor Elke, was Arik's wife. His other farfar – Jense – was smith. He squinted at his mother.

"Do you mean my mormor and morfar? *Your* mother and father?"

"Yes. On the *Stanford*."

Mother rarely spoke of the ringship in the sky, but she answered Tem's questions when he asked. On a clear night you could see it, always in the same place. Mother had tried to explain why it didn't move, like the moon and stars and planets did, but he hadn't understood.

"Are they coming to visit?" he asked. "I thought the sky people weren't allowed to visit us. That's why you can't go back, isn't it? Because you broke that rule?"

"I did break that rule, and I might be in some trouble for it, but I can go back any time I like. I'm a citizen of the *Stanford*. As are you, because you're my son. I was thinking I would take you to see your grandparents. Do you remember their names?"

Tem thought for a second, then shook his head.

"My mother's name is Marivic. My father is Shol."

"Does that mean your last name is Sholsson?"

Mother laughed. "No. My last name is Ganzorig. Last names are different on the ringstations." She used the English word for the ringships, instead of the Norse *Hringr-kjóll*.

"Ganzorig. That's a strange name. I'm glad my last name is Espersson."

"It's Mongolian. Mongolia was a country very far that way." Mother pointed east.

"Who lives there now?"

"No one. Just animals."

"Are you sure? Maybe giants live there. Or mushroom men."

"Maybe. You could be right. Nobody has been there in a long time."

Tem ate the last of his bacon and scooped up the rest of his porridge with his fingers. Mother offered to get him a spoon. He shook his head.

Metal spoons gave food a strange taste; he preferred to eat with his hands.

"So what do you think? Would you like to fly to the ringstation and visit Mormor Marivic and Morfar Shol? You have every right to, as a citizen."

"Do they speak Norse?"

"No. But you know a little English. And you could learn more."

"Maybe," said Tem. "I'd have to ask Farbror Trond and Farfar Jense. They need me at the bellows."

Mother scowled. "There are plenty of boys to pump the bellows. And girls too, if they'd let them."

"They'd let them," Tem said. "None want to."

Mother shrugged. "I can't say I blame them." She stood and stretched, catlike. "I'll talk to your grandmother today."

"Today?" said Tem. "Are we going to visit soon?"

"I think we should. You're not scared of a little adventure, are you?"

"No. I'm not scared."

"Good."

He dipped his bowl in the wash-bucket, scrubbed it clean with his fingers, and put it on the rack to dry.

"How do the ringships stay in the sky?" he asked. "Why don't they plunge to the ground?"

It wasn't the first time he'd asked the question, nor the first time Mother had tried to explain 'geostationary orbit.' She switched to English halfway through, and her words became sounds that passed through his head without meaning.

Tem went directly to the smithy after breakfast, but found the door shut and the furnace cold. He hung about near the bellows station until Nine-Finger Pieter came by and saw him.

"Trond and Jense are hunting today, with your father. Did Esper not tell you?"

"He left early," Tem said, feeling hurt. Why hadn't Mother told him? And why hadn't Father invited him? He was old enough to tag along on a hunt; he had his own small bow. He tried to hide his feelings.

"You look ragged, boy," Pieter said. "It was Hennik that did that to you? Shall we find him and teach him a lesson?"

"Really?"

"Yes, really."

They found Hennik at the dairy, where he worked with his uncle, Harald the cheese-maker. They could not touch him while he worked, so they waited until midday break, and followed Hennik at some distance, staying out of sight. The blond boy went to the river, retrieved his pole from a hiding place, and cast for brown trout. The river was wide and gentle this time of year, but still made enough noise so that Pieter and Tem were nearly upon Hennik before he turned and saw them.

Hennik dropped his rod and ran, but Nine-Finger Pieter grabbed him by the arm and tossed him to the ground. Pieter was not so strong and heavy as Trond and Jense, but years of the hammer had broadened his shoulders and thickened his forearms. Young Hennik had no chance.

"He attacked me first!" yelled Hennik from the ground.

Pieter lifted Hennik up and held his arms firmly from the back, so that Hennik faced Tem.

"Have a few swings, if you like," Pieter said to Tem. "Now might be a good time to apologize," he whispered loudly in Hennik's ear.

"You're hurting me!" Hennik protested. Pieter's hands were clamped hard onto Hennik's arms.

Tem stepped forward. He had enjoyed stalking and catching Hennik, but now he had no desire to pummel the helpless boy. Hennik was an idiot, and punching him wouldn't fix that.

"You're wrong, you know," Tem said. "I *will* become smith some day. I will forge a great sword, a soulsword, and you'll still be making *cheese*."

Hennik's face contorted. He opened his mouth with a retort, but no sound came out.

"Harald's cheese is very good," said Pieter reasonably, not loosening his grip. "There's no shame in cheese-making. Though I doubt this one will carry on the tradition. Not smart enough. Harald will choose someone else."

"Will you apologize, or do I have to hit you?" Tem asked. Pieter squeezed Hennik's arms with all nine of his iron-strong fingers.

Hennik looked away. "I'm sorry," he mouthed, though any sound was drowned out by the gentle splashing of the river against the rocky beach.

"What was that?" said Pieter, gripping harder into Hennik's fleshy arms. Hennik yelped.

"I'm sorry!" Hennik blurted. "I'm sorry for saying Trond isn't your real uncle, and I'm sorry for saying you won't be smith."

Tem took a step back, nodding. Pieter let go. Hennik stumbled to the side, rubbing his arms.

"You're lucky young Tem is so kind and fair," said Pieter.

"He struck me first," Hennik mumbled, picking up his rod and heading back toward the village. At a safe distance, he turned. "You'll always be small and weak!" he yelled, pointing at Tem. "I take it back – you'll never be a smith!" He turned and fled.

"Chase?" Pieter asked. Tem shook his head. Pieter arched one eyebrow. "You were too easy on him."

"I *did* attack him first," Tem admitted.

Pieter shrugged. "You had your chance. You're on your own now. But I don't think he'll bother you anymore."

Nine-Finger Pieter walked back to Happdal quickly, taking long strides and not looking back to see if Tem was keeping up. Tem matched the apprentice smith's pace for a while, but eventually stopped in his tracks. Why was he rushing back to the village? The smithy was shuttered; there was no work for him today. He doubled back toward the river. Hennik had a good idea, to cast for trout. Tem had his own rod hidden away; he would find it and steal Hennik's spot. Trout fried in butter was one of Mother's favorite meals.

Tem returned home to find Farmor Elke sitting at the table, scowling.

"Where's Mother?" he asked.

"Out back. What have you got there?"

"Trout. Look how big this one is!"

Farmor Elke grunted, unimpressed. His grandmother's eyes were pale blue, like Father's. Farmor stood, took the three fish, and laid them carefully on the cutting block. "Car-En had a talk with me. Your mother says she wants to take you to the ringship."

"Just for a visit," Tem said. "To meet Mormor and Morfar."

"A visit? Is that what she said?" Farmor Elke sat back down. Despite her age, she moved smoothly and quickly, not like an old person. More than once she had chased Tem down to cuff his ear. Elke often pointed out that she only punished Tem when he deserved it. Her own mother, Mette, had thrown rocks at children for no reason at all. Then one cold autumn morning, long before Tem had been born, Mette was found in the woods, frozen stiff. Nobody had been sad about that – not even Elke. This was hard for Tem to imagine. He loved his own mother dearly, and his father nearly as much. He even loved grumpy Farmor Elke.

"What's this?" Mother had come in, and was looking at the trout on the cutting block.

"Dinner," said Tem. "Please?"

"The boy is resourceful," said Farmor Elke, as if he wasn't there.

"You're happy here, aren't you?" she asked, turning to face him.

"Of course I am," he said. He kept his eyes on Mother. Something was wrong.

"That's not the point, is it?" Mother said to Farmor.

"I have no idea what the point is," Farmor said.

"There's a larger world out there."

"So? What does *that* matter?" Farmor Elke snapped. His grandmother's voice always had an edge to it, but she rarely raised her voice. She was truly angry, not just irritated. "He has everything he needs here. His parents, his grandparents, plenty of food."

"He needs to learn," said Mother sternly.

"I'm right here," Tem said. "What's this about?"

"He *is* learning," Farmor retorted. "His uncle will teach him steel; his aunt, letters; his father, archery. You can tell him whatever nonsense you like about the stars and floating ships. What else is there?"

"I'm right here," Tem repeated, more loudly. "Stop talking about me like I'm not here."

"He's never met my parents. Or my friends. He knows nothing about life beyond this village."

"*You* left your parents behind," Farmor said. "And your friends." Tem thought this was cruel to say, even though it was true. Mother had had good reasons, even though he didn't understand completely, and suspected that he hadn't been told the complete truth of the matter. But that was Farmor Elke: her honesty verged on cruelty.

"It's not too late for him to meet them," Mother answered. "And he can make up his own mind about if…about *when* he returns."

"Careful," Farmor said. "You might slip and say something true."

"Stop talking!" yelled Tem, striking the table with his fist. Mother and Farmor started, and stared at him. "I'm right here! What's this about? Why are you arguing?"

"We should wait until his father returns," said Farmor Elke, ignoring him. Mother's face tightened.

Tem stomped to the ladder and climbed to the loft. Soon he heard and smelled the trout frying in butter. He heard Farmor Elke leave (without saying goodbye, but that was not unusual), and soon after that Father returned from the hunt. Father had killed a boar, Tem overheard. Farbror Trond would clean it and bury it over hot coals to slowly roast overnight. Despite Happdal's growing population, the woods were thick with game. Hunting parties rarely returned empty-handed.

Tem waited in the loft for Mother to call him down for dinner. Waiting became sulking; his parents started eating without him. They spoke quietly to each other. About him, he supposed. He inched close to the edge so he could eavesdrop.

"Would you be safe there?" Father asked. "The man who tried to kill you – would he try again?"

"I'm not scared of Adrian," said Mother. "I never was. I stayed here to be with you."

"What about the intervention rule? I thought the sky people weren't supposed to interfere with the lives of villagers."

"Tem is both a villager and a sky person by birth. And there's no rule against villagers visiting ringstations, as far as I know. Per Anders is already on the *Stanford*, after all. Surely *you* could visit because you're my husband and Tem's father. And Non-Interventionism was never meant to be a permanent policy. It's simply a precaution until repopulation officially starts. Which it probably has – it's been ten years."

Tem scooched back from the edge. Visiting the ringship did sound like a good adventure, but in truth he did not care if he went or not. He didn't know his mormor and morfar, so he could not miss them. Farmor Elke was right – he was happy in the village. He was happy to pump the bellows until his arms burned and his hands ached. He was proud of the thick calluses that covered his palms and fingers.

What was everyone upset about?

When he heard them clearing the plates, he ventured down the ladder.

"There's my son!" said Father. "Were you hiding up there in the loft? We saved you a trout. Thank you for catching our dinner."

"You knew I was up there."

"Yes, I did. And you wanted to stay up there, so we let you."

Tem ate his fish in silence. Mother patted his head. He wanted to ask her what she and Farmor Elke had been fighting about, but he couldn't find the words.

Tem watched Father clean his bow. His father was tall and strong. Next to burly Farbror Trond, Father looked slender, but that was a trick of the eye. Tem had seen Father lift a dead stag over his shoulder with little effort; he was tremendously powerful. Tem hoped he would grow to be as strong, but so far he more resembled his mother: short and slight.

"Come with me," Father said. "There's still light outside. Let's see if the moon has risen."

They walked to the edge of the village, passing the hive field, and came to a wide clearing ringed with oak and beech trees. It was where the villagers celebrated *Jonsok*, the midsummer solstice.

"Have you heard of the Burnings?" Father asked.

Tem nodded. Farfar Arik's brother Bjorn had been the last to undergo the Burning ritual. There were still Afflicted among them, but no longer were the women Buried and the men Burned. Instead, the sick were cared for until they died. Tem wasn't sure why the tradition had changed, but it had happened around the time Mother had come to Happdal, a year before he had been born. He was glad the tradition had lapsed, though he knew that many in the village (including Farmor Elke) resented his mother for bringing change.

"Before Car-En arrived," Father said, "we did not know why some became Afflicted. Her people – the sky people – helped us. We have fewer sicken each year, and by the time you are grown, the Affliction will be part of our past."

"Are they smarter than us? The sky people?"

Esper smiled and shook his head. "No. Well, maybe they're smarter than your uncle."

Tem punched his father in the leg. He knew that Father and Farbror Trond teased each other mercilessly, but he wanted no part of it. He loved them both too much, and did not like teasing.

"The point," said Father, putting his arm around Tem's shoulder and pulling him close, "is that the sky people have a great deal of knowledge, and they are willing to share it."

"Smiths hoard their knowledge," said Tem. "Farfar Jense did not teach his own son the fifth secret of godsteel until Trond was full smith, and a man. And both Farfar and Farbror guard their secrets from the other smiths – Orvar, of Skrova, and Völund, of Kaldbrek."

Father's body tensed at the mention of Kaldbrek; that village had a sour history with Happdal.

"The sky people see knowledge as something to be freely shared. I agree with them," Father said. Tem nodded. He could see the sense in that. "Your mother thinks you should spend some time with them. Meet your mormor and morfar. Learn their language. See what life is like on a ringship."

"What do *you* think?" Tem asked.

His father sighed. "I will miss you. But I agree with her."

Tem stepped away from his father. "How long a visit are you talking about?"

"At least a year. Maybe longer." Father gazed at him, unblinking.

"A *year*? Who will pump the bellows?"

"There will always be boys to pump the bellows."

Tem shook his head fiercely. His father did not understand. The bellows was *his* job. It was what he must do to become apprentice, and then smith. It was his *path*.

"The bellows will be there when you return," said Father, more softly. "I know you want to become smith, like Trond. Nothing would make me prouder."

"You *don't* understand!" shouted Tem. "You never wanted to be smith yourself, so how can you understand?" With that he turned and walked home, taking long strides. Like Nine-Finger Pieter, he did not look back. It was disrespectful toward his father, and he felt bad for that. But unlike Farmor Elke, Father would not chase him down and cuff his ears. Father never struck him.

The summer light was finally fading and the quarter moon had risen. It was a clear night. The stars would be brilliant. The *Stanford* would be clearly visible, a bright, unmoving ring in the southern sky.

He wouldn't go. He would stay in Happdal. The sky people could have the sky to themselves.

CHAPTER TWO

A week passed, and there was no more talk of the sky people or visiting Mother's parents. Tem pumped the bellows, and hoped that everyone had forgotten about the whole thing. Farbror Trond and Tante Lissa invited him over for dinner; Farmor Elke joined as well. Everyone was nice – *too* nice, he thought. Tante Lissa give him a bag of honeyed nuts, and Farmor Elke made cloudberry pie for dessert. Tem was polite, but the kind treatment and treats worried him (it was not his birthday, *Jonsok* had long passed, and it was some time before the harvest festival). He avoided the adults and played with his young cousin Sigurd. Farbror Trond and Tante Lissa's son was already a challenge to wrestle. Sigurd liked nothing better than to punch people in the face and laugh uproariously – and his punches *hurt* – but he could take punishment as well as dish it out. Though Sigurd could not yet speak, he could wield a small hammer skillfully (his father pointed this out frequently, to anyone within earshot). It was easy to imagine young Sigurd as smith; he seemed born for the job. Tem, with his slight build, would have to work much harder to reach his goal.

Another week went by; no one mentioned the ringship. Maybe Farmor Elke had won out. Tem felt relieved but also disappointed. He *was* curious to meet his mormor and morfar. What kind of people were they? Were they kind and intelligent, like Mother? Children weren't always like their parents. None of Farmor Elke's children (Father, Farbror Trond, and Tante Katja) were anything like their mother. Tem was more like his grandmother – fierce and fiery. On second thought, Tante Katja *did* have a temper. Mostly, his aunt was quiet and studious. But when she angered, as sometimes happened when Tem's attention wandered during lessons, she could be sharp. And there were stories of her youth....

His aunt had never married, and lived in a small one-room house she'd built behind Farbror Trond's own grand house. His uncle often said he would fill his own home with children, and once that house was full, build a second house to fill with even more children. Tem had overheard that Farbror Trond's wife was pregnant again, though to Tem's eyes Tante Lissa looked the same – a little fat.

Tante Katja, on the other hand, had no interest in family, and spent her days reading books scavenged from the Builder ruins. She had explained to Tem that the ancestors of the ringstation people had once lived on the ground, and built great cities, before they had fled to the skies. Most of the books were in a language called German, which Katja could read but not speak. A few were in Old English, which was similar to the language Mother spoke. Mother had insisted Tem learn to speak English as well as Norse, but he could only read and write a few words in the former. Katja said Norse was no longer a written language – there had once been Norse books but they were all lost, crushed and buried by the glacial wall that had forced their ancestors south along the Ice Trail.

In the late afternoons, after the smithy work was done, Tem studied his letters with Tante Katja. At first she had bribed him with promises of berry juice and sword-fighting lessons, but eventually he had come to enjoy the lessons with or without the bribes. Tante Katja was a strict teacher, but when they had finished she told him stories. She insisted that the stories were true, but the tales were so outlandish that Tem assumed she must be making them up, insisting on their verity for dramatic effect.

Tem sat at a writing desk. The days were still long, and the afternoon light was strong enough to penetrate the yellowish windows and illuminate Tem's handmade paper. For this sort of practice he used reddish-brown ink made from iron salts mixed with oak gall resin. For special projects Katja let him use blue-black ink made from boiled hawthorne branches, iron salts, and blackberry juice. His quill, a slender iron nib affixed to a long black goose feather, had been fashioned by his uncle.

"Let's see you write the pattern," said Tante Katja.

"I already know it," Tem said.

"Let's see you write it again."

Tem sighed and dutifully wrote out the pattern: a sequence of letters, numbers, and symbols that made no sense to Tem. Tante Katja knew no better what it meant, but she had memorized it, and insisted that

Tem learn how to reproduce it exactly, with no mistakes. She refused to explain why this was so important.

She examined his work carefully. "Good," she said finally, patting him on the back.

"Can we spar now?" he asked.

"Not yet. Write me a story first."

"A story? I don't know enough words!"

"You know thousands of words."

"I mean I don't know how to write those words."

"It doesn't matter. Don't worry about writing them correctly. Just write something. It doesn't have to be very long, or even true. Make something up."

Tem grabbed his own hair. What she was asking was impossible.

"I'll be back in a while." She left him alone in the house.

Tem sat and stared at the pattern written neatly on the parchment. He put it aside to dry and placed a new sheet on the desk. What could he write about?

Tante Katja came back after a long time. He had written two lines. She told him to read them aloud.

"One day I would like to visit my mormor and morfar on the ringship," he read. "But first I will become smith, and make a fine sword."

"Good," said his aunt. "Most of the words are spelled wrong, but I can make it out well enough."

"Do you know why Farmor doesn't want me to go?"

Tante Katja sat on a wooden stool. "She's afraid you won't come back."

"That's silly!" said Tem.

"Not really. You might like it there. The sky people have many wondrous things. Elke is right to fear that you might stay."

Tem shook his head vigorously. "They don't have a smithy there," he said. "Do they?"

"I don't think so."

"Then why would I stay? Have you met Mother's parents?"

Tante shook her head. "Never. I've never been to any of the ringships."

"Aren't you curious?"

Katja shrugged. "A little. But I'm happy here. The ringships are wondrous, but so are the Builders, and I'm learning more about them every day."

"Like what?" Tem asked.

"They had great sporting events. Like the ones we have at Harvest Festival and Summer Trade, but with thousands of people from all corners of the Earth."

"Which sports?"

"Hundreds. Most I don't recognize, but they had foot races, and wrestling, and a kind of sword-fighting, and many games with balls."

"Did they play the drowning game?" Tem asked.

"No," Tante said. "Their games were tamer than ours."

Tem nodded. That fit with what he knew about the Builders. They were clever, and there were a lot of them, but they hadn't been a strong people.

"You're going, you know," she said.

"Where?"

"To the *Stanford*. Car-En's ringship. They're going to take you."

"Who is?"

"Your parents."

"How do you know?"

"Hadn't you noticed? Esper has been making food for the walk. He's prepared enough smoked trout to feed an army."

Tem furrowed his brow. There *had* been a great deal of food preparation in his home lately.

"Farmor won't let them take me," said Tem. "Nor will Farbror Trond. He and Farfar Jense need me at the bellows."

"You're going," Tante insisted. "Someone else will pump the bellows. You're right about Elke, but Trond will side with your father – he always sides with Brother over Mother when he has to choose. And Esper has decided some time on the ringship will do you good."

"But *why*?" said Tem, pouting.

Tante slapped him lightly on the side of his head. "To put some knowledge in there. Your mother wants more for you than village life."

She took him to the yard between her house and Farbror Trond's house, and there they sparred with wooden swords. Tante Katja was strong and fast and loved to fight. She had cut off her long blond hair years ago so that her braids would not whip around, distracting her. Now her hair was close-cropped, raggedly cut by her own knife. She was still pretty, and not that old, but she showed no interest in men. Sometimes she took another woman in her bed, but only for a night or two. Farfar Arik had given up on Tante Katja starting a family, and seemed happy enough with Tem and Sigurd for grandchildren (and there was little doubt that Sigurd would one day have little brothers and sisters). Tante Katja was happy with her books and weapons, and most accepted her that way. Only Farmor Elke disliked Tante Katja's way of life, and called her lazy and shiftless, resenting her own daughter for reasons Tem did not understand.

"Swing your sword *down* to block," said his aunt, after clipping him in the calf. "Don't try to lower your hilt to the ground. There are only five blocking positions – it's not that hard to remember."

"Sorry."

"Don't apologize. Just parry." Tante Katja swung her wooden blade straight down toward his head, holding nothing back. He blocked upwards, holding his sword at an angle to deflect the blow. Their wooden swords were of equal length, but he held his with both hands, while she used only her left, weaker hand.

"Good." She swung low again, and this time he parried correctly. He countered quickly with a strong thrust to her midsection, connecting.

"Ow!" His aunt stepped back and rubbed her lower abdomen. She had an old wound there, he remembered now.

"Sorry!"

"It's okay." She paced and rubbed the spot where he'd struck her. "You're getting faster. That's good."

Tem grinned. Though he hadn't meant to strike her old wound, he could count on one hand the times he'd snuck past her defenses.

"Don't get cocky," she said. Still fighting with her left hand, she tapped him three times in rapid succession: his arm, his shoulder, a thrust to his belly. His sword flailed, failing to block anything. "You're still slow. Don't watch my sword. Watch my eyes, and let the edges of your sight track my movement."

That night, Mother climbed to the loft to tuck him in. He often resisted tuck-in time, as he knew other boys his age did not receive such coddling. But tonight he allowed it. He wanted to speak alone with his mother.

"Tante Katja said that I'm going to the ringship, whether I want to or not."

"Don't you want to go?" she asked. "You said you wanted to meet your mormor and morfar."

"I don't know if I want to. I don't want to lose my spot at the bellows."

She tousled his hair. "You won't lose your spot. Your uncle and grandfather run the smithy. They love you and favor you. How could you lose your spot?"

"What if I'm on the ringship for a long time? Father said I might stay for a year."

"It does make sense for you to stay a long while. You'll need to improve your Orbital English, and it will take time to get to know your grandparents. And I'm hoping you'll make new friends."

"What if I want to come home?" Tem asked.

"Don't worry," said Mother. "We won't leave you there alone. I'm going to stay with you until you're settled."

"What if I don't get settled?"

"You worry too much. You're going to love it there."

"What if I don't?"

Mother stroked his hair. She loved him, but she didn't understand how much he yearned to become full smith. She wanted him to go to the ringship and learn new things, but he had *already* chosen his path: he would learn the Five Secrets of godsteel and forge fearsome weapons.

"Mother?"

"Yes?"

"I'm going to be smith. After Nine-Finger Pieter, I'll be next."

She smiled. "Of course you will."

She still didn't understand. But that was all right.

He had accepted that he could not fully control his own life. If Mother and Father and Farbror Trond all thought that he should go to the ringship, then he would go. Maybe, while he was there, he would learn how the sky people made their weapons.

A year was not so long. When he was ten, he would return to Happdal and resume his real work.

CHAPTER THREE

There was a feast in the longhouse to see them off: roasted pig, fresh bread, gravy, baked trout, smoked eel, blackberries with cream. Everyone attended. Those that could not fit in the longhouse sat on the steps, or outside at long wooden tables.

Tem sat next to his father at the head of the table. Farfar Arik was trekking the Five Valleys, forging alliances and trade agreements with neighboring villages, so Father sat in his chair as acting jarl. For that reason he would not join Tem and Mother on the ringship until Arik returned. Tem suspected Farmor Elke's influence might also have something to do with Father staying behind. It would be too hard on Farmor to see both her favorite child and her grandchild leave for a year's journey, especially with her husband still gone. Father would join them on the ringship as soon as he could.

There was a flying machine that would take them to the ringship, but it was far to the north. The long walk to the flying machine might be treacherous, and Tem had hoped to have Father at their side. Still, they would not be defenseless. Mother had her feather-blade, and Tem would bring his own bow and arrows. The journey would take at least two weeks, but they had packed plenty of provisions: smoked fish, oat cakes, aged cheese, nuts, and dried berries. The first days would be the hardest. They would climb the High Pass, descend to the flatlands, and cut through the Blood Forest. After that they would reach open country. It would be colder up north. Mother said the flying machine (she called it a 'mule' for some reason) was on the outskirts of old Builder ruins, a city that had once been called Bremen. It was far enough north to have ice and snow year round.

Tante Katja pulled him aside during the feast. She had dark circles under her eyes, and a crease between her eyebrows.

"What's the matter?" Tem asked.

"Nothing. I just want to talk."

Tem waited for his aunt to say something. She opened her mouth to speak, then closed it.

"Are you worried about us? We'll be fine. Mother has made the walk before."

"A long time ago," said Katja. "And she had powerful sky magic then. She doesn't have that anymore."

"But now she knows the land."

Katja nodded impatiently. "You're right. You'll both be fine. That's not what I wanted to talk about. I'm worried...about the pattern. Who you'll show it to, once you get to the ringship."

"I won't show it to anyone," said Tem. "It's secret – I know that."

Katja shook her head. "No. It's important that you share it. I'm just not sure with *who*."

"Can't I just ask Mother?" Mother knew a great deal about Tante Katja's past adventures, and he was sure Tante trusted her.

"Yes – you should ask her. But I want you to use your own judgment too. The pattern is powerful. It could be dangerous."

"Why?" Tem asked. "It's just writing."

"No, it's much more than that."

"How will I know who to trust?"

Tante sighed. "I don't know," she said. "You'll have to decide for yourself who is trustworthy. Just be careful, and get to know them first. Some people are skillful liars."

Tem nodded. Out of the corner of his eye he saw that Farmor was serving blackberries with cream.

"Go," she said, patting him on the head. "Get your dessert. And be with your father. He'll miss you." She kissed him on the cheek. "So will I."

"Come visit me then."

"Maybe," said Tante, but he could tell by her expression that she would not. There was something about the ringships or the sky people that scared her. She was fascinated by the Builders, but had no interest in meeting their actual descendants.

After the food had been eaten, most went home. His parents' friends wished him good luck. Too many people patted him on the head. The village children wished him luck too – even Hennik. Oddly, the older boy seemed to bear him no malice. Maybe he was just happy to see Tem go.

It was late, yet the remaining elders continued to drink and talk. The more they drank the louder they spoke, as if the mead and *öl* made them deaf. He found Mother and asked her if he could go to bed. Farbror Trond volunteered to walk him home, even though Tem knew quite well how to get home himself. His uncle said a few goodbyes, then took his hand and led him out of the longhouse and past the feasting tables. The main road was well lit by the gibbous moon. Though Tem had seen his uncle drink immense tankards of mead, Farbror did not act drunk, and walked without swaying, gently holding Tem's hand in his giant rough palm.

"I have something for you," said his uncle, when they reached Tem's home. Farbror Trond pulled a slender object from his boot and handed it to Tem. A longknife. Tem drew the blade from its fur-lined sheath and examined it, speechless.

"Godsteel," said Farbror. "One of my finest."

Tem tried to say something, but the sounds that came out of his mouth were not quite words. "Thank you," he finally managed.

"I hope you have no cause to use it, except to impress your friends."

"If I have any friends."

"You will," Farbror said. "You have that gift, just like your father. People love you, even though they don't always know why."

Tem looked up at his uncle, who was kind, but quite wrong. Tem did not have any gifts. Farbror Trond and Farfar Jense both had great strength. Father could see clearly even on the darkest nights. Farmor Elke could smell as well as any wolf (she did not think anyone knew this, but Tem had figured it out). Tem had no special gift.

Farbror grasped his forearm in the way that one man greeted another. Tem tried to grasp his uncle's forearm the same way, but his hand was too small.

"Say hello to Per Anders, if he still lives," said Farbror Trond.

"Come visit me."

His uncle shook his head. "My place is in the smithy, and with my family."

★   ★   ★

They set out early the next morning, while most still slept off the previous night's celebration. They said a final goodbye to Father.

He said he would follow them soon. Mother did not say anything in response, and Tem did not know what to think. He wondered what Farmor Elke had threatened in order to make Father stay.

They hiked along the river in the early morning. Mother set a fast pace. By the time they reached the Three Stones, the sun had risen just enough to give them light, but not enough to warm the ground.

"It's cold for late summer," he said.

"It's not cold," Mother said. "Can you feel your toes?"

Tem wiggled his toes inside of his wool socks and leather boots. "Yes."

"When it's cold, you won't feel them anymore. For the last day or two you'll feel like you're walking on two numb stumps. Hopefully we won't get frostbite. But even if we do, *Stanford* Medical will fix us up."

"What's that?" asked Tem.

"Doctors. Good ones."

"Better than Ilsa?"

"Ilsa does the best with what she has. She saved my life once."

Tem nodded. He knew the story well. The old crone's honey tonic had brought Mother back from the brink of death, when a bad man had tried to kill her.

By midday they reached the guard station, which was little more than a fire pit and a hastily built shade structure. The brothers Askr and Alvis greeted them.

"Hello, Car-En!" Askr was the more talkative one. Alvis was taller, but seldom spoke.

"Hello, Askr. Hello, Alvis. Any sign of Kaldbrek men?" Mother asked.

"None," said Askr. "Where are you going?" he asked in a friendly tone. The guards were stationed there to watch for raiders, not to pen in Happdal villagers who wanted to travel. Two guards were insufficient to fight off a raiding party, but Alvis carried a longbow and a quiver of whistlers. Tem didn't see the point of it – there hadn't been a raid since Kaldbrek's foul old jarl had died years ago – but the guard station was manned at all hours. Farmor Elke insisted on it.

"To the mule station – where there's a flying ship," Mother answered. "I'm taking Tem to visit the ringship, to meet my parents."

"You can just…go up?" Askr asked. "Can anyone fly up and board a ringship? Would the sky people let *me* on?"

"I have no idea. I haven't been on the *Stanford* in a long time. They've probably developed a policy by now. Want to come along and try?"

Tem couldn't tell if Mother was serious, but Askr rubbed his short beard and pursed his lips. "Is Per Anders still there?" he finally asked.

"I think so," Mother said. "I don't know if they've cured him."

"I'm tempted," said Askr. "I'm curious about the sky people. Maybe I will follow you when my shift is over." Askr was tall, and a good tracker, and Tem didn't doubt that he could catch up with them if he followed. Askr turned to Alvis. "What about you, brother? Would you come along? Any desire to see the sky ship up close?"

Alvis shook his head. "The sky is for the sky people."

Askr grinned. "My older brother has no love for adventure. But I'll accompany you to the High Pass. My legs need a stretch."

Askr joined them, taking long strides, using the shaft of his spear as a walking stick. Mother was more relaxed with Askr in tow, and she told him about life on the ringship. Askr had many questions; Mother answered them all. Some things Tem already knew: tens of thousands of people lived on the *Stanford*; they grew meat in jars instead of slaughtering animals; in the central hub you could float in the air like a feather. His attention shifted to the climb. Askr's pace was even faster than Mother's, and Tem had to move his own legs twice as quickly to keep up.

From the ridge they looked down on the green valley that was home to Kaldbrek.

"Are you old enough to remember when Kaldbrek came to Summer Trade?" Mother asked.

"No, but Alvis is," Askr said. "Will you follow the Upper Begna north?"

"Yes."

"Be careful. Svein and his men hunt and fish the headwaters."

"I will," Mother promised. Svein Haakonsson, Kaldbrek's young jarl, was cruel and bloodthirsty. So said Farfar Arik.

Mother gave Askr a warm embrace. "Thank you for joining us. Maybe we'll see you in a few days."

"May the Red Brother protect you." Askr smiled and waved to Tem before walking away.

Mother was quiet as they descended into the valley. The shady trail wound its way through immense spruce. Occasionally they passed through a sunnier open area, dotted with copses of silver birch and old knotted oak. Closer to the Upper Begna, the forest once again thickened. They heard the river before they saw it, though not much before; the snow had melted long ago and there had been no recent storms. The trail ended ten paces from the river bank. A huge fallen spruce spanned the water – a natural bridge. Age had worn away most of the bark, and sections of the great tree were rotted soft. But it was still solid enough to cross, at least for two as light as Mother and himself.

"Will Askr follow us?" Tem asked. Mother was eyeing the fallen tree.

"I doubt it. I think he just wanted to impress his brother."

"Then why did he ask you all those questions while we were walking? Alvis wasn't even there."

Mother shrugged. "He's curious. But he's courting Elika, and so is Grundar. Askr isn't going anywhere."

"She'll pick Askr," Tem said. Grundar had been a bellows boy too, long ago, but had never been chosen as apprentice. Maybe that's why Grundar was always scowling.

"Only if he's around. She can't pick him if he's gone off to live on a ringship."

Mother chose not to cross the water, and instead led them north on an overgrown hunting trail. After an hour or so of walking Tem could no longer hear the river; the path had veered slightly east. "We have to cut back in," said Mother. "I think this trail leads into the next valley, and then to Skrova." She sighed, hands on hips. "We probably should have crossed back at the big log."

"Don't worry," Tem said. "I don't think we're that far from the river."

Mother patted his shoulder. "I'm not worried. I have you to help guide me."

This was meant to reassure Tem, but it didn't. He had no idea where the flying machine was. And mother had never tried returning to her home in the sky.

Even off the hunting trail, the going was easy. The tall spruce were the bullies of the forest, hogging all but the tiniest slivers of light, and the undergrowth was paltry. Still, Tem stepped carefully, not wanting to twist an ankle. They had a long walk ahead. To pass the time, he and Mother played a counting game: How many types of animals could they see or otherwise identify? They spotted deer (a doe and two fawns), several squirrels, a jay, a birch tree filled with siskin, and best of all, a wildcat. They caught the bushy-tailed tabby unawares, stalking a woodpecker whose racket had concealed their approach. When the cat finally noticed them, it turned and stared wide-eyed for a long time, only fleeing when Tem took a few steps forward. The wildcat and the woodpecker brought the count to six.

The river was narrower here – they were nearing the streams and creeks of the headwaters – but still too fast and deep to easily cross. He suggested they head north and look for another fallen log. Mother agreed. The undergrowth was thicker here, and the ground marshy, and the going was slower. Tem tried to ignore the moisture seeping into his boots.

"Listen," Tem said. Mother froze; they heard a distant crash from the far side of the river. "A boar?" Tem asked. Mother put her finger to her lips. The crashing got louder, then quieter again; the beast was heading upriver. Now they heard men yelling and dogs barking. Hunters, pursuing their quarry. If it was a boar they were chasing, the men's lives were at risk. Tem had seen a tusk wound, deep and ragged. Three years ago Old Lars had taken a tusk to the calf. Strangely immune to pain, the old man had ignored the wound, which festered. Finally Ilsa sawed it off, while Lars calmly watched. Now the old man's lower leg was made of oak. Tem was glad there was a river between them and the hunt.

"This way!" cried a rough voice, much closer now. Mother ducked behind a brake of goat willow and fern. Tem did the same.

"It's wounded," said another man. The second voice was calm and flat, lacking in emotion.

"You stuck it," said the first. "A good shot, Svein. We'll eat well tonight."

Tem's eyes widened. Mother gave him a hard look. *Be silent.*

"We won't eat unless we finish the job," said Svein from across the river. He sounded so close. Were they well hidden? The thicket of goat willow was sparse, and the ferns grew close to the ground. "A dead boar does us no good if it rots in the brush."

"The dogs will find it," said the other. "They're hot on the scent."

Tem heard the men moving away. He started to stand, but Mother put her hand on his shoulder. They waited, silent, until the sounds of men and dogs were long gone.

"We should go south," said Mother quietly, "until we see a safe crossing. Even if we have to go all the way back to that first log. Then we'll cross the river, and head west until nightfall."

That made sense to Tem. The hunters had gone north, so going south would increase the distance between them. He shadowed Mother, just a few steps behind, watching her heavy backpack and the back of her head. Her straight hair, glossy brown except for a few strands of gray, was cut shoulder length. It had been longer when Tem was little, with no gray at all.

Something whizzed past Tem's head. Mother crumpled and fell. Tem rushed to her side. She groaned and twisted around, trying to see the back of her leg. A long arrow had pierced her hamstring.

"Sorry I had to shoot your mother, little boy, but she *is* trespassing. I have the right to defend my lands." Svein took a few squelching steps toward them; his boots and trousers were soaked through. Kaldbrek's jarl was younger than Tem expected, and uglier. A wispy beard only half covered his weak chin, and a long scar cut across his right cheek.

Tem grabbed the hilt of his longknife. Farbror Trond was wrong – the blade would be used for more than boasting.

Svein laughed. "Give me that, if you want to live. Tell him. Tell your brat to give me the knife." It took Tem a moment to realize that Svein was addressing Mother.

Mother grimaced and nodded. She grabbed his hand and squeezed it. Reluctantly, Tem pulled the longknife from his belt and tossed it, still sheathed, in Svein's direction.

"Obedience is a good quality in a boy," Svein said. "I was obedient too, when I was your age. When you become a man you may do as you wish. Unless you end up a slave." The scar on Svein's cheek flashed white when he grinned.

A burly black-bearded man trundled up behind the young jarl. "Cut off the shaft but don't yank on it," commanded Svein. "I don't want her bleeding out. Carry her back to the village. Tie the boy's hands and make him walk behind."

"What about the boar?" asked the black-bearded man.

"Leave that to me and the dogs."

"What should I do with them?"

Svein stared. Tem wanted to look away from the jarl's narrow blue eyes, but he willed his gaze steady.

"Take them to Völund," Svein said. "He'll know what to do."

CHAPTER FOUR

09.08.02737, Advance Field Station One, Earth

Lydia finished taping the girl's ankle and patted her on the knee. "There. You can walk on it, but don't run for a few days. Okay?"

"Okay," Maggie said. She was six, the first and now oldest child to have been born at AFS-1. Lydia refused to call the research station by its common nickname: 'Vandercamp.' She tolerated Adrian Vanderplotz, but she wasn't going to pander to his ego. The man's personality was big enough without naming the whole place after him. Lydia wasn't sure who had coined the moniker in the first place (probably Adrian himself), but she'd been annoyed when Xenus had started using it. It was still a point of contention between them.

"Can I jump rope?" Maggie asked.

"No. You can't jump rope. Just let it heal – be easy on it. Check with me in a few days and let me take a look."

"I will." Maggie was adorable: black hair, brown eyes, a cute little nose. She was a mix of Asian and European ancestries, the first Earth-born child in nearly one hundred years. No – that wasn't true. There were the villagers, of course, and without the villagers there would be no research station in the first place. But Maggie was still special. Some children had migrated to AFS-1 with their families, and other children had been born since, but Maggie was the first Repop child.

Maggie gingerly slid off the table and hobbled toward the door. "Thank you, Dr. Lydia."

"You're welcome."

Lydia returned the tape and scissors to the supply closet and took a quick inventory. They were low on disinfectant cream (which she could synthesize) and several elemental printing inks (which she couldn't). Using her m'eye she added the inks to the order queue. Every few weeks the *Stanford* sent a crate or two via mule. Someone, usually Xenus and Lydia together, had to pick up the supplies at the mule station with the hovershuttle. It was a long trip, several hours there and even longer back with a full load, but the scenery was spectacular. It was frigid that far north, but one of the engineers had designed a cozy modular environmental dome for the shuttles. Still – the winter trips were dicey.

She checked her schedule. No appointments for the rest of the day. There rarely were; in general the community was in excellent health. Still, drop-ins were common, mostly children with scrapes and bruises. The children seemed reckless and accident-prone compared to her own childhood, but that could be a trick of memory. Or it could be a real cultural change; space culture was cautious because life in space was dangerous ('P.M.C.' stood for Paranoid Maintenance Culture). Maybe these children, growing up in an environment to which they were naturally adapted, knew on some level that they could let their guard down. Or maybe the culture of the *adults* had changed, and the children were picking up on that. A technical mistake on Earth usually meant a do-over; in space it could mean the deaths of thousands of people.

She closed up the clinic, not locking anything – not even the supply closet had a lock – and pinged Xenus. He was at home, probably reading ringstation news feeds about AFS-1. Lydia didn't approve – Xenus was obsessed with the opinions of the ringstation denizens. Political bodies on the *Liu Hui* and the *Alhazen*, and even some voices from the generally apolitical *Hedonark*, took issue with the very existence of the field station. It was jumping the gun on Repop, they said. There were carefully negotiated treaties that governed the various research and planning phases that preceded, or *should have* preceded, what everyone assumed would be the careful, deliberate, conservative repopulation of the home planet. It was a once-in-a-species chance at a do-over.

The other ringstations were right to be concerned. AFS-1 was a research station in name only. It was, in fact, a settlement. Children had been born there. People considered it their home. Not every resident was involved in research, and many worked on projects that were little more than show: a pretense concealing the raw desire to *live on Earth*. Lydia understood that. She'd been among the first to volunteer.

The morning light was bright; Lydia adjusted her m'eye lens accordingly, filtering out most of the UV and some of the visible spectrum. Earth's ozone layer was intact, but she had never grown used to the intensity of direct sunlight. It was nothing like the yellowish-white 'sky' on the *Stanford*, also real sunlight, but redirected by mirrors and filtered through layers of translucent alumina. The vastness and intense colors of Earth's real sky had at first induced vertigo. These days she could look up and not panic, but she still used her m'eye filters as a crutch.

She passed between an open vegetable plot (summer squash, lettuce, high-protein corn) and a makeshift geodesic greenhouse fabricated from lengths of bamboo, printed carbonlattice connectors, and permeable bioplastic. The structure probably wouldn't survive a powerful storm, but they had gone ten years without strong weather. AFS-1 was sheltered in a broad valley, several hundred kilometers across, at the base of the mountain range that had once been known as the Italian Alps. The entire region was covered in a thick layer of volcanic ash from Campi Flegrei, which now partially constituted the easily tilled, moisture-retaining soil of the vegetable plots. The supervolcano had erupted in several places within the Phlegraean Fields cauldron, with the *Solfatara* crater eruption being the most spectacular. That event, more than anything else, had marked a point of no return for Earth's briefly hyper-connected global civilization. The date 02387 had been one of the few that stuck in Lydia's mind from her childhood history lessons. Exactly three hundred fifty years ago.

As she rounded the path that led to the dome she shared with Xenus, an alert flashed in her m'eye. *Emergency meeting in the Shell.* She changed course, heading directly to the field station's largest and most permanent structure. The Shell was an immense spiraling iridescent dome, guide-grown from an organic material that closely resembled the shell of a mollusk. The experimental building process was one of many inventions to be prototyped at the *Stanford*'s 'Hair Lab' and later implemented at AFS-1 (the hovershuttle was another, as was Lydia's portable medical synthesizer). To build a shell structure, a carbonlattice frame was draped with nutrient fabric, then moistened and exposed to sunlight. The fabric itself was seeded with minerals, polysaccharides, and a microorganism engineered to excrete a conchiolin matrix filled in with layers of calcium carbonate. The resulting material was light, extremely strong, waterproof, permeable to air, temperature regulating, and UV-protective while still being translucent.

She entered the Shell through a doorless archway, shivering as she adjusted to the cooler temperature of the interior. Warm reddish-brown light passed through the walls. The inside of the Shell reminded Lydia of cathedrals she'd seen in old films, with their high ceilings and colored glass. The *outside*, by contrast, looked like a gargantuan snail on its side.

Xenus, Adrian, and Shane were already there, seated at a large wooden round table toward the rear of the structure. She hadn't wasted any time getting there; had there been a meeting before the meeting?

"Hello Lydia," said Adrian Vanderplotz. "Please have a seat." The Station Director was in his sixties, but his black hair had only a few streaks of gray, and his face was smooth except for light lines around his mouth and eyes. He'd had at least one rejuv – maybe two.

"What's the emergency?" Lydia asked bluntly. She didn't like being the last to arrive, or the least informed.

Adrian didn't flinch. What he lacked in empathy he made up for in unflappability. "We lost a signal. Two signals, in fact. The Harz team."

"Which Harz team?" asked Lydia, taking a seat. There were currently three pairs of anthropologists observing villagers in the mountainous region that had once been known as New Saxony, only a few hundred kilometers south of the glacial line. The researchers always worked in pairs – never alone. Not since Car-En.

"The Kaldbrek observers. Rosen and De Laurentiis," Xenus said. "They went dark around the same time, approximately eight hours ago."

"Why am I just learning this now?" Lydia asked. She knew both researchers personally, and Aaron De Laurentiis was a friend.

"I just found out myself," said Xenus defensively.

"This needs to stay between us," Shane said. Shane Jaecks, the head of security, was a thick man, solid muscle. He was also intelligent, a fact often overlooked due to his appearance and simple, direct manner of speaking (which Lydia suspected was an affectation; he *liked* to be underestimated). Shane scratched his bald head. "We don't want people to panic. It might just be a glitch."

"How long are we going to wait?" Lydia asked. "They could be in danger." Of the three villages under observation, the denizens of Kaldbrek were the least predictable; their chieftain was young and brash. If the observation team had been detected they might now be prisoners. Or worse.

"That's not the only explanation," Adrian said.

"What do you mean?" Adrian just looked at her. Finally it occurred to her what he meant. They could have defected, like Car-En.

"You were friends with De Laurentiis," said Shane.

"I still am."

"Yes. Sorry. How well do you know him?"

"We were at the Academy together. Class of '24."

"Do you think he's the type to...."

"Defect? No." She was telling the truth. Aaron De Laurentiis loved his work; he'd been elated to receive the field position. But so had Car-En. She had gone over Car-En's desertion many times in her mind.

"That's not why you're here," said Xenus. He was protecting her; he didn't want her to think that Shane was interrogating her. But Shane was just doing his job. She knew why she was here. If there was a rescue mission, they would need a doctor. Xenus was present because he was Research Coordinator; ultimately the safety of Rosen and De Laurentiis were his responsibility.

"To answer your question, we're not going to wait," Adrian said. "We're leaving within the hour. Can you be ready?"

"Who else is going?" she asked.

"Just you and I," Shane answered. "The hovershuttle can hold five comfortably, but if there are wounded they'll take up more space. We'll both have dart rifles and disruptors. Are you trained?"

"I can point a disruptor. I've never fired a rifle."

"Fine," Shane said, "no rifle for you. More room in the shuttle."

"How long will it take to get there?"

Shane shrugged. "At top speed? A couple hours. Might be a rough ride – think you can handle it?"

"I can handle it." AFS-1 was roughly equidistant from the three known 'New Iron Age' settlements: the villages in the Harz mountains, a community in Israel, and an ancient town on the Mediterranean island of Sardinia. To get to the Harz region they would first need to cut through alpine valleys until they reached the forested flatlands of the central continent. Going southwest first, to the coast, and cutting *around* the mountains would make for a smoother ride, but they didn't have time for that.

"Good. It's settled," said Adrian. "Good luck. Return safely and quickly. We'll expect continuous contact and open m'eye feeds."

"Wait a minute. What else do we know? What was the last telemetry from the Kaldbrek team?"

"Not much," Shane said. "They were both in the actual village – which they shouldn't have been – then nothing. No m'eye data, no biostats, no location."

"Their kits were destroyed?"

"Or malfunctioned. Or were deactivated on purpose."

"Simultaneous malfunction seems unlikely," Lydia pointed out.

"I agree."

"Let's stop going around in circles," Adrian said. He was already getting up. "We don't have enough information, so enough guessing and speculating. Go find out what happened."

Xenus watched Adrian silently. He should be the one calling the shots in this situation. Xenus realized this, surely, but didn't want to butt heads with Adrian. It didn't make her think any less of him; Xenus was right to avoid turning this into a power struggle.

Xenus touched her arm as they headed toward the archway. "Be careful, okay? Svein is dangerous." Svein Haakonsson was the young chieftain, *jarl* of Kaldbrek. More than one team had recorded Svein meting out cruel punishments for minor infractions: floggings, half-drownings, even amputations. Culturally, Kaldbrek was less civilized and more brutal than the other Harz villages. No one knew why, but the subject was energetically debated within the department.

"I will be," she promised. She kissed him and ran her hand through his short hair. She considered asking him what she had missed at the pre-meeting but thought better of it. There was no time to waste.

Lydia donned her bioskin, packed her supplies, and met Shane at the hovershuttle bay, where he was stocking the shuttle with food canisters, g'nerf bars, and water cubes. He wore flexible armor over his bioskin and had a dart rifle slung over his back. His belt was equipped with a neural disruptor, a long carbonlattice blade, and an array of compact grenades in a variety of shapes and colors.

"Expecting a fight?"

"Always. There's a suit of armor in the backseat – try it on and see if it fits."

The armor was lighter than she expected, and didn't restrict her movement.

"Will this stop a sword?" she asked, half-jokingly.

Shane stopped and stared, box of g'nerf bars in hand.

"Sorry," she said.

"I'll do what I can to keep us safe, but I don't know what we're getting into. I don't like it."

"We don't really have much of a choice. Rosen and De Laurentiis might need our help."

He nodded without making eye contact, and resumed his packing. She picked up a pack of water cubes and handed it to him.

"Did you ever hear from her? Any message?" Shane asked.

"Hear from who?"

"Car-En."

The question caught her off-guard. She *had* heard from Car-En. Penelope Townes had told her, in secret, that Car-En was alive and well, living in Happdal; she'd fallen in love with one of the villagers. Car-En had destroyed or deactivated her kit, thus cutting off all contact with everyone on the *Stanford*. For two years everyone except for Lydia and Car-En's parents (who Townes had also informed) thought that Car-En had died, perhaps in an accident, perhaps murdered by the villagers she had been observing. Lydia, Marivic, and Shol had dutifully kept Car-En's secret, but each of them had mourned in their own way. It was *as if* Car-En had died, and it was impossible to not take her friend's decision personally, as rejection, even if Car-En *had* fallen in love with a handsome Viking-like villager.

Two years later, AFS-1 had gotten around to assigning a new observation team to Happdal. Surprise surprise, Car-En was alive and well. Not only alive, but married to a villager named Esper, and very pregnant. Lydia had known that Car-En had wanted to have children one day but had always considered it a *far off* possibility. The news triggered a storm of emotions: happiness for her friend, jealousy, anger, and a deep sense of unease. Car-En had not wanted to be discovered. For some reason (Townes had been vague about why) Car-En especially wanted to hide her whereabouts, and even the fact that she was alive, from Adrian. Why was that? Why was Car-En hiding? Or *what* was she hiding?

Adrian had not visibly reacted to the news that Car-En was very much alive. This seemed suspicious. Most people who knew Car-En were elated, or at least interested. Over the years Lydia had kept track of her friend via the Happdal research team. She had even considered at one point trying to make contact. But she had decided against it. Car-En had made her choice, romantic and foolish as it was. She seemed happy, and Lydia made peace with it.

And then Marivic had died. The death of Car-En's mother left Lydia feeling raw and exposed. Not only did she mourn the loss of Marivic (always a friend – but even more so after Car-En had disappeared), she mourned the fact that mother and daughter had never reunited, had never had a chance to say goodbye and one last 'I love you.' Car-En and Marivic had not had the easiest relationship. The saddest thing was that Marivic had never met her grandson. Now Shol was alone, and would probably never meet his grandson either. The whole business left Lydia feeling hopeless. She tried not to think about it.

"Yes," she heard herself say.

Shane lifted one eyebrow. "You *did* hear from her?"

She wondered if he already knew, and was testing her. But he seemed genuinely surprised.

"I always knew she was alive. Penelope Townes told me."

"Townes? Why didn't she make it public?"

"You'll have to ask her that yourself."

Lydia felt lighter suddenly. She rolled her shoulders back. Secrets were toxic, and this was one less she had to carry. And what did it matter? Everyone knew that Car-En was alive. Everyone knew that she had chosen life with the villagers over an academic career on the *Stanford*.

Shane grunted and furrowed his brow.

"Why did you ask?"

"I was just thinking about her. I never met her, but I've always been interested in her case. What she did was so…drastic. Leaving all her friends and family behind. Why do you think she defected?"

"She didn't *defect*. We're not at war with the villagers."

"What would you call it?"

"Falling in love. That's what happened."

Shane shoved in one last box of g'nerf bars and secured an elastic net over the storage compartment. "You think that's all there was to it?"

"Isn't that enough?" She wondered if Shane had ever fallen in love himself.

Shane took the driver's seat (without asking), and soon they were shooting across the open countryside, just a few meters above the grasslands. Lydia tried to relax and enjoy the scenery through the transparent envirodome. On her supply runs with Xenus they had often taken the southern route along the Mediterranean coast, traveling 'top-down,' wind in their hair. That was fun at lower speeds, but Shane was pushing the hovershuttle close to its top speed. Within twenty minutes they were a hundred kilometers north of the field station, already climbing into the mountains. Shane piloted the hovershuttle proficiently, but after hitting a few rough patches she realized that *she* was the more experienced pilot. She did, after all, have close to a hundred supply runs under her belt.

"It's a smoother ride at about fifteen meters," she said. "Especially over the rocky bits."

Shane said nothing, but slowly lowered the control wheel. The turbines whirred softly beneath their feet; the altimeter rose to fifteen. She shot Shane a glance as the turbulence subsided. He kept his eyes locked ahead. That was okay. She could handle his poker face – just as long as he was open to suggestions.

They followed, roughly, the line of an expressway that had once run north–south through Europe. Rain and tough grasses had long since broken up the asphalt, but the outlines of the route were still traceable where the road had been carved out of the terrain, or by piles of stone or crumbled brick that had once been roadside buildings. As they climbed, the scenery became even more breathtaking: green hills forested with evergreens; towering mountains in the background capped with snow that never melted. They passed through ruins hidden in a long valley. Lydia activated the historical layer on the map display. Aosta, an Italian city. Some of the stone ruins were Roman, but the area had been a human settlement since the Late Neolithic. Lydia shivered. So many lives and generations, all forgotten.

"What is it?" Shane asked.

"The ruins. I never get used to it."

He nodded. "Souls of the dead."

"Exactly," she said. "That's what it feels like." She started to say *poetic*, but stopped herself. He *had* meant it figuratively, hadn't he? He had to have. She watched his face for a moment, but his expression was inscrutable. She didn't know him at all. She wondered if she should feel more nervous about this mission. Would he keep them safe? She *felt* safe around him, but as Security Director he was probably trained to engender such feelings of trust and confidence. But those feelings didn't actually make her any safer. They were heading into a dangerous situation. She resolved to be more alert, to keep her wits about her, and to not psychologically outsource her protection to Shane. She was responsible for her *own* safety.

"I have ancestors from this region," Shane said. "A little north actually. Swiss. It's one reason I volunteered. To see if I would feel anything. A connection to the land, or something like that."

"Did you?" she asked. "Do you?"

He shrugged. "Not really. Maybe. I do feel something, but I don't think it's particular to this region. I think it's just…Earth. Living on land."

"It took me a few years to adjust." It felt like an admission. She had only ever talked to Xenus about her vertigo. The open skies hadn't bothered Xenus at all.

"Same here," Shane said. "I kept my eyes on the ground for six months. Literally – I didn't look up. Except at night, to see the *Stanford*."

She laughed. "I was the same way."

Shane slowed the hovershuttle as they approached the base of a towering mountain. The rusted, decrepit remains of a vast metal arch spanned their path. Beyond that was a huge pile of concrete rubble.

"What's this?" Lydia asked.

"It used to be a tunnel. Mont Blanc."

"Look," said Lydia, "there's still an opening. See, on the right? We could send in a drone." The storage compartment contained a case of a dozen insect-like drones. The mini-drones could be operated remotely or set to autonomous mode.

Shane shook his head. "Even if it's not collapsed, the air won't be breathable. It's quite long – over eleven kilometers."

"We could seal the dome. It would save time, right?"

"I don't think so. We can go much faster in the open."

An alert flashed in her m'eye. It was from Adrian, emergency priority, addressed to both of them. They must have been out of direct contact for a while. "Main screen?" she asked. Shane nodded. She routed playback to the shuttle display. The recording was of both Adrian and Xenus, from Adrian's office. At the sight of Xenus she felt a flash of guilt. Part of her mind started to analyze the emotional reaction, but she shut it down. Now wasn't the time.

"The bioskin telemetry came back online." It was Xenus talking. He looked tired and gaunt. "They're both alive."

"That's the good news," said Adrian. "The bad news is that they're both in bad shape. Biostats are showing elevated stress, and acute physical pain for Rosen. And his bioskin – Rosen's – has been damaged, a major rip or tear."

"Get there as fast as you can," Xenus said. "They're in serious trouble. No need to report – we're tracking you. Just...hurry up."

The recording ended.

"Torture?" she asked.

"I hope not," said Shane. His eyes flicked as he accessed his m'eye. "I'm finding an alternate route."

Lydia touched the neural disruptor strapped to her belt. Even at top speed, they were still hours away. To physically torture another human being...only one word came to mind. She pushed it aside; the word reeked of cultural chauvinism, even xenophobia. It was exactly the kind of judgmental, prejudicial word the department tried to avoid when discussing the villagers. But the word kept pushing its way to the front of her mind.

Barbaric.

CHAPTER FIVE

Tem's parched throat ached. He tried to say something...*hello*...but only managed a croak. He was in a basement, with a dirt floor and rough stone walls. Dim rays of light shone through cracks in the heavy trapdoor at the top of the ladder, enough to illuminate the bucket filled with his own piss, a pile of iron bars, a rusty pickaxe, and a dull hatchet. If he were stronger he might be able to use the tools to escape, to rescue his mother, and to kill Svein. But he was weak.

Völund, the smith, had thrown him down here. He had twisted his ankle when he landed on the packed earth; now the swollen joint throbbed painfully. At least they hadn't bothered to tie him up. He had gingerly climbed the ladder and pressed on the trapdoor. It hadn't budged, not even a little. Perhaps something was weighing it down.

Hours ago, he'd heard screams. He worried that they were his mother's. It had sounded like a man screaming, but he couldn't be sure. Where was Mother? What had they done to her?

He had cried at first, quietly. He didn't want to give them the satisfaction. He didn't call out for help. He would fight them, any way he could. He had not surrendered, *would* not.

The light from above dimmed, then darkened. Nightfall. He heard men enter the smithy. They lit a lantern, and Tem could see a little. They spoke in hushed voices, but he caught a word here and there. *Spy. Punishment. Sky people.* What did that mean? His mother was a sky person. Were they devising some punishment for her? Later he heard *eagle.* Did they think the sky people could fly? Were they so ignorant? The men left, and it was dark again.

He fell asleep, curled up on the cold dirt floor. He awoke to faraway sounds of men shouting, and terrible screams. Someone was being tortured, and dying. Eventually the screams stopped, only to start again, which elicited raucous laughter from the men, who started to chant a single word. *Salt! Salt! Salt!* Tem pressed his hands against his ears to drown out the screaming and the chanting, but it only muffled the terrible sounds. His bit his own lip until he tasted blood.

Finally the screaming and chanting stopped. Whatever had happened was done. If they had killed his mother he would kill them all, slowly, with hot iron.

He lay on his side for hours, shivering, staring wide-eyed into the darkness.

★   ★   ★

The creak of the trapdoor woke him. The light was blinding.

"Get up, boy! I have work for you." Tem could only see the backlit silhouette of the large man, but he recognized the voice. Völund, the smith.

Cold water splashed on his face. Desperately, he licked what he could. He wiped his face with his hands and licked the dirty water from his palms.

"Get up here quick before I haul you up by your hair!"

Tem looked for the hatchet. It was still there, lying on the dirt in the corner, near the bucket. Maybe if he was lucky, he could take out Völund with a single throw.

Völund laughed. "Go ahead, give it a go. I'll only cut off one of your toes as punishment. I'll use that same dull axe."

Tem climbed the ladder carefully, favoring his sore ankle. He flinched when Völund touched his shoulder, but the smith only steadied him.

"Where's my mother?" said Tem.

Völund didn't answer, but instead handed Tem a clay jug. "Drink. You'll need your strength today."

Tem took the sloshing jug. He wanted badly to raise it to his lips and drink. "Where is she?"

"Alive and well. A prisoner, like you, but unharmed."

"Give me your word," Tem said. "Swear on the Red Brother's hammer."

Völund frowned, smoothing his long mustache. His hand looked like a piece of blackened wood, more scarred and burned than even Jense's. "Boy, don't give me orders. I don't know if they let you talk back to your elders in Happdal, but if you do it again I'll cuff you."

"Swear that she's all right, and I'll do as you ask."

Völund's hand shot out, quick as a marten. Tem ducked, but the smith's palm caught the top of his head and knocked him to the ground. The clay jug shattered on the stone floor.

"I warned you," Völund said. "Now you'll go thirsty."

The smith went to his worktable, grabbed his hammer, and turned back toward Tem. Tem gathered himself onto his hands and knees, preparing to spring away. He would not let himself be crushed like a beetle. But the smith did not raise his hammer.

"I swear on my hammer, and on the Red Brother's hammer, that your mother is unharmed."

Tem stood.

"There, are you happy?" Völund asked. "Are you ready to work?"

Without waiting for an answer, the smith pointed to the furnace. "Light it. I know you know how. I know who you are, Tem Espersson. From now on you work for me. Not as an apprentice, mind you. Servant and bellows boy. But if you work hard, I'll treat you fairly."

Tem stared at the smith mutely.

"Be quick about it! Once the fire is lit you may drink from the quench bucket. It's fresh from the river."

Tem lit the fire, then drank until his throat muscles ached from the effort of swallowing. The cold water from the quench bucket tasted only a little metallic. He did as Völund ordered, sweeping the floor and pumping the bellows. When Völund wasn't looking he tried to peek out the smithy windows, but they were too high. He missed Mother badly; the feeling was a tightness in his stomach and throat that wouldn't go away. He wondered if Father and Farbror would come for them, as they had come for Tante Katja in the story. But they hadn't found Katja. Jense had found her, and nearly killed her. But in the end, everyone had made it back to Happdal. That was the important part.

He decided to bide his time until he felt stronger. Once Völund let his guard down, he would try to escape and find Mother. Until then, he would do as Völund ordered, and keep his mouth shut. The smith did not seem so terrible, and there were worse places to be kept prisoner than a smithy. There were examples of Völund's craft on the worktable and the cooling rack. The workmanship looked crude to Tem's eyes, inferior to Jense and Trond's standards. But it was far better than anything Tem could make. He had only been allowed to pound on a hot pig iron bar to make it flat. Once his arms were big from pumping the bellows for many years, he would be taught to truly work iron, and then, much later, steel.

"Is this your blade?" asked Völund. Tem's heart jumped. The smith held the longknife Trond had given him.

"That's mine!" Tem yelled. "Give it to me!"

Völund laughed. "This blade is far too good for you. Happdal must be rich, to waste godsteel on a boy."

"My uncle made it," Tem said, forcing himself to calm down. Yelling at Völund would do no good.

"I know," said Völund. "It bears his mark. It's not as good as Jense's work, but your uncle is learning."

He's better than you.

"This blade has no balance. Here…feel this one." Völund picked up a different longknife from the worktable and handed it to Tem, hilt first. Tem took it, suppressing the urge to stab Völund. Tem was not strong enough to land a killing blow. He would probably not even pierce the smith's hide vest. Instead, he examined the blade. It was unpolished and unsharpened, and the hilt was only plain bone, with no leather wrap. Still, it felt good in his hand. It was a plain mudsteel blade, but Völund was right; it was well balanced. Better, in that respect, than the longknife Trond had given him. Tem handed it back without a word.

"Ha! So I'll get no praise from you. Fine – I know my own skill. If you keep your head down maybe I'll teach you something. Perhaps one day I'll let you hold Faen." Völund pointed to an immense greatsword mounted on the wall. "That blade has killed six men."

All day, he worked. He pumped the bellows, swept the flagstones clean, and sorted coal into bins by size. In the evening Völund gave him food (stale rye bread, sour goat's buttermilk, a boiled pig's foot) and made him climb down to the basement to sleep. The next morning Völund gave him a bucket of potatoes to clean and peel. The knife was dull, and Tem found a whetstone and sharpened it himself. Völund noticed, and didn't stop him, but made sure Tem returned the knife when he was done. This single note of caution heartened Tem; Völund might not fear him, but at least he did not think him placid.

And Völund was right; Tem would murder him, if given the chance. Or so Tem told himself.

Not once was he allowed outside. A dark-haired girl came and emptied his waste bucket (he said hello to her, but she did not answer and would not even look at him). Völund fed him twice that day and let him drink freely from an earthenware jug. He was no longer hungry, but he missed the sun and the outdoors. Even more so, he missed Mother.

Unlike the Happdal smithy, the bellows station was inside, right next to the furnace, hot and uncomfortable. Where were the Kaldbrek bellows boys? Were they jealous of him – the prisoner who had taken over their job? He would be jealous, in their place. This led him to wonder what Völund wanted with him. Did the Kaldbrek smith hope to learn Trond's and Jense's secrets through Tem? He would tell Völund *nothing*. But the smith did not ask him questions, and instead continued to assign Tem chores.

"When can I see my mother?" Tem asked, toward the end of the day. He had finished every task assigned by Völund.

The smith continued to sharpen a longknife on the treadle wheel, not looking up. Tem swept the already clean flagstones for several minutes. Then he repeated the question.

Völund lifted his foot from the pedal. He held up the blade and examined its edge. "Not yet," he said.

"Then when?"

Völund glared at him. Tem held the smith's gaze, but he could not stop his body from recoiling. The smith's face softened. "She fine," he said. "Your mother is unharmed. Don't worry about her."

Tem watched Völund's face closely. Grownups were skillful liars. It was easy to know when children were lying (little ones especially – their voices took on a sing-song quality and their eyes went in all directions). But children learned to mask these telltale signs as they grew older. Tem himself had already learned to do so.

Later, Völund gave him a thin iron rod and a hammer. "Heat it," he said, "and show me how you strike."

Tem stuck the bar in the furnace until the end glowed yellowish-orange, then grabbed it with the tongs and placed it on the anvil. He struck it only twice before Völund corrected him. "Choke up," the smith said. "The hammer is too heavy for you." Tem gritted his teeth and adjusted his grip. He knew that Völund had given him the smallest hammer, and still it was too heavy. When would his arms grow? The smith laughed and patted his back. "Don't worry, you'll grow soon enough. Sweeping won't grow your arms, but the hammer will."

For dinner that night Völund brought him a stale crust of rye as usual, but also a jug of whole milk with the cream still in (instead of the sour, watery milk left over from butter-making). He wondered again where the other bellows boys were. Maybe there weren't any. Maybe that's why Völund had stolen him, so that he could have an apprentice one day.

That night he cried himself to sleep, thinking of Mother. The tightness in his stomach and throat wouldn't go away. He missed her badly, and feared for her. The men of Kaldbrek were cruel. Mother was strong, but she couldn't fight a whole village. Where was Father? He and Farbror would come looking for them. But what if Father had changed his mind, and stayed in Happdal, as Farmor Elke had wanted him to? In that case Father would expect Tem and Mother to be gone for a long time. Many months, or even a full year. Maybe Father wasn't coming at all.

CHAPTER SIX

Lydia and Shane hid in the spruce forest about ninety meters back from the bonfire, watching through infrared binoculars. Three of the insect drones, much closer to the fire, were sending them visual feeds.

Alexi Rosen was dead, murdered in a gruesome ritual. He'd been stripped and tied facedown to a wooden cross, his back ribs gaping open on each side of his spine. His lungs, pulled through the open wounds, hung limply alongside his ribcage.

A few drunken men still loitered about the clearing, but most had dispersed. One of the long wooden tables had been overturned. A mangy dog sniffed at the scraps.

How long had Rosen suffered? It was impossible to know. His bioskin had stopped transmitting data twenty minutes after the message from Xenus and Adrian. He'd been dead when they'd arrived. Lydia could only hope he hadn't suffered for long.

"Look," said Shane. Three old women approached Rosen. They untied him from the cross and covered his body with a swath of burlap, handling his heavy corpse easily. Once he was wrapped they carried him away. The dog trotted after them.

Lydia checked the bioskin telemetry from Aaron De Laurentiis, Rosen's research partner. The other researcher was still alive. His vitals signs – adrenaline, heart rate, and blood pressure – were all dangerously elevated. She called up a top-down display in her m'eye; De Laurentiis's location showed as a blue dot. He was only one hundred twenty meters away, just west of the clearing.

She lowered the binoculars and turned to Shane. He pointed toward De Laurentiis's position. "I'm sending in the drones now."

"Patch me in."

The drone feeds appeared in her m'eye. The insectile robots were closing in on a sturdy wooden structure with no windows, guarded by two men holding heavy spears. Three meters and closing. One meter. Abruptly the view went dark – the tiny drones were squeezing in through cracks in the wood. Moments later the visual feed returned: two figures, a man and a woman, both bound hand and foot, a reflective glint of silver from the man's uniform.

"The bioskin – that's him," she whispered. "What should we do?" Shane didn't answer. Lifting the binoculars again, she surveyed the clearing. The bonfire was dying. The remaining men had either left or fallen asleep in the tall grass.

"The woman…who is she?" Shane asked.

Lydia refocused on her m'eye. The bound woman was asleep on her side, turned away from the drones (the insect-bots were now perched on the wall, perfectly still). "I don't know, but I'm guessing she's in trouble. Maybe she stole something, or slept with the wrong person."

"I thought these villagers didn't care much about infidelity," Shane said.

"I don't think it's a crime punishable by death, but someone might have gotten jealous."

Shane grunted. "If she's locked up with De Laurentiis, it's serious. I'm guessing tomorrow night there's going to be another ritual."

"So you think we're safe for the night?"

Shane shook his head. "We're nothing like safe. We're going to end this now and get out of here."

They pulled the close-fitting bioskin hoods over their heads. The skins color-shifted as they moved; with the camouflage and the darkness they were nearly invisible. Shane carried his dart rifle; Lydia held her disruptor in her right hand and a utility knife in her left. She followed closely behind Shane, crouched low and moving quietly just as he had instructed.

Shane moved quickly, staying in the cover of the trees until the last possible moment. Lydia checked the time in her m'eye: 2300 hours. Not that late, but most of Kaldbrek had gone to bed. They passed the bonfire undetected, closing in on the wooden structure where De Laurentiis was held captive. She could see the guards now with her own eyes. Shane knelt and aimed his dart rifle. It was a long shot – over fifty meters. One of the guards crumpled. The other straightened up, looked around, then lowered his spear in their direction.

"Quick," whispered Lydia, "before he alerts the others." Shane aimed carefully, taking his time. The remaining guard shouldn't have been able to see them at this distance, not in the dark, not with their camouflaged bioskins, but he was moving toward them. No, he was *sprinting* toward them, pulling back his shoulder to hurl his spear.

Shane fired. The guard kept running for a few seconds before his grip slackened. He dropped the spear and crouched, hands on knees, breathing heavily. He stood, drew a knife from his belt, and staggered toward them.

Shane swore under his breath, then leapt to his feet and ran toward the guard. At ten meters he fired his neural disruptor. The guard collapsed. Shane stood over the body, pointing the disruptor, until he was sure the man was down. Shane waved Lydia over and she joined him, heart pounding against her sternum.

The guard was still alive – that much she could see with her infrared. He'd wake within the hour, or much sooner if he was resistant to the dart sedative. "Let's move," she said. Shane was already entering the windowless wooden structure. She followed cautiously, disruptor raised. Shane was sawing away at De Laurentiis's bindings.

"Help," croaked Aaron De Laurentiis. Thin to begin with, he now looked emaciated. But he was alive. The bioskin had told them as much, but she felt a flood of relief seeing her old friend with her own eyes. De Laurentiis squinted at her.

"It's Lydia. It's good to see you, but stay quiet for now."

Shane helped De Laurentiis to his feet. The researcher looked shaky. Her m'eye indicated that he had a fever; she would check for infection when they got back to the hovershuttle. Dehydration was also likely.

"Where's Rosen?" De Laurentiis asked. "They took him away."

"Can you walk?" Shane asked. De Laurentiis nodded.

Lydia looked at the other captive. "What about her?" The woman was bound and gagged, but had rolled over to face them. She was small-framed for a villager. In the dark it was impossible to make out her features, but somehow she looked familiar.

"Not our problem," Shane said.

"Who is she?" Lydia asked.

De Laurentiis shrugged. "We couldn't talk. We were both gagged."

The captive woman tried to say something through her gag.

"We should free her," Lydia said.

Shane shook his head. "Non-intervention. You know the rules. We have to leave. *Now.*"

The woman thrashed on the ground, yells muffled by her gag. Shane shot her with the disruptor. She went limp.

"Was that necessary?" Lydia asked.

Shane was already heading out the door, practically carrying De Laurentiis. As soon as Shane was out of sight, Lydia knelt and cut the rope binding the woman's ankles and wrists. She folded the utility knife and left it next to the prisoner's limp body. Whatever the woman had done, she didn't deserve what had happened to Rosen. No one did. She felt sick at the thought of telling De Laurentiis that Rosen was dead, and had been tortured. She ran and caught up with the others.

Shane led them on a circuitous route back to the hovershuttle, avoiding the flickering remains of the bonfire. Apparently he wasn't ready to tell De Laurentiis either; the bad news could wait. Adrian was trying to patch in via her m'eye. She ignored the alert. That could wait too. Adrian probably wanted to congratulate them, but she didn't feel ready to be congratulated. Not until they were back at the hovershuttle, at least, and maybe not even then. There was no cause for celebration; Alexi Rosen had been tortured to death.

She felt sick. A moment later she was on her hands and knees, emptying the contents of her stomach onto the soft undergrowth of the spruce forest. The mildly sweet taste of half-digested g'nerf bars mixed with her own stomach acid only increased her nausea. She dry heaved until her stomach muscles ached.

"Shane," she said weakly. He hadn't stopped. They weren't that far ahead – she could see them as blue dots in her m'eye display. Why hadn't he stopped? Shakily, she stood, and walked slowly in the direction of the hovershuttle.

She took her time, savoring the physical relief that followed vomiting. According to the drones, nobody was chasing them. It was peaceful here in the woods. The late summer night air was pleasantly cool. She heard crickets, running water in the distance.

Something about the female prisoner....

She considered opening a patch to Xenus but decided against it. He was probably with Adrian, and she wasn't yet ready to talk to Adrian. There was no need to apprise them of the situation; all her feeds were open. They could see what she saw, hear what she heard. They had witnessed her vomiting. The thought made her laugh. "Serves you right," she muttered to nobody in particular. She checked the feed status in her m'eye. They *weren't* open. She had turned them off right before slashing the second prisoner's bindings.

When she reached the hovershuttle, Aaron De Laurentiis was lying flat on the back passenger bench under a synthiwool blanket.

"You okay?" Shane asked.

"Fine. Thanks for asking."

"We should go," he said. He was already seated behind the control wheel.

"Not yet," she said. "I want to give De Laurentiis a quick exam. And he probably needs a hydration drip."

"Can you do it in flight?"

"Not as easily. Not the way you drive."

"I promise I'll keep it at fifteen meters. Smooth as silk."

She boarded. Shane spun the turbines before she was even fully seated. The hovershuttle lurched upwards. "Watch it!"

Shane slowly brought the hovershuttle to fifteen meters, closing the twin hemispheres of the envirodome as they rose. Soon they were flying south at two hundred kilometers per hour.

They reported to Adrian and Xenus. Xenus had many questions about Rosen, but they didn't know any more than he did. He had all the information they did, via the feeds and drones. Rosen had been brutally tortured and murdered, reasons unknown. Adrian claimed he knew the name of the ritual. *Rista örn*, he called it. The blood eagle. Maybe De Laurentiis could tell them more, but for now the surviving researcher was out cold. Lydia had given him a sedative along with a broad-spectrum antibiotic.

"Who was the woman?" Adrian asked. "The other prisoner."

"We don't know," Shane said. "Neither does De Laurentiis."

"She didn't look like a villager."

"We followed protocol," said Shane, sounding defensive.

Lydia replayed the sequence in her m'eye. It was hard to make out the woman's features in the heatmap infrared image. She froze a frame where the woman was staring at them, then edited the image with a visible light interpretation filter. She recognized the woman instantly.

"Shane!"

"What? What is it?"

The patch to Adrian and Xenus was still open. She would have to tell him later. But they needed to turn around. *Soon.*

The color interpretation wasn't perfect – the program had chosen too light of a skin tone. And the woman in the picture was older and thinner than Lydia remembered her.

But there was no doubt in her mind. The other captive was Car-En Ganzorig.

CHAPTER SEVEN

The next day, in addition to his chores, Völund gave Tem time at the anvil. "Make a knife," he said, giving no instruction beyond that. Tem did the best he could. He had watched Trond and Jense make dozens of knives, and knew what steps were involved, but his hands would not obey his mind. He hammered the heated rod to flatten it, but it bent. Trying to correct his mistake, he only managed to further twist the metal. Parts of the iron were too thin, other parts too thick. Völund watched him, saying nothing. At least he did not laugh. Tem kept reheating and striking the metal, grimacing at the ugly thing that in no way resembled a knife.

Völund finally spoke. "Warm metal won't yield. Put it back in the fire until it glows *white*. If the fire isn't hot enough, you know what to do."

Tem returned the metal to the fire, added more coal to the furnace, and stoked the bellows until his arms ached and his skin was slick with sweat. When he pulled the mangled scrap of iron from the fire, it glowed light yellow, and when he struck it, it *did* yield more easily. He struck it again and again. Each shower of sparks further purified the iron. Dusk fell, and still Tem worked the metal. His ears hurt, and every strike jarred his bones.

After thousands of blows, Tem stopped to rest. Völund grabbed the metal with his own tongs and held it up to the lantern light. Tem's work was crude, but the result did resemble a knife. An ugly knife, but a knife nonetheless.

"Terrible," said Völund, but the smith was smiling. Tem kept his own face stony, but inside his heart was bursting with pride. He had made his first weapon.

★   ★   ★

Darkness fell. Völund opened the trapdoor and gestured for Tem to descend, but did not close the door above him. Tem obeyed, despite his growling stomach. Would he get no dinner tonight? Someone – a young woman from the sound of her voice – came into the smithy and spoke quietly, but urgently, with Völund. Tem thought it might be the dark-haired girl. Tem overheard her address the smith as 'Farbror.' So the dark-haired girl was Völund's niece. He trapped the fact in his mind, hoping to use it later.

"Tem, come get your food!" Völund called out. Tem climbed back up the ladder.

It *was* the dark-haired girl, and she'd brought him dinner: a bowl of stew, a mug of creamy milk, and a thick slice of buttered bread. He drank half the milk in one swallow, not even minding the grassy, goaty taste.

"You may sit with us," Völund said. Tem balanced the bread atop the bowl and carefully carried it and the mug to the table. The girl glared at him.

"Saga is jealous that I let you use the hammer today."

Tem took a bite of the buttered bread, keeping his eyes down. It was crusty and sour and delicious.

"She would call herself my apprentice, but she had no talent. I tell her smithing is a *man's* job, but she won't listen. She tugs on my belt like a little girl, harassing and bothering. Once I made the mistake of giving her the hammer. You should have seen the mangled mess she made. Tem, compared to my niece, you are a *master* smith." Völund laughed heartily. Tem risked a glance at Saga. Her skin had paled and she stared at the table fiercely.

"I told her she can pick up my hammer when I die, but not a day before then. And even when I'm with the Three Brothers, I'll frown from the afterlife, and never bless her work."

Tem chewed his bread and wondered why Völund was so cruel. Perhaps he hated Saga's father, and took it out on the daughter. Siblings could go to war. Even Father and Farbror Trond fought at times. There had been a fight about beards once....

"Then I hope you die *soon!*" Saga yelled, rising to her feet and making as if to strike her uncle. Despite his size and strength, Völund flinched. He recovered quickly and swatted at Saga.

"Go! Bring breakfast in the morning. Don't be so sensitive. You have other talents. It's not my fault smithing is not one of them."

Saga slammed the door behind her. Völund patted Tem on the shoulder. "Don't worry about her. She loses her temper easily. Now finish your food, then sleep. Tomorrow your arms will ache, but there's more work to be done. You'll make another knife, and one the day after that, and again until you've something to take pride in. Your shoulders will burn, but you'll get used to it." Völund rose and returned to his workbench. Tem ate his stew in silence while Völund straightened his tools. When he finished he went to the ladder.

"If you want me to be your apprentice, I need to see my mother. I need to know she's all right."

It was a lie – he would *never* willingly be Völund's apprentice – but if there was leverage to use, he would use it.

Völund did not look up from his work.

There was a cry from outside, and footsteps, someone running.

The door swung open, letting in a gust of cool night air. It was Saga, eyes wide with terror. Völund leapt to his feet and grabbed the greatsword Faen from its place on the wall. Someone pushed the girl from behind; she fell forward onto the hard stone floor. Tem heard the crack of bone. Tall men rushed through the door. Völund shouted and drew Faen from its fur-lined sheath, but one of the men leapt forward and sliced Völund's throat with a longknife, turning the smith's shout into a gurgle. A sheet of blood fell down the front of his hide vest. Tem scrambled under a table, but a strong hand grabbed his arm and dragged him back. He cried out.

"Tem! Calm down. You're safe now."

It was Father. His face was painted brown with clay and dirt. His longknife glistened with Völund's blood. Behind him stood Askr, sword drawn.

"Quickly, we need to go," said Askr. His face was also painted, but Tem remembered him from the guard station.

Tem pulled his arm free from Father's grip and went to the drawer where he had seen Völund stash the longknife Farbror Trond has gifted him. On the way he passed the smith, who stared at him wide-eyed, mouth agape.

"You're lucky," Tem said. "This is a good death for you." In truth he felt bad for the smith; Völund had not treated him so badly in the end. But he did not yet know Mother's fate. If she was injured, and Völund had any part in that, then this death was better than the smith deserved.

He found his longknife. "Ready?" Father asked. Tem nodded.

Saga stared at Tem as he passed. She was clutching her elbow, and her lip was bleeding.

"Are you all right?" Tem asked.

She spat, landing a glob of blood-streaked mucus on Tem's trouser leg.

"Quickly," said Father, "and quietly." Men were shouting in the distance.

They fled into the darkness.

CHAPTER EIGHT

Shane stared ahead, shoulders tense. Lydia had insisted, then implored, that they go back. She'd even considered grabbing the control wheel, or disabling him with the neural disruptor, but she was afraid of crashing the hovershuttle and killing them all. At two hundred kph it would be a quick and definitive death.

Stay calm. He'll listen to reason.

"It was her," she said. "I'm sure of it."

He relaxed a little, perhaps sensing her desperation. Maybe he was thinking that as long as she was talking, she wouldn't try anything stupid.

"You can't be sure," he said. "You haven't seen her in person for ten years. And nightvision can be deceiving."

"You saw the corrected image yourself. I showed you the comparison pictures – don't tell me that didn't look like Car-En."

"That's not enough to go on. Like I said, first priority is returning to Vandercamp and getting De Laurentiis medical care. Then we can share what we've learned with Adrian and request a second mission."

"I told you – we *can't* tell Adrian. Car-En doesn't want him to know...."

"What? That she's still alive? He already knows that from the Happdal feeds."

"Look, for some reason she wanted to stay hidden. I just want to be careful."

"Lydia, I don't mean to offend you – but you sound paranoid. Even if it *was* her, what danger could Adrian possibly pose to Car-En?"

This was going nowhere – they were talking in circles. She turned in her seat and checked on De Laurentiis. He was still asleep. His monitor bracelet showed normal blood pressure and only a slight fever. Glucose was within range. Potassium and magnesium levels were low, but not dangerously so.

"He's out of the woods," she said, refilling De Laurentiis's electrolyte drip.

"Good," said Shane.

She wasn't giving up on getting Shane to turn the hovershuttle around, but she needed a new tack. Shane was right that they didn't have a way to positively identify Car-En. She should have instructed the drones to look for a sample; a hair or even an eyelash could have confirmed her identity. Or an iris scan. But the insect-bots had defaulted to following them back to the shuttle, and were now stowed in their carry case.

The night before they had flown only a short distance before landing. Shane had nearly flown them into a tree, and hadn't argued when Lydia insisted that they rest for the night. They'd slept in the grounded hovershuttle, Shane soundly, her fitfully. Several times she'd checked on De Laurentiis. At one point the field researcher had woken up and asked about Rosen. She had responded by giving him another sedative. With the stress and the drugs it was possible De Laurentiis's mind wasn't yet forming memories, and she only wanted to tell the grim story once. Or maybe not at all – maybe that task could fall to Shane.

At dawn they continued home, heading southwest along the remains of a major expressway. According to the hovershuttle's navigation display, it had once been called *R45*. Now, far to the west, she saw ivy-covered stone towers peeking through the trees, a castle or a church of some kind. Stone buildings had outlasted metal ones. All the skyscrapers had fallen long ago, rusted away, concrete foundations broken up by roots and washed away by centuries of rain. But some ancient castles and cathedrals remained, seemingly impervious to the passage of time. She briefly considered looking up the castle's history, but she already knew the gist of it. Long ago, people had built the structure for some military or political reason, and now they were all dead.

Earth's globally connected civilization had disintegrated, and terrestrial population had plummeted from billions to thousands. Ringstation peoples and culture had lived on, a branch of humanity that somehow flourished even as the main trunk died. A handful of 'primitive' hunter-gatherer peoples had also survived: those who had rejected contact from technologically advanced societies. And then there were the villagers, the few anomalous groups who had weathered the

Survivalist Age with mostly Iron Age technologies and a smorgasbord of belief systems and social structures which the ringstation anthropologists were just beginning to understand.

What would the villagers do if they found such a castle? Would they move in? Who was to say it wasn't already inhabited? It was unlikely the survivors they knew about were the *only* survivors. The vast majority of Survivalists had killed each other off or starved to death, but pockets of humanity persisted here and there. Surely not all the survivors had been discovered. The thought made her shiver. As barbaric as the Harz villagers sometimes appeared, they lived in a structured society with social norms. There might be humans out there who were truly feral, devoid of language or formal culture. Devolved people, intelligent but completely animalistic.

"Maybe we can check it out on the way back," Shane said.

"Check what out?"

Shane's eyes flicked back and forth as he read from his m'eye. "Looks like it was called Löwenburg Castle. Some kind of monastery. Surprised you didn't look it up – you've been staring at it for the last five minutes."

"It worries me what might live there," she said.

"My guess would be bears. At least when winter comes around. Looks like a good place to hibernate."

Shane was probably right. There might have been feral humans long ago. But without societies – even primitive ones – they would have died out.

A few hours later they could see the Alps in the distance. De Laurentiis woke up and started asking questions. Shane told him about Alexi, leaving out the most gruesome details. For a long time no one spoke. *Had they been close?* It was a stupid question – of course they'd been close. Even if they hadn't gotten along well, they'd worked together, camped together, faced danger together.

"They're not all like that, you know," said De Laurentiis. His voice was hoarse.

"Like what?" Shane asked.

"Cruel. Violent. It's Svein's influence. The jarl. And a few other men. Mostly they're good people. Kind. Not much different than us."

Tactfully, Shane didn't answer. It was obvious to Lydia that the villagers were *significantly* different from them, but she didn't want to contradict De Laurentiis, who seemed to derive comfort from the thought that the villagers were similar to ringstation folk.

"He's insane. Mentally ill, I mean," continued De Laurentiis. "Paranoid and delusional. But also highly functional, and a control freak. If someone else were jarl, Kaldbrek would be different. The jarl sets the mood of the village. No, more than the mood – the ethical norms."

"Who would be a better jarl for Kaldbrek?" Lydia asked, mostly to humor the researcher.

"Egil," De Laurentiis answered without hesitation. "Egil the Bard."

"I thought he was exiled," Lydia said. Years ago she had closely followed the reports and recordings from the Harz observers, anxious for news about Car-En. Egil's exile was a story that had stuck in her mind, though she couldn't remember the reason for it. Hadn't he killed someone?

"He was," De Laurentiis confirmed. "He lives in Skrova now. But the last few years he's been allowed back to visit. He's still loved and trusted by most people in Kaldbrek. Much more than Svein."

"Then why did Svein let him back?" Shane asked. "It sounds like he's a threat. Especially to someone suffering from paranoia."

"That was something we were trying to figure out," said De Laurentiis. Once more they lapsed into silence, a moment of respect for Rosen. They climbed for a while, until Shane led the hovershuttle into a wide alpine valley. Soon they would be home.

As they raced over the verdant landscape, Lydia wondered how Car-En had been captured in the first place. Had there been a raid? Were there other prisoners? Car-En had a son.... Where was he? Trying to rescue Car-En would probably be construed as intervention by Adrian. Penelope Townes, the anthropology Department Head, might be willing to overlook it; she knew Car-En personally and she outranked Adrian. But rescuing other villagers would definitely cross the line. Lydia didn't care. If Car-En's loved ones were in danger, she would try to save them too.

★   ★   ★

Xenus looked wrecked. He hugged Lydia for a long time. "I'm sorry," he said. "That must have been horrible."

They were in the Shell, along with Adrian and Shane. De Laurentiis was back at his dome, resting.

"I'm okay," said Lydia. "We're all okay."

"Alexi Rosen isn't okay." The anger in Adrian's voice was tinged with hysteria. Lydia had never seen him so agitated. Still, compared to Xenus, Adrian looked well-rested. His black hair was neatly combed; his skin, already tan from the Mediterranean summer, looked deeply bronzed in the warm light of the Shell.

"Can we sit down?" Shane asked. "I'm exhausted." He took a seat at the round table without waiting for a response. Lydia sat as well, leaving an empty seat between herself and Shane. Xenus and Adrian sat across from them.

"How were they captured?" Adrian asked. "This never should have happened. And why did you disable your feeds? I specifically told you – asked you, rather – to keep them open."

Adrian had addressed the question to Lydia, but Shane answered. "We did leave them open. We only turned them off when De Laurentiis was secure and we were on our way back."

Adrian tapped the carbonlattice tabletop with his knuckles. Lydia wondered if he had done the same thing she had: corrected the image of Car-En and then recognized her. What had happened between them? She briefly wondered if they'd had an affair at some point, before Car-En had been awarded the field research position. Maybe it had gone sour, and Adrian hadn't been able to move on. Is that why Car-En had wanted to disappear?

"So what happened?" Adrian asked again. "How were they captured? Why was Rosen killed?"

"De Laurentiis isn't ready to be debriefed," said Lydia. "He was severely dehydrated when we found him – practically delirious. I suspect an amebic GI infection." None of this was quite true. De Laurentiis was exhausted but not delirious. And she didn't know why he had a fever. Mentioning 'amebic infection' was a precaution; evoking intestinal distress tended to make people back off. For the moment she just wanted to protect her weakened friend from an aggressive debriefing. Adrian, in his agitated state, might press too hard.

"So you have no idea," said Adrian, scowling.

"We'll find out," Shane said. "Our first priority was to get De Laurentiis back home in one piece."

"Your first priority is to protect this field station," Adrian said.

Shane didn't respond. What was Adrian suggesting? The mad jarl of Kaldbrek, hundreds of kilometers to the north, was no threat to them.

"Look," Xenus said, "we'll talk to Aaron when he's ready. He's been through hell. Lydia, how long do you think he needs before we debrief him?"

"At least forty-eight hours."

"Fine. We'll talk to him then."

"*If* he's well enough," said Lydia.

"What about this other prisoner?" Adrian asked. "What do you know about her?"

"Not much," Shane said. "We didn't get a good look at her, and De Laurentiis hadn't talked with her. They were both gagged."

"She didn't look like a villager," Adrian said, looking directly at Lydia. *He knew!*

"No way to tell," said Shane, "but it might make sense to go back. Find out who she is."

Adrian nodded. "I agree. How soon can you leave?"

"I need to sleep a few hours, then resupply the shuttle. I can leave first thing in the morning."

"Lydia, you stay here and tend to De Laurentiis," said Adrian. "Let me know as soon as you think he's well enough to be debriefed. I want to talk to him myself."

Lydia shook her head. "I should go with Shane. The other prisoner might need medical attention."

"I can check on Aaron," Xenus offered. "Lydia, can you give me whatever protocol he's on?"

"Of course."

"So it's settled?" Shane asked. "I'd like to get some rest now. Lydia, meet me at 0600 at the shuttle bay?"

Adrian furrowed his brow. "Shane, can I speak with you for a minute?"

Lydia stood. After a second Xenus realized that Adrian meant *in private* and got up too.

★　　★　　★

Lydia and Xenus walked by the vegetable gardens, then past a few sets of habitat domes. Each group of seven domes had its own central clearing; the middle space was used for outdoor eating, bonfires, and other communal activities. Beyond the domes were storage sheds, greenhouses under construction, and dirt plots in various stages of development. Soon they reached the edge of Vandercamp, overlooking a broad meadow of high grasses and pink wildflowers. On the other side of the meadow, near a clump of trees, a group of children played some complicated tag-like game. More than once Maggie had tried to explain the rules to her – the game involved keeping track of several things in your head while simultaneously chasing and evading the other players – but Lydia had never quite grasped it.

"Penny for your thoughts?" Xenus asked.

"Actually I was thinking about that game they're playing. I guess I need to distract myself right now."

"Understandable." He plucked a tall reedlike weed and wove it into a spiral pattern.

"I wasn't totally honest with Adrian," she said. That was an understatement. She'd lied through her teeth.

"You're protecting De Laurentiis. I get it. He needs to recuperate – especially if Adrian is going to personally debrief him."

So it had been that obvious? She wasn't sure if she was a terrible liar or if Xenus just knew her well.

"Well…that, but something else too."

He looked up. "What?"

"I recognized Car-En. The other prisoner. It was her."

He squinted. "Car-En Ganzorig? Really?"

What other Car-En do we know? she almost snapped, but suppressed her sarcasm. It was shocking that Car-En was being held prisoner in Kaldbrek. She gave Xenus a moment to adjust to the thought.

"Why didn't you tell Adrian?" he finally asked.

She clenched her fists. "I think Car-En is scared of Adrian. I don't know why. But she didn't want anyone else to know that she was alive. She must know that we've seen her – after all, she was a field observer herself – but she doesn't know about Vandercamp, and she doesn't know that Adrian is here, on Earth, only a few hundred kilometers away."

She braced herself for a reaction similar to the one she'd gotten from Shane, but Xenus had gone pale.

"Why is she scared of him?" he asked.

"I don't know."

Xenus stared across the meadow; Lydia followed his gaze. It felt as if the day had been going on forever, but it was only early afternoon. The complicated tag game had ended; most of the children were making their way back across the meadow. Lydia looked for Maggie, but she didn't appear to be among them. Good – that meant she was staying off her ankle.

A thought occurred to her. "Do *you* know?" she asked. "Why Car-En is scared of Adrian?"

"There were rumors," he said, confirming her suspicions.

Lydia checked her m'eye to make sure her feeds were off, looking over her shoulder for good measure. They were alone.

"What rumors?"

Xenus took a deep breath. "That Adrian was furious when Car-En stopped taking his orders. That he lost it."

"Lost it...and what? What did he do?"

"I heard that he tried to kill her. Through her bioskin...some kind of medical override. There's no evidence, no charges even. Just hearsay."

"Who told you?"

"I can't remember. It was just something that was going around the department. It was ten years ago, when Car-En disappeared, and before the Happdal observers were reinstated."

"Why didn't you tell me?" She tried to suppress the emotion in her voice, but failed.

Xenus turned to her, eyes wide. "You're angry? It's just a rumor! It doesn't mean anything! You *know* me – I'm not the kind of person to go around spreading unsubstantiated claims. At the best, it's gossip, at the worst, slander. Look, Adrian nominated me for this position. I trust him."

He spoke earnestly. She believed him, right up until the end. The last sentence, he didn't believe himself. He'd looked away as he said it.

"Really? You trust him?" Maybe it was unreasonable to push him, but she didn't feel reasonable right now. Last night, she'd seen a man with his lungs yanked out of his back. Then she'd abandoned a friend to potentially meet the same fate. At least she'd freed Car-En. The thought gave her a moment of hope. Car-En had always been tough, and years of living with the Harz villagers could only have made her tougher. She *had* to be alive.

"Look," Xenus said, "Adrian is manipulative, and probably more narcissistic than average. So maybe I don't trust him entirely. But he's not a psychopathic murderer. I trust him not to *kill people.*"

The children were approaching, waving at them. They both waved back.

"I guess we can talk about this later," she said.

But she didn't mean it. She had already decided what she would do. If there were sides to be taken, she would take her friend's side. She still loved Car-En, and would do anything to help her.

CHAPTER NINE

Tem sprinted through the forest, close on his father's heels. Only a little of the full moon's light filtered through the canopy. At times Tem ran blind, trusting Father to see for both of them. Askr brought up the rear, crashing through the underbrush like a boar.

Strong hands grabbed him and lifted him into the air. Father had stopped, catching Tem in his arms to avoid a collision. Askr skidded to a halt, bumping into them lightly.

"Quiet," Father whispered. "Listen."

Tem heard nothing, not even crickets. They had scared everything away.

"Are we safe?" Tem asked. In the darkness he could only see the outline of his father's form.

"For now."

"You killed Völund."

"He tried to take you as a slave."

"He was teaching me."

Father was silent.

Askr kneeled, breathing heavily. "Is this the place?" he asked. Father said nothing, staring intently into the darkness.

"Where is Mother?" asked Tem.

A warm hand touched his cheek, then she was hugging him from behind. "I'm right here." Quickly, Mother ran her hands over his head, neck, chest, and legs.

"I'm fine," he said.

"He seems uninjured," Father said.

"You killed his captors?" Mother asked. She had heard them – she knew about Völund. She must have been hiding, waiting for them in the darkness, listening. Tem could not read her tone. Would she be happy or sad when Father confirmed the smith's fate?

"Only one," Father said. "It was quick. I did not think about it. The man tried to steal my son."

Mother exhaled. Still, Tem did not know how she felt. It was hard to tell without being able to see her face. He wished he could see in the dark, like Father.

"How did *you* get away?" Tem asked. "Did Father rescue you too?"

"No. I was helped, but I'm not sure who...never mind. I'm here and we're all safe. I escaped and was trying to find my way back home. I'm lucky your father can track as well at night as during the day. He found me." She grabbed Father and held him tight, then pulled Tem in and hugged them both hard. Tem pressed his face against her and inhaled deeply. They stayed that way, clutching each other, for a long time. Mother released her grip first. "Let's go," she said. "I'm ready to be home."

★   ★   ★

They marched for hours. The moon crossed the sky. Tem had many questions, but his elders walked in silence. He wondered what 'home' meant to Mother. They were heading back to Happdal – that much he could tell. Did that mean the ringship plan was scuttled? Would life return to normal? Or when Mother said 'home' did she mean the *Stanford*?

After as much silence as he could bear, he asked Mother a question. "Who helped you escape?"

Her tone was softer than he expected. "A ghost helped me. Someone from my past."

"A real ghost?"

"No, not a real ghost. But someone I didn't expect to see. I still can't believe it was her."

"Who was she?" Tem asked.

"You'll meet her, I think, in time."

A ghost from Mother's past – that meant life on the ringship. So maybe Mother did plan to take them there after all.

"I miss Farbror Trond," Tem said, "and Tante Katja." In case there was any doubt about how *he* felt about the situation, he wanted to make himself clear.

"I know you do," said Father, patting his head. "We'll be home soon. You'll see them."

His pace slowed. Askr dropped back with him, while Mother and Father walked ahead, speaking to each other in hushed tones. Askr, with his long legs, took slow strides so as not to leave Tem behind.

"You're lucky," Askr said. "It could have been much worse."

"Luckier than Völund, I guess."

"He was a slaver – he deserved to die."

"I think he just wanted an apprentice," Tem said. "He didn't even have any bellows boys."

"Then he could have invited you to apprentice with him," Askr pointed out.

Tem knew that wasn't quite true. Perhaps Orvar, smith of Skrova, could invite him to apprentice; Skrova and Happdal were on good terms. But relations were foul between Happdal and Kaldbrek. There were no goods traded, no marriages, and no apprenticeship exchanges.

"It wasn't Völund who captured me," Tem said. "It was Svein, and his hunting companion."

Askr muttered something, maybe a curse against Svein.

"What?"

"Nothing. I'm just glad we got you back. We were following your tracks north – we planned to join you on the ringship. Esper missed you and your mother too much...he couldn't wait for Arik to return. Trond agreed to sit in the jarl's chair, and we set off to find you. We saw signs of trouble at the river, and guessed what might have happened. We saw what Svein had done...perhaps I should not speak of it. The young jarl of Kaldbrek is bloodthirsty and black-hearted. We hid and watched. After the sky people came, we saw that someone had escaped. We followed the tracks and found Car-En. She told us you were still a prisoner."

"Wait, slow down," Tem said. "You were going to the flying machine? To fly to the ringship?"

Askr nodded. "Car-En said the sky people have an open culture, and that I might be welcome there. She didn't know for sure, but it can't hurt to ask."

Tem looked ahead. His parents had stopped. He waved. Father waved back.

"So you want to live on the ringship?" Tem asked. "What do you think it will be like?"

"I don't know. But if I can visit, why not? The people there can perform miracles. I'd like to see the place with my own eyes."

"What about Elika?"

Askr stared at him. "What? What does she have to do with anything?"

"Mother said you were courting her."

"Did she? Well…perhaps she's right. But my chances are no worse if I seek adventure and then return. Maybe better. Life in Happdal is good, but we're only one village in a vast world. I yearn to see it. Don't you?"

"No, I don't. I just want to stay in Happdal and become smith."

"You're still too young to apprentice," Askr said. "There will be plenty of time for that later."

"Völund didn't think I was too young."

They climbed the ridge. Soon they would summit, then descend into the narrow valley that housed the Upper Begna. They had not slept at all but Tem did not feel tired. In the early twilight Tem could now see faces as well as forms. Father had wiped most of the clay and dirt from his face but the remaining dark streaks gave him a wild look.

Tem wondered what was happening in Kaldbrek. Did Völund's death mean the two villages were now at war? As jarl of Happdal, what would Farfar Arik do when he returned? Farfar avoided bloodshed when he could, but maybe that was impossible now. Surely Svein would not accept Völund's death without retribution. The men of Kaldbrek would come, with swords and axes, and kill Happdal men until they felt the score was settled. If they came before Arik returned, Happdal's defense would fall on Farbror Trond's shoulders. Tem wondered what he would do if *he* were jarl. He thought on this while they walked, until the sky was light. No good answer came to his mind, and he was glad he was not jarl.

They walked south along the high ridge. To the west lay the narrow valley that was home to Kaldbrek; the steep valley to the east was cut through by the Upper Begna. They passed the old lookout: a large flat stone perched on an immense boulder. A boy had been murdered there, many years ago, by Svein's father Haakon. Young Karl Hinriksson had killed Haakon in retribution, poisoning him. All this had happened before Tem had been born. The two villages had feuded for generations, even before Farfar Arik's time. Always a killing, and a killing in return. Who had started it? A Kaldbrek man, according to Happdal lore. But was the story different in Kaldbrek? Did it even matter who had started it? More important was how the conflict would end. Tem saw only two solutions: make a permanent peace, or the complete slaughter of one village by the other, including every man, woman, and child, so that not a soul would be left to take revenge.

There had been an uneasy peace for years, but that was over. Father had slit Völund's throat. Tem had seen it with his own eyes.

Father grabbed him and threw him to the ground behind a twisted, windblown tree. Father was crouching, looking south, gesturing to Mother and Askr to hide.

Tem heard a distant buzzing noise, like a giant fly. He peered out from behind the stunted tree and saw what looked like a flying raft coming toward them. There were two figures riding the raft, a man and a woman. The woman waved to them.

"Who are they?" he whispered.

"Ringship people," said Father.

"Why are we hiding? Are they dangerous?"

Father was already standing up, nocking an arrow. They'd been spotted; there was no use in hiding. Still, Tem stayed down, and looked at the ground. He did not want to see another death today.

"Don't shoot!" Mother yelled. Tem looked up. Mother ran forward and stood between Father and the approaching raft. Father lowered his bow. Askr held his spear at the ready, but did not pull back his arm to throw.

The flying raft came to a stop twenty paces away, and landed softly. The buzzing noise stopped, and once again Tem could hear the morning songbirds. A woman stepped out of the vehicle. She was about Mother's age, with freckled skin and hair the color of burnished copper.

"Car-En," the woman said. "It's Lydia."

Mother stared at the woman, her arm outstretched back toward Father, palm open, signaling him to hold his fire.

"It *was* you," Mother said.

They made camp, cooked breakfast, and talked. The ringship man was thick-limbed, though not as tall as Father, nor as broad as Farbror Trond. Tem guessed he was a warrior. A dark rod was slung across his back, and he carried a knife at his belt – one similar to Mother's feather-blade.

The ringship people offered their strange food, which, as far as Tem could tell, was a kind of grain flour congealed into a square. Mother accepted one of the squares, as did Askr, but Father declined politely, and Tem shook his head when the woman offered him one. Both the woman and the man readily accepted and ate the aged cheese and honeycomb that Esper had brought along, but declined the deer jerky. That was fine with Tem – more meat for him.

"It's not bad," said Askr, gnawing off a corner of the congealed grain square. "A little sweet. A mild flavor. I think you'd like it. Change your mind?" He broke off a piece and thrust it in Tem's direction.

"No thank you," said Tem, through a mouthful of salty deer jerky.

The others were speaking in English, too fast for Tem to understand. He caught a few names: *Svein* and *Völund*. There was another word that sounded like a name: 'Adriun.' Father did not speak, but listened closely, and Tem was sure he understood most of what was said. Father learned quickly. Father and Farmor Elke had the quickest minds in the village; everyone knew that. Tem was bright, but not as bright as them.

He watched Mother. Her brown cheeks were flushed and her eyes open wide, like a hawk's. The ringship woman's words had angered her. Mother said the name again – 'Adriun.' A man's name?

"Can you understand them?" he said quietly to Askr.

Askr shook his head. "Not a word. Though if they wanted to, they could speak Norse. I remember Car-En made herself understood when she first came to Happdal. I was just a boy but I remember it well. She was difficult to understand, but somehow she knew our language."

Tem nodded. Mother had told him about the translators. He was beginning to feel frustrated and left out.

"Can you speak more slowly please?" Tem asked, more loudly than he meant to.

Everyone looked at him.

"Or speak in Norse?" he asked in a softer tone.

"Sorry, Tem," said Mother, moving close to him. "I promise I'll explain everything later."

"What's going on? Who are these people?"

"They live to the south, many days away. I've known Lydia for a long time, but I thought she was still on the *Stanford*."

"Ringship people live on Earth?" asked Tem.

"Apparently," Mother said, looking at Lydia. The ringship woman looked embarrassed.

"What's your name?" the ringship man asked Tem, speaking slowly in English. His accent was different than Mother's but Tem understood the question.

Mother shot the man a look and put her hand on Tem's shoulder. Tem shrugged it off.

"My name is Tem Espersson." He didn't fear the ringship man, not with Father nearby.

"We can take you to the mule station in less than a day," said Lydia, also speaking deliberately.

Tem flinched. He didn't want to go to the ringship. He wanted to go home. He missed Farbror Trond and Tante Katja.

The ringship man raised an eyebrow and said something in English. Mother responded, and soon the adults were back to talking rapidly among themselves. Tem angrily bit off a piece of jerky. "Maybe I'll just go home now," he muttered in Norse. Only Askr heard him, and grinned.

Tem wandered away from the cooking fire and the adults gathered round it. Things were changing too fast – he didn't like it. It was getting harder to imagine his life as he had always planned it. With the possibility of Svein and his men raiding, the smithy would be busy, and no one would have time for Tem. Surely he would work the bellows station, but nothing beyond that. He had fantasized telling Farbror Trond that Völund had given him time at the anvil. Maybe Farbror would do the same? He would say to his uncle: *How can I learn without a hammer in my hand?*

But the Happdal smiths would not listen to him, not with war coming. Farbror Trond and Farfar Jense would be busy at the anvil themselves, with no time for teaching.

Tem looked back at the others. They were still huddled together, speaking intently. Even Askr, who did not speak a word of English, was paying attention to the conversation. Tem kept walking, slowly, until he reached the trail that sloped down the mountain toward Happdal. He looked back once more. Still, nobody saw him. Why did they even bother to rescue him, if he was then to be ignored? Even Völund had paid him more mind than this. The work had not been so bad, sweeping the floor and sorting the charcoal by size. Saga – Völund's niece – he'd thought she was pretty. She must hate him now, for what Father had done. He checked his trousers and found the spot where her spittle had dried.

Shielded from the wind, the trees stood straight a little farther down the mountain: thin white birch, shrubby rowan, some smaller spruce. Below him sprawled the great green mass of the older spruce. As he descended the canopy closed overhead. He was sleepy. He wondered vaguely if the others might notice his absence and worry. They would be coming this way anyway. The time would pass more quickly if he took a short nap. Yawning, he sat with his back to a great old spruce, nestled between two sloping roots. He would only close his eyes and rest for a minute or two. Mother and Father and Askr would wake him when they came down the trail. Would the ringship people still be with them, riding their raft?

⋆ ⋆ ⋆

When he opened his eyes again, a bearded old man was staring at him, inches from his face. Tem cried out. The man's hand shot forward and smothered Tem's mouth. His hand smelled like wood smoke. The old man raised an oaken cudgel. Tem froze. Slowly, the man withdrew his hand. His long beard was forked and twisted like the chin fur of a winter lynx.

"Silence, boy." The old man's voice was harsh, but also sonorous.

"Who are you?" Tem asked. In truth he did not care. He wanted to hear the man speak again.

"Don't worry – I'm no ghost. Just an old poet, following the deer trails," the man said. "Now follow me. No harm will come to you."

CHAPTER TEN

It had taken Lydia and Shane several days to track Car-En, even with the help of the search drones. When they did find her, it was clear that she no longer needed their help. Cutting the ropes had been enough. Car-En had escaped, and was now reunited with her son, husband, and another villager.

Her old friend looked strong and healthy, but older. Car-En's skin had once been smooth and coffee-colored; now it was weathered and brown, with crinkles around her eyes and mouth. Maybe motherhood had aged Car-En, or maybe it was living without the benefits of technology. Any bloodstream nanodrones would have long ago stopped functioning and been reabsorbed into her body. Certainly those were replaceable. And Car-En could easily get a rejuv, if she wanted. It had worked for Adrian Vanderplotz – he was in his sixties and didn't look a day over forty. But maybe Car-En didn't care how she looked.

"Deer meat?" said Car-En's husband, holding out a strip of ruby-colored dried flesh. Esper's English, while heavily accented, was easily comprehensible. Lydia could see why Car-En had fallen for him. He was beautiful: tall, lean, long flowing hair, captivating light blue eyes, and not yet thirty from the looks of him. Despite his youthfulness he carried himself with assurance and maturity (more so than Xenus, and Xenus was nearly forty). Esper looked too young to be a father, but his son was right there. The boy was handsome too, dark-haired with delicate Eurasian features. He'd been quiet; he was probably in shock. From what Car-En had said the boy's rescue had involved bloodshed. Car-En had been vague about the details, and neither Lydia nor Shane had pressed.

"No thank you," said Lydia, smiling. The uncooked deer might be laced with parasites. Esper did not seem offended and handed the strip of meat to his son.

"When was the field station established?" Car-En asked. So far, their reunion had amounted to a cool exchange of information. There had been no warm words, no embrace. They'd been good friends once, long ago. Part of Lydia was giddy to be this close to Car-En, but she suppressed the feeling. Obviously Car-En did not feel the same. And Lydia had yet to share the worst of the news. There were two things she needed to tell Car-En, and she dreaded both. She made a split-second decision to come clean, at least with one of the facts.

"Adrian Vanderplotz is Station Director," Lydia said. Car-En did not react immediately. This was surprising; Car-En had never been one to conceal her emotions. Living among the villagers had changed her.

Esper looked first to Car-En, then to Lydia and Shane. "The one that tried to kill her?" he asked. "*That* Adrian?"

"He was never charged with a crime," said Lydia.

"If I meet him, I will kill him," Esper said matter-of-factly. It did not seem like an empty boast.

"So he knows I'm alive," Car-En said icily.

"Yes."

"Does he know where I am right now?"

Lydia noticed that Shane was keeping a close eye on both Esper and Askr. Her partner's body language was relaxed, but ready. The two groups did not yet trust each other.

"No," said Lydia. This was more or less the truth. Her feeds were off. This would irritate Adrian, but Privacy of Perception was a fundamental right, part of the *Stanford*'s human rights charter. Adrian knew the mission, and he had probably figured out that Car-En had been the second prisoner held in Kaldbrek. But he didn't know that Car-En and her son had already escaped, and that Shane and Lydia had tracked the rescue party to this high ridge.

Car-En watched Lydia carefully, then lowered her shoulders and sighed. Esper and Shane, who had been staring each other down, broke eye contact.

"He may try to kill me again if he gets the chance," Car-En said. "He's a psychopath. If he tries anything...." Car-En's voice had a tone to it that was new to Lydia. Motherhood, or maybe living on the planet's surface, had toughened her. Lydia briefly wondered if she should be worried for Car-En's safety, or for Adrian's.

"Are you and the boy all right?" Shane asked. It was a good instinct, changing the subject away from Adrian. "Did they harm you?"

"I'm okay," said Car-En. "Tem hasn't complained, but he's limping a little. I want to look at his ankle when we get home."

"I could look at it now," Lydia said. "I've got medical supplies in the shuttle. We could scan it – he might have a hairline fracture."

"Ilsa will treat it when we get home," Car-En said, looking away. That stung. Car-En knew Lydia was a doctor. Or did she? Lydia had been studying medicine ten years ago, but she hadn't yet been practicing.

"Maybe we should let her help Tem," said Esper, gently touching Car-En's knee. "From what you've told me, they have good medicine. If he's hurt...."

Car-En softened. "You're right. Yes, please take a look at his ankle. And thank you."

The boy said something loudly in the village dialect. The translation flashed in Lydia's m'eye; Tem was asking them to speak in his language – *Norse* – so that he could understand. The village dialect was a mix of Old Norse and Corporate Age Norwegian. Lydia had studied it briefly while first watching the Happdal research feeds. So had many others on the ringstations; Car-En's research had been immensely popular. Still, she didn't know enough to speak the dialect without the aid of her translator.

Car-En comforted the boy and offered a few words of explanation. Tem seemed surprised that people from the ringstations were living on Earth. Of course this had also been a surprise to Car-En; she gave Lydia a look that left little doubt how she felt. But what did Car-En expect? She had made her choice, throwing her lot in with the villagers. Life had gone on for everyone else, despite the fact that Car-En had chosen to live in an information vacuum. Repop, for better or worse, had begun.

Shane asked the boy his name. Tem answered confidently, chin up and looking Shane right in the eye. The boy had some of his father's swagger.

Car-En had told them she was taking Tem to the *Stanford*, to meet Car-En's parents and possibly to attend school for a while. Lydia hadn't yet worked up the courage to tell Car-En about Marivic. She wanted to share the sad news with Car-En privately, not in front of her son. For a moment, Lydia surrendered to self-pity. It wasn't fair that *she* had to be the one to tell Car-En that Marivic was dead. *She should already know.* But how could she? Lydia closed her eyes for two seconds and tried to accept reality as it was. Despite the fact that Car-En had left her old life behind, despite the fact that Lydia had not seen Car-En in ten years, her old friend was now right here in front of her, and it was Lydia's responsibility to tell Car-En the truth. She resolved to do so at the first opportunity, as soon as the two of them had a moment alone.

For now, maybe she could help in other ways. With the help of her m'eye translator, she addressed Tem in Norse and offered the family a ride to the mule station. The hovershuttle wouldn't be able to take everyone at once, but they could make a couple trips; there and back would only take a few hours. Adrian might not approve (technically their mission should be over – the second prisoner was safe), but officially it wasn't intervention. Car-En was, after all, still a ringstation citizen. And so was Tem, by right of birth. Generally, in cases where parents were from different ringstations, the child acquired citizenship rights within both societies. Lydia wasn't sure about the legalities when one of the parents was a villager – there was no precedent – but the reasoning was sound.

Her offer, which she considered to be quite generous, fell flat. The boy was scowling. "Looks like he doesn't want to go," Shane said, glancing at Car-En.

"It's not up to him," said Car-En sharply.

"Shouldn't he have a say in the matter?" Lydia asked. She immediately regretted her words. It was none of her business. It was too late; Car-En's face had darkened.

"You know nothing about our lives." Car-En's voice was cool and calm, but Lydia felt as if Car-En were screaming, inches from her face.

"I'm sorry," Lydia said. "I just meant—"

"It's really no problem to give you a ride," Shane interjected. "It would only take a few hours." *Bless him.* It was the second time he had come to her rescue during this conversation.

"I am not coming," Esper said. "I need to defend Happdal – our village. Svein will come for me."

"Then maybe you should be somewhere else when he comes," said Car-En.

Esper shook his head. "Svein would prefer my blood, but will slaughter others in my stead. I will come to the ringship as soon as the matter is settled."

"You will make peace?" Shane asked.

"No, not this time. You can't make peace with a madman."

Car-En was looking around. "Where is Tem?" she asked Esper in Norse. Askr responded, pointing to the trail that descended east down the ridge. Car-En cursed and stood, scanning the tree line below.

"He'll come back," said Esper. "He's just off for a stroll – he was probably bored."

"Unless he went home," Car-En said. "He knows the way."

Lydia almost offered the help of the drones, then thought better of it. She would help if asked.

Shane stood and scanned the area (without turning his back on Esper and Askr, Lydia noticed). Askr jogged off in the direction of the trailhead where he had last seen Tem. Lydia returned to the hovershuttle and brought up the control interface for the drones, should they be needed. While she hoped the boy was safe, she was relieved to postpone the difficult conversation with Car-En. She had imagined their potential reunion in many ways, but never like this. What right did Car-En have to be mad at *her*? Car-En had been the one to leave, abandoning her family and friends. But that wasn't the way emotions worked, was it? People felt how they felt.

Shane raised his rifle, then lowered it. Askr was returning, Tem in tow. Behind them followed a tall gray-haired man, rail-thin, carrying a heavy wooden staff. His long gray beard was braided into two forks; his rough woolen clothes were frayed and dirty. Lydia guessed who it might be, and immediately sent a hound to compare her visual feed with the field observation archives. A moment later her guess was confirmed; it was Egil. De Laurentiis had called him 'Egil the Bard,' the one who'd been exiled from Kaldbrek by the young jarl Svein.

Esper closed the distance in a few seconds, drawing his knife as he ran. Tem raised his hand and shook his head. Good – it seemed the man had not harmed the boy. Shane watched warily, rifle lowered but at the ready. He was on edge. *She* should probably be more alert and amped up than she was; her emotional preoccupation with Car-En was crowding out her awareness of basic safety and security. These villagers could escalate to violence quickly, sometimes without warning. Had the real Vikings been the same way? She had a vague notion that the original Nordic warriors (when not raiding the British Isles or Europe) had conducted themselves peacefully, with complex traditions in place to resolve conflicts and avoid bloodshed. The Harz villagers appeared to lack such social structures, at least between villages.

Egil raised his free hand, palm open. Lydia and Shane joined the others, gathering around the old man.

"I am Egil, of Skrova. I found the boy alone, asleep in the forest, and thought it wise to return him to you. The woods are not safe this summer."

"How did you know he was ours?" Esper asked.

"I've been following you," said Egil.

"Why?" Askr asked, with some hostility. "And for how long?"

"Business with Kaldbrek is business of mine," Egil answered. "Svein is my responsibility."

Car-En laughed ruefully. "Then you are irresponsible. Svein runs wild."

"I know," Egil said. "It is a problem." He tugged on the left side of his beard, then the right, looking at Lydia and Shane in turn. "Who are they?" He addressed the question to Esper. "Not from the Five Valleys, I think." He peered over Lydia's shoulder at the hovershuttle. "And what is that?"

"There is much you don't know, old man," Esper said.

"Maybe so," said Egil, "but the same is true of you. There is new danger in the woods, a dark horror. You would be wise to hear me out, if you value your life."

CHAPTER ELEVEN

Lydia grabbed her medical supply bag, tossed in a block of water cubes and a few g'nerf bars, and joined Shane. Egil would lead them south along the ridge. Shane had suggested they go on foot; it was best to minimize the number of villagers exposed to the hovershuttle.

Egil walked slowly, surveilling the path ahead. Shane brought up the rear, rifle at the ready. Egil had refused to elaborate on the nature of the 'dark horror,' insisting it was easier to just show them.

Ahead, Egil and Car-En's husband spoke in hushed tones, too quietly for Lydia's translator to pick up. The boy held Car-En's hand. The tall villager Askr walked next to them, using his heavy spear as a walking stick. Now and then Askr turned back and flashed Lydia a toothy grin.

Lydia kept expecting that Shane would insist they return home. Their mission was complete; their offer of help, while not outright rejected, had not been accepted. There was no real reason for them to be here, investigating Egil's cryptic warning. Well, she knew *her* reason: she desperately wanted to make things right with Car-En. She had no idea how to do that, and before she could even begin she had to tell Car-En that her mother, Marivic, was dead. There was no avoiding her moral responsibility in the matter.

Lydia stole a glance at Shane. He wore a brimmed cap to protect his bald head from the summer sun; at this altitude the ozone layer provided little protection. He walked deliberately, rifle pointed down, eyes forward. What was *his* motivation? Curiosity maybe. Or was he just indulging her?

"Look, there's something I need to tell you," Shane said, without making eye contact. He spoke quietly, dropping back a few steps from Askr. His tone was serious. Did he suspect a trap? Was the 'accidental encounter' with Egil a ruse? She didn't want to end up like Alexi Rosen.

"Are we in danger?" she whispered.

He glanced at her. "I don't think so. Not from *them*, if that's what you mean." He gestured ahead with his rifle. "Unless you know something I don't."

She thought about it. Car-En was angry, about Adrian, and maybe something else too, but she wouldn't *hurt* them. "No, I trust Car-En. What is it?"

"Remember when Adrian wanted to talk to me alone, after our debriefing?"

She nodded. She had almost asked him about it, but had strategically decided not to. She wouldn't win Shane's trust by being nosy. Now she was glad she had held her tongue. "What did he want?"

Shane exhaled through his nose and clenched his jaw. "Basically he wanted me to make sure Car-En ended up dead," he said quietly. "He didn't say so in as many words, but that was clearly the ask."

Shane's statement was shocking, but on some level Lydia wasn't surprised. "What did he say *exactly*?"

"He recognized Car-En from our feeds, but he wasn't completely sure. He wanted me to confirm her identity. He said that she was no longer a ringstation citizen, and that to help her would constitute intervention."

Lydia hadn't told anyone about cutting Car-En's ropes, and her feeds had been closed. So Adrian must have assumed that Car-En was next in line to be ritually murdered, and had sent Shane as a witness to confirm Car-En's demise.

"And if you confirmed her identity, but she was still alive... then what?"

"Well, he was vague. But he said that if Car-En had recognized you, that she could potentially be a threat to AFS-1, a security risk. That didn't make sense to me, but he refused to explain. 'Neutralize the threat' was what he said."

"What did you tell him?" asked Lydia. She was gripping her bag so hard that her hand ached. She switched hands and flexed her fingers.

"I told him I would assess the situation – with AFS-1 security as the top priority. He seemed satisfied by that, so he must have thought I was agreeing to his implicit request."

"But you weren't," she said. She needed to hear him say it.

He glared at her. "I'm not a murderer. The reason I'm telling you this is...well, you might be right about Adrian."

"Of course I'm right about Adrian."

"Then what do we do about it?"

The question startled her. It had never occurred to her to *do* something about Adrian. Over the years, under his leadership, she had come to admire him less and less. Now she didn't trust him. But he was the Station Director. What could be done? Ostensibly Adrian reported to Penelope Townes; AFS-1 was part of the anthropology department and Townes was Department Head. But there was little, if any, communication between the two. Effectively Adrian was the captain of his own ship, reporting to no one. As long as he turned over his research results and nobody got hurt, the status quo would remain undisturbed.

But now someone *had* been hurt. Alexi Rosen was dead.

"Does Townes know about Rosen?" Lydia asked.

"She must," Shane said. "Adrian would report it. Wouldn't he? Rosen has extended family on the *Stanford* – he has to report it."

"Maybe *you* should contact Townes."

"And say what? 'In case you didn't hear, one of our researchers died.' I'll look like a fool if she already knows." Shane's eyes flicked rapidly – he was checking something in his m'eye. "Nothing about Rosen in the *Stanford* feeds. If Townes knows, she hasn't yet made it public."

"You can be more subtle than that. Just prepare a report detailing security reforms for field researchers – referencing Rosen – and deliver it to her."

Shane nodded. "I've already been making notes for a report."

"What do you think Townes will do if she finds out Adrian is withholding information?"

Shane shrugged. "Maybe nothing. It's only been a couple days.... Adrian might be able to talk his way out of it. And who knows what kind of agreement those two have in place."

"What do you mean?"

"There was some talk years ago, when Adrian resigned as Department Head and Penelope Townes took over. It didn't make sense. Nobody thought Adrian would ever resign, much less accept a position where he was reporting to Townes."

"But he got what he wanted. *Vandercamp.*"

"Sure. I'm just saying – some people were suspicious. They thought maybe Townes had something on Adrian."

She thought about what Xenus had told her – the rumors that Adrian had tried to kill Car-En, using the bioskin as a remote endocrinological weapon. What if Penelope Townes had known?

Egil and Esper had stopped; Egil was pointing at something. Lydia moved to the front of the group, brushing by Car-En. The terrain was rocky here; the meager flora consisted of thorny weeds, scrub brush, and twisted, windblown elfin-wood. Forty meters ahead, a strange, stunted black tree clung to the rocks. Shane started toward it.

"No closer!" Egil shouted. "They bite, and they kill."

Lydia zoomed in with her m'eye. The black tree was in motion. Furry black spiders the size of her hand were crawling over the sprawling network of roots.

"Spiders?" said Esper. "This is the great horror you speak of? They are large, yes, but surely they can die." He had already nocked his bow and was pulling back a long shaft tipped with sharpened iron.

"You'd be wise to hold your fire," said Egil quietly. "They'll swarm us, and kill us all. I've seen it happen."

"They're poisonous?" Shane asked.

"Yes," said Egil, "and flesh eaters. Look – can you see the bones?"

Following Egil's sight line, Lydia did see a pile of bones, stripped clean of meat but not yet bleached by the sun. From the looks of the clothing the victim had been a villager.

"Who?" she asked.

"Tófi, of Skrova. He came with me to this place. He was curious when I told him of the Black Tree, and wanted to see it with his own eyes. It was the last thing he saw."

"He attacked the spiders?" Shane asked.

"He kicked them away," said Egil, "and crushed one with his boot. The rest were over him in seconds. I could do nothing."

"They didn't attack you as well?" Shane's tone was not accusatory. He was merely assessing the situation, trying to quantify the threat. But the question struck a nerve.

"What could I do?" Egil shouted. Flecks of spittle flew from his mouth and caught in the forks of his beard. From the corner of her eye Lydia saw Tem back up against Car-En's leg. Several of the spiders froze and looked in their direction. "What could I do?" he repeated, more quietly. "It would not have saved him to die as well. *This* is what I am doing – warning *you*." He looked at Lydia with the last word.

Tem stepped away from his mother and held up his hand, palm facing toward the strange black tree.

"It's hot," he said. "Can you feel it?"

It was early afternoon on a warm summer day, but Lydia's front was still warmer than her back. Tem was right.

"The Black Tree burns without fire," said Egil. "It always has, since I first discovered it."

"It's not really a tree, is it?" Shane said. He had detached the scope from his rifle and was using it like a telescope. "More like a...actually I can't tell what it is. The structure is organic but the material isn't. Could be carbonlattice or something similar."

"Let me see," Lydia said. Shane relinquished the scope and squinted at the spider-covered mass.

The physical magnification was superior to her m'eye zoom. The central mass of the structure was about a meter high, roughly dome-like, with at least five thick, black tendrils radiating outward. From each main tendril there were dozens of narrow offshoots, and from each of those, numerous black vines. From each vine sprouted thousands of fine black strings or threads. Whatever plants had once lived in the area had been absorbed by the black web; here and there the vines formed masses over what must have once been stunted elfin-wood trees or shrubs. The extended web covered a rough circle with an approximately twenty-meter radius. The spiders – there were hundreds of them – moved languidly over the black mass.

"They're growing," said Egil. "When they killed Tófi, they were only this big." The space between his finger and thumb was about seven centimeters. "They feasted on his flesh, and grew."

"Did they build the web?" Shane asked. "Or whatever it is."

Egil grunted. "No, the Black Tree was here before the spiders. I don't know where they came from. Perhaps from the tree itself."

"I want to take a sample," Shane said. "One of the spiders, and some of the black material. Do you have a sterile sampling kit?" Lydia looked in her bag. She did. She handed the cylinder to Shane.

"You're a fool," said Egil.

"I'll be careful."

Shane took ten paces toward the black structure, knelt, aimed his neural disruptor, and pulled the trigger. As far as Lydia could tell, nothing happened. Shane adjusted a setting on the weapon, carefully aimed, and fired again. Still nothing.

Shane stood and cautiously took another few steps toward the black writhing mass. A few of the arthropods froze and watched him, but none approached. He raised the weapon, still standing, and fired. Nothing.

"Is his weapon broken?" Tem whispered.

"I don't know," Lydia said.

Shane retreated slowly, without turning his back on the spiders.

"You're a *lucky* fool," said Egil, as Shane rejoined them.

"Did your disruptor malfunction?" Lydia asked. "Do you want to use mine?"

Shane shook his head. "I ran a diagnostic. It's working perfectly. Those things should have been out cold for at least a few minutes."

"So what happened?"

Shane holstered his disruptor and scratched his temple. "Whatever those things are, they're not biological. Somebody made them, and somebody put them here. And given what happened to poor Tófi, I think we're safe in making an assumption."

"What assumption?" Car-En asked. She'd pulled Tem close, holding him tightly against her leg.

"Those things are a weapon. They were created to kill."

"To kill who?" Tem asked. "And who made them?"

Shane adjusted his cap and peered in the direction of the spiders. "Those are good questions."

CHAPTER TWELVE

As afternoon slipped into dusk, it became clear to Tem that they would not be continuing home to Happdal until the next morning. Father and Askr went off for a quick hunt. Father scolded him when he tried to tag along, sending him back to help Mother prepare the camp. He had expected as much and did not bother protesting.

Tem gathered branches from the stunted elfin-wood to construct raised beds for himself, Mother, and Father, using the longknife Farbror Trond had given him to do the cutting. The sky people busied themselves with their floating raft; Tem guessed it might also serve as a night shelter. Egil just sat there by the smoldering coals of the breakfast fire, staring into space. Tem asked the old man if he would like help preparing his sleeping site, but Egil shook his head. There would be no rain tonight, he said, and he was too old and tough to be affected by the cold ground. Tem shrugged and left the graybeard to his ponderings.

Father and Askr returned with a brown hare, shot through the neck with a single arrow. Tem asked whose kill it was, but Father merely smiled. Surely it was Father's; Askr had only his spear. They had already gutted it, but gave it to Tem to skin and cut into strips. Tem did so quickly and efficiently, once again using the knife given to him by Farbror. He was happy to be using the gift, but the blade still needed a name. It made sense to name the knife after a deed, but neither Bedmaker nor Hareskinner sounded impressive. After the meat was prepared he carefully wiped the knife clean on some leaves, then polished the steel dry on his trouser leg.

Askr stoked the coals and added dry wood. They cooked the hare meat on long sticks held over the fire. Egil told his story. His tale began before Tem had been born, when the young jarl Svein had exiled Egil from Kaldbrek.

"I met your father and your brother on the road," Egil said to Father. "I'd been beaten. My face was bloodied, and they'd cut off my hair to shame me. Your brother Trond was kind to me. He gave me water. Your father told me to go to Happdal and ask your mother Elke for mercy."

"Did you?" Father asked.

"I did. I feared Elke, because of what we had done to the lookout boy. I thought she might have me killed, or even kill me with her own hands, but I didn't care. My heart was black."

"Looks like she spared you," Mother said, pulling a strip of roasted hare meat from her fire-blackened stick. "You were lucky."

Egil shrugged. "Maybe. What is luck? I'm still here. Elke took mercy on me. She fed me and gave me shelter. The next day I decided the Red Brother still had a use for me, and I vowed to discover what that use might be."

"And what did you decide?" Father asked.

Egil stroked the forks of his beard, first the left side, then the right. "It wasn't my decision. But after wandering the Five Valleys for several weeks, I had an inkling."

"Did you receive a sign?" Askr asked. "An omen from the Red Brother?"

"No, nothing like that. The thought developed slowly. First I knew I must go to each of the villages. From Happdal I went to Skrova, and spoke with Jarl Jakob...."

"Jakob the Bold was second smith of Happdal!" Tem blurted. Egil the Bard paused, swiveling his gaze toward Tem.

"Let the man speak," Father said.

"I know of Jakob the Bold," said Egil, narrowing his eyes and pointing a crooked finger at Tem. "I will tell you his story later, if you hunger for it. But *this* Jakob was, and still is, jarl of Skrova. A wise man. He gave me smoked fish and venison, and told me I was welcome in Skrova, as an advisor to him. He was delighted to steal me from Kaldbrek. I would eventually make my home there, in Skrova, but not yet."

"Where did you go next?" Tem asked. It was not just the story, but the bard's voice that Tem wanted to hear. His speech was harsh, like rocks scraping together, but one could not help but listen to it. Certainly Tem would ask to hear the story of Jakob the Bold, for he knew little of the second smith beyond his name, and the tale would keep the bard talking. Tem wondered if *he* could one day learn to speak that way, so that no one could turn away. Too often when Tem spoke it was as if he had not spoken at all! There was a power there, in being impossible to ignore. Tem looked over at the sky people. The copper-haired woman and the thick bald man sat next to each other on a silvery blanket, quietly listening. Even the sky people were entranced by Egil's voice.

"I went to Silfrdal, and then to Vaggabœr, and met with the jarl of each village."

"I remember the people of Silfrdal from Summer Trade," Father said. "They brought fine silver jewelry and wares, and fur capes. But of Vaggabœr I have only heard stories."

"And yet Vaggabœr is only a two-day walk from Happdal," said Egil. "Don't you find that odd?"

"Is it true that their smith is a woman?" Tem asked, for he had also heard stories about Vaggabœr.

"Her name is Hulda," Egil said, "and she is stronger than your father, if not your uncle."

"Nobody is stronger than Farbror Trond," Tem said. The bald ringship man raised an eyebrow at this. Tem glared at him.

Egil continued. "Hulda is also jarl. Before her it was Heidrun, sister of Hulda."

"A woman jarl? *Two* woman jarls?" Tem exclaimed.

"Yes. In Vaggabœr they make little of differences between men and women. Or perhaps the men and women are simply more alike – their women are strong of body. Hulda is strongest, but not by much."

"What happened to Heidrun?" Mother asked.

"Killed by a panther, while hunting boar," said Egil. "Though Heidrun slew the beast even as her own blood watered the dirt. She stabbed it in the eye with her dirk, and now her sister Hulda wears the pelt as a girdle."

The bard pulled his cooking stick close to his face, examining the long strip of hare meat. After a sniff he put it back over the flames.

"Do not char your meat, old man," Askr said. "It will be dry and tasteless."

"Then it will suit me well," said Egil, "for I am old and dry myself. But my work on this world is not yet finished, and neither is this tale, so hold your questions and let me finish.

"As you mentioned, young Esper, you remember the people of

Silfrdal from Summer Trade. Generations ago, in the time of Jakob the Bold," – he shot a glance at Tem – "the five villages of the Five Valleys were united. One people, all who suffered on the Ice Trail when the glaciers swallowed our homeland. The old bards sang our heritage songs and told our stories, and people remembered and rejoiced together. Together, we mourned our dead. Together, we shared our hopes.

"Now, we are fractured. Young Tem here has never been to Silfrdal, or Vaggabœr, and he only knows the people of Skrova from Summer Trade."

"And Harvest Festival," Tem said. Mother shushed him.

"And Harvest Festival," continued Egil, unperturbed. "And he has only been to Kaldbrek by way of poor luck. Happdal is the only way of life he knows. He is impoverished, in that way."

Mother nodded in agreement.

"A calamity has occurred, this fracturing," Egil said, "and when I looked for fault, I found the blame squarely on my own shoulders. When Haakon still lived, I served him, and allowed him to make an island out of Kaldbrek. Outsiders became enemies. I tried to be the voice of reason, to blunt his cruelty with good sense. But his mind was too twisted. I failed.

"Not only did I stand by and watch while Kaldbrek severed ties with Happdal and Skrova, but I failed to take on an apprentice. Who will carry on the few scraps of knowledge I have acquired when I die? No one. It's too late. And I am the only one, in all the villages. The old bards of Happdal, Skrova, Silfrdal, and Vaggabœr expired long ago. There is no one left!"

The last few words came out choked, and the bard wept. No one else made a sound. But there was not much moisture left in the old man and soon his weeping ended. When Egil continued, his voice was stronger than before.

"So it came to me, what I must do. I would travel through the Five Valleys for the rest of my days, singing the songs and telling the stories that lived inside my skull. Maybe some would be remembered. Maybe new ties could form between the villages. This was the Red Brother's use for me."

A tiny piece of fat fell from Tem's stick and sizzled in the flames. Out of respect for Egil no one spoke for a long time. Tem watched the sky woman. He could see a question forming on her lips but she did not want to break the silence. Finally she could no longer suppress herself, and spoke.

"Are there other villages you have not mentioned?" she asked. "Are there more than five?"

Egil shook his head. "Five valleys, five villages. Why do you ask?"

"We only knew of the three. Not Silver-dal and…."

"Vaggabœr. Silfrdal and Vaggabœr. Even from your great ringship you can't see everything."

"Would you like to visit?" the sky woman asked. "Your stories…we would like to write them down."

"No." said Egil. "My place is here in the mountains. If the Red Brother's hammer ever tames Svein, then I would accept your invitation. But not until then."

Tem yawned. Talk of visiting the ringship tired him. He whispered to Mother that he was going to sleep and retreated to his cot of sticks, a few paces back from the warm fire. The others continued to converse, but their voices ran together in Tem's ears. What would they do? Who would go where? They talked and talked. Mother came and put a blanket over him. The blanket was light and flimsy, but warm, and soon he slept.

★   ★   ★

Tem woke early under a starry indigo sky, with the faintest glow of dawn beyond the eastern range. He'd slept well under the lightweight silvery blanket. Mother must have gotten it from the sky people's floating raft. He carefully folded the shiny material and tucked the silver square under his stick cot.

His dream mind had been active, and without delay he gathered the items he would need. First, a long stick: not as straight as he would like but it would do. He carefully opened Father's pack, moving slowly so as not to wake him, and borrowed his extra bowstring. Most of the silky string, woven from Father's own hair, he wrapped around the end of the stick. With the last bit he formed a slipknot noose.

Once, he looked back at camp. Still slumbering, all of them, except the old man, who stirred and switched his sleeping side. The bard's eyes snapped open. Tem froze; was he seen? Egil closed his eyes and was still again. Tem turned back toward his task.

By the time he reached the Black Tree, twilight had yielded to dawn. Tem approached, light-footed, until he could see the spiders. They moved languidly over the black branches, more calmly than the day before. Tem silently rejoiced. It would be easy to catch a slothful bug.

From his pocket he pulled a strip of sticky hare meat that he had saved while skinning their dinner. Even then an inkling of the plan had scratched at his mind. He sniffed the uncooked meat: ripe but not yet rotten. "Do you like hare?" he whispered, creeping closer. "The sky man could not catch you, could he?" He grinned, imagining the pride on Father's face, marveling at Tem's cleverness. Then he disciplined himself, and sharpened his senses. There would be time enough to celebrate after the hunt.

Tem slowed, first counting to ten between each pace, then to twenty, then fifty. Counting in his head reminded him of the bellows. At twenty paces the spiders still paid him no mind. The heat of the Black Tree was like a forge furnace, cutting through the cold dawn air. From here he had a good view of Tófi's yellowish bones. He considered the Skrova man's last moments. Was it terrible to die from spider venom?

Tem tossed the strip of meat underhanded. It flew farther than he meant it to, landing on one of the black vines near three of the black bugs, each one the size of Tem's foot. The three spiders scurried to the morsel and devoured it with high-pitched clicks of delight. One of the spiders ripped off a shred of meat and retreated to eat in solitude, but a fourth rushed in and stole the scrap.

Tem checked his pocket. He had two strips of meat remaining. Delicately, he tossed another. The scrap of hare meat fell short, falling only a few paces from Tem's feet. None of the spiders noticed. Tem sighed and prepared to aim the last piece.

Tem had not meant to sigh aloud, but his exhalation seemed to reflect off the eastern range as if he had shouted. One spider in particular noticed him, and approached. Moving smoothly and quickly, like water, Tem extended the stick so that the noose hung between the spider and meat. His quarry halted and raised a black forelimb, as if waving. Tem eased the stick back, so that the bottom of the noose touched the ground directly in front of the bait. The spider stepped through the noose and bit into the ripe hare flesh. Tem yanked the stick sharply, and ran for his life.

He dared not look back, but ran as fast as his feet would carry him. The stick felt light in his hand; the noose must have slipped. Well, he had tried. He wasn't stupid enough to try again – surely the swarm was now agitated. He risked a quick glance back. Just shrubs and stunted elfin-wood, no black mass of spiders pursued him.

He slammed into something, and fell. The stick flew from his hand. As it arced through his field of vision he saw the large black spider caught in the noose, flailing its legs in the air. He *had* caught one.

"Fool!" said Egil. He brought the butt of his staff down on the black bug, crushing it. Still the legs moved. Egil raised his staff again.

"No!" Tem shouted. "Don't destroy it. The sky people wanted one, to bring to their ringship and examine."

Egil hesitated, glaring at him. "Are you bit?"

"No."

"Let me see you." Roughly Egil lifted Tem to his feet and examined him, paying special attention to his bare hands and forearms. Tem watched the black spider, still caught in the noose, mostly crushed but still waving a single leg.

"Well, I don't see any bite marks," said the bard. His morning voice was low and gravelly.

"I told you, I'm fine." Tem pulled away from Egil's calloused grip.

"Very well. Bring your prize and let's show the others. Take care... it doesn't quite look dead."

★　★　★

Everyone gathered round and stared at the now-expired spider. Mother had already scolded him. He had guessed she would, but he had not expected her eyes to well up with tears, and now he felt guilty. Father stared impassively at the black bug without so much as a knowing wink in Tem's direction. If he was proud of Tem he did not show it.

"I'll get a sterile bag," the sky woman said. "It's too big for a sample kit."

The bald man – Shane – nodded in agreement. "May I take a closer look?" he asked. It took Tem a moment to realize the question was directed at him. Tem nodded. The man unfolded a slender black blade and poked gently at the eight-legged beast. "Hmm."

"It puzzles you?" said Egil in Norse.

"It looks biological," Shane answered, after a pause. "Natural, I mean. Not a machine. Not a...device."

"I know what a machine is," Egil said. "I have seen the Builder ruins. I have even read some of their books. Why would you think this spider is a machine?"

"It didn't react to my disruptor."

"Your weapon must be broken," Askr suggested. "Or perhaps the spiders are immune, as they are to their own venom."

Shane shook his head. "My weapon is functioning perfectly. I can demonstrate on you if you like."

"I'm sure that won't be necessary," said the copper-haired sky woman. She had returned from the raft with a transparent bag.

"Anyway, you can't develop immunity to neuro-disruption fields," Shane said. "It doesn't work that way. The field affects insects, worms, anything with synaptic transmission of any kind. Even non-chordates."

Tem didn't understand many of the words, but he had an idea. "Could it be part flesh, part machine?" he asked. A mix of things, like Tem himself.

The ringship people exchanged a look, but neither answered him. The copper-haired woman knelt by the spider, holding the transparent bag open. Shane pushed the bug into the bag with the flat of his blade, never touching it with bare skin.

"There," said the woman, sealing the bag. "We'll take it to the lab."

"Thank you, Tem," the man said. "Car-En is right – you put yourself in too much danger. But the sample will help us."

"Foolish," added Egil. "Stupid, not brave."

"Enough," Father said. "The boy has learned his lesson."

Tem *hadn't* learned his lesson – he was ecstatic to receive the thanks from the ringship man – but he did not contradict Father. Instead he nodded and kept his eyes down.

★   ★   ★

Tem ate a cold breakfast with the ringship people while Father, Mother, Askr, and Egil broke camp. They had other food besides the dry grain squares: dried fruits called apricots and plums that grew in their southern land (much sweeter than the mountain berries Tem was used to), and a sweet paste they called *goo*, and cubes of water sealed in a tasteless but edible material. Shane showed Tem the various compartments, levers, knobs, and buttons inside the floating raft, which was called a *hovershuttle*. It rode the air by virtue of two great horizontal wheels that spun at a great speed. Would Tem like to ride in it?

The copper-haired woman spoke quietly with Mother. They were too far away to overhear, but Tem watched them closely. Mother either did not like the woman, or was angry with her. To Tem the sky woman seemed harmless and sweet, but he would not put his full trust in her unless Mother did so first. Shane seemed like a solid sort, even if he did not believe Farbror Trond was the strongest man in the world. How could he know? He had not seen Tem's uncle. Perhaps Shane would come to Happdal and wrestle Trond – then he would understand. Maybe the sky man would tell what Tem had done, catching the spider. Even better, Egil would tell the tale, for he was a bard. He could even sing it, the song of Tem the Spider Catcher!

"Are you dreaming of gold and glory?" Father had approached without Tem noticing. Tem blushed. Father had read his face as easily as tracking a bear in the mud. "Listen," Father said, "I must bid you goodbye. I will join you on the ringship as soon as Svein is dealt with."

"What do you mean?" Tem asked.

"You and Mother are going to the ringship," Father said. "Lydia and Shane will take you there in their vessel – quickly – you will arrive within the day. By tonight you'll have your own room, hot food and a cozy bed. And you'll meet your other farfar.

"Don't look so sad, my son. I'll be there as soon as I can. You're going on a great adventure. You're not scared, are you? You'll have Mother, you'll have Trond's blade at your belt. Have you given it a name yet? I know you'll miss village life. The smithy will be there when you return. I promise. Trond and Jense will save a place for you. I'll make them swear it. Now here, take this." Father handed him a small leather bag, tied closed. Tem knew his Father's possessions by sight, but he had never seen this bag before. "Don't open it until you're on the *Stanford*. Promise?"

Tem took the pouch and nodded. "I don't want to go," he mumbled, but in truth he had already resigned himself. Briefly he had hoped Mother and Father had changed their minds, but clearly they had not. So he would do his year on the ringship, then resume his plan. It was simply what he must do.

★   ★   ★

Father and Askr would return to Happdal. Egil would continue his wanderings, telling his stories and singing his poems. Tem hoped, but did not dare ask, if Egil would compose *Tem the Spider Catcher*. The bard had seen the events with his own eyes; surely Tem's brave deed was worthy of a song? But it would only be a first verse, for the end of the spider story was not yet known. It occurred to Tem that Egil should speak with Tante Katja when he was next in Happdal; Katja studied Builder things, and she had had her strange adventure. Maybe she would know what the spiders were. But Egil was already waving his staff, yelling farewell, leaving with Father and Askr. Tem, Mother, and the sky people clambered into the hovershuttle. Shane took the steering seat, while Lydia busied herself at the control panel.

"Ready?" Shane asked, looking back at Mother and Tem. Mother nodded.

He spun up the great wheels, blowing dust and leaves in every direction. Tem squinted. The hovershuttle slowly rose into the air.

"We're flying," Mother said, squeezing his arm. She looked happy, which surprised Tem.

CHAPTER THIRTEEN

Lydia had been piloting since their last stretch break, and was glad to be back at the controls. The task required her full concentration, and cleared her mind.

"There's a storm system coming in from the North Sea," Shane said, frowning at the display panel.

"Can we avoid it?" Car-En asked from the backseat, speaking quietly. Tem was asleep, his head resting against the side of the envirodome.

"No," Shane said. "It's going to pass right over the mule station. Our best bet will be to land and sit it out. I'll let the OETS crew know we'll be delayed."

It was a clear summer day, blue skies over green steppes. It was hard to believe foul weather was imminent, but she trusted the *Stanford's* weather forecasting. Fierce storms were more common in the winter, but it was cold year round this close to the glacial wall.

The trip was going well. Car-En was in good spirits, and had been quite talkative before Tem had dozed off, pointing out herds of migrating caribou, grazing woolly cows, and a pride of lions probably descended from zoo stock. Lydia hadn't yet told Car-En about Marivic. She kept meaning to, but Tem was always close by. Now might be a good time, with Tem asleep, but she didn't feel up to it. Maybe it was best to wait until they weathered out the storm. Once they arrived at the mule station, Lydia could take Car-En aside and share the difficult news, and apologize for not telling her sooner. Then Car-En and Tem would be up and away; Lydia wouldn't have to deal with the aftermath. She felt guilty for thinking such a thing, but it wasn't Lydia's fault that Car-En had missed her own mother's death. She hated being the messenger.

"Slow down – there's no rush," Shane whispered, leaning toward her. Lydia eased off the accelerator; the hovershuttle adjusted its forward angle back a few degrees. She'd been approaching two hundred kph, nearly maximum speed with their current load. It was hard to judge speed on the open steppes.

"Sorry." He was right to caution her; even a minor accident could put them in a difficult and dangerous situation.

"Want me to drive?" Car-En offered. "Doesn't look that hard."

"It's not," Shane said, "but it's easy to go too fast. Especially out here in the open." They'd flown over forests north of the Harz mountains, then skirted the ruins of Hanover. Between their current location and the mule station there was nothing but open grasslands.

Lydia checked their course in her m'eye. "Are you sure we can't outrun the storm?" Even at the leisurely pace of one hundred kph they would arrive at the mule station, near the ruins of Bremen, within ninety minutes.

"We could try," Shane said, glancing back at Tem, "but I think it would be safer to go slow and sit out the storm if we need to."

Lydia brought up the satellite feed in her m'eye. The windstorm was moving alarmingly quickly over the North Sea. It would land any minute, and be on them within the hour. She adjusted their course slightly north, toward the Aller river. They could follow the Aller west to the Weser, which passed directly by the mule station.

"So I noticed you haven't reported to Adrian," Car-En said. "Unless you've been sneaky about it."

"There's no need to," said Lydia. "We'll be back at AFS-1 tonight – we'll bring him up to date then."

"You mean *Vandercamp*," Car-En said, darkly sarcastic. "Look, you can report to Adrian if you need to. Just don't tell him I'm with you. Not yet. Wait until I'm on the mule. Once we're on the *Stanford*, we'll be safer."

"We'll just update him later," Shane said. "It's fine."

"You know it's not fine," said Car-En. "He's a control freak. It's *dangerous* to leave him out of the loop. Believe me, I know. I learned the hard way." Tem stirred in his sleep and mumbled something. Car-En stroked his hair until he settled.

"If you were scared of Adrian," Lydia asked, "why did you want to return to the *Stanford* in the first place?"

Car-En looked at her sharply. "I stayed in the village because I fell in love, not because I was afraid. I know Adrian's dangerous, but I'm not going to let him control my life. It's time for Tem to meet my parents, and to get a better education."

"Do you think you'll return to Happdal?" Shane asked. Lydia was beginning to realize that changing the subject was a frequently used conversational tactic for Shane. For a man specializing in conflict he was good at avoiding it.

Car-En was quiet for so long that Lydia thought she might not answer. "It depends on Esper," she finally said. "If he were willing to live on the *Stanford*, I wouldn't mind staying there. I miss my parents." Lydia cringed. She had to tell her *now*. "It will be nice to have some modern comforts too – village life is strenuous – but mostly I miss the people I left behind." Car-En paused in a way that Lydia thought might mean that *people* might include Lydia herself.

"Car-En, there's something I need to tell you. It's important."

"What?"

"Hold that thought," said Shane, "look over there."

Lydia slowed the shuttle. Several hundred meters ahead, a group of figures stood atop a low hill. Zooming in with her m'eye, Lydia could make out four men, two women, and a child, all dressed warmly in furs and hides, wearing leather backpacks. With them were three large dogs or domesticated wolves. The entire group, including the wolf-dogs, stared back at them.

"Who are they?" Tem asked, rubbing his eyes.

"I don't know," Shane said. Lydia eased the shuttle forward, closing their distance to fifty meters. The group watched their approach, curious but not obviously frightened.

"Mother, they look a little like you." Tem reverted to the village dialect.

It was true; the women did look like Car-En, brown-skinned with wide faces and flat noses. Car-En's features were more European, and her build was slighter, but there were some similarities.

"Mongolians?" Shane suggested. "Some of the horsemen lived traditional lifestyles right through the Corporate Age. They could have survived Depop."

"I don't think so," said Lydia. "They look more like Inuit." She dispatched a hound to gather historical images. "They could have migrated from North America over the ice sheets."

The child waved at them. Tem stood up in the backseat, slightly rocking the shuttle, and waved back.

"Not too close," Shane cautioned, "and don't land." Lydia slowed their advance to a crawl, stopping at twenty meters. The craft hovered two meters from the ground. "A little lower," Shane said, "so we're at eye level."

"Can we open the dome and talk to them?" asked Tem.

One of the men flicked his hand in their direction. The three wolf-dogs leapt forward, racing toward them. Tem screamed. Lydia yanked the steering stick and twisted the throttle. The turbines roared, thrusting them upwards. One of the men pulled back his arm and hurled a heavy antler-tipped spear in their direction. The weapon soared toward them, then crashed into the envirodome, cracking the reinforced glass. The impact rocked the craft. Lydia struggled to keep them level.

The dogs barked wildly from below. "Get us out of here!" Shane's hands twitched toward the steering column.

"I've got it!" Lydia yelled. Carefully she brought them higher and away from the hostile group. Ten meters up and one hundred meters away she brought the shuttle around so they once again faced their attackers. The dogs had returned to the group and the spear-thrower had retrieved his weapon. The child continued to wave, while the adults watched impassively.

"Not very friendly," Car-En said.

"The boy is," said Tem. "Can we do that again?"

"They seem to have a non-engagement policy," Shane said. "Maybe leftover from the Survivalist Age. It might have kept them alive."

The hound had returned with hundreds of historical images. The group's clothing style did seem to be Inuit; their furs were probably caribou. The leather backpacks didn't match any traditional design, but that didn't mean much either way. Obtaining a genetic sample would provide more information, but trying to do so seemed unwise.

"It's cold in here," said Tem.

Cold outside air was seeping in through the cracked dome. "Dammit," Shane muttered. "We better get going."

Lydia pointed the hovershuttle northwest and gradually accelerated. Tem looked back and waved until they were out of sight.

★   ★   ★

Soon they reached the Aller river, twisting its way west. Ahead the sky was dark. Already Lydia was having trouble flying in a straight line. "We'd better land," she said. "The wind is getting crazy."

"The storm will be on us in five, ten minutes," Shane said, checking the display panel. "Can you set us down behind those trees?" He pointed to a copse of poplars near the river. "That should give us some cover."

Lydia eased the shuttle to the ground next to the hardy trees. The tall poplars had survived the dryer, colder climate, sprawling out from their tidy riverside plantings. Fallen yellow leaves whirled up around them as they landed. Even as the turbines slowed to a stop the loose leaves eddied higher, buffeted by the storm winds.

"Are we safe here?" Tem asked.

"I think so," Car-En said. Lydia appreciated that Car-En did not blindly reassure her son. The world was dangerous, and Tem knew it, and did not expect others to guarantee his safety. It was a good, practical attitude.

"Anyone hungry?" Shane asked. "We've got g'nerf bars."

"I'll try one," said Car-En.

"Vanilla-cream, cocoa-cinnamon, or mixed fruit?"

"They can be a little speedy," said Lydia. "They're loaded with micronutrients. You might start with half of one."

"I'll be fine. Cocoa-cinnamon please."

"Can I try whichever one I didn't have before?" Tem said.

"Just give me one of each – we'll work it out," said Car-En.

Shane handed out the g'nerf bars and some water cubes. Car-En distributed hard cheese, smoked trout, and dried berries from her bag, then pulled out a corked jar and waved it in front of the boy.

"No!" Tem yelled. "Don't!"

"What is it?" asked Lydia, alarmed.

"Fermented fish paste," Car-En said. "Best to wait for open air, but it tastes pretty good once you get used to it. This is Elke's recipe."

"Your mother-in-law?" Shane asked. "Do you get along?"

"Well enough. Better since Tem came along – the first year was rough."

"Farmor is mean," Tem said, "unless she likes you."

Car-En laughed. "It's true. And she doesn't like your mother, unfortunately. But she's good to you. I can't wait for you to meet your other grandma."

Lydia tried to swallow the lump in her throat. She couldn't wait any longer. "Car-En...what I was meaning to tell you before. A few years ago...."

"What?"

"Your mother," said Lydia. Car-En's eyes went wide. Lydia found herself hoping, against logic, that Car-En somehow already knew. But she couldn't – there was no way. "There was an accident...."

"What kind of accident?" Car-En asked quietly.

"Environmental control."

"Did she suffer?"

"Not for long. She froze. It would have been quick."

Tem looked up at his mother. "Mormor died?" Car-En pulled him close and nodded, somber but dry-eyed.

"What about Shol?" Car-En asked.

Lydia sighed and wiped the tears from her cheeks. "He's fine. He's good! He's healthy, still working, still tinkering. He'll be happy to see you. He'll be happy to meet *you*." She reached back and squeezed Tem's knee. "I'm sorry I didn't tell you earlier. I wanted to."

"It's a hard thing to say."

"Marivic and I became good friends," Lydia said. "Especially after you...after you decided to live in Happdal. I think spending time with me made her feel closer to you. I still miss her."

"When did she die?"

"Four years ago."

"Four *years*." Car-En closed her eyes and exhaled slowly. "She's been dead for four years, and I didn't know."

Tem hugged his mother tightly. "I'm sorry."

The rain came down, at first a pitter-patter on the dome, then a torrent of heavier droplets. Yellow leaves stuck to the wet glass. A rivulet of water trickled inside from the crack where the antler spearhead had fractured the dome. Lydia turned on the heat. Minutes later the dome interior was comfortably toasty.

"Now it's *hot*," Tem said.

Shane fed their food scraps into the fuel cell's compost tube. "That will keep us going for a little while. After that we might need to go outside and forage."

Lydia stretched as best she could within the confines of the dome. They might ride out the storm comfortably. Part of her was disappointed; she had been harboring a silly fantasy about *surviving* the storm with Shane, forced to huddle together for warmth. Maybe it was time to admit to herself that she was attracted to him. Maybe she would even do something about it. Xenus wouldn't be happy, but neither would it be an act of betrayal. Lydia and Xenus had never agreed to exclusivity when it came to intimacy, friendship, or anything else. She wasn't sure how Shane felt. He seemed to like her, but nothing he had said or done could be interpreted as flirting, even if she took a wildly optimistic attitude. She guessed he was a one-partner-at-a-time sort.

"What's that?" Tem asked.

Three large animals, partially obscured by the trees and rain, were watching them.

"Maybe woolly cows?" Lydia said.

One of the animals trotted a few paces toward them, then sat back on its haunches.

"That's no herbivore," Shane said.

"Is it a dog?" Tem asked.

Now all three animals were closing in, with a distinctive canine gait. Two of the creatures were roughly two meters high at the shoulder. The third was half again as large.

"Too big to be dogs," said Lydia, not quite believing her eyes. They were close enough to see clearly; the animals *were* dogs, if unnaturally sized. The huge beasts were thick-limbed and broad-chested, with shaggy black coats and tawny paws.

"Mastiffs of some sort," Shane said.

There was a no pets policy at AFS-1. They had enough food to feed themselves, but not much extra. The denizens of the *Stanford*, on the other hand, kept a menagerie of domesticated beasts including dogs, cats, rodents, snakes, and birds. The dog breeds tended to be the smaller sort; ringstation culture put a premium on lightness. But Lydia was sure that no human pet had ever reached the size of the beasts approaching them, not even during the Corporate Age peak of recreational genetic tinkering.

"Looks like the European megafauna have returned," Shane said.

"What do they *eat* to get that big?" Tem asked.

"Probably whatever they want," said Shane. "Caribou and woolly cow, I imagine. We've seen both in the vicinity."

The largest giant mastiff circled around their perimeter, flanking them. One of the others came closer. Towering over the environmental dome, it sniffed at the hovershuttle, flaring its nostrils. The dog's hot breath clouded the glass. Car-En paled and pulled Tem close. "Does this thing have weapons?" she asked.

"None external – it's just a transport vehicle," said Shane. "I have a neural disruptor if we need it, but the glass might interfere."

The mastiff lifted a wet, tawny paw and placed it atop the dome, rocking the craft.

"Whoa," Shane said, "it's strong."

"Get us out of here," said Car-En.

"No way we can fly until the wind calms down."

The huge dog tapped experimentally on the dome, heavy black claws rapping against the glass like small hammers.

"Can he break it?" Tem asked.

"I don't think so," Shane said.

"The spear already cracked the glass," Tem said, sounding worried.

"That was a concentrated point of impact, and a lucky shot. Sit tight, kid – we'll be fine."

Car-En clutched Tem with one arm. Her other hand moved to the hilt of her knife.

The biggest mastiff closed in. It sniffed, then opened its massive jaws and tried to bite the dome. Looking up they could see directly into its maw, gums mottled black and pink, rainwater streaming down its yellowed fangs. The dome was too wide and the glass too smooth for the animal to get purchase. Lydia exhaled, then gulped for air – she hadn't realized she'd been holding her breath.

"Are you getting this?" Shane asked. Lydia nodded, tagging her m'eye stream for later retrieval. Some people saved all of their feed data, but Lydia preferred to delete old streams by default and rely on natural memory unless there was a particular reason to document an experience. Like now.

Failing to bite through, the humungous mastiff struck the dome with its forepaw. This was no tap; it meant to shatter the glass. The existing crack from the spear fractured longer. The third dog trotted up to the front of the craft; they were now surrounded.

"What now?" Lydia asked.

"Just wait. They'll probably lose interest in a minute or two," Shane said.

That seems optimistic. Lydia held her tongue; Shane was probably just trying to reassure the boy.

The biggest dog backed off a couple meters and circled the craft, as if examining it.

"It looks like it's thinking," Tem said.

The boy's comment triggered a memory. "Didn't the Russians experiment with intelligent war dogs?" Lydia didn't want to worry Tem, but keeping them all alive was the top priority.

"I was just having the same thought," Shane said.

The alpha closed in, this time from the rear, and locked its jaws on the hollow rim of the shuttle. A horrible cracking, shredding sound filled the dome as the dog's fangs pierced the hard polymer casing of the rear bumper.

"It's okay," said Shane, "that doesn't compromise our ability to fly. The bumpers provide buoyancy in case of water landings, but they're not essential to operations. That thing can chew all it wants."

Jaws still locked on the craft, the beast locked its forelegs and tugged hard. The shuttle lurched backward, scraping along the ground.

"Open the dome and shoot it!" Car-En yelled. "Now!"

Shane shook his head. "That would be suicide. The others would be on us too quickly."

"Then give me your dart rifle. I'll tranq the big one and you use your disruptor on the others."

"No way. The tranquilizer takes at least a ten-count to work, and on something that size…."

The mastiff pulled again; this time the shuttle moved a full meter. It was pulling them toward the river.

"It's trying to drown us," Car-En said. "We can't just sit here and do nothing!"

"We'll float," said Shane. "The bumpers are compartmentalized. Just keep it together. It can't get to us."

"How long before it figures out it needs to pierce the other compartments to sink us?" Car-En had a wild-eyed look that Lydia had never seen before. "*Look* at that thing. Look into its eyes. It's fucking smart, and it wants to eat us."

Shane was already watching the mastiff, calmly assessing the situation. Lydia's own heart was ready to leap out of her chest.

Tem has escaped from his mother's grasp and clambered up the backrest of the rear bench, getting as close as possible to the giant mastiff. He rapped on the glass of the dome.

"Tem, quit it!" Car-En yelled.

"I'm just trying to distract it!"

Steadily, the giant war dog pulled them toward the river. The two other dogs joined the effort, placing their forepaws on the front rim of the shuttle and shoving it forward with coordinated pushes. The wind had picked up and was blowing the rain at a forty-five-degree angle onto the south side of the dome. Lydia peered out at the river. The Aller flowed slowly but looked icy cold. The outside temperature had dropped to just above freezing. At any point the rain could turn to snow.

"Shane, what's the plan?" Car-En asked. "Talk to me." She had grabbed Tem and was restraining him. The physical exertion seemed to calm her.

"Lydia, get ready to start the turbines."

"It's too windy – we'd blow right into the trees."

"Just be ready. Please trust me."

Because of his vast experience fighting genetically engineered Russian war dogs? She suppressed her sarcastic thoughts and faced forward in the driver's seat. "I'm ready."

With one final tug the mutant mastiff pulled them down the shallow bank into the river. Immediately the current pulled them downriver. The beast waded next to them, seemingly unaffected by the cold, and bit into one of the side bumpers with a crunch. The craft listed to the left. Tem cried out, panicked.

"Hold on to him!" Shane yelled.

"I am!" Car-En had the boy in a bear hug.

"Lydia – hit the turbines. Full power."

She had never tried a takeoff from the water, much less with the shuttle partially submerged. How much water had seeped into the bumper compartments? With four people and provisions they were already close to max carry capacity.

"Now!" Shane yelled. Lydia slammed her palm flat on the biometric starter and twisted the throttle with her other hand. The turbines started to rotate beneath them. The water frothed on all sides. The giant mastiff ignored the rough water and bit down on one of the forward compartments, cracking the hard polymer with its fangs.

"We can't take off if it's holding on to us. It's too strong!" Car-En, looking frantic, let go of Tem and grabbed at Shane's dart rifle. "Open the dome. Open it!"

Shane pushed Car-En back with a straight-arm thrust. He was thrice her weight and immensely strong; Car-En slammed into the rear bench backrest, coughing and clutching her chest.

"Don't hit my mother!" Tem screamed, red-faced with rage.

"Everybody calm down!" Lydia bellowed. White foam splashed up around them, blinding them on all sides. Did the beast still have its jaws locked on the shuttle? The back of the shuttle lifted higher, but the front end stayed down. Lydia's forehead slammed into the glass dome. Tem was shouting something. She could hear Car-En gasping for air.

"Forward! Full speed!" Shane was yelling at her. She tried to analyze his instruction and predict the result. "Now!" Backward was not a good idea. The shuttle didn't have enough thrust to escape the dog's jaws; if they reversed thrust the dog might pull down and flip them. Then the turbines would push them even deeper underwater. If the dome cracked they'd drown. "Lydia – now!"

Full speed ahead. She pulled back the steering stick, leveling them out. The turbines had displaced a huge amount of water on all sides; they were surrounded by a wall of white foam. She could see the dog now, eye to eye. The mastiff's brown eyes bulged in rage as she pushed the full thrust of the craft into it. They were going nowhere.

"Keep going! The water's too deep – it doesn't have purchase. It can't swim against us."

She didn't believe it but she couldn't think of a better plan. She stole a glance at the battery gauge; at this rate of expenditure it would be dead in a few minutes.

The shuttle slowly pushed forward. The dog-beast released its jaws and they twisted away, then up. A few seconds later they were ten meters above the water, buffeted by the winds, looking down on what could be a large pet swimming in the river. The wind and the turbines roared.

"I feel sick," Tem said. He looked pale and sweaty.

"Anyone injured?" Shane asked.

Lydia wiped her hair away from her eyes. Her hand came back wet and red. Shane was already opening a first-aid kit. She blinked away the blood until he pressed a cool white cloth against her forehead.

"Is she okay?" Car-En asked.

"Can you see straight?" Shane asked. She could, more or less. With the rain and the wind she could only see about a hundred meters ahead.

"Take it slow," said Shane. "We'll check for concussion later." She felt nauseous, but that was probably just from the turbulence.

For the next few minutes she steered, white-knuckled, keeping low to avoid the worst of the buffeting winds, checking the altimeter every few seconds to make sure she didn't run them into the ground. Ten minutes later the storm blew over; they were left with a steady downpour. Tem, who had been moaning in the backseat, was now quiet. "He's asleep," Car-En whispered.

"I'm sorry I shoved you," Shane said, turning back to look at Car-En. He sounded like he meant it. "You okay?"

"I'm fine. I forgive you. It was...a moment. I panicked a little."

"Better than freezing up. What about him?" Shane nodded at Tem, who was sound asleep with his head in Car-En's lap. "Think he'll forgive me?"

Car-En shook her head. "Not likely. Not for a while. He's very protective."

"Hmm."

"I'll talk to him later – explain you were just trying to keep us all safe."

"I'd appreciate that."

"Shane, can you wipe my forehead again?" Blood was trickling down her left temple.

"Sure." He did so, gently.

"Can you check our total weight? I'm worried we took on water."

Shane tapped the display a few times. "A little, but we're still under max capacity."

Lydia nodded. "Good. But it feels heavy. We need to land and find something to feed the fuel cell. Unless you've got something handy."

"Would it take fermented fish paste?" ask Car-En. Shane laughed a little too loudly.

"Don't you dare."

"We could sacrifice a couple g'nerf bars," Shane suggested.

Lydia nodded. "Sounds good – better than stopping in this mess. Use the mixed fruit. Nobody's going to eat those anyway."

Shane rummaged around in one of the supply compartments. "Got 'em!" He opened the compost tube and inserted the two ration bars, wrappers and all. "That should do it."

They flew in silence for another ten minutes. Lydia's head throbbed steadily, a dull ache synchronized with her heartbeat. "I think we should switch soon."

"Anytime," Shane said.

They cleared the storm. Ahead, Lydia saw the gray platform of the OETS station. The unwieldy acronym for Orbital Earth Transport Shuttle sounded like 'oats' when pronounced. That, and the fact that the reusable transport rocket was short, squat, and extremely tough had led to the nickname *mule*, which had stuck.

Car-En shook her son gently. "Tem, wake up. We're almost there."

"What is it?"

"Look over there. That's how we're getting to the *Stanford*. See those little rocket ships?"

Tem rubbed his eyes and blinked. "Those are the mules? Will one be big enough for all of us?"

"It will just be you and me."

"Do you know how to steer it?"

"I won't need to – the flight will be controlled from the station."

"By who?"

"The mule crew. They live there some of the time. The rest of the time they live on the *Stanford*."

"Will you know them?"

"Maybe. Probably not."

"Will they speak Norse?"

"Nope," she patted his head. "But don't worry, your English is getting much better."

Lydia brought the shuttle down gently on the landing platform, not far from the two mules. Three of the OETS station crew, wearing green and black uniforms, came to greet them. Bracingly cold air rushed in as she opened the envirodome. Everyone climbed out of the shuttle and stretched.

"What happened?" A short black-skinned woman was surveying the damage to the shuttle.

"A close encounter with the local fauna," Shane said. "Something new – some kind of engineered dog."

"Looks more like a shark," said the woman, examining the bumper damage. "Glad you made it in one piece." She extended her hand to Shane. "I'm Petra. OETS station shift leader, for the moment. You must be Shane."

"Enjoying life on Earth?" Lydia asked. The woman grimaced, noticing Lydia's forehead.

"Lydia, right? We're enjoying our shift just fine. Looks like you've had more excitement than we have. How are things at Vandercamp?" So, the moniker had spread to the *Stanford*. "Have enough to eat?" It sounded like she hadn't heard about Alexi Rosen. Adrian was keeping a tight lid on things. She made a m'eye note to follow up with Shane about the security report to Townes. She wouldn't let Adrian keep Rosen's murder a secret. Petra was staring at her. "You okay?"

"Sure. Just a little shook up."

"Who's this?" Petra was looking at Tem.

"That's my son," Car-En said. She took a step forward, moving between Tem and Petra.

"Sorry, I didn't mean...." Petra trailed off, staring at Car-En.

"My name is Car-En Ganzorig."

One of the other mule crew, a slim man with a full beard, gasped. "I watched your feeds," he said.

Tem glared at the man.

Petra raised one eyebrow. "Your son, you say."

"He'll be visiting the *Stanford*."

For several seconds nobody said anything. Petra broke the silence. "If you consent to a full medical scan and decon, I don't have any issue with that."

"We consent," said Car-En.

"My father is coming later," Tem said, "and our friend Askr. They'll want to come up as well." Tem stared at the squat rocket ships as he spoke.

"I'll have to check with Townes, since they're not citizens," Petra said. "But if you vouch for them, I'm guessing she'll okay it. Looks like we'll be having some visitors."

"Update your kits with the latest Happdal dialect," Car-En said. "Esper speaks some Orbital English, but not Askr."

"Anybody hungry?" the bearded man asked.

Lydia used the OETS station facilities to shower, then disinfected and bandaged her wound. As a precaution she took a neuroprotective medication for the head injury; she couldn't yet rule out a concussion. She dressed in one of the generic green and black one-piece uniforms she found folded in a drawer. It was a little big, but preferable to her own bloody, sweat-soaked clothing. She found the others eating hot soup in the mess hall.

"Want a hot cocoa?" Shane asked. She nodded. "I'll get it for you."

Lydia sat next to Car-En. She wanted to put her arm around her old friend, but didn't dare.

"Thanks for the ride," Car-En said.

"It was nothing. I'm so sorry about Marivic."

"Sorry you had to be the one to tell me. That couldn't have been easy."

"How long will you stay on the *Stanford*?"

"At least a couple months. I want Tem to get to know my father. After that we'll see how it goes." Tem had finished his soup and was exploring the mess hall.

"It will be a big adjustment," Lydia said. "For both of you, but especially him."

Car-En nodded. "I know, but he needs to see an alternative to village life. His world is too small now. All he can think about is blacksmithing. I want him to see…I don't know…more possibilities."

"Maybe he'll still choose to be a smith," Lydia said.

"You're just saying that because your last name is *Heliosmith*." Car-En grinned, and Lydia felt a flash of hopeful joy. Just as quickly Car-En's countenance darkened. "Look, what are you going to do about Adrian?"

"I don't know. Shane and I need to discuss it."

"Fine," said Car-En. She grabbed Lydia's hand and squeezed it.

"But don't *just* discuss it. You need to do something. I'm worried about your safety."

"Don't worry about us. We can handle Adrian."

"Don't be so sure," Car-En said. "As long as Adrian is alive and in control of *anything*, he's a problem. If you don't do something, I will."

Lydia wasn't sure what to say to that. It sounded like a reckless threat, but she didn't want to get into an argument with Car-En.

Shane returned with a cup of steaming cocoa. Car-En left to check on Tem.

"What was that about?" Shane asked.

"I'll tell you later," Lydia said. "We'll have time to talk on the ride home. And there's plenty to discuss."

CHAPTER FOURTEEN

Tem liked the mule crew, and was sad to say goodbye. Petra, the black-skinned one, had given him chocolate, the first sky food he found tolerable. There was much more chocolate on the *Stanford*, she said, and hundreds of other foods that would be new to him. Merus, the skinny bearded man, was a little *too* friendly (especially to Mother – it made him wonder if Father would be jealous), but Mother didn't seem to mind. When Merus learned that Tem was interested in swords he challenged him to fight with sticks, but gave up as soon as Tem poked him hard in the belly. Tem had trained with Katja, and fighting the ringship man was like fighting a baby. In fact it was *easier* – even his little cousin Sigurd fought better. He wondered if all the ringship people were so weak and unskilled. Still, he grew to like Merus, especially when the man showed him pictures of Vikings, which he claimed were Tem's own distant ancestors. The swords in the pictures *did* look like Trond and Jense's blades, but the Viking helmets were adorned with ridiculous horns. If the pictures were true then his ancestors had been fools. No wonder most of them had perished.

The third crew member was the least effusive; thus Tem found him to be the most interesting. Javier, slight with dark brown skin, spoke quietly but with confidence. Javier did not offer Tem any gifts, but deliberately answered all of his questions, speaking slowly enough so that Tem could understand his English. Javier even used a Norse word here and there. Somehow the ringship people knew some words in Norse even though they did not speak the language. Javier explained that he used a false lens over his eye to ask a machine that gave him the words. Later he asked Mother if he could have such a thing; it would help his studies. Mother at first pretended to not know what he was talking about, then changed the subject.

Tem was given a small private room, and washed himself in an even smaller room that streamed hot water from a tube. Mother washed his hair with a pungent soap that she insisted stay on his scalp for a long time, and afterward she combed his hair with a fine comb for what seemed an eternity. His old clothes were taken and new ones given. The new sky clothing fit too tightly and felt too soft against his skin.

Petra gave him medicine to take (though nothing as horrid-tasting as Ilsa's concoctions) and examined his body from head to toe, even drawing a small amount of blood with a stinging device she pressed up against his arm. She pronounced him in good health, which he already knew, but his old clothes never reappeared. His blade they did return, though Petra did not approve of a young boy carrying such a weapon. Mother ignored Petra's protestations, which delighted Tem.

For the voyage they donned heavy clothing that would protect against *radiation*, dangerous invisible energy that was stronger in space. Attached to the bulky travel uniform was a helmet and face shield that enclosed the head entirely. Tem felt claustrophobic when he first tried it out, but soon adjusted. Petra said it was important to feel comfortable; the trip was quite long. As first they would feel very heavy as the ship picked up speed. Later, as they escaped Earth's gravity well, they would float in the air like dandelion tufts.

The 'mule' flying ship, upon inspection, was quite complex. At a distance it had appeared much like a turnip or potato perched on three squat legs, but a closer look revealed a pair of wide ducts (which Javier said sucked in air to use as fuel – and as a bellows boy Tem understood this), several doors which disappeared entirely when closed, three large 'thrusters' which propelled the craft by spitting flame down against the ground and pushing the mule into the sky, and a number of tiny thruster side nozzles that could be used to change direction. Surely the craft could not fly just by using *only* air for fuel – didn't it also burn charcoal to create the great flames that must be required? Javier explained that the main fuel was something called *hydrogen slush*, a kind of special air forced into liquid form. When Tem asked if the mule was heavy, Javier responded by lifting one leg of the craft, which was twice as tall as Farbror Trond, several inches off the ground. The hull was made of the same stuff as Mother's feather-blade – carbonlattice – and until loaded with fuel, cargo, and passengers, the mules were so light that they would blow away during storms unless secured to the launch pad with strong cables.

There was no set schedule; they could leave when ready. The *Stanford* would track their flight and assume control of the OETS around the midpoint of their voyage. Mother wanted to talk to Lydia alone, so Shane and Javier took Tem on a tour of the station facilities. They strolled past a field of sunlight-harvesting black panels, steamy glass houses filled with miniature fruit trees and sprawling vegetable vines, and tanks that collected and purified rainwater. One room was filled with the tanks and machines used to create the hydrogen slush (though most of the supply was produced on the ringstation and muled down). Did the mules fly only to the *Stanford*, or to the other ringships as well? The OETS were in service to the *Stanford*, Javier told him, but both the *Alhazen* and the *Liu Hui* had contributed to the engineering effort to create a viable SSTO, and the mules were at their disposal as needed. Javier was explaining what 'SSTO' meant, but Tem's mind was already full. He asked to be shown the 'rec room' which Javier had mentioned in passing.

The recreation room was not as exciting as Tem had hoped. It consisted of some tables and chairs, several sofas (the first Tem had seen but their purpose was obvious), a number of small machines, and large screens on each wall. Most of the games had many complicated rules or took a long time to learn, but one called ping-pong was simple enough. For a long time they played with Tem and Shane as a team against the more experienced Javier. Eventually the men tired and sat on the sofa talking while Tem explored closets and bins filled with puzzles, toys, and contraptions beyond his understanding. Tem pretended to be interested in the games and toys while using the opportunity to eavesdrop.

"What were you saying about Adrian?" Javier asked.

Shane did not answer immediately. Tem assumed he was looking in his direction, and feigned a deep interest in a bin of tiny multi-colored blocks. "Car-En made it clear that she thinks he's dangerous, and that we're crazy to allow him to continue to run AFS-1."

"And you would say that he 'runs it' now?" Javier asked.

"He does," Shane admitted. "He's extremely controlling. The fact that our feeds have been closed for the past few days will incite him to rage."

"But surely he knows you're here? Or someone does?"

"Yes, Lydia let Xenus know. But we've been avoiding reporting to Adrian."

"What would your alternative be? How would you displace Adrian?"

"Officially? An appeal to Townes. As Department Head she's still nominally in charge. But they might have…an arrangement. I'm not sure."

"And unofficially?"

There was a moment of silence that made Tem wonder if the men fully trusted one another. Or maybe they had noticed he was listening? He struggled to keep his gaze fixed on the tiny colored blocks, which, like many of the sky people things, were both lightweight but strong, and snapped together in various ways, and *would* interest him if not for the more interesting conversation nearby.

"I don't know," Shane said. "If we do have to…improvise…are you sympathetic to our situation?"

"Yes," Javier said, "as long as nobody is injured."

"Tactically, you're in a key position," Shane pointed out.

"We're aware of that. Should I talk to Petra?"

"No, not yet. Let's see how things play out." Shane stood, stretched, and crossed the room to where Tem was playing with the blocks. He knelt and mussed Tem's hair. Tem was surprised to find he did not mind the gesture; Shane did not quite feel like family, but nor was he a stranger. "More of those on the *Stanford*, and plenty of other toys. Let's go find your mother."

"Where is the spider I caught?"

Shane raised an eyebrow. "Lydia has it. She's taking it back to her lab at the field station."

"She's going to take it apart?"

"Something like that."

"Will you tell me what it is, when you find out?"

The bald man gave him a long look. Tem wondered if he was about to hear a lie.

"Maybe. It depends on what we discover. Sometimes it's dangerous to know things, and I want to keep you safe."

"I already know some things," Tem said, thinking of the secret pattern Katja had insisted he memorize. "Powerful things."

"Like what?"

"Maybe I'll tell you one day," Tem said, and began to put the tiny colored blocks back in their container.

★ ★ ★

The interior of the mule was smaller than Tem expected. Javier explained that most of the space was dedicated to fuel, machinery, and cargo. There were only two seats, though when necessary two more could be transported in 'nap tubes' that fit neatly into the cargo compartment. Since there were only two of them making the trip, the cargo area was instead loaded with lightweight carbonlattice crates. When Tem asked what the crates contained, Javier opened one and showed him: samples of local plants and insects, some seeds, a few books recovered from the nearby Builder ruins and a cache of ancient gold and silver coins. "For the museums," said Javier, grinning, "though you could fairly call it looting. Though the past owners will hardly miss their treasure, and there are no more nation states to claim property rights."

"*I* claim the treasure for Happdal," Tem said. "The sky people have the sky, but the Earth belongs to us."

"You claim the entire Earth for your village?" Javier looked surprised, but did not dismiss Tem's claim outright. "How far does Happdal's territory extend? Surely the OETS crew can claim the ruins of Bremen?"

Tem pondered on this. He did not want to be timid if he was representing all of Happdal, perhaps even all the Five Valleys. What would make Farfar Arik proud? "Our rights extend north to the river, west to the ocean, south to the sea, and east to Mongolia." Of these boundaries only the river he had actually seen, and Mongolia he had only learned of recently, as the source of Mother's last name.

"Which river?" Javier asked. "The Aller? That's a wide swath of territory. You drive a hard bargain – perhaps there is still some Viking left in you. But okay, I accept your terms. I claim the ruins of Bremen and everything north of the Aller for the *Stanford*. Should we shake on it?"

Tem shook, searching Javier's face for condescension but finding none. "It is agreed," said Tem. "I will tell Jarl Arik when I see him."

★   ★   ★

Everyone gathered to bid them farewell. Shane and Lydia looked serious, as if they had just received some ill tidings. Petra, Merus, and Javier were in better spirits, excited by the pending flight. Javier helped Tem fasten the clear helmet to the neck ring of his heavy uniform. Petra did the same for Mother, and checked that they could both breathe easily. If necessary, they could remove the helmets during flight; the cabin was also filled with air. The suits and helmets were to provide additional safety. Tem, who had long thought Mother to be overly concerned with safety, was beginning to realize that, compared to the other sky people, Mother was carefree, even reckless.

Tem and Mother clambered into the mule and positioned themselves in the reclining seats. Petra closed and sealed the door. Mother pulled straps across his body, fastening him securely to the padded chair. For a long time they sat still, saying nothing. Tem listened to his own breathing. The air was supplied to his helmet by tubes woven into the fabric of his uniform. He imagined tiny bellows boys pumping the air. Mother took his hand and squeezed. What if they missed the ringship, and kept flying into the blackness of space? Would they reach a distant star, or run out of food and die? No, not food – air. Javier had explained there was no air in space; they would need to port the air they breathed, stored in their uniforms and compressed into tanks. They had a limited supply. He hoped that Mother could steer the mule, in case they got lost.

He heard a hissing sound inside his helmet, then a woman's voice. "Tem, can you hear me?" It was Petra, speaking in halting Norse. "It's almost time to take off. I'm going to count down from ten. Then the mule will rise, and you'll feel very heavy for several minutes. Just relax and lie back in your chair. Okay?"

Could she hear him if he spoke? "Yes," he said.

"Good. Here we go. Ten, nine, eight…."

The mule came to life. When Petra reached zero a violent noise shook Tem's body. The mule lifted from the ground. Through the viewing port Tem saw only blue sky. Mother withdrew her hand and positioned her arms on the padded armrests of her reclining chair; Tem did the same. As Petra had warned, his limbs felt heavy, but the effect was tolerable. A bird shot past above; something fast, maybe a swallow. Were there birds on the ringship? Maybe there were creatures he had never seen. He inhaled deeply, with some difficulty. They were rising quickly. His body was pinned to the seat.

"Mother?" Could she hear him?

"Try to relax. Soon you'll be weightless." Her voice sounded strained.

He closed his eyes and breathed. It was all he *could* do; each breath required conscious effort. Again, like pumping the bellows, but now his own lungs needed filling. He counted each breath, one count for in and one for out, until he reached one hundred.

"It's getting easier now," he said, opening his eyes to an indigo sky. For some time they traveled in silence, the sky darkening, Tem's body lightening.

"Look," Mother said, pointing to the left, "that's the *Stanford*."

On a clear night he had seen the ringships in the southern sky, rings of light that held their position even as the stars swept across the night bowl. But now the *Stanford* looked different. Even far away the ringship looked vast, many times larger than he had imagined it. There were spokes – eight of them – like a waterwheel, and along the spokes and the outer ring were thousands of points of bright light. The rest of the hull was covered in some sort of silvery fuzz. Contraptions protruded along the ring and the spokes, increasing in density at the central hub, a smaller inner ring lined by massive angled mirrors. A wave of fear passed through Tem's gut. There were so many things he didn't know: about life in space, about the sky people's machines, about *how everything in the world had happened*. There was a word for that – Katja had told him. History.

Mother undid his straps. He felt buoyant and relaxed. "We've stopped accelerating," Mother said. "Soon we'll turn around and begin to decelerate. We'll have a wonderful view of Earth."

"But we're still moving, right? We're still going toward the ringship?"

"Yes, but at a constant speed. You'll learn about that in Physics, at school. Velocity, acceleration, mass, force, momentum. I think you'll like it – especially the Newtonian laws. They'll be useful to you too – you'll be a better smith once you learn them."

Tem said nothing. He did not look forward to what Mother called *school*. Learning new things was fine; it was the other children he worried about. How many would he need to fight to earn their respect? Maybe they would be soft and friendly, like Merus. *Easy to intimidate.*

He thought back to his agreement with Javier. Probably Javier did not have the authority to cede so much land to Happdal, but someone on the *Stanford* did. The ringship would have a jarl, or the equivalent. It gave him a thrill to imagine himself as the representative of Happdal, gaining territory for his people. Why not the whole Earth? Why not the skies as well? Who would stop him? It was true that not *all* sky people were soft (Mother was tough, so was Javier), but compared to the stock of the Five Valleys they were an inferior breed. They had better weapons, but weapons could be taken and turned.

He checked himself; why was he imagining conquering the sky people? He was half sky person himself. Instead, he would be an ambassador of peace. That's what would make Father and his grandfathers proud.

The sky darkened further; now Tem could see stars beyond the brilliant torus of the *Stanford*. Again he heard a voice in his helmet.

"Prepare for turn and deceleration. How are you two doing?" It was Petra again. He could see her face clearly in his mind's eye. He'd been surprised at how dark her skin was. Before Petra, Mother was the darkest person he had known, and Mother's skin was brown like earth, not black like coal.

"We're doing fine," Mother answered. "Haven't been weightless in a long time."

"Ten years, right?"

"Almost eleven."

"Okay, here you go. After the turn I'm handing you over to the *Stanford*. They'll guide you in. Safe travels."

"Thanks, Petra."

Tem felt the mule shift position in short little bursts. After a minute he saw a curve of blue at the edge of the viewing port.

"What's that?"

"That's Earth," Mother said. "That's our home."

The mule continued to turn until the entire view port was filled with the blue and white sphere. He could see clouds, water, and mountains.

"Where's Happdal?" he asked.

Mother pointed. "Do you see the big boot, with the toe pointing down? Start there, then move your eye to the left, until you reach the ice."

"The white part?"

"Yes. Now move your eye back to the right until you see a large mountain range. Do you see that? Those are the Harz mountains, where we live."

"The Five Valleys?"

"Well, there are many more than five, but yes."

"That's...so small."

He could hear a smile in Mother's voice. "You're right. Very small."

Tem marveled at the size of the Earth. What he had thought of as the entire world was only a tiny part. And yet, according to what Mother and Katja had told him, there weren't many people left. Most of them lived in space, on the ringships. It was comforting to think that even though the Earth was vast, Tem might still play an important role.

But would that role be as smith to Happdal? That had always been the way Tem had seen his life unfold, but now that path seemed unambitious. The thought that his deepest conviction and desire might shift so easily shocked him. He felt nauseous.

"Mother, I feel sick."

"If you think you're going to throw up, I'll take off your helmet. Close your eyes and breathe slowly."

Tem did as Mother instructed. The wave of sickness passed, only to be replaced by fatigue.

"Is it okay if I sleep?"

"I'll wake you up when we arrive."

★   ★   ★

He awoke with a jolt of the mule. The Earth still filled the view port, but no longer entirely. Instead, his home appeared as a giant blue and white ball.

"Are we here?"

"We're docking."

"I still feel light."

"You won't feel gravity again until we go through one of the spokes to the main ring. And even then it won't be gravity, but centripetal force. We're docking in the central hub."

The mule slowly backed into a large room of sorts, and a door slid closed, blocking the view of Earth. The craft came to a full stop.

"Can we get out yet?"

"No. The docking bay has to pressurize."

"What would happen if we opened the mule door right now?"

"We'd be fine, as long as we kept our suits on."

"What if we took them off and opened the door?"

"Before the docking bay was pressurized and warmed? We'd suffocate, and freeze, and our bodies would leak fluids."

"What if I held my breath and closed my eyes?"

"You'd still die. But you don't have to worry about it – we can get out now." Mother took off her helmet and reached over to help him, but Tem waved her off and unfastened himself. Just as he began to float up from his seat, the mule door opened with a hiss. A pretty young woman wearing a blue and black uniform grinned at him from just outside. She had orange hair and freckles.

"You must be Tem," she said in Norse. "Welcome to the *Stanford.*"

Ingrid (the orange-haired woman) and Oscar (an olive-skinned man with a round, friendly face) led Tem and Mother through a long twisty tube, propelling their weightless bodies with handholds affixed along the inner surface of the passage. The large room that Tem had seen while docking was nowhere to be found; the mule door had opened directly into the tube. Ingrid and Oscar moved effortlessly, touching the handholds lightly. Car-En and Tem struggled to keep up, frequently bumping into the sides of the tube. The impacts didn't hurt; the silvery material yielded like stiff cloth. Ahead, Ingrid stopped to wait for them.

"We'll stop by decon first. It won't take long. Then some new clothes, then medical. Have you thought about which nanodrones you want?" The orange-haired woman spoke Norse with a strange accent, but without the odd delay and garbled pronunciation Tem had heard from Shane and Lydia.

"Have the options changed much in the last decade?" Mother asked.

"Not enormously. The standard package includes plaque scrubbers, cancer killers, immune assist, and a diagnostic array. Hormone regulation and epigenetic modulation are optional."

"I don't want anything that can be controlled remotely," said Mother.

"Not even local control? You'd be the only one with access."

"Nope. Autonomous only."

"Sure, okay. What about for Tem?"

"Nothing, if that's an option."

"He'll need his vaccines."

"Sure, but no bloodstream drones."

Tem did not know what this meant, but was relieved that nothing was going into his blood. Mother was protecting him, as she always did. Still, he wanted to make his own decisions when possible.

"Do the drones make you stronger?" he asked Ingrid, pushing off one of the handholds and sailing through the air.

"Well…some types of nanodrones assist and encourage muscle repair – even growth – so I suppose they could."

"I want that kind."

"Those aren't for children," Mother said.

"I'm not a child," said Tem. "I'm almost ten."

"Here, you're a child." Mother's voice did not invite further argument.

Decon was a series of sponge baths, violet lights, more hair combing, several small cups of foul-smelling pellets which Tem was asked to swallow whole (he made the mistake of chewing the first batch), and more stinging devices pressed up again his arms and shoulders. Mother was by his side the entire time, assuring him he would only need to undergo this procedure once. Still, at the end of the ordeal he felt woozy and light-headed.

"I'm tired of being weightless," he said, trying to squirm into the gray pants and green shirt Ingrid had given him.

"It won't be much longer," said Ingrid. "We'll descend to the outer ring soon. You'll start to feel your own weight about halfway down the spoke."

"How did you learn Norse?" Tem asked, fumbling with his belt buckle. "You speak it well."

"I'm a student of ancient languages, specializing in modern hybrids. I've studied the Happdal dialect going back to Car-En's earliest feeds."

"Her whats?"

Ingrid looked at Mother hesitantly.

"I haven't really explained my prior role as a field anthropologist to Tem."

Ingrid nodded. "It might be a good time to bring him up to speed. You're famous here – he's going to get a lot of questions."

"Famous?"

"Penelope Townes will brief you. She's waiting on Slope-4, with your father and a few others. Svilsson is there too, with his daughter. She's about Tem's age."

"I'd like to see my father first. Alone. Just him and myself and Tem. Can you arrange that?"

"Sure. I'll do it now."

Oscar floated into the room, carrying Tem's longknife. "Here's this," he said, offering the sheathed blade to Mother, hilt first.

"That's Tem's knife," said Mother. Oscar looked confused, even when Tem held out his hand. Reluctantly he handed the blade to Tem, shaking his head. Tem took the longknife and tucked it into his belt, grinning.

Ingrid led them through another tube. Oscar stayed behind, saying he would analyze Tem's *results,* which he seemed eager to do, an attitude Mother either disapproved of or found repugnant, given the look on her face. In any case Tem was happy Ingrid was still with them. He drifted next to the orange-haired woman with Mother bringing up the rear. The tube opened into a tiny room with rows of cushioned seats. They strapped themselves in. Tem guessed that the direction his feet were facing would soon become *down.*

"Ready?" Ingrid asked.

"Let's go," said Mother.

Ingrid's eyes flicked back and forth, then she blinked rapidly. The tube port slid closed and the room began to move.

"Feel it yet?" Ingrid asked thirty seconds later. Tem shook his head, but then he *did* feel something. Weight. Once again his body knew which way was down. For a moment he felt extremely heavy. Ingrid unstrapped herself and stood. "We're here." Tem tried to move but his body refused.

"I'm stuck!" Tem cried out. Mother helped him up, and with some effort he found that he could stand. Still, his legs felt like jelly. "Am I... *heavier* than I was?"

Ingrid laughed. "No. You'll feel heavy for a few minutes, but you'll get your legs back."

The port slid open. They stepped into a room filled with sunlight and sprawling plants. Water trickled down a stone wall in irregular rivulets, weaving between ferns and mosses, feeding a shallow pond beneath the glass floor. A small, tanned man dressed in white stood to greet them. He stared at Mother, then at Tem, then back at Mother. Mother took a hesitant step forward. The man embraced her and held on tightly, eyes squeezed closed. He was crying.

It was his morfar. It had to be. Though the man looked younger than Arik and Jense.

"Shol," Mother said, "this is Tem. Your grandson."

Shol released his grip on Mother and stared at Tem.

"He looks like you," Shol said.

"I look like myself," said Tem. He rested his hand on the hilt of his blade and stood up straight.

Morfar Shol's eyes widened. "He *is* your son."

CHAPTER FIFTEEN

Lydia flew most of the way back, while Shane worked on his security report detailing the circumstances of Alexi Rosen's murder. After lunch they switched places and Lydia reviewed his work. The report did not *announce* Rosen's death, but merely referred to it, making the assumption that the reader had already been briefed, and proposed additional security measures. If they delivered the report directly to Adrian, he might bury it and invent a convenient story in regards to Rosen's disappearance. Rosen's friends and relatives would inquire – maybe Adrian had already concocted some tale involving accident or illness. It was dangerous to do an end-run, delivering the report directly to Penelope Townes. But Rosen's family deserved to know the truth.

"What do you think?" Shane asked. Ahead, the late afternoon light reflected off the distant Alps.

"It's perfect...for what it is. We're doing the right thing, right?"

Shane shrugged. "Adrian will consider us enemies as soon as Townes confronts him. Are you ready for that? He's dangerous when cornered."

"Should we talk to Xenus first? Give him a heads up? Adrian will assume he's in on it."

"That's a good idea. I won't send the report until we brief Xenus."

They landed the shuttle to rest and eat, and over a dinner of water cubes and g'nerf bars decided it would be safer to camp rather than pushing through to Vandercamp (Lydia had stopped arguing with Shane over the AFS-1 moniker – it was easier just to go with it). They were somewhere in what had once been eastern France, rolling green hills and open fields. The crumbling ruins of a church steeple crowned a nearby hill.

"These might have been grape fields once," Shane said, chewing ruefully on a g'nerf bar. "I wouldn't mind some real food right about now. And some wine."

"Vandercamp '33 isn't bad."

Shane winced. "Really? You drink that stuff?"

Lydia shook her head. "No, not really."

He leaned over and kissed her gently. His lips tasted like vanilla-cream.

"Oh!" she said. She had been expecting a question about her relationship status with Xenus, but apparently he wasn't concerned about that.

"Oh?"

She kissed him back.

They took a few minutes to make camp, which was easy. The hovershuttle-kit tent set itself up with a simple command. The heated tarp below the tent would keep them warm and dry. Shane told the drones to maintain a fifty-meter security perimeter.

For a moment they lay in the tent and watched the stars through the mosquito netting.

"Those Russian war dogs," she said, thinking back to the attack at the river. "I thought we were going to die."

"Car-En lost it," Shane said. "I thought she'd be cooler under pressure."

"I thought Tem was going to jump out and fight them!"

"He would have," said Shane, nestling closer. "That boy doesn't know fear. It worries me."

"Do you think he doesn't get scared, or just that he's courageous in the face of fear? He's different than our children. And by *our* I mean…."

Shane laughed. "I get what you mean. Vandercamp kids. You're right. He's nothing like them."

She kissed him. He kissed her back, not so gently this time. Soon they had slipped out of their bioskins. He was heavier and stronger than Xenus, bigger in every way. His weight and size electrified her, even though he moved gently and slowly.

"You can be rougher if you want."

It turned out that he did, and when she finally fell asleep it was in a hot haze of pleasure and pain.

PART TWO
THE ALGORITHM
CHAPTER SIXTEEN

Tem bounced lightly on the balls of his feet, waiting for his opponent to strike. In his right hand he held a saber, a thin sky-alloy blade. This one was flexible like steel, but lighter, though not as light as carbonlattice, nor as stiff. His left hand gripped a *main-gauche*: a short, dull composite blade with a rounded tip, used only for blocking. Tem's own longknife was far away, tucked in a drawer back at Morfar Shol's apartment.

His opponent was bigger and taller, a full-grown man, his face obscured by a fencing mask. The man didn't bounce and hop about like Tem, but moved deliberately, with heavy, plodding steps. Tem had at first been fooled into thinking his opponent was slow, and had paid the price. The man had quick reflexes and impeccable fighting form, honed by years of practice.

His opponent lunged. Tem held his ground, refusing to react. The lunge was a feint; his opponent was not yet close enough to reach him, even fully extended. The man recovered and took a step forward. Now he was close enough to strike. Tem readied himself.

The man took a heavy step forward and lunged low, committing fully. Tem parried in *septime*, his blade angled down but still pointed at his enemy. His opponent disengaged, whipping his blade around and coming in toward Tem's chest. Tem parried again in *quarte*, bringing his *main-gauche* forward to reinforce the block. His opponent's saber scraped against Tem's carbonlattice parrying dagger, less than a hand's width from his chest.

His opponent recoiled; Tem followed immediately with a quick low thrust (blocked), then another (also blocked, easily). He would have to do something clever to get through his enemy's defenses.

Tem rapidly shuffled back five paces, then charged, waving his saber wildly and yelling. At the last possible second he threw his *main-gauche* as hard as he could. The short blade bounced off his opponent's mask. Tem lunged low and deep, extending all the way, angling the tip of the saber upwards. The point made contact, right in the stomach. A green light flashed on Tem's side of the score board. One point.

Per Anders tore off his mask, indignant. "You can't do that! Yvette, did you see that?"

Some of the other fencers in the gymnasium paused to look at them. Yvette, their instructor, strode over. "What happened?"

"He threw his dagger!" Per Anders sputtered.

"*Main-gauche*," Yvette corrected. She was strict in regards to terminology. Tem didn't mind. English, French, Italian, Japanese…most of the words were new to him anyway. At first he had been astonished at the number of languages spoken on the *Stanford*, but now he just accepted it and tried to learn as quickly as possible. "Tem, did you throw your *main-gauche* at Per Anders?"

"Yes," Tem admitted. "You never said we couldn't."

"Well, you can't. That's not allowed. Please don't do it again. Point deducted."

Underneath his mask, Tem grinned. Of course he knew it wasn't allowed. But he had broken Per Anders's concentration; he would have an advantage for the remainder of the bout. And even though Per Anders was his best friend on the *Stanford*, Tem still liked to beat him.

"You little turd," said Per Anders in Norse.

"What was that?" Yvette asked.

"Nothing."

Per Anders won the bout, five to three. Still, Tem considered it a victory. Before today he had never scored more than a single point against Per Anders.

Tem showered and changed in a private room (he felt too self-conscious for the communal showers) and met Per Anders afterwards. They walked to a nearby outdoor café and ordered ice cream, just as they did on most Saturday afternoons. Per Anders was an old friend of Father and Farbror, and the first villager to live on the *Stanford*. Father, Mother, and Farbror Trond had found Per Anders wandering in the woods, sick and confused, a 'mushroom man.' *Stanford* Medical had cured him of the 'mycological brain parasite,' but some lingering effects remained.

"English or Norse?" Per Anders asked, digging into his mint chip.

"English," said Tem.

"English, always English. Fine."

"Ingrid will speak Norse with you. She always wants more practice."

"Ingrid is boring," Per Anders said. Tem knew he didn't mean it; Per Anders was quite fond of the orange-haired woman. He suspected that Per Anders might have had his romantic advances rebuffed.

"You gave me the choice, so I choose English." He took a bite of his chocolate ice cream. As Petra has promised, there was plenty of chocolate on the *Stanford*. As for the cream part, Tem wasn't so sure. He had yet to see a cow on the ringship, and he'd explored widely in the three months since he'd arrived. The *Stanford* had a huge open main level filled with parks, restaurants and cafés, apartment buildings, and the grand buildings of the Academy. The slope levels (Starside and Earthside) contained more of the same, with the fancier dwellings and establishments higher up. The lower 'Sub' levels of the ringship housed manufacturing facilities, fab labs, storage areas, sprawling farms (with no dirt, somehow the plants thrived on mist and purplish light), and thousands of machines that kept the whole place running. Both Morfar and Per Anders had shown him around, but on many days he just wandered off on his own. Mother didn't seem to worry. If you got lost (which he had, many times), all you had to do was find a tram on Sub-1 and take it back to Elon, the station nearest Morfar Shol's apartment.

Per Anders scowled but answered in English. "Very well. Tell me more about your plan."

So far Tem had only confided in Per Anders. Who else could understand? Per Anders had grown up in Happdal, but for the last ten years, more than Tem's entire life, he'd lived on the *Stanford*. No one else knew both worlds. Well, maybe Mother did, but her loyalties were divided.

"Well, first I need to get rid of my accent. People still look at me funny when I open my mouth."

"That's because you're funny looking," said Per Anders, grinning. Tem didn't mind. At times Per Anders acted like a child. The ringship doctors had done their best to cure him, but the mushroom spores had riddled his brain through and through. Ingrid said it was good for Per Anders to have a friend Tem's age; they were at 'similar developmental stages.' Tem didn't quite see it that way. Per Anders was the superior fencer, but Tem already had the mental edge.

"Your hair is funny looking," Tem said. He could have come up with something meaner, but he didn't want to hurt his friend's feelings. Besides, it was true: Per Anders wore his long gray hair and beard loose and unkempt. That, combined with his height and broad shoulders, caused most sky people to eye him suspiciously and grant him wide berth. Tem, on the other hand, rarely got a second look. The sky people came in all skin shades, and, like Tem, they were mostly of slight build. It was a relief to no longer be the only brown boy among a sea of pale faces. "Maybe you should cut it, and shave off that creature growing on your chin."

"And look like the child people? I think not."

"Fair enough," Tem said. He wondered when he would be able to grow his own beard.

"So, learn to speak like them. Then what?"

"Then I find the ringship's jarl."

Per Anders ate the last of his ice cream, shaking his head. "I told you, they don't have a jarl."

"Well, not a jarl *exactly*. I mean the person in charge."

"You don't understand," said Per Anders. "They don't have a chieftain. The have *councils* that decide how things will go on different parts of the ship."

"Well, there must be one council in charge then. A group of leaders."

"Not really. There's an Over Council, but they exist mostly to help the other councils talk to each other. Ingrid explained it to me. They're not really in charge."

"So who leads them?" Tem asked, putting the last of his ice cream aside. His tongue had accumulated an unpleasant coating.

"No one! Everyone! I don't know. But somehow the ringship stays in the sky."

"Who's in charge of what happens on Earth?"

"Ah, I have an answer for you there. Repop Council. Repop for *repopulation*."

"What's that?"

"Putting more people on Earth."

"Aha! So they plan to take over Earth. You see, my plan *is* important."

Per Anders looked hurt. "I never said it wasn't."

"So," Tem continued, "I will meet with *Repop*, and confirm the agreement I made with Javier. Make it official."

"You really think they'll grant you everything south of that river?"

"The Aller. Maybe they will. But the point is that they need to acknowledge our territory and respect our borders. No more spying."

Per Anders grunted. His friend agreed on the topic of the field researchers. It was wrong for the anthropology students to stay hidden, to trespass without permission. If they wanted to perform an exchange, as Skrova and Happdal sometimes did, Tem guessed that Jarl Arik would agree to it. Tem was visiting the *Stanford*; why not let a young person from the ringship try out life in Happdal for a while? But the sneaking about was wrong, and needed to stop.

In truth this wasn't the only reason to meet with the ringship leaders, but he wasn't yet ready to confide the whole of his plan to Per Anders. It might disturb his friend to hear the truth.

"You think they'll listen to you?" Per Anders asked, scratching his chin through his beard. "You're only a boy."

"A young wolf is still a wolf," said Tem. He would make them listen.

When Tem returned to Shol's apartment he smelled a familiar scent; his morfar was cooking ratatouille. "I'm home!" he yelled. "Is Mother here?"

There was no answer from the kitchen, which did not alarm Tem. Morfar ignored interruptions when he was concentrating. Tem plopped himself down in a puffy chair and turned on the screen. Mother didn't approve of screen watching, but Morfar Shol allowed it. It was good for Tem's English, after all.

Morfar emerged wearing a yellow apron and carrying two glasses of beer, the smaller of which he handed to Tem. This meant Mother was *definitely* not home. Ringship beer did not make you wobble the way Happdal mead did, but Mother still frowned on it.

"Put on the Hub channel," Morfar said. "The Reavers game starts in ten minutes." The Reavers were a lacrosse team; they played in one of several zero-gravity arenas in the central hub.

"Where's Mother? Will she be home for dinner?"

"She didn't say," said Morfar, avoiding eye contact. Mother was gone from the apartment more than not. While Tem and Morfar Shol had become good friends almost instantly, things had been tense between Mother and Morfar. At first they'd seemed happy to see each other, but lately Tem had heard heated conversations at night, when they thought he was sleeping. During the day they spoke only tersely.

"Well, she hates lacrosse," Tem said. Mother would be sorry to miss the ratatouille though – she loved Shol's cooking. He would make sure there was some left for her.

They watched the game and ate dinner. While Morfar Shol cleaned up, Tem practiced writing his letters (with pen and paper) and reading (on his tablet). It felt as if he had only just gotten started when Morfar came into his bedroom and told him it was time to sleep.

"But I'm not sleepy."

"You'll get sleepy when the lights are off."

"Will you sit and talk with me for a while?"

"Of course."

His bedroom was much smaller than the loft, but the bed was comfortable. After he'd changed into his pajamas he called for his morfar.

"How's school going?" Morfar asked, sitting on the edge of the bed. "Are the other students treating you well?"

"I haven't had to fight any of them. They're much friendlier than I thought they'd be."

"Good, you shouldn't have to do any fighting. Are your teachers keeping you busy?"

"Mr. Kan is my favorite. He teaches math. And Yvette is strict but I like her."

"Fencing, right? Did you beat Per Anders today?"

"Almost."

His grandfather dimmed the lights; the spectrum shifted to a warm reddish tone.

"Morfar?"

"Yes?"

"How would I go about meeting with the Repop Council?"

"What? Why would you want to do that?"

"Can anyone just go?"

"Anyone can observe a council meeting. Not in person, but you can watch the feeds. The Repop meetings are public. Most of them are, anyway."

"I want to meet with Repop. On behalf of Happdal."

His grandfather frowned, but Tem could tell he was considering the request seriously.

"The meetings are just for the council members, unless they're meeting with academic experts or advisors, or emissaries from other ringstations."

"What's an emissary?"

"A representative. Like…a messenger."

"I'm a messenger from Happdal. I have something important to tell them."

"And what's that?"

"Can you help me meet with them?"

Morfar pulled Tem's covers up to his chin. "Just focus on your studies for now. Don't worry about Happdal. From what Car-En says, your father and other grandfather are wise men. I'm sure they're taking care of everyone."

"Will you help me meet with the council?"

Morfar sighed. "I'm not sure if I can do anything. But I'll look into it."

"Thank you, Morfar Shol."

*　　*　　*

The next day at school, during first break, Tem's class split into two teams for a soccer match. Tem had been surprised to discover that among the many unfamiliar ways of ringship life, the game of *fótrknöttur* was essentially unchanged. The ringship children had a different name for it − soccer − and the ball was harder and rounder than the pig bladder ball Tem was used to, but the rules were the same. It was a relief. Even fencing was only vaguely similar to fighting with wooden swords. Soccer was the only activity in which Tem did not lag behind his classmates.

Tem's class consisted of about twenty children between the ages of nine and eleven, both boys and girls and a couple whose gender he could not determine. Tem was among the youngest, but the ringship children were smaller than village children. Nobody towered over him as many of the village children had.

Some of the older children ran off to continue a long-running fantasy game that included wands, capes, and funny hats. A few others stubbornly continued working on their projects inside. That left eight who were interested in soccer, a decent four to a side. Five or six per side would be better, but four-on-four worked nearly as well if they played with the tiny one-meter goals and no goalkeepers.

The field was artificial grass, and very flat. The ball traveled much faster and straighter compared to Happdal's lumpy dirt *fótrknöttur* field, which doubled as the festival grounds and was well trampled. Tem had adjusted quickly, discovering he could make longer, more accurate passes on the level turf. Most of the time he passed to Marcus, who was nearly as fast as Tem. The pair had developed a reputation as effective forwards.

Marcus and Zinthia were the two captains today. Zinthia picked Bruno, a ball-hog who always shot on goal regardless of distance or the position of the defenders. Predictably, Marcus picked Tem. They alternated picks until Marcus was left with Falder, who had only just turned nine, rarely got a foot on the ball, and was pleased to be included at all.

Marcus pulled them into a huddle for a quick strategy session. "Falder, you play defense. Just stand in front of the goal and kick the ball away if it comes close. Tirian, you play center. Stay close to Zinthia. I'll play right wing. Tem, you play left."

"Why don't I ever get to play forward?" Tirian whined.

"You do a good job in midfield. Just hassle Zinthia."

"She'll shove me if I get too close."

"Then call foul. Don't let her push you around. Okay?"

Tirian nodded. Marcus was good at getting people to do what he wanted. He did this mostly by encouraging them, focusing on their strengths. The truth was that Tirian was too slow to play forward effectively, but Marcus hadn't pointed that out.

Zinthia tossed a gold coin into the air for the toss, and won it. Right away Zinthia passed to Haley, who immediately shot the ball forward to Tengza. Tengza dribbled up the field and shot the ball into the goal while hapless Falder stood by.

"Gooooaaaaaal!" yelled Tengza. Marcus grimaced.

Tem started with the ball at the midline. Passing back and forth with Marcus, they advanced up the field, until Zinthia intercepted a pass. She kicked the ball upfield to Bruno, who blasted it past Falder, scoring again.

Back in the huddle, Marcus did not scold them. "They're overpowering us. Let's change things up. Tirian, fall back to defense and help Falder. I'll play midfield. Tem, you play forward. When I pass to you, get past Bruno and score."

Tem nodded. Marcus was not one to stick with a failing strategy.

Again, Tem started at midline, this time alone with the ball, facing Zinthia. Her light blond hair and pale skin reminded him of the village children. She frowned at him briefly, then looked past him. She'd noticed their changed field positions. Giving her time to think was a bad idea.

Instead of passing back to Marcus, Tem charged forward with the ball. Zinthia moved to block him. At the last possible instant Tem flicked the ball back to Marcus, then sprinted upfield and left. Marcus chipped the ball over Zinthia's head to Tem – a perfect pass. All Tem had to do now was dribble by Bruno, who stood resolutely between him and the goal. Tem dribbled forward, feinted to the left, and tried to run the ball past Bruno on the right. Bruno jogged backward, not committing, staying well positioned in front of the tiny goal. Tem didn't have a clear shot. Once again he moved forward and feinted, trying to get Bruno to charge him.

Like a marten, Haley snuck up behind him and stole the ball. He lunged to get it back, but she had already kicked the ball upfield to Tengza. "Too slow!" Haley taunted, running up the field.

Tem was many things, but slow was not one of them. He sprinted back toward his own goal, knocking Haley aside. She yelled in protest but Tem kept running. Tengza and Zinthia were passing back and forth, moving closer to the goal. Marcus tried to intercept while Tirian and Falder fell back to defend. Tem imagined he was a young wolf, sprinting through the winter woods in pursuit of a white hare. Zinthia, with her white-blond locks, was the rabbit. He charged her, knocking her down and taking the ball.

"Foul!" Zinthia yelled from the ground.

"Take it easy, Tem," said Marcus.

Tem blushed. "Sorry."

Zinthia was already up. She had grabbed the ball and strode toward the goal. "Penalty kick. It was in the zone."

Tem looked to Marcus for help, but his friend just shrugged. "She's right."

For the penalty, they swapped out the minigoal for the standard-size net. Six meters across with a sturdy-looking carbonlattice frame, the goal was light enough for the children to move.

"I'll be keeper," said Tem, as Tengza and Haley positioned the full-sized goal.

Zinthia placed the ball carefully on the ten-meter mark. Tem checked that he was centered between the goal posts, then took a couple steps forward, remembering Mr. Kan's lesson on angles and arcs.

"That's not allowed," Zinthia protested. "You have to stand between the posts."

Tem looked to Marcus, who nodded. In truth soccer had a few more rules than *fótrknöttur*; the village children did not concern themselves with fouls and penalties (if someone played too rough, they were simply kicked out of the game). Reluctantly Tem stepped back to the line. At least this way he would have a little more time to judge the path of the ball.

Zinthia backed up. Tem tried to stare her down, but Zinthia did not make eye contact. She ran to the ball and matter-of-factly kicked it into the left corner. Tem lunged but came nowhere near the ball.

"Three-zero," Zinthia said. She jogged back down the field, leaving Tem and his teammates to swap out the standard goal for the minigoal.

"You made her mad," Marcus said, grinning. "Maybe we can score now."

Marcus was wrong; Zinthia's tactics and execution were only enhanced by her anger. After the penalty kick her team switched to an offensive style. Zinthia, Haley, and Tengza passed flawlessly on offense, while Bruno hung back, defending their goal like an angry bear. By the end of break the score was six to one.

"At least we scored," said Marcus cheerfully, patting Tem on the back. Marcus had scored their only goal on a pass from Tirian.

"Sorry I didn't play well today," Tem said.

"Zinthia got under your skin. She's clever that way. Don't let her get to you."

★   ★   ★

Several days later they were assigned to new project teams. Tem and Zinthia were on the same team, along with Bruno, Shelley, and Abelton. Their task was to build an arbalest, an oversized crossbow used in ancient Builder wars. Instead of wood (which was rarely used as a building material on the ringship – there were trees but no forests), they used a semi-flexible material called woodish, almost as strong as carbonlattice but heavier and less hard. For instructions they were given only a reproduction of an ancient blueprint. The document consisted of beautiful but inscrutable handwritten notes, diagrams, and illustrations. They had one week to complete their siege weapon, after which point there would be a contest for distance, accuracy, and shots fired per minute.

"Who speaks French?" Zinthia asked. She had naturally taken charge; no one had challenged her. Tem decided he would be better off observing. He could probably learn more that way, and he guessed that in time, if he was smart about it, Zinthia might become an ally. Underneath her brusqueness he sensed she was curious about his life on Earth, though so far she had feigned disinterest, while the other children had questioned him voraciously.

"I speak a little," Shelley said. "My grandmother speaks it fluently and she taught me a few words."

"What does *fer* mean?" asked Zinthia, squinting at the blueprint. Shelley shrugged.

"It must mean iron," Abelton said. Like Tem, Abelton had light brown skin. Both boys were nine and were about the same size. "Ferrous means iron, right?"

"What's iron?" Bruno asked. After a moment Tem realized the question was not as stupid as it sounded. Metal was simply not used as a building material on the ringship.

"There's iron in your red blood cells," Zinthia said. "You'd be dead without it."

Tem sat next to Zinthia and examined the blueprint. The handle of the ancient weapon had been constructed from wood, but the actual bow part – the limbs – were made from iron. *An iron bow.* Why had he never thought of such a thing? Who would be strong enough to wield it? Nobody, apparently. That's why the hand crank was needed to pull back the string. The whole apparatus made Tem's mind race with possibilities.

Tem looked up. They were all staring at him. "Did they have crossbows in your village?" Zinthia asked. "Did you ever make one?"

"No. My father makes bows – wooden ones. And I've worked with iron, but only to make knives and swords." The last part was an exaggeration – he had yet to make his first sword. "I've never made an iron bow."

They were silent, waiting for him to say more.

He looked down. "But we don't have any iron, so it doesn't really matter." Thinking of Father and Farbror Trond and Farfar Jense gave him a lump in his throat.

"I wonder if we could get some," said Abelton.

"If we could, could you fashion the metal into the right shape?" Zinthia was staring at him intently.

"I would need a furnace, and an anvil, and hammer and tongs. A smithy."

"What's an anvil?" Bruno asked.

"I'll bet we could set something up in one of the fab labs," Zinthia said. "I'll ask my dad about it. You can come over after school if you want – we'll ask him together."

*   *   *

Zinthia and her father, Svilsson, had been among the first to greet them the day they'd arrived on the mule, along with an older woman named Penelope, who had quietly spoken with Mother. Zinthia had seemed standoffish and suspicious even then, so much so that her father had admonished her. Svilsson himself was an odd man, tall and pale, quiet, his face locked in a serious, slightly menacing expression. After introducing his daughter he had said little during their small welcoming party. Several times Tem had glanced at him, accidentally making eye contact. Each time Svilsson had nodded gravely, as if they shared a secret.

Zinthia lived with Svilsson and Genta in a palatial apartment on Starside Slope-2. From their balcony you could look down on the entirety of the visible arc of Main: parks and creeks, sculpture gardens, shops and outdoor cafés, the handsome white Academy buildings, even the colorful apartment building where Morfar Shol lived.

Genta, a slim black-skinned woman, emerged from the living room, carrying two tall glasses filled with a bright green beverage. The colorful drinks complemented her yellow dress.

"Zin? Limeade for you and your friend? What's your name, dear?"

"My name is Tem."

"Oh! The Earthling. Welcome, and pleased to make your acquaintance. Limeade?"

"Thank you."

Genta was gone just as quickly, a blur of yellow.

"She's pretty," Tem said.

"And she knows it," Zinthia snorted.

"You don't like her?"

"She's all right. I just wish my mother and father were still together."

"Where's your mother?"

"Over there," Zinthia said, pointing to a green and aquamarine apartment building not far from Morfar Shol's. "I stay with her on weekends, but there's more room here."

"Why don't they live together anymore?"

"My mother said my father didn't talk enough. But Genta doesn't seem to mind. She can talk enough for two people."

Zinthia showed him her room, filled with bins of carefully organized toys and many shelves of books. She had more possessions than all of the village children put together.

"What do you do with all this stuff?" he asked.

"Honestly a lot of it just sits on the shelf. If you see something you want you can probably have it. I go through phases...right now I'm drawing and painting"

She showed him her paintings, which were mostly of animals. "Do you have bears on the ringship?" he asked. "We have bears in the forest near our village. Sometimes Father hunts them with his bow."

"He kills them?" Zinthia look horrified. "Why?"

"To eat. Why else? Bear meat makes you strong."

Svilsson came home soon after. He kissed Zinthia on the top of her head, saying nothing, and nodded at Tem as if he had expected to see him.

"How was the council meeting?" Zinthia asked.

Svilsson grunted, glancing at Tem. "Is there more of that limeade?"

"Ask Genta, she made it for us. Dad, we have a question for you. At school we're making an arbalest, and we need to make metal limbs. Can we—"

"Hold that thought," Svilsson said. "I'll be back."

Zinthia scowled as her father left the room. "He'll forget. Let's follow him."

"What council is your father on?"

"Repop," Zinthia said. "He's an anthropologist." From the kitchen they heard Genta's cheerful voice. "Darn it, now she'll be telling him about her day for the next hour. We need a distraction."

"We could build a fire," Tem suggested, regretting it immediately. His mind was racing from the fact that Zinthia's father *was on the Repop Council*. He wasn't thinking clearly.

Zinthia frowned. "That's a little extreme."

"Does Genta follow sports? Maybe there's something on the screen she'll want to see."

"No. Sometimes she watches fashion programs, but she can watch those anytime."

"What if we change the subject?"

"What do you mean?"

"Can we get your father talking about something that bores her?"

Zinthia scratched her head. "That's a good idea, actually."

Tem strode into the kitchen. He stood next to Svilsson and Genta, looking up expectantly. Genta paused mid-sentence. "Yes? Do you want some more limeade, dear?"

"What did you discuss at the council meeting today?" Tem asked Svilsson.

Svilsson glanced quickly at Genta before answering. "I don't think you'd be interested."

"Of course I'm interested. I'm from Earth. The point of Repop is to discuss putting more people on Earth, right?"

"Well…yes. In the long term, anyway."

"But there's already a ringship settlement. I mean a *ringstation* settlement. I met two people who live there – Lydia and Shane."

Svilsson looked uncomfortable. "That's not a settlement exactly. It's a field station for research."

"For researching my village, right?"

Svilsson cleared his throat. "Among other things."

"So, you see, I am interested. What did you discuss today?"

Genta smiled and placed her half-full limeade glass on the counter. "I'll leave you two to it." As Genta left, Zinthia squeezed in the doorway past her.

Svilsson sat on a tall stool and looked at Tem steadily. "In fact, we discussed the research station. It's called AFS-1, and it's where your friends are from."

"Are they okay?"

"Mostly, they're fine."

"Did you talk about the spiders?"

Svilsson sighed.

"What spiders?" Zinthia asked.

"I'm not allowed to discuss it," Svilsson said.

"I was *there*," Tem said. "I was the one who caught it!"

Svilsson nodded. "I know."

"So? Don't I get to know what they are? The bald man – Shane – he thought they were a kind of machine."

"*What* spiders are you talking about?" Zinthia asked, clenching her fists.

Svilsson looked at each of them in turn.

"Near our village," said Tem, "there's a tree – or something like a tree – that's covered in spiders as big as my hand. Bigger! I captured one, and Lydia – the ringship woman who lives at the research station – said she would study it and tell me what she found out. I think your father already knows." It wasn't quite true – he had only spoken to Shane about the spider – but he did suspect Svilsson knew something.

Zinthia turned to Svilsson. "Well, do you? You have to tell us! You heard him, she promised Tem she would tell him. So if you know something you have to tell us."

"And I want to meet with Repop," Tem said. "I have a message." Svilsson raised an eyebrow. "An important message," Tem continued. "Life-or-death important."

Tem and Zinthia glared at Svilsson, who pursed his lips and furrowed his brow. "I'll submit your petition to the council," he said to Tem.

"What about the spiders?" Zinthia asked.

"If you're granted an audience, you can submit your questions to Repop." Svilsson picked up Genta's limeade from the counter and took a sip. "Now what's this about an arbalest?"

*   *   *

Svilsson recommended they go to the Hair Lab and commission a project. According to Zinthia, the Hair Lab was the most eccentric of the fab labs, and in a way the most prestigious. Engineers were always on the lookout for projects that could net them acclaim or notoriety, and Svilsson thought there might be a few historical construction enthusiasts who would be interested in metalworking. Tem explained that all he needed was a furnace and the tools; he could do the work himself. Svilsson shrugged and repeated the advice. The Hair Lab was their best bet.

"Why is your father so secretive?" Tem asked. They were on the Sub-1 tram. Tem had called Morfar from Zinthia's apartment and gotten permission to stay out longer. Mother was out again and would not be home until late.

"I got the sense he wanted to tell you," said Zinthia, "but he takes rules very seriously. If he was sworn to secrecy then we're not going to get it out of him. Can you call this Lydia woman?"

"I wouldn't know how."

"I'll see if I can find out. There's only one research station on Earth as far as I know. Maybe we can get ahold of her and ask her about the spider-thing."

They sat in silence as the tram sped toward their destination. Tem was surprised at how normal it all seemed. Two months ago he had known only his small village, the mountains, and the forest. Now here he was, living on a giant spinning ringship in space, among *thousands* of people, surrounded by Builder miracles. He didn't call them Builders out loud, but that's how he thought of the ringship people. They were the descendants of those who had built the ancient ruins. It wasn't fair to group everyone together, he supposed. From what he could tell, the ringship dwellers saw the Builders the same way he saw the Vikings: distantly related but quite different.

They got off the tram at Colosseum. Tem followed close behind Zinthia, his face less than a pace from her white-blond hair. Zinthia, occasionally consulting a map on her tablet, led them through wide passages past sprawling markets and shops. The ceilings of Sub-1 were immensely high; it felt as though they were outside. This effect was enhanced by the elaborate landscaping connecting and sometimes covering the buildings: ferns, flowers, shrubs, palm fronds, high grasses, creeks, pools, fountains, waterfalls, trails, hidden benches, and bamboo huts.

"What are those little houses for?" Tem asked.

"Public use. You could spend the day working in one if you wanted, or even sleep there."

For a long time they wandered, Zinthia consulting the map and Tem asking questions, until they reached the Fabrication District. They found themselves in a busy alley lined with galleries and showrooms. Peering through windows, Tem saw blueprints projected on walls, miniature models of machines and ships, and a fantastic array of machines whose purpose he could not guess.

"Prototypes," Zinthia said. "Sub-1 just has the display galleries. The actual fab labs are on Sub-2. We need to find a way down."

With the help of Zinthia's tablet they found a sloping walkway. Passing through two sets of sliding doors, the air became hot and thick. A colossal blue butterfly briefly landed on Tem's shoulder before fluttering off. On all sides they were surrounded by flowering vines, thick fronds, and twisting trees. Here and there Tem could see through the dense weave of plants to the curving surface of the tube itself, which glowed with a warm violet light.

"What kind of forest is this? I've never seen any of these plants before. And why is the air so thick? It's hard to breathe!"

"It's a jungle tube," Zinthia said. "A micropark. C'mon, let's hurry."

Descending through the dim, warm passage toward Sub-2, Tem found his adventurous spirit slipping. He wished he was back home having dinner with Morfar and Mother. He missed Mother. What was she so busy with? She'd said only that she was 'getting organized' and 'catching up with old friends.' If Mother had old friends, why couldn't

Tem meet them? He'd briefly wondered if she had a lover, but that didn't make sense. Mother loved Father, and had never shown the slightest interest in any of the other village men. Could she have met someone else? It made no sense.

Something scurried across their path. "What was that?" Tem asked.

"A squirrel maybe? Or a rat?"

"There are rats on the *Stanford*?"

"Sure, there are all kinds of wild animals. Mostly small ones. Rats, mice, birds, snakes, lizards, frogs, voles, weasels…small animals. No bears or tigers or cows or horses. Don't worry, they're all chipped and vaccinated. The microdrones take care of that."

"Poisonous snakes?"

"Quit worrying, the planners wouldn't put poisonous snakes in a park."

They emerged into Sub-2. The yellowish-white glowing ceilings were still fairly high, but unlike Sub-1 this level felt *inside*.

"Which way?"

"Hair Lab – this way. We're close. Sixty meters star, then turn right and another two hundred meters spin."

Directions on the *Stanford* had taken some getting used to. Instead of north, south, east, and west, the ringship dwellers used star, Earth, spin, and counterspin.

No one paid them any mind as they entered the cavernous building. Dozens of partitioned bays gave the open space a loose, maze-like structure. Young men and women rushed past them, intent and purposeful.

"Where do we start?" Zinthia asked. She looked overwhelmed.

Tem grabbed a young man by his sleeve. Irritated, the man pulled his arm away.

"What do you want? Are you lost? Go to one of the yellow kiosks. You can look at a map."

"I want to commission a project. It's for my school."

The young man's face softened. "Sure. The yellow kiosk is still the best place to start. Just tell it what you want and it'll talk you through the submission process."

"Thank you. I owe you. My name is Tem Espersson."

The young man nodded and resumed his errand, but looked back over his shoulder at Tem.

"Why did you tell him your name?"

"So he'll remember me."

As promised, the yellow kiosk answered Zinthia's questions in an odd, polite voice that sounded neither male nor female.

"What is the nature of the project?" it asked.

"You better tell it," Zinthia whispered. "You're the ironworker."

"We need to build flexible iron limbs, each approximately half a meter in length," said Tem, speaking more loudly than he meant to.

"Iron is not a recommended building material," the kiosk replied.

"It has to be iron or steel," Tem insisted. "And we'll need a furnace – very hot. And an iron anvil, and iron tongs and hammer."

The kiosk paused a moment before answering. "I will refer you to a specialist," it finally said. "Please provide your contact information."

"Tem?" Zinthia said.

"What's our contact information?"

"Tem, look." She was pointing at a small group of devs in an open bay thirty meters away. A short, brown-skinned woman was listening intently to a tall, much younger woman; the latter was gesticulating wildly and looked excited.

"Isn't that your mom?"

Tem blinked. Zinthia was right. The shorter brown-skinned woman was undoubtedly Car-En Ganzorig, his mother.

CHAPTER SEVENTEEN

22.11.02737, Advance Field Station One, Earth

Lydia and Xenus, on their evening walk, passed by the new, huge landing pad. "Why did they make it so big?" Xenus asked. The grading alone had taken three weeks. Now the giant concrete slab, over one hundred meters square, was complete except for cosmetic work around the edges. Even in the soft moonlight the structure was brutish and ugly. "The OETS platform isn't even a third that size."

"Maybe it's for a bigger mule," Lydia said.

Xenus squinted at the platform suspiciously. He'd been stonewalled by Adrian when he'd requested detailed specifications on the project. Despite the ongoing investigation into the Rosen cover-up, Adrian Vanderplotz was still Station Director.

"At least we won't have to make those long supply runs anymore."

"Of course we will," Xenus retorted. "We don't have refueling facilities. They can't land a mule here. Besides, I like our supply runs."

Lydia smiled tightly. "Me too." She hadn't told him about Shane. She'd meant to. She *planned* to, if he asked. But with each passing week she felt guiltier. Perhaps if she'd brought up her tryst with Shane right away, it wouldn't have been a big deal. But three months later, bringing it up would seem like a confession. Xenus would be hurt and distracted, and he didn't need that. Maybe it would be worth the discomfort and hurt feelings if she were still seeing Shane, but she'd barely spoken to the Security Director since that night.

Interim Security Director. Shane had been demoted, thanks to Adrian's preemptive letter of resignation on Shane's behalf. Instead of shouldering his share of the responsibility for Alexi Rosen's death, Adrian had pointed the finger at Shane and tried to wash his hands of the matter. That hadn't worked; Penelope Townes had opened an investigation into why Adrian had delayed notifying Alexi Rosen's family. But this hadn't saved Shane; the department, advised by Repop, had already begun their search for a new AFS-1 Security Director. Shane had not protested, and was stoically performing his interim duties without complaint.

"What's this meeting about?" Lydia asked. Streams of people were converging, all heading toward the Shell. "We haven't had a station-wide meeting since...I can't even remember."

"Since Rosen's funeral."

Of course. Only three months ago, but some part of her mind had suppressed the memory.

"I have a bad feeling about this," said Xenus.

Xenus was alone in his feelings of foreboding; all in all the Vandercamp mood was festive. Many of the domes and nearby trees were already decorated with colorful winter lights. Children noisily burned off their after-dinner energy in games of tag. Overall there was a sense of anticipation. The Station Director had an important announcement 'that would affect all of them.' Most had chosen to interpret that promise optimistically.

At night the Shell was lit by long ropes of glowing cables snaking along the spirals. The dim orange light was flattering; Xenus looked almost boyish, his fatigue and tension temporarily erased. The uncertainty around Adrian's investigation was getting to him. If Adrian were forced to step down, Xenus might be nominated for Station Director. They had discussed it; Xenus wanted the position. But for the moment, Xenus reported to Adrian, and they both reported to Penelope Townes. Lydia wondered what was keeping the investigation in limbo. Was Repop still collecting information, or did Adrian have dirt on Townes that he was leveraging to delay the process?

They sat toward the front, in curved wooden pews. Adrian was nowhere to be seen. So...a dramatic entrance. What in the *hell* did he have to announce? The safe bet was that it had something to do with the landing pad. Direct, more frequent deliveries and transport to and from the *Stanford* would be a life changer. But Xenus was right; a slab of concrete did not make a mule station. The rockets ran on hydrogen slush, and Vandercamp could produce no more than minute amounts of the stuff with their current facilities. Definitely not enough for liftoff. The single-stage-to-orbit vehicles represented a brilliant feat of engineering, but they were a first-generation technology. The mules needed refueling on *both* sides of the trip.

The lights pulsed, and quite suddenly Adrian was standing behind the podium.

"Welcome!"

His voice was amplified, booming and loud. Xenus leaned over and whispered, "Is his voice usually that deep?"

"Welcome, citizens of Vandercamp!"

Xenus was right – this close she could hear Adrian's natural voice beneath the amplified version. The latter was definitely lower, and had a *vast* sound to it, beyond the Shell's natural reverberation. She glanced at Xenus. His mouth was hanging open. It took her a minute to understand why, but when she did her own jaw dropped. Adrian had just said *Vandercamp* instead of AFS-1.

Adrian was grinning widely. "I know, I know! I've been trying to get rid of that nickname. But if you can't beat 'em...."

Lydia heard herself make a sound that resembled a growl.

"Friends, tonight is an important night. November twenty-second, 2737, will be remembered by historians. Tonight is the night when our research station becomes something more. Unofficially, the transformation has already occurred. Let me ask each of you a question."

Lydia glanced at Xenus. His mouth was no longer hanging open; now he was scowling suspiciously.

"Who here," continued Adrian, "thinks of Vandercamp as only a research station? Is this a temporary place to work, then return home somewhere else? Or is this place...." Adrian paused. He brushed the side of one eye.

"Is he...is he *fake crying*?" Lydia whispered. A woman to her right shushed her. She glanced around, and saw serious, earnest faces. They were buying it.

"Or is *this* place your home? Some of you brought your children here. Children have been *born* here, dozens of them. Is Vandercamp just a *research station* to them?"

She twisted around so much that her neck hurt. People were nodding. Others were tearing up. Somehow, Adrian had managed to strike an emotional chord. She had vastly underestimated him. Xenus was shaking his head. "Is he going to...."

"Friends, tonight is the night we come into ourselves. When we admit what we are to the rest of the world. We are not a *satellite*. We are not a *research station* – at least not only that. We are our own place. We are a *community*.

"Tonight I have given official notice to the authorities on the *Stanford*, to the Repopulation Council and to the Over Council, that we, citizens of Vandercamp, are an *independent* community."

In the silence that followed, Adrian slowly lifted his arms, as if embracing the entire hall.

"Friends, we are our own place now. To make it official, we'll hold a general referendum. Then…we'll have our work cut out for us. We'll need a new constitution. I've drafted one but it will need your approval. We'll need a new organizational structure. I'm stepping down as Station Director – we're no longer a station! We'll have a general election as soon as we can reach consensus on what the new leadership looks like.

"It may seem rash of me to have started this process unilaterally, but I promise you this is the only way it could have been started…."

From outside a faint roar was getting louder.

"What's that?" Lydia stood and looked back toward the entrance. People nearby looked up at her, a few looked back in the direction of the noise, but most still had their eyes on Adrian. She saw a mixture of reactions, but nothing resembling outrage. Some were nodding. Somehow this preposterous idea was being communicated as *reasonable*. She sat back down and leaned in close to Xenus, whispering, "Why is everyone just accepting this?"

"It's a seductive idea. And they don't know about what he did to Car-En – they trust Adrian. A few months ago *we* trusted him." She thought back, tried to remember how she had felt toward Adrian months ago. No, she had never fully trusted him.

Adrian droned on for minutes; she couldn't focus, couldn't make meaning from the sound of his words. The roaring had stopped. Her stomach tightened into a dense pit. The stench of fuel exhaust filled the Shell.

"Someone's coming," said the woman who had shushed her earlier. Adrian was looking toward the entrance, smiling, making a beckoning motion with his hands.

"Friends," his voice boomed. "Allow me to introduce the newest members of our community – the *Liu Hui* contingent."

Lydia gasped. Two columns of men and women were marching down the aisle. They were tall – over two meters on average – and clad in black matte uniforms. Each was equipped with a utility belt: disruptor pistols, compact sabers, luminators, and devices she didn't recognize. Their faces were hard, unsmiling. This was a military force. As the soldiers progressed up the aisle, a ripple of uneasy vocalizations followed. But no shouts, no screams. Lydia herself wanted to cry out, but couldn't. Her throat was thick, her jaw clenched shut. She grabbed Xenus's hand and squeezed.

"Please don't be alarmed. These people are our friends. You'll know them all by name soon enough. You'll break bread and drink wine with them. You'll introduce them to your children. For now, we need new friends. We need to make it clear to all the ringstations that we are serious about our declaration. We are no longer under the control and supervision of the *Stanford*. Our friends from the *Liu Hui* will make sure that's understood."

The black-clad soldiers gathered in formation on either side of the podium. Superficially they were a mix of ethnicities, predominantly Asian but also European and African. Differences in skin color and facial features where overwhelmed by similarities in size and build. "I knew they were bigger, but..." said Xenus.

"They're terrifying," Lydia said. Each ringstation had a slightly different version of the Standard Edits; the *Liu Hui* version emphasized height and strength. This was in direct contrast to the smaller, lighter phenotype preferred by denizens of the *Stanford* a smaller habitat with fewer resources.

Two of the soldiers were opening a large crate; she hadn't noticed them carry it in. Oddly, it was a non-standard size. She was familiar with the mule crates and this wasn't one of them. One of the soldiers, a blond, blue-eyed giant with craggy features and a full beard, joined Adrian at the podium.

"Friends, let me introduce our newest ally, Regis Foster." Adrian stepped off into the shadows. Foster nodded and pushed the microphone aside.

"I realize this is all happening very fast. I appreciate you welcoming

us into your community." His voice was clear and sonorous. "We've
brought a small gift, something to share from the *Liu Hui*. We hope you
like it."

The soldiers were now moving up and down the aisle, smiling,
handing out *bottles*. Lydia, close to the aisle, could see a label with Japanese
characters. Each bottle was filled with a clear golden-brown liquid.

"Please, open and drink, there's plenty to go around. Have some and
pass it along."

Without even questioning, some were opening the bottles and
drinking the contents. Some squinted or puckered their lips after
swallowing. A smoky, brackish smell permeated the Shell.

"Our finest whiskey, aged in authentic salvaged wooden barrels.
Rare and expensive."

A bottle came to Xenus. He sniffed it, raised his eyebrows, then took
a swallow. "Mmm...ooo...wow."

"I can't believe you just...."

"What? They're not going to poison us." He handed the bottle to
Lydia. It was real glass. The container – how much had it weighed in
full? Way above the maximum allowed for a mule crate. She passed
the bottle to the woman next to her. The woman, who she knew only
vaguely, avoided eye contact but took the bottle and drank from it.
Her eyes had a faraway look, disassociated. Everyone was in shock.
Lydia stood.

"I'm getting out of here. Are you coming?"

Xenus shook his head. "I'll see you back at the dome. I'm gonna see
how this unfolds."

Lydia half expected one of the black-uniformed soldiers to grab her
on the way out, but no one stopped her. Were people looking at her,
judging her? She kept her eyes down until she was outside, well away
from the Shell. For a second, breathing the cool night air, surrounded
by colorful winter lights, she felt normal.

The grounds were quiet; the children had gone to bed. Lydia
wondered idly how the news would be broken to the adults who had
stayed at home to care for the children. *Oh, by the way, at the general
meeting...there was a military coup.* She grinned at the absurdity of the
situation, but at the same time she had a pit in her stomach. They were
in deep trouble. Did Adrian really think he could get away with this?

How would the *Stanford* react? And what *could* they do? There had never been anything resembling a military conflict between the ringstations. Diplomatic dust-ups, yes, over asteroid mining rights and orbital positions and the like, but never even the threat of violence. The *Stanford* didn't even maintain a standing military force. This was more than a coup; it was a historic shift in ringstation politics. For centuries there had been absolute solidarity among the spinning worlds. As humanity on Earth had gradually wound down (due to generations of reduced fertility, centuries of economic recession, and finally the supervolcano and resulting famines that had pushed humanity into Survivalism), the ringstations and other spinships had formed a loosely unified exo-community, each with sovereignty but having more in common with each other than with the Earth-dwellers. Now there was no *other* on Earth. The empty, ecologically rejuvenated planet was a shining jewel waiting to be taken. The ringstation Repop Councils, slow-moving and cautious, were supposed to have prevented disputes among the orbiting worlds. Earth settlements would be carefully planned, ecologically sustainable, seeded from multiple ringstations and accountable to them all. Some had perceived AFS-1 as a violation of Repop principles; it was a settlement in all but name. Of course the *Liu Hui* would react.

But why *here*? Why hadn't the *Liu Hui* started their own research station, somewhere else? Earth was vast and unpopulated; there was nothing but room.

She passed the last of the domes and gardens. On the platform ahead, silhouetted in the moonlight, tall figures moved below a long grounded ship. The *Liu Hui* transport looked nothing like the squat upright SSTO mules. It had a sleek horizontal body, like a thin beetle. Three thick cylindrical rings surrounded the body; a dozen telescoping lander legs kept it off the ground.

As she neared the platform she heard voices speaking in Mandarin. Had they seen her? She veered so that her approach was concealed by a sprawling old olive tree. With a m'eye command she engaged her translator.

A man with a deep voice barked out a question. Her m'eye displayed the translation a moment later: *Will she debark?*

Only if [unknown]. So far the community seems accepting...pliant. Another man, but this voice was soft and soothing. She hid behind the olive tree, not thirty meters away. Even with her implant volume maxed the translator was having dropouts.

The low voice: *Just as well. Her appearance can be...alarming.*

The soothing, simpering voice: *She is monitoring the events. Vanderplotz prepared the population well.*

He'd better have. He owes us. What is the status of [unknown]?

Wait a moment. I'm getting an alert from the proximity drones. We have a guest nearby.

Lydia's breath caught in her throat. A moth had landed on the trunk of the olive tree, right near her face. Without thinking she slapped her hand against the trunk, smashing the insect with a brittle crack. Palm smarting, she sprinted away. She ran until her lungs hurt, listening for pursuit. At thirty meters she risked a quick glance over her shoulder. At fifty meters she stopped and turned, hands on her knees and gasping for breath. A tall figure stood next to the olive tree, watching her. Slowly, he raised one hand in greeting. She stood straight. The figure beckoned for her to return. She turned and ran.

She found her dome empty; Xenus wasn't home yet. Was the Shell meeting still going? Her mind raced. She sat on the polished bamboo floor and tried to think. The only thing that was clear was that she was in over her head. *Breathe...slow down.* Maybe she should have had a slug of whiskey.

She opened an audio patch to Shane. He connected immediately.

"Where are you?" she asked.

"The meeting just ended. Everyone is confused and drunk, stumbling around like zombies."

"Don't go near the platform."

"What? Why not?"

"Just get over here, okay? It's important."

She heard someone at the door. She stood, closing the patch without saying goodbye. Frantically she searched the living circle for something to use as a weapon, but saw only throw pillows, lamps, framed paintings, carved wooden sculptures...creature comforts. She grabbed an intricately carved wooden giraffe by the neck and hefted it over her head. Maybe she should have left the patch to Shane open.

"Whoa, whoa! It's me!"

It was Xenus, hands raised in defense. Slowly, she lowered the giraffe.

"We've got a problem," she said.

"I know. I was there."

"No, it's bigger than that. Sit down. Shane's on his way."

★   ★   ★

Shane swept the dome and the surrounding area for surveillance drones, then set up his own defensive perimeter. Xenus, visibly drunk, made tea.

"Do you need an enzyme shot?"

"My nanos are working on it, and so is my liver. I'll be fine in a minute."

"How much did you drink?"

"One more glass after that first swallow. There was a sort of meet-and-greet."

"Getting to know your new prison guards?"

Shane shushed them. "Give me a few more minutes."

Five minutes later Xenus, pale but steady, poured them green tea. They sat on pillows, legs crossed, in a neat triangle. For an instant it seemed just as likely that they would discuss their relationships as plan a resistance movement.

"What's so funny?" Xenus asked.

"Nothing. Sorry. I think I'm in shock."

"Lydia, what did you see?" Shane asked.

She told them about the ship and the two men, and the mysterious *her* who would not be debarking, and that they had caught her eavesdropping.

"I don't think they sent any drones after you," said Shane. "Or if they did, they're very small and very smart."

"I smashed a moth-sized one. It didn't seem particularly sophisticated."

"Could have been a decoy," Shane said. "But let's assume we're safe and secure for the moment. So...what do we know?"

The question hung in the air until Xenus broke the silence. "Adrian has declared Vandercamp an independent settlement. And he's got backup from the *Liu Hui*."

"But *who* on the *Liu Hui*?" Shane asked. "Their Repop Council? Those uniforms looked generic. It could be a private security force."

"I don't know," Lydia said. "That ship...it looks like new tech. I can't see an independent group developing something like that."

"Why not?" said Xenus. "Private interests have historically pushed technology forward when governments have lagged. It happened with Earth space programs more than once. And the Ringstation Coalition hasn't developed any new ships since the mule."

"So that's an unknown," Shane said, rubbing his bald head. "What about Adrian? Why is he doing this?"

"That's easy," said Lydia. "Stay in control. Become a dictator. He hated reporting to Townes."

"But it looked like the investigation was coming to nothing," Shane said. "I took the heat for Rosen's death." He said it matter-of-factly, without resentment. She wanted to reach out, to touch his arm and comfort him. Shane felt responsible for what had happened to Rosen, though there was nothing he could have done to prevent Rosen's demise short of pulling the field researchers altogether. Which might, in fact, still be a good idea. It would defeat the whole purpose of having an advance research station, but did that even matter anymore?

"Maybe he's had this planned for months, or even years. Since well before Rosen's murder," Xenus said.

Shane raised his eyebrows. "It's possible."

"What the hell are we going to do?" Lydia asked. She directed the question at both men, but ended up looking at Shane. So did Xenus.

Shane grunted, then slurped his tea. "We stay quiet and observe, for now. Let's see what Adrian's intentions are. He seems to be taking a soft approach to this coup. I'm wondering if he'll allow free passage to the *Stanford*. He hasn't jammed orbital patches. I already spoke with Townes."

"You did?" Lydia hadn't even thought to try.

"Yes. They know what's going on down here. They're nowhere close to formulating a response, but the councils are in emergency session."

"So something could go down fast," said Xenus.

"I doubt it. Look, you should know that Townes has already put me in charge of citizen safety. I'm not sure there's much I can do if the *Liu Hui* thugs start bashing heads, but it's my priority to try."

Xenus nodded. "Of course."

"So if you were thinking about making a hovershuttle dash to the OETS station, I can't join you."

Xenus looked at Lydia. "I think we're staying put. Right?"

"Right," Lydia said, thinking that if Shane wasn't going, *she* wasn't going. The thought came with a flash of guilt.

"What do you know about politics on the *Liu Hui?*" Shane asked Xenus. Did *Shane* feel guilty? He didn't seem uncomfortable or awkward. Maybe he assumed she'd already told Xenus about that night, and that there was no issue. Or maybe he just didn't care.

"Their government structure is more hierarchical and centralized than the *Stanford.* Their *Zhōngyāng* council makes most of the decisions. The other branches of government – legislative and judicial and military – all report to the *Zhōngyāng.*"

"There's a military branch of government?" Lydia asked.

"It's more like a safety and security branch, but the word means military. *Jūnshì.*"

She was reminded of why she loved Xenus. He was brilliant and well-educated, but also humble. He wasn't the type to lord his knowledge over you. She'd had no idea that he was intimately familiar with governmental structures and systems on the *Liu Hui.*

"Do you think…are these troops *jūnshì?*" Shane asked.

"I don't know. They might be. Or, like you said, they might be a private force."

"What else do we know about this woman?" Shane asked. "The one on the ship. You think she might be in charge?"

"It sounded like it. One of them said…he said that some might find her appearance *alarming.*"

Shane stood and paced around the room.

"What?" Xenus asked. "Does that mean something to you?"

"Maybe. I've heard rumors.… It's probably unrelated."

"What rumors?"

"Have you heard of the Crucible program?"

"The name rings a bell," said Xenus. "A late Corporate Age brain emulation experiment, wasn't it?"

Shane nodded. "More or less. But it was more than that. The host was implanted with a machine parasite – the Crucible – that gradually grew a mirror nervous system…mimicking and virtualizing every axon and dendrite."

"Sounds invasive," Lydia said.

"Wait a minute," Xenus said, "I *do* remember. The idea was to solve

Smooth Transition. Transfer consciousness to an emulated state without identity divergence. But it didn't work. The program was discontinued."

"The program was discontinued, but not for technical reasons," said Shane. "There were ethical concerns."

"How does this relate to our current situation?" Lydia asked. They didn't have time for a leisurely review of Corporate Age weird science.

Shane looked at her. "Believe me, I hope it doesn't."

Xenus's eyes flicked back and forth as he looked something up. "After the initial host died, the machine parasite – which now contained the host consciousness within a sim – lived on. If a second host ingested the parasite, the process repeated itself."

"But the first consciousness still existed?" Lydia asked. "Which one controlled the body?"

"That's where the ethical concerns came in," Shane said. "The idea was that each Crucible would become a community of minds, sharing the perceptions and motor control of the current host. In reality, some of the primary hosts became jailers, refusing to cede any control."

"Mind parasites," said Xenus. "It reminds me of that mycological infection – the villager who was treated by *Stanford* Medical. What's his name?"

"Per Anders," Lydia said. She had studied the case. "But I still don't get how this relates. Can you get to the point?"

"Sorry. Like I said, it's just a rumor. But I heard that a few of the Crucible subjects might still be alive."

"They'd be centuries old," Xenus observed.

"The quantum cores would be centuries old," Shane said, "but who knows how many host bodies would have been used up during that time. The rumor is that one of the Crucible subjects ended up on the *Liu Hui* in the military branch. Special forces in particular."

"*Kǒngbù Wǔzéi*. The terror squid," said Xenus. "Rescue and counter-terrorism specialists. Seems like every ten years or so we need them for some reason on the *Stanford*."

"Didn't they intervene during the *Hedonark* catastrophe?" Lydia said.

Shane nodded. "They saved thousands of lives. But get this – the reason they're called *squid* is supposedly because one of their leaders cybernetically enhanced herself with additional flexible appendages."

"What...like squid arms?" Lydia asked. "You think there's a *squid woman* on that ship – that's who they were talking about? And that she's hundreds of years old?"

"I'm just speculating."

"Squid woman or no squid woman, you're saying we should do nothing? Just wait it out?" Xenus sounded impatient, maybe even panicked. She wanted to comfort him but she didn't want to make him look weak in front of Shane.

"Observing isn't the same as doing nothing," Shane said. There was an edge to his voice as well. Shane's eyes flicked as he checked something in his m'eye.

"What is it?" Lydia asked.

"My drones just went offline."

Lydia and Xenus both stood. Thinking more clearly this time, Lydia walked calmly to the kitchenette and grabbed a long carbonlattice knife from the knife block. Xenus gave her a disapproving look. Shane already had his disruptor pointed at the door.

Two loud knocks.

"Open it slowly," Shane said.

Xenus, even paler than before, did as Shane had instructed.

Adrian Vanderplotz stood in the doorway. Lydia caught a momentary glimpse of a black-clad figure behind him, already walking away.

"Xenus, glad I caught you. Do you have a minute to chat?" Adrian looked flushed and happy. Military takeovers seemed to suit him. "And Shane, it's good that you're here too. May I come in?"

Xenus stepped aside. Adrian came into their home as if he owned it. Lydia put down the knife, but not before Adrian saw it.

"Hello, Lydia. No need for *that*, I'm sure. This isn't what you think it is. In a few months you'll be thanking me. Maybe even sooner. Ah... tea. That sounds good right now. Would someone mind pouring me a cup? The whiskey...too strong for an old man like me."

No one moved to serve him.

"I see." Adrian turned to Xenus. "I anticipated we might not see eye to eye. I thought I should come to you first."

"You didn't come to anyone first," Xenus said. "You acted unilaterally. You've made an enormous mistake. This will end up as nothing more than a huge, embarrassing diplomatic problem. Congratulations on committing career suicide."

It was a good retort. Even Shane looked impressed.

Adrian laughed. "Your way of thinking is outmoded, Xenus Troy. From Day One you've seen the *Stanford* as the mothership. But that's not the way it is. The truth is we've always been independent. I'm just making it official."

"Who are your friends?" Lydia asked. Her voice sounded shaky, but it was better than standing there mute.

"I already told you – they're from the *Liu Hui*," said Adrian.

"Are they *Kǒngbù Wúzéi*?" she asked impulsively. "Is the Squid Woman here?"

Adrian smiled tightly. "Serve me some tea, and I'll explain everything."

CHAPTER EIGHTEEN

Tem, sitting next to Mother, surveyed the council members' faces, trying to distinguish friend from foe. Svilsson – Zinthia's father – was a familiar face, and he guessed that Svilsson would not have arranged the meeting only to thwart him. He also recognized Penelope Townes, with her long gray hair and green eyes; she had been among the first to greet them when they arrived on the *Stanford* via mule. Townes smiled whenever Tem looked in her direction. Mother did not seem to trust her. Mother did not seem to trust *anyone* on this council. He had asked to bring Morfar Shol as his guardian (the council considered him too young to not have a family member present), but Mother had insisted. She was incredulous that he had been granted an audience in the first place, and at first forbade him to attend, but Tem had persuaded her.

"If I don't represent Happdal, who will?" he had asked.

"It's not your job – you're just a child. Arik, your father, your uncle, Elke…they can take care of themselves and everyone else."

"They don't know that the sky people have come to Earth – to *live*. I'm the only one who knows. Well, you know, but…." He had stopped short of accusing Mother of having mixed loyalties, but he had seen the hurt on her face. She was quiet for some time before answering.

"I know you're trying to do the right thing," Mother had said. "But the reason I brought you here…well, there are many reasons, but one is so that you can be safe and *enjoy* yourself. You know, *be a kid*. I didn't see you getting involved in politics. What do you intend to discuss with the council, anyway?"

"Our village land rights and territory. Someone has to speak for us. Except for Per Anders, I'm the only one on the *Stanford* who was born in Happdal. It's my responsibility."

She'd sighed and hugged him. "They won't take you seriously."

But she said he could attend the meeting, *if and only if* she was there with him.

If Repop had a leader, it was the old man with the long white mustache who had introduced himself as Kardosh. His eyes looked friendly, but it was impossible to tell if he was smiling; his mustache concealed his lips. Something in his manner reminded Tem of a fox. After bringing the meeting to order, the fox cleared his throat and looked directly at Tem.

"We have a guest today. Tem, son of Car-En Ganzorig. I am sure you all know *of* Car-En, even if you do not know her personally. It suffices to say that without Car-En's research we would know nothing of the people of the Five Valleys. But it is her son, Tem, who has requested an audience with the council today."

"I'm sorry," said a young woman with straight brown hair, "why have we invited a *child* to a council meeting?" Tem glared at the woman but she kept her eyes fixed on Kardosh. He made a mental tally – *foe*.

Kardosh answered cheerfully. "This nine-year-old happens to be in a unique position. He is the only Earth-born villager who is aware of the full extent of our terrestrial presence and activities. He has some questions and he deserves our complete attention and *respect*. Is that something you can offer, Polanski?"

"Of course," Polanski said, still avoiding Tem's gaze. "I was just asking."

"Let the boy speak for himself," said a man with narrow features and dark brown skin.

"As Bala says," said Kardosh, "let the boy speak for himself. Tem?"

The council members looked at him – even Polanski. He glanced at Mother for reassurance, but Mother was staring ahead, jaw clenched.

Tem took a deep breath and spoke. "My name is Tem Espersson, son of Esper Ariksson and Car-En Ganzorig. My uncle is Trond Jensesson, sixth smith of Happdal. My grandfather – my farfar – is Arik Asgersson, Jarl of Happdal. His wife – my farmor – is Elke Mettesdóttir. My other farfar is Jense Baldrsson, fifth smith of Happdal. My morfar is Shol...." He paused, what was Shol's surname? Was it also Ganzorig? "Shol of the *Stanford*—"

"Really? Is this necessary?" Polanski interrupted.

Tem continued without pause, raising his voice. "My mormor was Marivic. I am here to speak for Happdal and the people of the Five Valleys. I have three demands," – Polanski snorted at this, while the others looked at him dubiously – "and they are as follows. First, immediately cease all

spying operations on Happdal and the other towns of the Five Valleys."
He had considered making demands only on behalf of Happdal. What did
he care for the accursed souls of Kaldbrek? But the people of Skrova were
friends to Happdal, and the sky people were no less likely to cede to his
demands if he presented himself as the ambassador of the greater region.
It might even make them take him more seriously. "Your anthropologists
have been spying since before I was born." Conversations with Morfar
Shol had given him a clearer picture of Mother's activities before she had
married Father. "My existence itself is proof of that espionage. Do you
deny this charge?" He directed the question at Kardosh.

The old white fox opened his mouth as if to answer, but then closed
it and twirled his mustache. He shook his head slightly and gestured for
Tem to continue.

"We demand that you stop. As a gesture of good faith we will invite a
cultural enjoy...." He paused. He had learned the term from Morfar Shol
but the council members looked confused.

"I think you mean *envoy*," said the man with dark brown skin – Bala –
not unkindly. Polanksi stopped smirking after a dark glance from Kardosh.

"Yes, thank you. A cultural *envoy*. An exchange, starting with one
person each, growing to more as the trust between us grows." He liked
the sound of that. Offer the carrot with the stick, as Farfar Arik said. If he
understood the sky people, they craved knowledge more than power. The
arrangement would balance power between the Five Valleys and the sky
people, but it would not take away what they considered to be the greatest
prize: the means to observe and study how the villagers lived, spoke, and
thought. How could they refuse? He had thought it out carefully.

"What is the second *demand*?" Kardosh asked, sounding a little impatient.

Tem risked a glance at Mother, then wished he hadn't. Brow furrowed,
lips pursed, she looked at him as if she didn't know him. Well, she didn't,
entirely. She knew him as her son, but she did not know or understand
the man he was trying to be.

"The second demand is that the *Stanford* and the entire Ringstation
Coalition officially acknowledge and respect our territorial borders. I,
Tem Espersson, representing the Five Valleys, claim the land surrounding
our home as follows: north to the Aller river, south to the headwaters
of the Danube, west to the Rhine, and east to the Elbe." He had pored
over maps to learn the sky people's historical names for the rivers (none

of which he had seen, save the Aller; the Nyr Begna and Upper Begna were the only rivers he knew). The claim was less ambitious than the handshake deal he had made with Javier (Morfar Shol had laughed when Tem had recounted the story), but was still far larger than they could use in a hundred years, even if each woman bore a dozen children. That seemed a good thing to Tem.

"I think we've heard quite enough," said Polanski. "Kardosh, this child is wasting our time."

Kardosh frowned. "We can spare a few minutes more. At the very least, I'm curious. We'll hear the boy out."

"Acknowledge your borders how, exactly?" Bala asked Tem.

Tem froze. He had not thought to elaborate. He began to speak, hoping he would not spout nonsense. "You shall not trespass on our lands without permission from a jarl. We will respect your borders as well, the mule port and the ringships...the ring*stations*."

Polanski smiled slyly. "Written permission, or verbal?" Was she goading him?

"Either," he said, unsure. What did it matter?

"What if one jarl grants permission and another refuses it? Who has the final authority in your lands?" Polanski asked. Perhaps she *was* goading him, but it was a valid question. He had not thought it out.

"We will not consider it trespassing if you have permission from any jarl."

"And who has given you authority to speak for the villages? The jarls? Your mother?" Polanski raised an eyebrow at Car-En.

"Enough with the questions," interrupted Kardosh. "What is the third demand?"

"Excuse me," said Polanski, "I was speaking." Kardosh raised an eyebrow but yielded. Tem did not yet understand the hierarchy of the council, but it appeared that Kardosh did not yield absolute control. Then again, neither did a jarl. Only a fool of a leader refused to be challenged and questioned. "Let us assume that you have spoken to the jarls, and they've chosen you as their representative. What if we don't comply with your demands? Are the jarls threatening us?"

"Is this really necessary?" Bala asked, glaring at Polanski. "He's just a boy."

"I think it is. If Tem wishes to be taken seriously, he should have thought more carefully about his so-called *demands*. The villagers are not in a position to dictate terms."

"If you think you hold all the power, you're a fool," Tem said. "And if you had ever met my Farmor Elke you would not dare speak to me that way. There are fierce folk among my kin."

"Enough!" bellowed Kardosh. "Tem, please state the third item on your list, be it demand or request."

Tem paused before speaking, looking each council member in the eye. "Happdal is in danger. The jarl of our neighboring village has gone insane. He is savage, bloodthirsty, and deranged." He let that sink in.

Kardosh nodded knowingly. "We are aware of that. He murdered one of our researchers."

Tem hadn't known that. He wondered who. It must have been one of the anthropologist spies. Had Mother known the victim? It explained why Shane and Lydia had been in the region, so far north of their home near the sea. They had come to collect their dead. "Svein Haakonsson is not only a murderer, but also a slaver. I myself was captured and enslaved until my father rescued me."

"We can't interfere, if that's what you were going to ask," Polanski said. "We have a strict Non-Interventionist policy in regards to the villages."

"A what?" asked Tem.

"Never mind," said Kardosh. "What is it exactly that you want?"

Tem suppressed a smile. He now realized what Polanski had meant by *Non-Interventionist policy*. She had spoken too soon.

"What I want is perfectly in line with your current *policy*," Tem said. "I want a promise that you will not interfere, or even observe, when we deal with Kaldbrek."

"*Deal* with them?" Polanski said. "What does that mean?"

"When we exact our revenge. I am asking that you stay out of it."

"Okay, that's enough," said Mother, grabbing his arm. He twisted in his seat, wrenching out of her grip.

"Car-En, please," Kardosh said. "Let us at least offer a brief response. Your son is in a unique position."

Mother, fuming, let him go.

Kardosh looked around the room. He took a deep breath and sighed. As the air left his lungs he looked older. He was the oldest man Tem had ever seen. A moment ago he had seemed strong and vibrant; now he looked frail and gray. He turned his weary eyes on Tem. "Young Tem Espersson, thank you for addressing the Repopulation Council. I apologize on behalf of some of my colleagues who did not offer you the respect you deserve. Please know that this council takes your concerns seriously.

"We need time for discussion. But right off I can say that one of your requests has already been met. The terrestrial field research program has been suspended. Those we refer to as field researchers – and you call spies – have been called home. The man murdered by the Kaldbrek villagers – *tortured* and murdered – was a field anthropologist. Given the nature of recent events, it is unlikely that the program will be reinstated."

"What recent events?" Mother asked.

"This will be news to you, Car-En, but now is as good a time as any. Advance Field Station One, colloquially known as Vandercamp, is no longer associated with the *Stanford*."

"What does *that* mean?"

"It means just that," said Polanski. "They're independent. They no longer report to the anthropology department, or to Repop, or to anyone."

"I'm sorry," Mother said, "are you saying—"

"If I may," said Penelope Townes. The green-eyed old woman had been silent up until now, even brooding. Now she leaned toward Mother and Tem. She, too, looked tired and grim. "To be blunt, Adrian Vanderplotz has declared independence, and we're currently powerless to stop it. It's a preemptive coup. He was about to be removed from his position for misconduct."

"Powerless?" Mother said. "Why? Send down security with some disruptors and apprehend him. I'll go myself."

"It's not that simple," Townes said. "He's enlisted his own security force."

"That's impossible," said Mother, her voice rising. "I know the head of security myself – Shane Jaecks. He would never side with Adrian if—"

"Jaecks offered his resignation weeks ago. He felt responsible for Rosen's death."

"And you accepted?"

"I asked that he serve as Interim Security Director. Car-En, listen, Adrian recruited outside help from the *Liu Hui*. Military help."

Tem watched Mother's face carefully. At first, her anger had flared at the sound of Adrian's name. Mother had seemed angry since their arrival on the *Stanford*; it was her new baseline mood from which she fluctuated into hot rage or cool, simmering fury. This was disturbing, and at first he had taken it personally, but Morfar Shol had reassured him it had nothing to do with Tem. Mother loved him as much as ever. She would get better, said Morfar. She would not always be so angry. She was mourning the death of her own mother, and she was angry at herself for being absent. Morfar Shol had already forgiven her, and in time she would forgive herself.

Now Mother's face had a cool, calculating look. This scared him. Her expression had been the same when he'd asked her what she was doing at the Hair Lab. A project, she'd said, offering nothing more, deflecting Tem's follow-up questions. It was the first moment when he'd felt *outside* of Mother's circle. He'd always been her confidant, her ally, always on her side even when it was just a disagreement with Father. That moment had changed everything. Whatever Mother was up to, Tem wasn't invited.

It had hurt, even more so than her anger and foul mood.

It had also gotten Tem thinking about how he might want *different* things than Mother. Their interests would not always be aligned in life. Sometimes they might even be opposed. He had chosen to confide in Morfar Shol when preparing for the council meeting.

Mother rose from her seat. "We're done here, yes?" She was asking Tem. Tem nodded, and stood. He took a last glance at the council members before leaving the chamber. Polanski avoided eye contact, Kardosh nodded, Svilsson stared, and Penelope Townes gave a mouth-only smile. He was sure of one thing: his demands would not be ignored. Ridiculed perhaps, but at least discussed. He had stirred the pot.

They walked home on Main, through McLaren Park. Mother said nothing, but took his hand when he reached out. They walked, holding hands, past couples sitting under trees, families picnicking on colorful blankets, and pickup soccer games. "I'm hungry," Tem said as they passed an ice-cream stand. Mother bought them ice-cream cones and they sat on a bench to eat them.

"Your farfar will not be pleased," said Mother in Norse. "Unless you somehow managed to speak with him about your plan. Did he know?"

It was comforting to hear her speak the village language. Mostly, since their arrival, she had insisted on English.

"No," Tem said, "but I think Farfar Arik will be proud."

Mother laughed ruefully. "Maybe you're right. He approves of boldness."

"What should we do?" Tem asked.

"*We?* At the meeting you had your own agenda."

"It's important that we work together," he said, watching her face closely.

She smiled. "I know you're angry with me. I've been gone a lot, and there are some things I haven't shared with you. But it's all to keep you safe. I love you."

"Being safe isn't always the most important thing," he said. "Honor and loyalty are more important."

She shook her head. "When you're a parent, nothing is more important than keeping your children safe. But you know what? You're right about one thing. We should be working together. How do we do that?"

He looked out at the park. Everything he saw was pleasing to the eye, balanced and sculpted. He missed the craggy wildness of the mountains.

"When can we visit home, on Earth? You said that we could."

"This isn't very good," she said, looking at her ice-cream cone dubiously. She'd chosen a dark yellow color.

"Can we?"

"Remind me not to get curry next time. You answer my question first."

He thought about it, how much to confide in Mother. If he wanted her trust, he had to trust her. And she was a villager, after all. She had married Father and left her own home behind. That choice had cost her.

"Tante Katja taught me something. It's important, and I think it's powerful. She chose me to guard her secret."

"What secret?"

"It's a pattern she taught me to write, with numbers and symbols."

"A formula?"

"I think so." In mathematics he had only just started learning division. He was far behind his classmates, but he suspected even the brightest of them would not know what to make of the pattern. Perhaps Mr. Kan, his math teacher, might understand it.

"Did she learn it from one of the Builder books?"

"No. She learned it...."

"Where, Tem?"

The story Katja had told him was so farfetched that he had imagined it to be a tall tale, something to entertain him during his studies. But now he knew better what the sky people could do. What had seemed like magic was in fact complex technology. Were there no limits to their enhanced abilities and incredible machines? Katja's fantastic tale no longer seemed so impossible.

"She told me that she was captured, and lived for a time in another world. She met one of her ancestors there – Henning – and later a woman named Zoë who helped her escape."

Mother looked at him thoughtfully. At least she didn't have that patient, slightly bored look on her face that meant she thought he was making up a story. "And that's where Katja learned this...formula?"

"Yes. Zoë taught it to her. Somehow the formula was *how* Tante Katja was able to escape. But it destroyed the world she was trapped in, killing Zoë, Henning, and everyone else. Only Tante Katja survived, because somehow the world was *inside* of her body."

"And Jense brought her home to the village, and Ilsa cared for her until she woke up," finished Mother. That much of the story was established lore, known to everyone in Happdal. Father and Farbror Trond had returned at the same time, his uncle carrying Mother in his arms, unconscious and close to death. Ilsa had nursed both Mother and Tante Katja back to health.

Mother stood, tossing the remainder of her ice-cream cone into a nearby compost bin. She reached out a hand to Tem. He took it, and together they walked toward home.

"Did Tante Katja already tell you her story?" he asked.

"Some of it. I once saw your ancestor, Henning. At least what was left of him. He was a gast at that point – that's what the villagers called him. His mind had been taken over by a parasite. I watched him die, in the forest near the Silver Trail. Before he died he vomited up a black egg, and forced it down Katja's throat."

"A black egg? Was that the parasite? Why didn't you try to stop him?"

"I did. I attacked him, but he was already dying. I tried to help Katja, but she left while I was sleeping. I didn't see her again until we were both recovering under Ilsa's care. She told me her story, but she didn't mention anything about a formula."

"What was the egg? Who made it?"

"It was experimental Corporate Age technology. Something called the Crucible."

"What happened to it? Is it still inside of Katja's body?"

"No, I don't think so. I don't know where it is."

"Would Jense know? He's the one who found Katja up on the ridge."

"He might."

He wondered if the black egg Mother had spoken of might be related to the black tree and the spiders. He almost told Mother his idea, but in the end stayed quiet. It was a silly thought, and he had already received enough ridicule today. "What do you think Grandpa Shol is making for dinner?" he asked instead, switching to English. He'd finished his ice cream but it had only made him hungrier.

"I don't know, but I think it might be something special. He's very proud of you. He'll want to hear all about the meeting. Tem?"

"Yes?"

"Will you show me the formula that Tante Katja taught you? Can you write it out for me?"

He felt a tightness in his throat, and suddenly he was crying. Mother held him but he couldn't stop. He pressed his face into her shirt and sobbed uncontrollably.

"It's okay," she said. "You don't have to show me. It can be your secret with Katja."

"No," he managed to say between sobs. "I want to. I'm tired of keeping secrets." He would tell her everything.

If he couldn't trust his own mother, who could he trust?

CHAPTER NINETEEN

Umana closed her eyes and browsed her feeds, first all at once like a thousand-eyed spider, then individually when a flash of movement or sound caught her attention. Nothing in the settlement caught her interest. The people there had offered no resistance, dumbly lining up like cattle, doing as the vassal had instructed. There were murmurs of discontent (she heard everything), but no fighting. She had expected a scuffle at least. She'd been disappointed.

There were hints of a nascent resistance movement. Jaecks, the former Security Director, had tried to conduct a private meeting. His defenses had been primitive and laughable, an easy fence-hop. The meeting itself had been boring; the conspirators had simply decided to 'watch and wait.' There had been one brief thrill – they'd guessed her identity. On the *Liu Hui* her origins were not so much concealed as…*forgotten*. Human memory was short. To them, anything that had happened before their own existence took on an unreal, story-like quality. But she had *lived* through the history they'd learned in school.

A mind spoke up, one of the first-tiers. "My lady, the *Zhōngyāng* awaits your report."

She flicked the first-tier away. The council could wait. The *Zhōngyāng* still thought they controlled her, but now she had the ship. Giving her the *Iarudi* had been a mistake.

The mind persisted. "They are being quite insistent. What should I tell them?" Who was speaking? It was Zhan, one of her oldest. She considered a censure, for being annoying. But no, she had assigned Zhan to monitor communications from the *Zhōngyāng*. Zhan was only doing her job. Or was it *his* job? She could no longer remember; Zhan had switched avatars and genders so many times. The current one was a Siberian tiger (long extinct in reality – perhaps she would reseed them one day). The silky striped cat used an androgynous telepathic voice to communicate. How childlike.

"Tell them everything is proceeding according to plan. The vassal is obedient. The population is pliant."

"And the *Stanford*? Have they responded to the vassal's pronouncement?"

"They have," she said, feeling impatient. But Zhan did not have access to her senses, and had no way of knowing. "They will acknowledge the independence of the settlement on the condition of free passage: that any citizen may leave or return at any time."

"And will you grant it?"

"No one will leave unless I want them gone."

"Do I have your leave to relay this information to the *Zhōngyáng*? May I compose a report on your behalf?"

She considered it. Zhan's report would be flawlessly obsequious. If she composed the report herself, there would be a touch of haughtiness and arrogance, no matter how much she tried to conceal it. "Yes, you have my leave. Now begone." It was better if Zhan wrote the report. The council would never know the difference. They had no idea Zhan existed.

In one of her feeds, something caught her attention. Someone was watching the spiders. It was the old man with the forked beard, and a young woman with pale skin and hair the color of rich soil. The old man pointed and the girl nodded. Her face might have been pretty if not hardened by ill fortune and worry; her mouth turned down at the edges and her forehead was prematurely lined. It warmed her heart to see such a face; she had looked the same way herself, centuries ago.

She considered sending one of her children to kill the man. She'd seen him before, which meant he was nosy. He might be plotting something. But she liked the dour-faced girl, and her children had already eaten. They'd brought down a boar and picked the bones clean. They were so big now, nearly a meter across. In her thread womb they'd started so tiny. She briefly replayed the ecstasy of birthing them.

The old man and the girl retreated into the woods. She wished she had a drone to send after them, but they were hundreds of kilometers to the north. Her children were too big to follow them without being seen, and she had not thought to leave drones when she'd dropped off the spiderlings. If she sent one now, how long would it take to get there? She opened the thought to the thralls; a third-tier presented her with the answer moments later. A lance could make the trip in forty minutes. Very well. She sent ten of them.

Her children had returned to the black, stump-like mass. Of all the wonders on Earth this one fascinated her the most. Her progeny had discovered it, and now idled near it unless they were hunting, or acting under orders. So far all she knew was that the black mass was made of the same stuff as herself, as her children. She lifted her arm − one of her human arms − and examined the black lace of threads beneath her translucent skin. The threads were versatile, feeding off heat, light, sugar, protein − practically anything. But she'd never seen them outside of flesh, feeding off soil and sunlight like these did. Where was the core? Underground? More importantly, *who* was the core? Could she consume them? She had a great appetite for many things, but nothing more so than thralls.

Umana shifted restlessly in her throne. It was time to move, to stretch her many limbs. She hadn't left the ship, or even the cocoon, for days. Foster had cautioned her against making an appearance; he didn't want to spook the locals. Well, they seemed placid enough. Maybe it would do them good to see something out of the ordinary. The settlement had been seeded with stock from the *Stanford*, a ringstation with conservative genetic editing parameters. On average their citizens were small-boned, highly intelligent, and conflict averse: the perfect recipe for a sustainable, smoothly functioning collective. The *Liu Hui* population was bolder and more adventurous in their edits, choosing bigger bodies, bigger appetites, and more variation overall. Skin color was not limited to the beige-to-dark-brown spectrum, but included photosynthetic greens and burgundies. Additional sensory organs were commonplace, for magnetoperception, echolocation, cryptochromatism, or simply extra sets of ears or eyes.

But even *Liu Hui* denizens were taken aback by her current form. She would have it no other way. The smell of fear made her glad.

She commanded the cocoon to unseal. The relatively fresh air from the ship interior reminded her to bathe; she had acclimated to her own reek. Perhaps a swim would do her well. There was an ocean nearby − that would be a novelty. It reminded her of the nickname the young doctor had coined during the resistance cell meeting. The *Squid Woman*. She liked that.

The crew scrambled to attention as she emerged into the control bay. There were only three of them; the rest were engaged in security, surveillance, or diplomatic activities throughout the settlement. Chiang straightened his uniform and saluted. "C-commander...." he sputtered.

"At ease. I'm going for a stroll. I need some fresh air." A female crew member squinted, eyes watering. She sidled closer. "Something the matter? Are you homesick, little one?"

"No, Commander. Just...allergies, I think. The local pollen."

"Then inoculate yourself."

"Yes, absolutely."

"Open the bay doors."

Chiang cleared his throat. "Lieutenant Foster advised—"

"Silence!" she roared, enhancing her voice with subsonic, dissonant intervals. Chiang flinched. The girl clutched her abdomen, knees buckling.

The bay doors opened. Her inner lids closed to vertical slits as sunlight flooded the interior. With a pneumatic hiss the ramp extended and locked.

"I might go for a swim as well," she said in her natural voice. "When I return, make sure the cocoon is clean."

"Yes, Commander," said Chiang, as if nothing would please him more than scrubbing the detritus from her throne. Not that he would do the work himself. She imagined that particular task would fall to the delicate flower holding back her vomit. The youngling – Mèng was her name – had potential, if she was willing to eat bitter for a few years.

She stepped onto the crudely built landing pad. These were her first steps on Earth in a very long time. Memories of a half-dozen thralls rushed into her mind, but she pushed them aside in favor of her *own* memories: a little girl growing up in California's Central Valley, a parched, mineral-depleted agricultural region filled with pesticides and lung-eating fungi. She'd been a laborer's daughter, one of seven children, wearing dusty hand-me-down clothes. Food production had mostly moved to the depopulating cities, to vast urban greenhouses occupying entire city blocks, where organic greens feasted on growth-optimizing ultraviolet light and fish-waste-enriched water, *post-soil* agriculture. Some food was still grown outdoors, almonds and tree fruit mostly, but even those crops had eventually moved to the cities, replacing the ornamental stock. Her father's way of life had been dying. Her parents had struggled to steer her toward a better life. They'd encouraged her reading habit, and had introduced her to the few they knew among the lighter-skinned, landed intelligentsia. The gambit had worked; she had become an academic, a rising star in the field of full-nervous system emulation. *Brain* emulation had been solved, mostly, but the holy grail was Smooth Transition. The Crucible Program offered the best shot at immortality. Her body already ravaged by Valley Fever, she had volunteered without a second thought.

Someone was approaching. It was the vassal, with an entourage. One of them was her own man, Regis Foster. Foster towered over the vassal, but she loomed over all of them. Standing erect, she was nearly three meters tall. Her reach was more impressive: her two tentacle-arms, fully extended, spanned twenty meters. For now she kept her six manipulator arms coiled against her chest, with her two tentacles partially extended and held low for balance. As the vassal came within reach she extended a human arm, palm down. For a moment he looked confused, then bowed and kissed the back of her hand. Good, he had studied protocol. She appreciated the proper show of respect.

"Commander Umana," he said, "welcome to Vandercamp. When I heard you were debarking I came immediately to greet you."

"Thank you," she purred, adding infrasonic octaves. He did not visibly react, and she smelled no fear on him. Impressive.

"May I lead you on a tour of our town?"

Town – an interesting word choice for the anemic settlement, egotistically named *Vandercamp*. The vassal was ambitious.

"I think not. Let them see me at a distance first." She glanced up. Predictably, some of the settlers had stopped to gawk at the edge of the landing pad. She lifted and slowly waved a tentacle-arm overhead. Tentatively, a black-haired girl waved back, mouth agape.

"Of course. Are you well supplied? Do you need food or water?"

"I'm sure the crew would appreciate some fresh food delivered." The main force was already integrating with the settlement, sharing communal meals, and more importantly, communal work. "My people are contributing adequately?"

"They're very industrious."

"And well received?"

The vassal's face took on a neutral expression. So...they had yet to charm the locals. It might take some time. At least they weren't being attacked with shovels and compost buckets.

"I'm sure, in time...." said the vassal.

"Thank you for greeting me, Vanderplotz, but I was just about to go for a stroll."

"May I join you? I'd like to discuss our agreement. What is the status of...the situation to the north?"

"We'll discuss that soon. As for the stroll, I'm afraid you couldn't keep up."

★   ★   ★

She glided over the green plains. It was exhilarating to move this way, taking long, loping strides with her tentacle arms. For long moments, mid-stride, she hurtled through space until her forward tentacle found purchase in the soft earth. As vast as the *Liu Hui* was, there was nowhere she could run like this. There was nowhere else like Earth.

In less than thirty minutes she had traveled thirty kilometers south. Mountains loomed ahead. She opened a task to the third-tiers: offer her routes to the ocean, scenic and not too steep. Her thralls came to a rare consensus; there was a pass cutting southeast between the Alps and the Apennines. She would emerge near the ruins of Savona. She increased her pace, relishing the strain in both her real and artificial muscles. Fauna scattered before her: hare, shrew, and vole diving for cover; sparrow and crow taking to the air. She was careful not to crush any beast with her great strides. More than once a tentacle twitched at the last second before landing, avoiding a field mouse, warren entrance, or ground nest. The long arms had eyes of their own, and primitive 'minds' too, in a way. She was a collection of beings (though not a *collective*; there was a *single* mind in charge).

She did not kill for sport, or by accident, but she had no qualms about killing for the greater good. The vassal wanted the villages to the north exterminated. Unbeknownst to him, this had already been part of her greater plan. Humans had had their time on Earth. That time had passed. There would be no 'repopulation' of the home planet, if she had her way. And who could stop her? There were powerful forces on the *Liu Hui*, but they could be tricked. The councils and committees of the *Stanford* had already demonstrated their impotence and passivity; they had not even bothered to mount a blustery protest when the vassal had declared independence.

Her children would clean up the Harz villages, then move on to the Sardinians, the kibbutzniks, and any other strays. As for Vandercamp, she would graciously grant Free Passage, and most would emigrate to the *Stanford*. The stragglers would succumb to disease or starvation – she hadn't yet decided which. There might be other attempts at repopulation, but the 'Vandercamp disaster' would cool ringstation enthusiasm for decades.

There was only one Earth, and she meant to preserve and protect it. Only the ancient, isolated hunter-gatherer populations, resistant to cultural evolution and biological expansion for whatever reasons (perhaps wisdom), would she leave unmolested. They were as much a part of the zoological continuum as anything else.

In one or two hundred years the philosophy of repopulation would come to be seen as folly. Humans belonged on vessels of their own creation, *limited* by the hard and obvious constraints of living in space. It was a natural counterbalance to the expansive, acquisitive nature of the human mind. On the homeworld, humans had acted like locusts, devouring everything. She would not let the swarm return.

She was climbing now, avoiding the rubbly ruins of the old thoroughfare, mostly grown over with trees, in favor of the open green slopes on the eastern side of the pass. She saw the remains of a mountain village below. She was eager to submerge herself in the sea, but it would only take a few minutes to explore. Wood had rotted, steel had rusted; only stone remained. But the village was centuries old, and while many of the ancient stone structures had crumbled to rubble, others were recognizable: a bell tower, a wall, a row of houses. Curious, she scanned a wide area for elemental composition, focusing on metals. There was plentiful iron, rusted and dissolved back into the red earth. There was tin and copper, some of it in the same vicinity, indicating bronze artifacts, likely well-preserved. A small cache of gold, less than two hundred meters away, caught her attention. Gold had never completely lost its fascination for her. She could still picture her father's simple wedding band. As a young scientist she had collected antique gold coins. More recently, the *Liu Hui*'s asteroid miners had increased supply to the point where gold was now just another pretty metal, but she was still tempted to dig up the cache. She suppressed the urge and took a great leap toward her destination, launching herself into the air from spring-coiled long limbs. She flew fifty meters before her tentacles touched down, absorbing her significant weight with an S-shaped curve. The reckless nature of the leap thrilled her. For too long her physicality had been controlled and cramped. So had her personality. For decades she'd pretended to be less than she was. Now that she had the ship, and Earth, that time was over.

The *Iarudi* was a feat of engineering and artistry, the result of tireless experimentation. It was the first ship of its class and the *only* ship with a Natario-White drive, capable of compressing spacetime. It was not the most lethal ship in her fleet (technically the *Zhōngyāng*'s fleet, but they deferred to her, almost always unanimously, when matters of security were at hand), but it did have a *unique* weapon, yet to be field tested. So far, she'd left technical operations to her crew, but her first-tiers were rapidly absorbing the ship specifications. Soon she'd take the *Iarudi* for a solo ride.

She crested a hill and saw the reddish ruins of Savona spread out before her, and beyond that the sparkling, pristine Mediterranean Sea. She rushed down the slope and leapt through the rubble, taking longer, more aggressive strides as she approached her destination. She was less careful with her limbs; it did not bother her to crush rusted scraps or to crack cobblestones, accelerating the ruin's inevitable decomposition. She wished she could bring down a thousand years of rain and wind at once, to wash the landscape clean. Would that be enough? Ten thousand, maybe, to truly bury the last remains. Would she still be alive? She was only six, seven hundred years old. How old exactly? Six hundred fifty-eight, answered a third-tier. Yes, she'd been born in 02069, near Fresno, California, in what had then been the United States of America.

Finally, the beach was in sight. She leapt over the sun-bleached rubble of an ancient beachside hotel and hit the sand. Three strides later her tentacles were submerged in salt water. She slowed her pace, relishing the warmth of the sea. The southern horizon looked nearly flat; the curve of the Earth, so clear from orbit, was barely perceptible from this angle. Again, a flood of memories: beach visits with her family, looking out at the vast Pacific Ocean, imagining Japan on the other side. She dug her tentacles into the seabed, careful to not disturb any coral, and launched herself into a shallow dive.

What had once been a barren oceanic wasteland, polluted with plastic bottles, sunscreen, and ammonia from human urine, was now a thriving ecosystem, rich in brilliant corals, hundreds of fish species, and all manner of starfish, eel, anemone, crab, and mollusk. She sealed her nostrils and tentatively flushed her gills. It had been a long time, but the artificial organs still worked. Her lungs did not ache for air despite being empty and relaxed. The fish made way for her.

She swam to deeper water, bringing her six manipulator arms and her two human legs into play to assist her tentacles. With ten limbs there were many ways to swim, but she settled on a simple wavelike motion with her long limbs, relaxing the rest of her body. She was in no hurry.

After an hour of luxuriating, she emerged from the sea and stood dripping on the sand. The sun was low in the sky. She considered informing Foster or Chiang of her whereabouts. No, let them wonder if she had disappeared forever. Would they be glad, or would they panic? Maybe both.

A third-tier alerted her to a faint, unusual signal. She brought it into focus. A distress call, from one of her children. It was barely alive. She shivered with rage. Who dared assault one of her progeny?

There were coordinates embedded in the signal. She teased them out, brought up the location visually.

One hundred forty kilometers to the northeast. Vandercamp.

What was one of her children doing at the settlement? Who had brought it there? Who had injured it?

She quelled her rage. Whoever was responsible would die, but not before she had learned what they knew, and who they had told. No one – not even her own people – could know that she was mother to the spiders.

CHAPTER TWENTY

Lydia put out breakfast: fruit, boiled eggs, and brown sourdough bread. Xenus seemed distracted. He was scheduled to meet with Lieutenant Foster to assign work duty to the *Liu Hui* soldiers. Lydia was glad that Xenus had something to do; his position as Research Coordinator was now irrelevant. The field researchers had been immediately recalled when the news of Rosen's death reached the *Stanford*.

Regis Foster had insisted that his people would work, and thus integrate themselves within the community. This declaration had been met with skepticism, but when Xenus had tentatively delegated some grunt work to the soldiers, they had completed the tasks with diligence and gusto. The *Liu Hui* giants were acting more like friendly neighbors than an occupying force.

Still, Vandercamp was in upheaval. After the initial shock wore off, the residents began to question Adrian's intentions. There was not yet a consensus regarding what to do. It was confusing that the *Stanford* had so little to say about the matter. The Over Council's single 'condition' had been Free Passage: Vandercamp's independence would be recognized only so long as citizens were free to come and go, to travel freely between Earth and their home ringstation. So far, nobody had tried to leave, but neither had passage been forbidden. What would the *Stanford* do if this right was not granted? The councils had made no warnings, presented no consequences. Lydia wondered if Penelope Townes and the others were secretly relieved to be rid of Adrian. With the field research suspended, was the field station now a liability?

Or perhaps there was a darker truth. By disowning Vandercamp, the Repopulationists got their way. The charade of calling the settlement a 'research station' could be dropped.

Would the *Stanford* really cede control to the *Liu Hui* without any resistance? That didn't make sense. The *Stanford* councils must be buying time, hoping to lull Adrian and the *Liu Hui* force into complacency. AFS-1 was a valuable asset, a foothold on Earth.

"Shouldn't take long," Xenus said on his way out. "We'll see how they like compost duty."

"I'm sure they'll smile and thank you for the privilege," said Lydia, "but don't trust them."

"I won't."

Lydia cleaned up breakfast, took a quick shower, and was at the clinic thirty minutes later. She had a few appointments in the afternoon (a ten-year nanodrone refresh, two wellness checkups), but her morning was free. She wondered if any of the *Liu Hui* soldiers would drop in for medical needs. So far none had. Their ship must have its own facilities and staff. Certainly it was large enough – at least tenfold the size of the mules.

It still wasn't clear who they *were*, exactly. Academic and civilian contacts on the *Liu Hui* claimed no knowledge, and the newsfeeds were scrubbed clean. Direct inquiries to governmental channels had gone unanswered. Lydia doubted an operation of such scale could be mounted privately, and the soldiers *seemed* like official military. She'd heard them refer to Foster as 'lieutenant.' But the *Zhōngyāng* hadn't yet fessed up to invading Earth.

The most mysterious character was the Squid Woman. Lydia had pored over the feeds of Adrian greeting her on the landing platform. Vanderplotz had knelt and *kissed her hand*. While Lydia had seen extreme body mods before, the coiling tentacles were in a class of their own. She wondered about the woman's origins, and how much of what Shane had speculated was true. Was she really hundreds of years old, a relic from the Corporate Age? The thought chilled her to her bones. People didn't change (well they did, but only superficially, not deep down) and to imagine a living mind from that brutal, twisted period of human history… it scared her. It might as well be Genghis Khan, or Stalin, or some other brutal genocidal maniac.

Adrian had promised to explain, but in the end he'd given them nothing. He'd ignored questions about the *Kǒngbù Wǔzéi* and the Squid Woman, instead lecturing them on the greater good of a Vandercamp 'independence movement,' as he called it. They were making history, he'd said. They were pioneers, world-builders, visionaries heralding in a golden age on the homeworld. She'd barely been able to keep a straight face, but he'd been earnest, even fervent. Adrian Vanderplotz had swallowed a dose of his own medicine. He'd become a true believer. He'd been better off as a cynical bullshitter. All evidence pointed to Adrian having lost control to this Squid Woman, whoever she was. *Kissing her hand.*

She spent a few minutes straightening up the clinic and checking inventory. They had stocked up on fab inks and printing resins at the mule station, but who knew when they would get more. In her lab nook, she pulled a sample box from cold storage, set it on her worktable, and keyed in the access code. With a hiss the lid slowly lifted, revealing the contents within.

The jet-black spider-bot, or whatever it was, was not as damaged as she'd remembered. The old man with the forked beard – Egil – had crushed it with his boot, but aside from a slight flattening, the machine hybrid seemed undamaged. Its legs, curled up in a dying spasm, were covered in fine threadlike hairs.

It was not the first time she'd opened the box. Several times over the past few months she'd begun the process, fully intending to dissemble the specimen and discover its origins. But each time she'd simply stared at the arachnid for a minute or two, then returned it to cold storage.

She didn't want to touch it.

Shane had asked her about the analysis. She'd lied, telling him she was proceeding cautiously. He'd mentioned that the boy had asked to be kept apprised. Should they tell Tem what they discovered? The question was moot; she hadn't discovered anything.

Suppressing her dread, she donned sterile gloves, goggles, and a surgical mask. Carefully, she lifted the specimen from the storage box and placed it, still supine, on her worktable. It was heavier than she expected; the thorax and abdomen yielded like meat. There was nothing robotic about it. She wondered if Shane's disruptor had malfunctioned after all.

For a moment she turned away to retrieve a case of surgical tools from a nearby cabinet. When she turned back, one of the spider's legs had half straightened. She held still, watching. The arachnid didn't move – it still looked dead. Perhaps she had accidentally straightened the leg herself when she'd placed the specimen on the worktable.

She opened the instrument case and removed a scalpel. Where to start? Her knowledge of spider anatomy was limited, and who even knew if this creature was designed along natural lines? Slicing open the large abdominal cavity would be reckless. Instead, she carefully scraped off a few hairs from one of the legs. She carefully dropped the black threads into a biosampler, then snapped the tube closed, autoactivating the analysis process.

There – at least she'd started. She stepped back, removing her mask and goggles. If the threads contained biological DNA, she'd soon know. The spider twitched.

She'd seen it. Two of the legs had moved. But now it was still again. She took another step back.

Slowly, the spider came to life. Its legs spasmed and flexed. It clawed at the air and squirmed. In a single twisting motion it righted itself, and turned to face her.

It was looking at her.

She looked for the scalpel. She'd placed it down on the worktable – too far to reach. The spider crouched, as if preparing to jump. She raised her fists. If it came at her she would punch it.

The spider leapt into the air. Lydia screamed and ducked. It soared *over* her head, landing on the floor behind her. It scuttled out of the nook.

Shit.

She crept around the partition separating her lab nook from the exam and treatment area. The spider was nowhere to be seen.

She heard the tinkle of a bell; the clinic door had opened. A small mocha-skinned boy, no older than five, was holding his elbow. His tears had dried but his eyes were still red-rimmed.

"Mateo, stay still," she said.

He ignored her instruction and rushed toward her, words tumbling from his mouth as he explained the circumstances leading up to his injury. She held her breath and watched the space near his feet.

Now he was standing before her, looking up, expecting a response.

"We'll get it cleaned up. Does it still hurt?" He nodded. "We'll put some numbing cream on it."

"What are you looking at, Miss Heliosmith?" he asked, turning to follow her gaze. The spider scuttled across the floor and out the door. "What was that? A spider?" He turned back to her. "A really, *really* big spider."

She shut the clinic door, then cleaned up Mateo's elbow. After he had calmed down she walked him back to the group of children he'd been playing with. She saw with relief that they weren't playing alone; two men she recognized were playing chess nearby. She considered saying something, but what?

She found Shane doing maintenance on one of the hovershuttles. A tall uniformed woman, a *Liu Hui* soldier, was sweeping the concrete floor of the shuttle bay. The woman smiled and nodded at Lydia. Lydia smiled back, tightly, and sidled up to Shane.

"Is it safe to talk here?" she asked. The woman was out of normal earshot, but that didn't guarantee their privacy.

"Depends on what you have to say," said Shane. "If you're asking about drones, assume we're being monitored. There's some new tech in town and it's beyond my scope."

"Is there somewhere we can go?"

Shane glanced at the woman, who continued to sweep the clean floor. "Let's go for a walk."

They were more than two kilometers from the field station before Shane even bothered to take out his scanning device. Lydia sat in the shade of a sprawling copse of eucalyptus while Shane squinted at the tiny screen.

"We *might* be in the clear," he said, "but I can't guarantee it."

"The spider came back to life," she blurted.

He raised his eyebrows. Under different circumstances she would have laughed at the exaggerated expression. "*That* spider?" he asked.

She told him what had happened, including every detail she could recall.

"What did the biosampler say?"

"It hadn't finished processing when I left with Mateo. It should be done by now."

"Any idea where it came from?"

"Shane, it seems completely biological. Is there any other explanation you can think of for the disruptor not working?"

Shane frowned. "Well…maybe synthetic biology…a shielded nervous system…." He lifted his eyes. "Have you ever heard of that kind of tech?"

"No. But the *Liu Hui* has leapfrogged us in that department. Did you notice their ship didn't have a fuel tank?"

"I did notice," he said. "And I'm pretty sure they've got gnat-sized surveillance drones. Or smaller. The single motes don't have sensors big enough to pick up anything significant, but with the right reconstruction or recombination algorithm…."

"Motes? They have surveillance dust?"

"Pretty much," said Shane. "Though I can't prove it. The samples I've captured keep disintegrating."

Shane sat next to her, almost touching, and together they looked out toward the mountainous horizon. After several minutes Shane broke the silence. "Do you think the Crucible subject…what did you call her? The Squid Lady?"

"What about her?"

"Could she have *made* the spider things?"

"On their ship? It's big, but it's not fab lab big."

Shane became more animated. "The spiders could have started out small. Egil is convinced they're carnivorous – he called them 'flesh eaters' – and said they were growing."

"Even so, she would have had to get them to the Harz region somehow. Is there a public manifest for their ship?"

"I doubt it. I don't even know what it's called. But maybe I can check satellite surveillance for something matching the description. Hold on – I'll send a hound." Shane closed his eyes, concentrating, then snapped them open a few seconds later. "Crap."

"What?"

"My clearance has been reduced. I wasn't notified."

"Who reduced your security?"

"No idea. It might have been automatic when I was demoted."

"Or maybe the Squid Woman doesn't want you accessing her flight records. Her tentacles might reach to the *Stanford*."

Shane's eyes widened. "You need to leave. If there *is* a connection between the Squid Woman and the spiders, and that specimen makes its way back to her…it's possible it already has."

She'd been having the same thought. "Will you come with me?" The words spilled out before she'd thought it through. What was she asking exactly? Come with her or come with her *and Xenus*? She didn't really know. The part of her mind that had spoken only knew that she wanted Shane.

Shane's expression hardened. "No. I promised Townes I'd stay."

She sighed, relieved the decision had been made for her. She'd tell Xenus; they'd leave together.

"We'll be the first ones testing Free Passage," she said. "Xenus and I," she added.

"No…you and Troy won't test it. You'll just leave. You won't tell anybody, and you won't ask anybody. We'll get you out tonight."

CHAPTER TWENTY-ONE

After a few weeks, Tem was beginning to get a feel for school, and he enjoyed many of the projects assigned to him. His team came in second place in the arbalest contest, winning in the distance category, placing third in accuracy, but performing dismally when it came to reload speed. For this failure Zinthia was furious with Bruno. Bruno blamed Abelton, who had been responsible for the winch mechanism, but Zinthia pointed out that imprecisions in the flight groove had hurt them even more, and *that* part of the design had fallen squarely in Bruno's court. Tem didn't care who won. He was delighted that his iron limbs had propelled the bolts hundreds of meters along the green length of the skirmish field, over and over again.

A group of Hair Lab engineers had taken an interest in their project. The volunteer dev team had built a makeshift forge on Tem's behalf. Instead of a charcoal-fueled furnace they had provided Tem with a blowtorch. The anvil and hammerheads they had cast from molten iron. The latter they mounted on woodish handles, printed to conform to Tem's grip. With such tools the work had gone quickly. Tem wondered what Farbror Trond and Farfar Jense would think of the blowtorch. He could see Jense's scowl in his mind, but his uncle might be more open minded. He asked the engineers if he could take the blowtorch with him on his next visit to Earth (they knew about Happdal – they even knew Trond by name!) but they pointed out that the fire-spitting tube would be useless as soon as the gas tank was depleted. They did let him keep the set of hammers, custom-fitted to his grip as they were.

His class would keep the same teams for the next assignment, a 'cultural exploration' field trip to the vast *Liu Hui* ringship. Tem feared that Zinthia's anger with Bruno would make them all miserable, but Bruno, after briefly reverting to his old ball-hogging habits on the soccer field, had since won back Zinthia's favor with disciplined play. Zinthia could be forgiving when her followers followed instructions, and Bruno was happy to do Zinthia's bidding as long as he ended up on the winning team. Tem wondered if the same was true of himself – was he a happy follower, or a leader in his own right?

"I think Zinthia likes you," Marcus said one day after music class. Tem was learning to play the drums, while Marcus had chosen violin.

"I think she finds me useful," said Tem.

"No, that's not it," Marcus insisted. "She likes you. I can tell from the way she looks at you when you're not looking."

"She does?"

"Yep."

At that moment Abelton joined them to ask Marcus a question about bow technique. Tem looked up and *did* see Zinthia looking at him from across the room. She looked away quickly and said something sharp to Shelley, who was holding her flute as if it were a club. Shelley sheepishly adjusted her grip.

★   ★   ★

In addition to reading, writing, math, music, history, terrestrial and lunar geography, and introductory science courses, Tem had taken to studying basic metallurgy in his spare time. He'd started by looking up simple terms like 'iron' and 'steel' on the library consoles, but conversations with the Hair Lab engineers advanced his learning in leaps and bounds. Now that he knew how to get there, he'd taken to exploring the lab and observing the open projects after school. The engineers who had helped him with the arbalest project were delighted to have a young charge eager to soak up information, and were as generous with their knowledge as Farfar Jense was stingy. Soon Tem knew the difference between alloys and intermetallics (in the latter, elements were not randomly distributed but took on a well-ordered structure). He learned the various properties of the major non-ferrous metals (copper, zinc, aluminum, titanium, tin, nickel, and lead), the malleability and durability of the classic monetary metals (silver, gold, platinum, and palladium), and the effects of blending small amounts of manganese, vanadium, or chromium with iron and carbon to create high tensile or stainless steel.

He began to tell the engineers what he knew of *godsteel*, if for no other reason than to brag. They listened with such fervent intensity that he wondered if he was betraying the Happdal smiths, and feigned ignorance when they asked detailed questions. What was the exact process by which this steel was forged? What temperatures were used? How was the crucible constructed? Tem said he didn't know – he was merely a bellows boy, not even an apprentice. This much was true, his elders had alluded to the Five Secrets but had hidden the actual makings from his young eyes. Still, he could have shown the engineers his godsteel blade. He chose not to.

Mother was curious. Why was he spending so much time at the Hair Lab? He turned the question back against her. Why had she been there herself? She changed the subject and their intentions remained unknown to each other. Secrets, again. Still, he was glad he had shown her the pattern. It was a great burden lifted from his shoulders. He missed Tante Katja, but he did not miss her obsession with the mysterious equation.

★ ★ ★

Morfar Shol cooked them a paella with saffron-red rice and fat shrimp from the greenhouse ponds. They brought the meal up to the rooftop, and though the sun mirrors had gone dark hours ago they still had a fine view of Main, a length of twinkling lights curving up to the arced horizon. Zinthia and her father, Svilsson, were guests. For the first time that week Mother was joining them for dinner. Something was wrong – Mother and Morfar would not look at each other. But both were putting on a good face for Tem and the others.

"Delicious," Zinthia said. She had a way of speaking to her elders as if…as if *she* were an elder. Maybe it was because her father said almost nothing, and she'd gotten used to speaking in his place.

"Thank you," said Morfar. "The saffron is from the *Alhazen*. Nobody has managed to make the crocuses thrive on the *Stanford*."

"Do you think we'll see exotic foods from Earth, once Repop is farther along?" Zinthia asked. Svilsson and Mother exchanged a look.

"What would you have, my dear?" Morfar Shol asked. "Wild boar? It's one thing to shuttle a few grams of spice between ringstations, another to blast a hundred kilos of meat out of the gravity well."

"Boar is delicious," said Tem, looking to Mother for confirmation. She nodded absentmindedly.

"Did people eat sharks?" Zinthia asked. "Or whales?"

"They did," said Morfar Shol, "though they shouldn't have."

"I'd like to see a blue whale," Zinthia said. "I wouldn't eat it."

"I hear your class is going to visit the *Liu Hui*," Mother said.

"Yes," Zinthia said, "and some of their children are coming to the *Stanford*. We'll be there for almost a week. Is Tem going? He said he didn't have permission yet."

Morfar Shol looked at his plate, busying himself with his rice. His grandfather had already agreed to the trip, but Mother had avoided his attempts to secure her permission. Mother leveled her gaze at Zinthia, but Zinthia refused to look away.

"I haven't yet decided," said Mother. "There's been some trouble between the *Stanford* and the *Liu Hui*, and that worries me."

"What are you worried about?" Zinthia asked. "Do you think they'll take us hostage?"

Mother sucked in her breath. It was a joke, but Zinthia had gone too far. Mother and Tem *had* been taken hostage; the memory was close and raw.

"Zinthia, that's a rude question," said Svilsson. "Please apologize."

"I'm sorry, Car-En." She seemed to mean it. Her skin looked paler than usual, and tears welled up in her eyes.

"I'll decide soon," Mother said. "I know you'd very much like him to go."

"Who'd like more paella?" Morfar asked, brandishing a giant woodish spoon.

After dinner they moved down to Morfar Shol's apartment. Zinthia and Tem were responsible for clearing the rooftop table, while Morfar Shol prepared dessert. That left Mother and Svilsson alone. He wondered what they would talk about. Would they talk at all?

"Why is your father so quiet?" Tem asked, carefully carrying the huge paella pan.

"He's not always quiet. Sometimes he has quite a lot to say. Especially when I'm in trouble."

"My mother usually gets quiet when she's angry. It's a little scary."

"Your mother *is* scary," Zinthia said, eyes going wide. "I mean, she's *nice* too. I don't mean I don't like her. It's just…."

"You'd want her on your side during a fight?"

"Exactly," said Zinthia, looking relieved.

"Have you ever been on another ringstation?" Tem asked.

"No. I've never left the *Stanford*. You're lucky, you know, that you've traveled so much."

"I grew up my whole life in a small village!"

"But you've lived on Earth! There are only a few people who've lived on both Earth and in space. You're one of them."

Tem thought on this while they cleared the remaining dishes. Somehow living in a different place changed you. He hadn't meant to change, but he was no longer the same boy who had lived in the village, thinking only of becoming a smith. After seeing what was possible at the Hair Lab, the Happdal smithy seemed cramped and limited. He would always enjoy pounding iron, but the engineers had shown him miraculous materials: carbonlattice, metallic foams, conchiolin-mineral matrixes, transparent alumina, ultralight nickel sponge, chameleon fabrics, hydrophobic coatings, intelligent gels, vantablack surfaces, and plastimuscle. Some nights his mind assembled these parts into unusual weapons or armor, or vehicles, or even dwellings, and in the morning he scrambled to draw the fading contents of his mind's eye. Other times the visions prevented sleep. He was working up the courage to show his designs to the Hair Lab engineers.

He felt guilty, and still loyal to the boy who had had such powerful convictions. But he'd changed; he no longer felt the same desires. He would not abandon his family or his village, but his imagined future, making fine godsteel swords in the smithy for the rest of his days, was no longer clear. Now there was only fog.

"What are you thinking about?" Zinthia asked.

"My village. Earth."

"Are you homesick?"

"A little. I miss my father and my uncle. But mostly I worry that they miss me."

Zinthia nodded. "Parents miss their children more than the other way around."

Morfar Shol had baked raspberry tarts. They were small, but there were enough so that they each had their own, with three left over. Mother, Morfar, and Svilsson drank coffee; Zinthia and Tem drank spiced tea.

"I have something to say," Mother said. She hadn't yet touched her dessert. "I'm going to visit Earth."

"When are we going?" Tem asked.

"I'm going alone. It's still not safe for you in Happdal."

He had expected her to say that, but he wasn't going to give up without a fight. "I can defend myself. I have my own blade now."

"Your father killed Völund. Svein will be looking for retribution. You could be targeted."

"So could you. So could Father."

She nodded. "That's true. But I'm going to…." She trailed off and looked at Svilsson.

"Going to what?" Tem asked.

"You have work to do here," said Morfar Shol. "Your studies, for one thing, and if you return to Earth, who will represent Happdal to the councils?"

"I'd come back!" Tem said. Then, to Mother: "How long will you be gone?" His voice had a tremor he couldn't quash. Someone was touching his hand, squeezing it. Zinthia.

"No more than a few weeks," Mother said.

"I'm coming with you."

Mother, Morfar, and Svilsson looked at him with kind eyes. That made him angry; they did not even respect him enough to argue with him. He pushed the last of his dessert away dramatically and somewhat reluctantly, and stood. Zinthia pulled her hand back as if she'd been shocked. "You can't control me anymore. I have friends, you know." The words sounded ridiculous as they left his mouth. He was thinking of the engineers from the Hair Lab. Only a few had learned his name. "Powerful friends. I'll go to Earth if I want to!" He stormed off to his bedroom and slammed the door. For a long time he sat on his bed, but nobody came. He picked up a picture book but was too distracted to read the English words. There was a soft knock on the door.

"Go away," he said, not meaning it.

"May I come in?" It was Morfar. He'd been hoping for Mother. After a polite pause Morfar opened the door and sat on the bed.

"Are Zinthia and her father still here?"

"They went home. They said goodnight."

"I'm still hungry."

"Do you want another tart?"

Tem came to the kitchen and he and Morfar sat in a small nook and each ate another tart.

"Your mother will miss you. But she has to do this."

"Why? Because she misses Father? He could come here to visit."

"She's still grieving, you know. That's why she's been acting…that's why she might have seemed distant."

"Grieving?" It took him a moment to realize what Morfar was talking about. "Oh."

"For me, Marivic died a long time ago. But for Car-En it just happened."

"I'm sorry I stormed off at dinner."

"It's okay. Are you ready for bed now?"

Tem brushed his teeth and changed for bed, then went to Mother's room and quietly opened the door. At first he didn't see her. She was wearing a shimmering skinsuit, camouflaged to match the soothing amber tones of her bedroom. As his eyes adjusted he noticed the skinsuit was enhanced with external joints, and thin bands running parallel to her muscles. An elongated container or scabbard was affixed to each forearm. Mother was watching herself in the mirror, flexing her limbs experimentally. The suit looked lethal, and for a moment he saw not Mother but Car-En. Car-En instilled fear; he'd seen it in Zinthia's face. Quickly and quietly he closed the door.

An image came to his mind, blood spilling from Völund's throat, opened by Father's blade. Would Svein die the same way, at Mother's hand? Was Mother returning to Earth to take vengeance? Did he come from a family of killers?

Not killers…warriors. If Svein died the jarl would get what he deserved.

He returned to his bedroom and lay in the dark for what seemed like hours. When he finally slept it was a deep and dreamless slumber. He woke to the sounds of Mother and Morfar Shol eating breakfast. He rushed out to see them.

"Good morning!" Morfar said. "We called your name but you didn't wake up." It was a Saturday; there was no school. Tem shoved his tablet in Mother's face.

"Can you please give me permission to go on the field trip? I really want to go."

Surprised by his enthusiastic request, she smiled and touched her thumb to the tablet.

CHAPTER TWENTY-TWO

The clinic was Lydia's first stop. She eased open the door, listening intently, peering into the dark interior. Leaving the lights off, she crept to her lab nook. An indicator light on the biosampler glowed green.

The results indicated a synthetic sample – no DNA or RNA – but the black hairs scraped from the spider's leg *did* have a biological cellular structure. The spectral analysis revealed elements normally present in animal hair (carbon, silicon, sulfur), but also unusually high amounts of boron, iron, titanium, vanadium, and lead.

So…artificial life. The evidence pointed to something that had been *grown*. But who had grown it, and to what purpose?

She thought back to her encounter with the spider. Had it attacked her or not? She couldn't be sure; it might simply have been trying to escape. Shane thought the spiders might have been created by the Squid Woman. But why? They were too big for spying, especially if the *Liu Hui* soldiers were already using surveillance *dust*. The old villager – Egil – was sure the spiders were carnivorous, but maybe they killed only in self-defense, or to eat. How intelligent were they? How did they communicate?

She sent off the results to the *Stanford*'s general research archives, tagging the results *unknown synthetic lifeform*, and *Harz Mountains region*. As an afterthought she added *black tree*, and *Squid Woman*.

When she returned to her dome, Xenus looked up from a table cluttered with tablets.

"Where've you been? I was starting to worry."

He hadn't been worried enough to ping her. She caught herself – maybe he had. She'd gone dark as soon as Shane had warned her.

"Xenus, we have to leave. Tonight."

"What? Why? We can't leave…people are looking up to us."

He meant that people were looking up to *him*. And it was true. But still, maybe leaving AFS-1 was the best thing he could do. Let the residents of the field station see for themselves if Free Passage was a reality or a false promise.

"The spider came back to life and escaped from the lab. And Shane thinks the Squid Woman made the spiders, and that it's going to make its way back to her, and that we're in danger." It sounded like nonsense when she said it aloud. Xenus blinked rapidly, uncomprehending. For the next ten minutes she explained what had happened, in detail.

She put on some tea while Xenus paced around the dome. "Even if the spiders are somehow connected to the *Liu Hui*, to this…Squid Woman…why do you think we're in danger? They're bending over backward to make this a *peaceful* coup. Today I had a work crew of elite soldiers shoveling shit as if it was their true calling in life. Not a single complaint."

"We don't know who the Squid Woman is, or what she's capable of. Just because she hasn't killed anybody yet doesn't mean she won't."

"Well, okay," said Xenus, "I guess that's true. But we have to go on the evidence here. She hasn't given any indication of aggressive behavior…."

"She's displayed nothing but *dominant* behavior, which promises aggression if challenged. She made Adrian kiss her hand."

"She didn't *make* him. I saw the feed."

"He felt *compelled* to kiss her hand. This is Adrian we're talking about. When have you ever seen him defer to anybody? Look, they're armed to the teeth. No matter how peaceful they act, we're in a dangerous situation. The Head of Security is telling us to get out now. I think we should heed his advice."

Xenus looked as if he were about to say *Interim* Head of Security, but instead shook his head. His lips moved as he paced and thought. "What about everybody else? Just leave them behind?"

"If we leave, maybe anyone can leave."

"So we go openly? We don't try to sneak out? Because I thought that's what you were implying."

She had been implying just that. Shane had already worked out a plan to get them on a hovershuttle and two hundred kilometers away before anyone noticed. But Xenus was right. They wouldn't test Free Passage by sneaking off.

"Fine. We go openly."

"To where? The OETS station? And back to the *Stanford*?"

She nodded. "We'll be safe there. I'll let Petra and Javier know to expect us."

Twenty minutes later they were in the Shell talking with Regis Foster and a slight, tense-looking man named Chiang. Foster was leaning forward, elbows on the lacquered wooden round table, smiling at them condescendingly.

"We're leaving," Xenus repeated. "And we're leaving tonight. We're not asking permission – we're merely informing you as a courtesy. And you should know we've already made our intentions public."

Foster sighed. "I, along with everyone else, received your message. But it's not too late to change your mind. The community will be negatively impacted if you leave. Xenus, you're the key link unifying the settlers and the *Liu Hui* forces – your protectors. The work crews you've organized are about more than the work itself. It's the relationships that are important. People can see that we're here to help, not to take over. Have any of my crew complained, or caused trouble?"

"No," Xenus admitted, "but...."

"So continue to help us. A few more days at least. I'm asking...don't go yet. We need you. You're not going to make me beg, are you? I'm a proud man, Xenus Troy." Foster grinned. He was charismatic; Lydia found that part of her wanted to go along with his suggestion. She glanced at Chiang. The other man was sitting up rigidly, his attention elsewhere, eyes twitching in their sockets as if tracking an invisible fly.

Xenus stood. "We're going now. Thank you for meeting with us on such short notice." Lydia hurriedly stood up too.

Foster leaned back in his chair and sighed. "Well, if you insist. We can't stop you. Please take whatever food and other provisions you need. May I ask where you're going?"

"To the OETS station," Lydia said.

Foster raised an eyebrow, feigning surprise. "That's a long walk."

"We'll be taking one of the hovershuttles," said Xenus tensely.

Foster shook his head slowly. "There are only three hovershuttles for the entire settlement. I'm afraid we can't spare one."

Xenus was ready. "Then send an escort with us. One of your crew can fly the shuttle back to AFS-1 after dropping us off at the mule station."

Regis narrowed his eyes. Chiang brought his attention back to the meeting, clearing his throat.

"You have something to say?" Foster said, with an irritated glance at Chiang.

"Mr. Troy and Ms. Heliosmith make a reasonable proposal. I will assign a pilot to escort them. Are the hovershuttles difficult to operate?"

"Not at all," said Lydia. "I could teach someone the basics in ten minutes."

"And you won't wait until daylight? Your trip would be much safer." Chiang twisted his lips in what might have been an attempt at a smile.

"We'll use the luminators," Xenus said curtly. "We've traveled at night before. It's not a problem."

"Very well," said Chiang. "Someone will meet you at the shuttle bay shortly. I wish you a safe and pleasant voyage."

★　★　★

Xenus had lied – they'd never traveled at night in the hovershuttle. Lydia flew the craft slowly, less than fifty kph, using both the luminators and sonar to navigate. Every so often the high-lumen beams caught the reflective eyes of a ground mammal, frozen blind. They were flying high enough to ignore the fauna; mostly she concentrated on not flying into a tree or a cliff.

Mèng, their escort, sat quietly on the rear bench. They had waited alone in the shuttle bay for nearly twenty minutes, loaded, armored, and ready to go. Mèng had arrived, alone, just as they had decided to leave on their own. Lydia had persuaded Xenus to wait a little longer – it would be better if they could leave on good terms, and it was true that the research station needed all three hovershuttles, especially if the *Liu Hui* soldiers *did* allow Free Passage.

Mèng showed up right before their discussion escalated into an argument. She was young and not quite as tall as the other *Liu Hui* soldiers, though still a half head taller than Lydia. "I am Mèng. I will be escorting you to the OETS station."

★　★　★

As they coasted through a narrow valley, Xenus turned in his seat to face Mèng. "Are you warm enough? We can raise the envirodome if you like."

"My uniform regulates my temperature," Mèng said. Her black hair was tied in a single braid hanging straight down her back.

"You can relax," Xenus said. "It's a few hours at least to the OETS station. Longer, since we're traveling at night. You can sleep if you want."

"Thank you."

"Tell us about your ship. I've never seen anything like it."

Xenus had previously asked members of the *Liu Hui* work crews about the ship, but had received only polite evasions. Lydia didn't expect anything different from Mèng. The girl (she couldn't be older than twenty) seemed nervous, sitting up straight and speaking only when spoken to. She displayed none of the ease and casual camaraderie of the other *Liu Hui* soldiers.

"The *Iarudi* is an Alcubierre Class Versatile Transport," Mèng said. Lydia gripped the steering stick. Mèng had revealed more in one sentence than they'd learned in all the weeks since the invaders had arrived.

"Part of the *Kǒngbù Wǔzéi* fleet?" Xenus asked casually. His tone was perfect. She'd forgotten how skillfully manipulative Xenus could be. He hadn't been elected to Repop, or assigned as Research Coordinator, accidentally.

Mèng nodded. "Yes."

"Alcubierre Class...I haven't heard of that. New propulsion system?"

"Space compression."

"As in wormholes?" Xenus continued to sound mildly curious – a clever tactic. But Lydia was beginning to suspect there was something else going on beyond Xenus's disarming charm. Mèng was being far too forthcoming.

"Yes, the *Iarudi* is capable of generating a negative mass field."

"How fast can it go?"

"Conventional speeds, through compressed spacetime. Relative to its point of departure, the *Iarudi* moves superluminally." Mèng's voice was calm, matter-of-fact. Lydia had to concentrate to keep her eyes on the terrain ahead; she wanted to turn and stare at Mèng.

"How *much* faster than light, at maximum speed?" Xenus asked.

"I don't have access to that data. I'm only Second Navigator."

Silence. Lydia started to speak – she was going to suggest they stop and camp until dawn – but she stopped herself.

"Mèng?" said Xenus.

"Yes?"

"Are your feeds on?"

"No. I went dark about five minutes ago. When you started asking me questions."

All three of them were silent. Even without the cool breeze on her face, Lydia would have been wide awake from anticipation alone.

"Mèng," Xenus asked calmly, "are you defecting?"

Mèng responded without missing a beat. "If the *Stanford* offers me protection I will continue to answer questions."

"Did you just decide this?"

"I…yes. I've been looking for an opportunity. I volunteered to be your escort."

"Are we in danger? Does going dark put us in danger?"

"It will raise suspicions."

"Turn your feeds back on. I'll stop asking you questions."

Lydia stole a glance at Xenus. He was once again facing forward, staring out at the luminated terrain with a pensive expression.

"Should we stop and camp for a few hours?" Lydia suggested. "I could use some rest."

"Let's switch and keep going," Xenus said. "I'd like to make it to the OETS station before dawn."

★   ★   ★

She awoke on the back bench of the shuttle, cramped and dehydrated. Someone had covered her with a reflective metallic blanket; at least she was warm. She sat up and blinked, trying to acclimate to the daylight. It was well past dawn.

The shuttle was grounded in a flat meadow that might once have been farmland. To the east there was a distant mountain range, to the west gentle hills and a rocky outcropping jutting high into the sky. Mèng was making tea on a small electric stove, a few meters from the shuttle.

"Where's Xenus?" she asked. Mèng pointed to some shrubs twenty meters away. He was taking a piss. "Got it. So, Mèng, do you have a first name?"

Mèng pronounced a long vowel that Lydia's translator thought might mean 'feather.'

"I'm Lydia Heliosmith. Okay to just keep calling you Mèng?"

"That's fine."

She got up, stretched, and wandered over to Xenus. He was standing, hands on hips, staring at the towering rocks to the west. She hoped Mèng was out of earshot, but she couldn't rule out enhanced hearing or microscopic drones.

"Do you trust her?"

"Does it matter? She's either going to try to stop us or she's not."

"Why did we stop?"

"I nearly ran us into those rocks," said Xenus, pointing west. "I needed some rest."

She nodded – so he didn't trust Mèng – at least not enough to let her pilot the shuttle.

"Do you think she's telling the truth about their ship?"

"It's plausible. Engineers on the *Liu Hui* have been chasing negative mass fields for decades. Maybe they finally got somewhere."

"Wouldn't we have heard about it?"

Xenus shrugged. "Research transparency is the ideal, but a functional negative mass drive could upset the balance of power within the Coalition."

"Maybe it already has," Lydia said. "Our research station was just invaded."

"And not a drop of blood spilt. We didn't put up much of a fight."

"Do you think we should have?"

"I think we *are*," Xenus pointed out. "As of a few hours ago, we're harboring a defector. Given what she's already told us about the *Iarudi*, they might even consider her to be a traitor."

"Let's get going. I'll feel better once we reach the OETS station." She brought up an area map in her m'eye. They were about one hundred twenty kilometers south of their destination. The mountains she'd seen to the east were the Harz, home to the village of Happdal and the other 'Five Valleys' peoples. The rocky outcropping Xenus had nearly collided with had once been called the Externsteine. They were surrounded by the ruins of German villages and towns.

"Are your feeds off?" Xenus asked.

"I'm completely dark."

Xenus was watching Mèng. The girl sat on the ground, facing the towering rock formations, drinking tea.

"We could be starting a war here."

Lydia put her arms over his shoulders and kissed his unshaven cheek. His eyes were tired and bloodshot from the night flying. *War.* What did that even mean, between the ringstations? It was an archaic Industrial-Corporate Age term. But she shared his unease in regards to Mèng.

"Don't think about it," she said. "Let's just go. I'll fly the shuttle."

Lydia piloted the hovershuttle over forested green hills. Xenus had tried and failed to sleep, and was now back to questioning Mèng. At first he'd just stared at her, saying nothing, until she'd told him her feeds were off.

"I haven't seen you on any of the work crews," Xenus said. "You said you were a navigator?"

"Yes. I served on the ship."

"And the woman with the...cybernetic arms. Who's she?"

"Commander Umana. You can refer to them as tentacles. She does so herself."

"Does she have authority over Foster? And Chiang?"

"Chiang serves the Commander directly. Foster is ostensibly in charge of the mission – he reports directly to the *Zhōngyāng.*"

"So Foster isn't a squid?"

"No, he's regular Peace and Order. *Jūnshì,* not *Kǒngbù Wǔzéi.*"

"And what *is* the mission exactly?"

"To preserve the autonomy of the Vandercamp settlement, to prevent revanchism by the *Stanford.*"

"But we didn't ask for your help." Perhaps because of fatigue, Xenus was unable to conceal the bitterness in his voice.

"Your leadership *did* request our help," Mèng retorted.

"Adrian Vanderplotz acted unilaterally and without consent!"

"Xenus!" Lydia snapped. "Remember what's going on here."

Xenus muttered something and turned back in his seat. He busied himself with the touch display.

"Sorry, Mèng," Lydia said. "It was a long night."

"Hmm," Xenus said, a few moments later.

"What?"

"Proximity sensors are…we've got something tailing us. Five things, in fact."

"How big are they?" she asked. "Vehicles?"

"No, drone sized. They're closing fast."

"Does this craft possess security countermeasures?" Mèng asked calmly.

"Sort of," Lydia said. "Insect-sized surveillance drones, but in a pinch they can—"

"Deploy them," said Mèng, still icily calm, "immediately. Increase velocity to maximum and drop altitude."

"What's on us?" Xenus asked.

"Please act quickly," Mèng said. "We don't have much time."

Lydia looked over her shoulder. "I can't drop much lower." They were soaring over a close evergreen canopy.

"Descend to the lowest possible altitude. Please deploy the counter-measures."

Keeping one hand on the steering stick, Lydia opened the storage compartment and grabbed a handful of insect-bots, simultaneously issuing a *seek-and-destroy* command via her m'eye (*target* whatever objects were trailing them, *exclude* biological life forms). Each drone contained a few grams of concentrated explosives. It wasn't much, but it was all they had. The drones squirmed in her hand and buzzed to life as she tossed them over her shoulder. Out of the corner of her eye she saw Xenus turn to face their pursuers.

"If you can see them, we're already dead," Mèng said. "Watch the display."

"See *what*?"

"Lances. Commander Umana's favorite toy."

They cleared the trees. Lydia dropped the shuttle twenty meters in a single sickening plunge. An explosive pop from behind them was followed by a fainter echo in front. "Did we get one?"

"Confirmed," said Xenus, hunched over the display. "Only four in pursuit."

"We should evacuate," Mèng said, no longer sounding quite so calm.

"You mean stop the shuttle?" Lydia gripped the steering stick tightly with both hands, getting as much speed as she could out of the fully loaded hovershuttle. Evasive maneuvers probably wouldn't work; if the lances were at all intelligent they would triangulate a shorter path based on her turns.

"No," Mèng said, getting up in her seat.

"What are you—" Xenus reached out and grabbed Mèng's wrist. With a quick twist of her arm Mèng escaped his grasp and leapt from the shuttle in a smooth swan dive. Lydia gasped. They were going over two hundred kilometers per hour.

"Slow down!" Xenus yelled, crouching in his seat.

With a m'eye command she activated the autopilot, telling it to slow to one hundred kph. The quick deceleration slammed her into the dashboard.

"Now!"

She clambered to her feet and leapt from the craft. Her body armor tightened and expanded, deploying a neck wrap and temporary inflatable helmet. She soared through the air toward a patch of tall grass. *No trees, at least.* She closed her eyes. The impact was painless. She rolled once, twice, five times.

★   ★   ★

She lay on her back, the clear blue sky above. She was alive, and as far as she could tell, in one piece. How much time had passed? A rude explosive boom violated the silence. She closed her eyes and watched the insides of her eyelids for a while (a warm orange, lit by the bright sun). Experimentally, she wiggled her toes. They felt like they were wiggling, but she couldn't be sure until she took a look. That would require sitting up and taking off her boots – too much effort. She would rest a few more minutes.

★   ★   ★

Someone was standing over her, trying to wake her up. It was Mèng. The sky had darkened. She was cold.

Mèng's lips were moving.

"What?" she asked. "Speak up."

"You're concussed," Mèng said, shining the light of a thousand suns directly into her eyes.

"Stop!" She batted Mèng's light away.

"Nothing broken as far as I can tell," continued Mèng. "Your armor saved you."

"I'm fine," said Lydia. "Where's Xenus?"

"You're not quite fine," Mèng said. "I'm going to give you something."

"No thank you," Lydia said, but the *Liu Hui* soldier was already pressing something into her neck.

"Relax," Mèng said. "We made it."

"The Squid Woman won't be happy," said Lydia woozily, drifting back to sleep.

CHAPTER TWENTY-THREE

Egil climbed to the top of the viewing rock and arranged his belongings: lunch (bread, cheese, and pickled vegetables), a wool blanket, his knife, his oaken staff, and the long Builder spyglass. Egil felt a stab of guilt as he carefully handled the long bronze tube. Jarl Haakon, Svein's father, had stolen the Builder artifact from a Happdal lookout boy, years ago. The boy, Jesper, would be a grown man by now, if Haakon had not murdered him. Eventually, Egil told himself, he would return it to Esper of Happdal; it was Arik's son who had originally discovered the spyglass in the nearby ruins. But right now Egil needed the device.

Once everything was arranged to his satisfaction, Egil spent a few minutes cleaning and polishing the spyglass. He'd only recently learned the Builder name of the ruins where Esper Ariksson had found it. He'd discovered an ancient but well-preserved book with the names of towns and cities written out, and maps showing their locations. The mountains – the Builders had called them the *Harz* – had not changed so much over the centuries. Nor had the rivers. The Begna had been called the *Sieber*. The ruins to the east of Happdal, where Esper had found the spyglass, had once been a town called *Braunlage*. From the looks of the faded pictures, it had not been a serious town, but rather a place for men and women to cavort and drink *öl* and ski the winter snow. Where were they going, on their skis? Nowhere – it seemed they glided about for sport. Down the mountain, then back up again by way of a machine.

Egil set up the three-legged base and attached the spyglass. Even without it he could see that the spiders were active this morning. Active, and larger: each was now the size of a dog. The Black Tree continued to sprawl outwards (though up, very little – the central mass still resembled a stump). The tips of the black tendrils stretched almost to the base of the viewing rock. Fortunately the spiders tended to cluster near the central mass, paying Egil little mind as long as he was quiet. He doubted his high perch would provide protection if they decided to attack, but at least he could see clearly. If they killed him – well, there were only so many years left in his life to steal. His best days were behind him.

No, that was a lie. He still loved life. And his hunger for knowledge was greater than ever. He wished to visit the ringship while he still had some strength. Tall Alvis of Happdal had told him the sky woman had said that the ringship might welcome visitors. Was it true? To the north, there was a land port with a flying ship that could take you there. Or so the rumor went.

Had the sky people created the spiders? It was a likely explanation, though the sky folk he'd met – Lydia and Shane – had sworn no knowledge of the creatures. They'd seemed sincere. But there were *other* groups of sky people who might be responsible. The *Stanford* was not the only ringship.

He peered through the spyglass. Disconcertingly, one of the spiders appeared to be staring directly back at him. How good was their vision? What were their thoughts? Could they distinguish his face from others they had seen? Black-haired Saga, for example; did they recognize her? Völund's niece had accompanied him many times on his spying expeditions. Today she worked at the smithy. Saga's skills were meager, but she was getting stronger. She was as close to a smith as Kaldbrek had, now that her uncle was dead. Völund's death was a hardship, not just for the girl but for all the villagers, but the brute had gotten what he deserved. He should have let the boy go at the first opportunity. Egil could not fault Esper for cutting the smith's throat in order to rescue his own son. Egil wished Esper had killed Svein, too, while he was busy killing. Then Kaldbrek could start anew.

And who would be jarl if Svein were dead? Egil himself? He could probably win over the villagers, if he so chose. Egil had a gift: his voice was not pretty, but it could not be ignored. When he spoke, men tended to confuse Egil's words with their own thoughts. Women were not so easy to sway, but neither could they turn away when Egil spoke or recited a poem.

But no, he didn't want to be jarl. Nor would he be a good one. He preferred to advise, then wander the woods alone, left to his own thoughts. A jarl needed to be *there*, above all, surrounded by the folk. Such a life would stifle Egil.

Maybe it was time for a woman to lead. Such a thing was not unheard of. Vaggabœr had done well with Hulda as jarl, and Heidrun before her.

Egil returned his attention to the spyglass, chiding himself for wasting time on such musings. Svein was jarl now, and there was no good way to get rid of him. Svein's death would bring no goodness or joy to Kaldbrek. Young Karl Hinriksson had slain Svein's father, Haakon, and what good had that done? Like a wooden doll within a wooden doll, Haakon's evil son had become jarl. Not a soul in the wretched village had cared.

The spider *was* looking at him. And not just the one; several had frozen still and were staring at him.

Why did Egil care about Kaldbrek at all? He had no close family there, only a few distant cousins. He was better known and loved in Skrova, where he'd lived and made friends.

The truth? He'd been called back to Kaldbrek because of his poems and tales. The people, even if dull and benumbed to abuse, loved to hear about themselves and their ancestors – in Egil's voice. When he spoke or sang, they lost themselves. Svein, tyrant as he was, had known enough to give the villagers back their stories. Egil's exile had been rescinded.

He sat up and stroked his beard. Why were the spiders drawn to the Black Tree? He'd come across the mysterious black root structure years ago. On each visit to the high ridge he'd found the Black Tree larger, and exuding more heat. If anything, animals and insects gave it wide berth. Then, one summer day, he found the spiders swarming over the hot black tendrils. They'd made it their home. But why?

Suddenly the swarm of arachnids moved, westward, in the direction of Kaldbrek. Within a minute the Black Tree was as bare as he'd ever seen it. Only one oversized spider remained behind, watching him. His throat tightened as the swarm descended over the ridge toward his home village.

Were they, in fact, headed toward Kaldbrek? If that was the case he must warn them. Perhaps he could outrun the swarm. He was old, but he knew the way to Kaldbrek as well as any man or beast.

The lone remaining spider raised a forelimb. *Stay*, it seemed to say.

A sentinel.

Experimentally, Egil moved to the edge of the lookout rock. The spider scurried forward, but froze as soon as Egil stopped moving. He moved back to the center of the rock; the creature's posture relaxed.

A plan formed in his mind.

After a minute of searching he found what he needed. Slowly, he retreated to the back edge of the lookout rock. The spider matched him step for step, advancing. Soon, as he had planned, their mutual line of sight was broken. Now he must act quickly.

Crouching, he positioned himself at the top of the boulder's eastern slope. Several large stones at the base formed a set of natural steps. It was not the only way to clamber up, but it was the way he always came. A spider could probably climb any of the rock's sheer faces. He could only hope his foe would choose this route.

He heard a scurrying, scraping sound, and loose gravel hitting rock. Nervously, he glanced over his shoulder. Where were the sounds coming from?

The spider appeared directly below him. He had one chance.

He lifted the heavy rock above his head and hurled it down. Even as it left his hands he knew his aim was off.

The rock smashed into the dirt and rolled a short distance. The spider screamed – a terrible shrieking sound. He hadn't missed entirely – he'd taken out a leg.

The seven-legged spider scrambled up the rocks. Had he thought dog-sized? This one was more the size of a wolf. Egil grabbed his oaken staff.

He closed his eyes and swung the heavy stick. A vivid picture filled his mind's eye: long ago, he had swung his staff at Einar the Lame's skull, collapsing it like a rotten pumpkin. Would this be his last thought? Oh well.

Egil fell back on his butt, waiting for the poisoned fangs to sink into his calf or thigh. He felt nothing. He opened his eyes. The spider was nowhere to be found.

Clambering down the rock, the bard found the huge black creature sprawled out dead. His staff had connected with the foul thing's head, smashing three of its eight eyes into a slimy pulp.

"Ha!" Egil said. "Take that!"

But there was no time to waste. It was time to run like a much younger man.

★   ★   ★

He emerged from the brush scratched and bruised, his left ankle sprained, at least one rib cracked. He'd fallen twice. His chest ached, his lungs were raw, and his skin was slippery with sweat. Worst of all, he was too late.

He heard the screams of women and children. Even as he ran into the village, a young woman ran past him the other way, clutching a baby in one arm and dragging a toddler with the other. *Hide in the woods and survive.* Ten paces ahead a small boy writhed in terror, pinned by a spider. The beast sunk its black fangs into the child's neck. Nearby, a man lay facedown in the dirt. The back of his skull was missing.

He forced his dead legs to move. The spider reared back from its young prey. Egil swung his staff, eyes open this time, but the creature scurried back, hissing. Another man, Uffe the furrier, lunged forward and thrust his longspear into the beast's abdomen. The steel spearhead emerged coated in yellow slime.

"Grab a weapon, old man!" shouted Uffe. "You'll need more than your stick to fight these things." Uffe sprinted off in the direction of the well circle, toward the village center. Egil knelt by the boy. The lad was breathing laboriously; his skin was darkening blue. By the time Egil clasped his small hand, the boy's short life had ended. *Poison, then – and fast-acting.*

Egil stood, strangely calm. His sprint down the mountain had exhausted him so thoroughly that even the call of battle could not raise his blood. Still, he would fight. He had no choice.

Black shapes scurried in the corners of his vision. The dead were everywhere: mostly children, women, and the old. Thankfully, the spiders were not feeding. The blue corpses had not been eaten or torn apart. Maybe they would eat later, after the killing was done.

A boar-sized spider blocked his path. A rustling behind him – two more blocked his retreat. So it would be here and now that he died. Not without a fight. He raised his staff.

Machines, the sky man had said. The spiders were minions. But who did they serve?

A black monstrosity leapt at his face, fangs open and dripping. It hit him with explosive force. He tumbled backward. Quickly, there were two more explosions. He was covered in yellow slime and ropy black hairs.

Was he bitten? He wiped the goo from his eyes. A black shadow leapt away.

A *human* shadow.

The three spiders were dead, strewn to bits all around him. He was alive, filthy but uninjured. He coughed and wretched, disgusted. The smell was vile.

Someone had helped him. A shadow warrior.

With new energy he ran toward the well circle. He heard the shouts of men fighting, and inhuman shrieks in return. He heard more sharp retorts, and felt a glimmer of hope.

He reached the village center. Mayhem. Dozens of fallen men, poisoned blue. But the enemy was fractured, decreasing in number. He saw the shadow again, a swift movement to his left. A hallucination, induced by fatigue and terror? No, he was covered in sticky evidence. *The spider had exploded even as it leapt at him.*

He saw Jarl Svein plunge the point of his godsteel blade into the maw of a spider. If there was one man he would not mourn today, should he fall and turn blue.... If he could trade the dead boy's life for Svein's dark soul, he would do it in a heartbeat. The jarl saw him and yelled out.

"Fight, bard! If you care for your village and your kin, fight!"

A blast of light and sound drove Egil back. He forced his eyes open, but saw only blurry shapes. Five sharp retorts assaulted his ears in rapid succession, some overlapping. A fine yellow mist filled the air.

A single black spider crouched before Svein. The rest were dead, leaving a foul mess of remains. Behind the jarl, the air shimmered. For an instant Egil saw a woman, knife raised in the air. Then nothing – she was gone. The black abomination leapt at Svein. The jarl ducked and spun, lashing out with his blade. Two of the spider's severed legs sailed through the air. The wounded creature fell, stumbled, and came at Egil. He brought his staff down. Energy coursed through his old muscles. He was illuminated by rage.

"Die!"

The oaken cudgel connected with the spider's abdominal section, ejecting a pulse of thick ocher fluid. He struck it again and again.

"You killed it, bard." The jarl patted his shoulder, grinning. Svein's breath was foul, his teeth yellow, one black with rot.

"Where did she go?" Egil asked.

"Who, old man?"

"The woman. The shadow. She killed them. Didn't you see it? Didn't you hear it?"

Svein looked around, surveying the blue corpses. He shook his head. "A whole life of reciting divine poetry, and you don't recognize the work of the Red Brother? He blesses us, bard."

"No, this is not a god's handiwork."

Svein smiled, but his eyes bored into Egil. "Did you hope to see me poisoned today, like my father before me?"

Egil bit his lip. "No, my jarl. I rejoice that you live."

Svein looked away. "Let us gather the dead and prepare the pyre."

Egil sat on a low stone wall and watched the others work. No one dared scold him for sloth – the villagers feared the man with the forked beard as much as they craved his stories. Twenty-two dead, another nine injured. Of the spiders, less than a dozen had been slain by steel. The rest had been killed by the shadow.

Someone had sat down next to him. Saga, Völund's niece. The girl's face was smeared with dirt and blood.

"Who was she?" asked the girl.

"You saw her?"

"We'd be dead without her," Saga said. "One of the sky people?"

"It had to be," Egil said. "Though Svein seems to think the Red Brother kept us alive."

"I don't believe in the gods."

"What do you believe in?"

"Fire and steel. Wheat and water."

"The sky people are like gods," Egil said.

"But they're not." The girl spat in the dirt. "They're flesh and blood, like us."

"I'm not so sure," said Egil. "Those creatures that attacked us today – they were *made*. Crafted."

"But you saw their insides – they bled yellow."

"Even so. They were not natural."

Saga snorted disrespectfully. He didn't mind; her lack of fear was refreshing. "You don't know every creature that dwells in the mountains. How can you know what is natural and what is not?"

Egil nodded. "You're right, I *wouldn't* know, except that the sky people told me. They saw the spiders too."

Saga grunted and went silent. Egil tried to gather his will. He should help prepare the dead for burning.

"Would you do nothing, old man?" Saga asked. "Will you eat fate without protest?"

"What would you have me do?"

"The sky people are not gods. We can fight them."

"They're not our foes."

"If what you say is true, about the spiders, then we have enemies among the sky people. Who else could have made these creatures?"

Egil thought on this. Saga was right. Someone thought nothing of slaughtering them all. But they had an ally — the warrior who had appeared as a shimmer of light.

"Will you eat fate, old man?" Saga repeated, taunting him. He suppressed an urge to strike her. He was tolerant of disrespect only to a point. She saw him twitch, and grinned. "Go ahead! Try. See what happens, bard. Do you think swinging a hammer all day has made my shoulders weak?"

"You make shit steel," said Egil.

Saga laughed. "Better than no steel. I'm the best smith in Kaldbrek."

"Do you miss your uncle?"

Saga shrugged. "He was cruel."

Egil stood and brushed his hands together. "Let us prepare the dead."

She followed him to the well circle. The dirt had been raked over, but a stench still lingered.

He would go to the *Stanford*, if he could. He would not eat fate.

CHAPTER TWENTY-FOUR

Umana sealed herself into the cocoon to watch the battle unfold through seven hundred four eyes. Even for her that was too much; she thinned the feed to sixteen – the frontal eyes of the eight alphas. The cascade down the mountainside was exhilarating; her tentacles twitched in sympathetic resonance with the convulsive leaps of her offspring. She left a single beta to dispatch the curious old villager, not bothering to split her attention to glean the result. Even if he managed to escape, her children would pick off the stragglers.

They caught the hapless denizens of Kaldbrek by surprise. Gleefully, she signaled the alphas to commence the slaughter. Leap, bite, kill. Don't eat, not yet. *There will be time later to feast.*

She led the chorus of simple minds, working synchronously, with her own consciousness directing the semi-chaotic assault. With scores of bodies and dozens of minds at her disposal, her thread-brain resonated with the simple nervous systems of her spawn. Particles entangled in her womb were now woven into their sensory and motor networks. She didn't have, or need, complete control. Unlike the thralls, her children *sensed* what she wanted and obeyed. Out of love, she liked to think. Love for their mother.

Zhan wanted her attention. *Go away!* The first-tier insisted. *What is it?*

"Are you sure this is wise?" The tiger looked at her accusingly. The thrall couldn't see what she saw, but he could sense her arousal, and he had known what was planned.

"Go, unless you have something for me besides useless questions."

"They have survived for so long. Isn't that worth something? Shouldn't they be preserved, as a sort of living history?"

She laughed. "History? You can't be serious. They're cultural mutants. Descendants of imitators. They're not Vikings, if that's what you're thinking. They have no boats. They live in the mountains."

Zhan growled, and despite herself Umana felt a shiver of fear ripple up her spine. Zhan was powerless, but his avatar was deeply realistic. "They're not expanding," the tiger said. "What threat do they pose to your ambitions?"

"I am not *ambitious*, Zhan. I am principled. And as for expansion, *you* should study history more carefully. The curve is very gentle for the first few millennia. Then the explosion, then ruin. We won't be waiting that long. Earth will be a garden."

"A garden," repeated the tiger, with something like a purr. Did she detect a shade of sarcasm? Insolence? Zhan was valuable, but not indispensable. There were other first-tiers. She could pick a new favorite. She could put the tiger in a cage.

"What, from the *Liu Hui*?" she asked.

"The *Zhōngyāng* seemed satisfied with my report."

"*Your* report?"

"The report I prepared at your request, Commander," said Zhan, followed by a soft growl.

"Fine. Anything else?"

"A request from one of your associates – Manning."

"I'll deal with him later. As you sensed, I'm in the middle of something."

"Genocide. Yes, commander." There was nothing ambiguous about Zhan's sarcasm this time. Fine, she would censure him. But not now – there wasn't time. Annoyingly, the soon-to-be-irrelevant first-tier was still talking. "Though Manning insisted that you attend to the matter expeditiously. He says that you owe him."

"*Owe* him? For what?"

"For facilitating communication with the vassal."

"Zhan, now is not the time." She willed him gone. The tiger slunk away.

★   ★   ★

Her children were ravaging the villagers. Some of the men fought back, swinging bits of metal: spears, swords, pitchforks. A charming medieval melee, monster against man. A modern weapon – a single warhead – could obliterate the village in milliseconds. Her children were slow and laborious by comparison, but the slaughter must appear to be an act of nature, should anyone investigate. She doubted that anyone would.

One of the alphas had spotted something and was vying for her attention. The old man with the forked beard was *still alive*. Impressive. The alpha sensed her desire and went for the kill.

A stabbing ache behind her left eye – the feed went black. She scanned for the two betas she'd sensed nearby. Gone.

An efficient killer was lurking among the villagers. With all her remaining eyes, she searched.

There – a flicker of movement. The assassin was well-camouflaged: active visual masking and a muted heat signature. A sophisticated battleskin. Was the *Stanford* finally fighting back? This might be their way: surreptitious resistance, guerrilla warfare. But this skin was nothing like the standard-issue bioskins she'd seen the Vandercamp settlers wear. Could the killer be one of her own, an enemy from the *Liu Hui*? She had her share.

Three sharp detonations, three more of her children vaporized. This time, she saw it happen. The assassin was firing explosive darts from a wrist cartridge. She sent two alphas to chase down the killer. Her quarry slipped away. Her children had many eyes, but they were simple organs. Bile rose in her throat. She gnashed her teeth and indulged in a quick fantasy of entering the fight *with her own body*. No one could hide from her true eyes, no one could escape her true grasp. She would crush the assassin slowly, luxuriously, savoring the cracking ribs and the wet pops of organs bursting. Her tentacles lashed about the cocoon. *Refocus.* She inhaled the acrid scent of her own battle pheromones.

She activated the wasps. Nestled beneath the carapaces of the betas, the parasites came to life. The little bloodsuckers could sting, but that wasn't her intention. She had a different job for them.

The fighting men of the village were making a stand near the well – as much of a town center as this little shithole of a village had. Her remaining children fought with vigor and fury. In rapid succession, five more exploded. She sent the wasp swarm toward the anonymous murderer. Today she might lose the battle, but with a little luck she would win the war.

The swarm converged on the target. Her prey leapt away, ten meters in a single bound. A haptic exoskin, then, augmenting both strength and speed. She dispersed the swarm into a wide cloud, surrounding her quarry in a hundred-meter hemisphere. Slowly, she contracted the net. All she needed was a single drop.

In waves, she sent the wasps in. The assassin hurled a tiny pellet into the first wave; a blast of heat burned the wasp-drones to a crisp. The killer was well-armed. Umana inhaled deeply and blew out her breath with a low whistle, matched by a subsonic hum six octaves below. The sound calmed her. *Patience.*

The killer rejoined the fight, firing detonator darts into her children, slaughtering them. She signaled the survivors to retreat, but the murderer was ruthless and let none escape. The last alpha, facing the strongest of the villagers, refused to flee. The brute wielded a long blade coated in the yellow blood of her children. The acid would damage the steel, but that was poor solace. All but one of her children were dead.

A lone wasp landed on the killer's neck and slipped its long stinger through the fabric. Numb with battle lust, the assassin did not notice. The wasp took its prize and flew off. *Come home to Mother.*

The last alpha leapt; the man dodged and lashed out with his blade. The alpha would fight to the end. Through its eight eyes she saw the fork-bearded man. The alpha charged. By now the villagers could smell victory, and fought all the harder. The old man smashed her child with his wooden club, over and over again.

Her feeds went dark.

She closed her eyes and listened to her own breath and heartbeat. Blackness. Peace. She let the loss wash over her. Emotion was food, a source of energy. She feasted on sadness.

Three failures. First, the doctor capturing one of her children. Second, the betrayal of Mèng. And now this.

One by one, she would track down her enemies and extract her price. Soon the wasp would return, and she would analyze the assassin's blood and reveal their identity.

She unsealed the cocoon. The relatively fresh air from the navigation room rushed in with a hiss. Tentacles first, she emerged.

"Where is Chiang?"

"We'll summon him, Commander."

"Never mind. I'll do it myself." She pinged the little squid and found him in one of the habitation domes. Chiang was unconscious – still asleep. With the equivalent of a shriek she roused him. *Come. Now!*

It took him eleven minutes to dress and appear before her.

"What of the prisoner?" she asked without preamble.

Chiang gave his face a quick rub. "He hasn't said much."

"How persuasive have you been?"

"We've done nothing but ask questions. Foster has him – he's followed the *Zhōngyāng* prisoner protocol to the letter, as far as I know."

"Bring him to me."

"Lieutenant Foster?"

"No, you idiot. The prisoner."

"To the *Iarudi*? That's in violation of protocol. Ship internals are not to be—"

"Shut up!" she roared at a decibel level just short of bursting his eardrums. Chiang collapsed to his knees, clutching his ears.

"Please, Commander…."

"Do I need to repeat my request? Maybe I'm speaking too softly?"

"No, Commander."

"Very well. You know where to find me."

Chiang left. Umana retreated to her cocoon and visualized, in exquisite detail, how she would extract the Security Director's secrets.

CHAPTER TWENTY-FIVE

Lydia's ankle was sprained, possibly broken, but Mèng helped her walk, taking much of her weight. Her head throbbed, despite the analgesics Mèng had given her. She'd felt better in the moments directly after the crash, when she'd still been in shock.

Not crash, *assassination attempt*. Commander Umana, the Squid Woman, was trying to kill them.

She'd asked Mèng why. The girl had shrugged. "She's a violent person. Very unpredictable. She's powerful because she scares people."

"That can't be the only reason," Lydia had said. "The *Liu Hui* isn't feudal – it's a ringstation society, not a fiefdom run by warlords."

"Within the military things are different," Mèng had said. Lydia took her word for it. The *Stanford* had never had a military force. There was even talk of discontinuing the civilian police force – there was never much for them to do.

It was still early in the morning. They'd only traveled half an hour before the Squid Woman's lances had caught up with them. Lydia and Mèng had passed the smoldering wreckage of the hovershuttle on their way to find Xenus. If they hadn't all jumped, they'd certainly be dead. Now they were trekking across hilly green terrain, staying on the high ground.

"How do you know where he is?" she asked. Xenus hadn't responded to her pings.

"I put trackers on both of you as soon as we left the settlement," said Mèng.

"Really? Is mine still on? Where?"

"Best to leave it on. Just in case."

"Can Umana track us too?"

"No. The trackers are keyed to me personally. But with Commander Umana you can never be sure. We'll get rid of them once we find your husband."

"He's not my husband," Lydia said, wondering why she felt compelled to share this fact with Mèng.

They reached the edge of a small lake. Across the water stood an elegant castle. The structure was covered in vines, and sections of the roof had collapsed, but overall the place was in better shape than most ruins. She tried to send a hound to learn more. She couldn't. Her kit must have been damaged in the fall. She ran a quick diagnostic. Her m'eye displayed a long list of functions, status CURRENTLY NON-OPERATIONAL. The bioskin's temperature regulation was still working, but that was about it. No wonder Xenus hadn't responded.

"Your exoskin and communications – are they working?" Lydia asked.

"Mostly," Mèng said, squinting at the castle.

"You must have hit the ground hard – we were going pretty fast."

"My suit is military grade, and...."

"And *Liu Hui* technology is about twenty years ahead of ours. Don't be embarrassed to say it. It's pretty obvious."

"Mmm," said Mèng. Lydia realized she probably should have said *one hundred* years ahead. Interstellar propulsion research had stalled out on the *Stanford*, and from the sounds of it the Squid Woman's ship, the *Iarudi*, was in a class by itself.

"He must have taken shelter there," Mèng said, pointing across the lake. It was more of a palace than a castle: the stately buildings had both Baroque and Renaissance features. Despite soot-covered walls and a few sections of collapsed roofing, the palace had weathered the centuries well.

"Let's hurry," Lydia said, wincing as she tried to lead the way. "He might be badly hurt. Though it's a good sign he covered so much ground."

Mèng nodded uncertainly and took Lydia's arm.

* * *

Lydia was surprised to find that the grounds immediately surrounding the palace were neatly tended. In the place of formal gardens there were tidy rows of squash, greens, and herbs.

"Someone lives here," Lydia said.

"Quite a few people," said Mèng, pointing to other vegetable patches nearby. "Look over there – some kind of grain."

"Do you have a weapon?" Lydia was unarmed, with no gear besides her bioskin.

Mèng grunted, in the affirmative, as far as Lydia could tell, though she could see nothing resembling a weapon on Mèng's slender body. "Let's be careful," Mèng said, "but I think the gardens are a good sign. Whoever they are, they live together peacefully, and it looks like they have enough to eat."

The palace comprised three large buildings arranged roughly in the shape of a horseshoe. The main building was topped with a grand bronze cupola, possibly a belfry. Within the inner courtyard lay the remains of low walls that might have once contained a decorative garden. Lydia could imagine rows of colorful flowers, intricate topiary, and gushing fountains. Now the courtyard was home to vegetables, compost piles, and a crude, odiferous wooden structure.

"The peasants have taken over the castle," said Lydia, gingerly lowering herself onto a stump. Someone had taken the trouble to cut down a tree.

"Peasants...." Mèng repeated softly. "Were peasants religious?"

"Why do you ask?"

Mèng pointed across the courtyard. In the shadow of one of the smaller buildings sat a stone statue, roughly five meters tall: a beatific, fat-bellied Buddha. "He looks happy," Mèng observed.

The Buddha *did* look happy – deliriously so.

A bell began to chime in deep, long tones.

CHAPTER TWENTY-SIX

Egil plodded through the spruce wood, each step requiring a conscious act of will. He stumbled, barely caught himself with his staff. Saga reached out to help. He waved her hand away.

"I'd be fine, if I hadn't sprinted down the mountain."

"A lot of good it did us. You were too slow."

Egil let her have the last word. She was right, after all. They were on their way to talk to Katja Elkesdóttir, in Happdal. If the rumors were true, Esper's sister might be able to help them.

"The shadow woman – I think she was going to kill Svein," Saga said.

"I saw it too," said Egil. "She lifted a blade, but never struck."

"Why would she want to kill him?"

"Why do you think?" He wasn't trying to frustrate the girl – he had his own suspicions and was curious if Saga's line of reasoning would bring her to the same conclusion.

"Many people hate Svein."

"But more fear him."

"Hate *and* fear him," Saga said. "But hatred is not the same as murderous rage. Cruel as he may be, Svein kept us fed, and never killed man, woman, nor child of Kaldbrek."

"He fed you poorly," Egil pointed out. He excluded himself, for he had feasted in Skrova during Kaldbrek's leanest winters.

"My parents might still be alive if we'd eaten better, and I *do* blame Svein for that. A better jarl would have resumed trade with other villages. But that doesn't make me want to kill him. He's stubborn and brutish, but he didn't put a knife to my mother's throat. A sickness did that."

They walked in silence for a while, descending the northern ridge toward the Upper Begna.

"Mostly Svein just insults people and roughs them up," she continued. "Völund was the same, and nobody wanted to kill him…."

She was getting warm.

"…until Völund stole a child. The boy's father slit my morbror's throat without a second thought. And…wait…the mother – she escaped too!" Egil smiled.

"The shadow warrior, was she Tem's mother?"

"Yes," said Egil, tugging on the left fork of his beard and feeling a spring in his step. "By the Red Brother's hammer, that's exactly what I think."

"Are we at war with the sky people?"

Egil shook his head. "No. If the sky people truly wanted to kill us they could rain down fire from their ships until we were truly cooked. I think only a few of them mean us harm. Or perhaps just one."

⋆   ⋆   ⋆

Elke greeted them, if it could be called a greeting. Young children had run to fetch the village matron as soon as Egil and Saga had stumbled into sight. Elke held a basket of onions in one hand and a longknife in the other.

"You're still alive? What do you want, goat beard?" she called out from twenty paces.

"It's good to see you, Elke Mettesdóttir!"

"Are you hungry, old man? You can have one of these." Elke hurled an onion in their direction. It landed in the mud, splattering Egil's boot. It was not a good onion, Egil noted, but striped with mold, half-rotted.

"I'm here to see your daughter."

"My daughter? Ha! I won't lie – Katja has few suitors these days. But even so, an old goat like you has no chance."

"I must speak with her, Elke."

"Go away. Kaldbrek scum are not welcome here. How dare you show your face in Happdal, after stealing my grandson?"

"I did not take him," said Egil, feeling hopeless.

Saga stepped forward. "Twenty-two are dead in Kaldbrek. Two more will not survive the night."

Elke frowned, lowering her knife. "Who are you?"

"One of the living," Saga said. "What came for us may come for you. Will you let us speak with your daughter?"

⋆   ⋆   ⋆

Katja Elkesdóttir looked pale and tired, not well at all, but she greeted Egil with guarded curiosity and invited them into her small home. The single room was cluttered with Builder artifacts, mostly books but also dirt-caked contraptions, rusted tools, and bits of broken ceramic plates and vases.

"I see that you're a scholar," Egil noted.

"I've taught myself to read. Well, Zoë taught me, at first...."

Egil hadn't heard that name before, and said so.

Katja smiled sadly. "No one has – not from these times. She died a long time ago. Please, have a seat. I'll move these books. Tell me why you're here."

Egil did not waste time, but asked Katja what she knew of the Black Tree. Katja spoke freely. Her story was far more fantastic and vivid than the diluted rumors he had heard over the years. Katja told them that she had been kept prisoner in the mind of another, while her physical form was used as a slave. As a boy Egil had been told tales of a gast that haunted the Five Valleys, stealing food and occasionally bodies. Katja had *become* this gast for a time. Jense the smith, and a woman named Zoë (another slave inside the mind of the gast), had rescued her, but Katja had nearly died in the process. She'd coughed up a black egg, a Builder machine that contained the mind of her captor. Somehow (Egil could not quite follow it all), the mind of the soul slaver had been destroyed, and the black egg had grown into the Black Tree.

"Is the tree alive," Egil asked, "or is it a machine?"

"A machine of sorts," said Katja, looking more animated. Egil could now see that she had been pretty once, like her mother. Perhaps even more so. "But a machine containing worlds. Thousands of them! Perhaps more."

"That's impossible," Saga said. The girl had been sitting silently, scowling, but also listening intently.

"You have no idea what is possible and what is not," Katja snapped. "You're ignorant, just like everyone from your village."

"Please, Katja," said Egil. "Forgive us our ignorance. How can we know these things unless you tell us? What do you know of the spiders?"

Katja glared at Saga, but answered. "I heard about the big spiders, but I haven't seen them. I don't know what they are, or why they'd swarm on the Black Tree. They weren't always there."

"They grew to the size of dogs, and attacked Kaldbrek this morning. More than twenty people are dead."

Katja gasped.

Egil softened his voice, wanting to make an impression. Both Katja and Saga leaned in, captivated, drinking up his words. "We need to learn where the spiders came from, and if they'll come back. We can't just wait for another attack. We can't eat fate." He glanced at Saga. "We're going to go up to the ringship – the three of us – and ask for their help." He reached out and took Katja's hand. Her palm was cool and rough. "Will you go with us?"

"I've told you everything I know," said Katja, pulling her hand away. "You've told *me*, but not *them*," Egil said.

"What if the sky people created the spiders?" Saga asked. "You said so yourself that might be true. We could be walking into death's jaws." Egil shook his head. "They're a peaceful people, overall. Otherwise they'd have slaughtered us long ago. But there's a traitor among them. They'll want our help. They may *need* it."

"I do miss my nephew," said Katja. Saga looked away.

"And you, Saga?" Egil asked.

The black-haired girl met his gaze. "How do we get there?"

★   ★   ★

Katja went to find Askr or Alvis. She'd heard that the brothers had run into Car-En and Tem, and had spoken to them about passage to the ringship. Perhaps one of them knew the way to the flying machine that could take them up. In the meantime, Egil would look for Elke. Perhaps he could make peace, and procure some food for the trek.

He found Tem's grandmother chopping wood. Why was it that whenever he spoke to the woman she was holding sharpened iron?

"You look nervous, old goat," Elke said. She stopped chopping but did not put down her axe.

"You are the one woman impervious to my voice," said Egil. "Most are charmed, or at least calmed."

"If a smooth tongue was all it took I would have more than three children."

Egil laughed, hoping it was a joke. Elke cracked the faintest smile. "I was hoping to make peace with you, Elke Mettesdóttir. It was not I who stole your grandson and your daughter-in-law, but I apologize on behalf of Svein and the men who helped him."

Elke grunted. "I don't accept your apology, because it is meaningless and irrelevant. But I won't kill you."

Well, that was something. And the woman was finally putting down her axe. "I have seen your daughter-in-law," he said, hoping the gamble would pay off.

"Seen Car-En? I think not. She went home to her ship in the sky. I would say good riddance, if she hadn't taken Tem with her."

"No, she's on Earth. In the Five Valleys, no less. I saw her with my own eyes."

"Then where is my grandson?" Elke looked worried.

"Safe and well. Still on the ringship, as far as I know."

"What did my son's wife have to say for herself? Where is she now?"

"I don't know – not exactly. But she saved our village this morning."

He told her of the spider attack. Elke had heard of the spiders, and did not seem surprised, and reacted only when she learned that Svein still lived.

"Car-En had the chance to kill him, you say? And she didn't?"

"Yes, as far as I could tell."

Elke snorted in disgust. "That woman is soft and weak."

A few minutes later Egil, Saga, and Katja were following Raakel, a little blond girl, no older than six, on their way to the dairy. The girl had seen Askr there, talking to Raakel's aunt.

"Grundar will be glad you're coming to get Askr," Raakel said. "He doesn't like anyone else talking to Elika."

At the barn, broad-shouldered Grundar greeted them with a scowl. "He's out back, in the pasture, with the cows."

"And Elika," said the little girl.

"Yes, with Elika," Grundar said, scowling more deeply. "Run along."

The girl ran off, braids bouncing. "She looks like you, when we were little," Grundar said to Katja. "When your hair was longer."

They found Askr out back, sitting on a fence, watching a tall, graceful woman hand-feed a calf from a jug. Askr hopped down and greeted Katja warmly.

"Who are these two?" he asked. "I heard there was an old goat and a pretty raven looking for me." Saga blushed.

"They just wanted to watch you be lazy," Katja said.

"I don't think Elika needs any help," Askr said.

"It's true," said the young woman feeding the calf. Her height and beauty were striking, and Egil found it difficult not to stare. "His mother weaned him early, and I don't mind feeding him."

"Askr, weaned early?" said Katja, grinning. "I think not! He and his brother were suckling their poor mum's tits until they could talk." There was some color coming back to Katja's cheeks. Maybe she had just needed some fresh air.

Askr shook his head. "I won't take that bait, Katja. I wouldn't battle you with words any sooner than I would fight you with steel."

"Then you're a wise man, even if you are a coward."

"What do you want then? As you say, you've interrupted my lazy afternoon."

Askr told them what Car-En had said, that a 'mool' ship could take them to the ringstation, but he had only the vaguest idea of how to get there (go north, near a great river, not far from the ice wall).

"You can't lead us there?" Saga asked.

"I might have tracked them, but that was months ago. Besides, Car-En said the trek would take weeks. The snow will be here soon, and that far north the cold would kill us."

Saga frowned. "Is there another way to get to the ringship? There must be."

Askr gave Saga a curious look. "Why do *you* want to go, young raven?"

Elika stroked the calf's neck. "Perhaps she's curious."

"I can speak for myself, milkmaid," Saga snapped. "I'm going to the ringship because we need to learn why the sky people attacked us. Kaldbrek lost twenty-two souls today."

Elika went pale. "I'm sorry."

Egil gently placed his hand on Saga's shoulder, but the black-haired girl pulled away. "Don't touch me, old goat! You're a coward too. You're all cowards!" Saga's face had turned pink. "If no one else will go, I'll go myself!"

"What's this then?" A handsome blue-eyed man was striding across the pasture toward them; he'd come within a few paces without anyone noticing. The man brushed back his long brown hair and smiled. "Sister. Elika, Askr. Egil the Bard – it's good to see you again."

"Greetings, Esper Ariksson," said Egil, but his attention was on Saga. Her eyes had gone wide.

"You!" Saga screamed and leapt at Esper, clawing at his eyes. Esper raised his hands, but the mad girl was already on him, drawing long red scratches down his cheeks.

"Stop!" Egil shouted, grabbing Saga's arm. It was like grabbing an iron bar – the hammer had made the girl strong. "Help! Get her off!"

Askr, grinning stupidly, waded into the scuffle and grabbed Saga by the leg. Saga twisted her hips and swung her free leg like a club, catching Askr's chin with her boot. The lanky youth collapsed, snuffed like a candle. Elika screamed and dropped the milk jug. The calf backed into the fence with a panicked bleat.

Saga's fists rained down on Esper. Esper fended off most of her blows, still looking more confused than hurt. Saga reached into her shirt and produced a short, ugly black blade. Gripping Esper's throat, she raised the knife.

Egil raised his staff, but Katja was faster. A quick step forward and she had Saga's wrist, twisting her arm behind her back. Katja, for all her book reading, was still a warrior. Egil expected a cry of pain from Saga, but the raven-haired girl struggled silently.

"Get off my brother!" Katja yanked Saga's arm so far up her back that her wrist nearly touched her neck. Still, Saga did not drop the knife.

"You told me yourself that Völund deserved what he got!" Egil used his full, booming voice, and everyone, including the calf, looked at him, rapt. "Esper Ariksson is not your true enemy. Save your rage, Saga Vandasdóttir."

Saga relaxed her hand, letting the knife fall. Katja snatched it up and released the girl, who still straddled Esper. Egil had not known the girl's rage was so thinly buried.

"Was he kin? The smith?" Esper asked. Blood oozed from the scratches on his face.

Saga drew back her right fist and smashed Esper in the face. She raised her left and did the same. Before any of them could react she had pummeled Katja's brother five times, all the blows connecting like hammer strikes on Esper's skull. Esper was still conscious – why did he not fight back? Surely he could overpower the girl if he wished. Saga was strong from the smithy, but Esper could walk a full day with a dead stag across his shoulders.

"Stop!" Egil roared. It did no good. Saga was beyond reason.

Katja moved in, knife in hand, ready to end it. As strong as Saga was, Katja would make quick work of her. In his mind's eye Egil saw Saga on her back, lying peacefully in the green grass, her throat slit. In the corner of his vision the pasture itself moved, a wave of green. Saga, fist raised, crumpled in a heap. Esper was now unconscious, bleeding from the nose and eyes. Askr had not yet come to. Katja dropped the knife and pulled Saga's limp body off of her brother.

"Did she faint?" Egil asked.

Katja held two fingers to Saga's throat. "Her heart still beats."

A woman spoke. The voice came from Egil's left, where he had seen the pasture move. "She'll be out for a few minutes."

Elika looked confused. "Did you say that?" she asked, looking at Katja. Katja was looking at Egil.

"Car-En," they both said simultaneously.

Tem's mother came into view, her suit now the color of molten silver. She held a weapon, the same as the bald-headed soldier had tried to use against the spiders. Car-En pulled back her hood. Her hair showed more gray than when Egil had last seen her.

Car-En knelt next to her husband. She ran her fingers along his cheekbones and jawline, pressing gently. "Nothing broken, I think."

Askr moaned. Elika, coming to her senses, rushed to his side.

Within ten minutes, Saga, now conscious and quite furious, was tied to the fence. Askr was on his feet, rubbing his sore jaw. Katja had taken Esper to see Ilsa. Esper, dazed, not only from his pummeling, but also on account of seeing his wife upon awakening, had stumbled across the meadow clutching Katja's arm.

"You followed us, from Kaldbrek?" Egil asked.

"Yes," Car-En confirmed. "I apologize for staying cloaked – maybe it wasn't necessary. Old habits die hard."

In his mind, Egil had already forgiven her. Avoiding Elke was reason enough to stay invisible.

Car-En strode over to Saga. She loomed over the girl, confident and dominant. "You are Saga Vandasdóttir, of Kaldbrek?" The sky woman was of small stature, but something in her posture and the way she moved had changed. Even her voice was different – more commanding.

Saga answered Car-En with a defiant glare.

"My son spoke fondly of you. I think he had a crush on you," said

Car-En, smiling. Saga's face stayed blank. "I'm sorry you lost friends and kin today. But I am not your enemy, and neither is my husband."

"Your *husband* slit my uncle's throat as if slaughtering a hog," said Saga, sneering.

"He did what any father would have done."

"He didn't need to *kill* him. Völund was my only kin."

Egil cursed himself silently. How foolish he had been, to take Saga's words at face value. What kind of bard was he, to believe a young woman's words matched her heart? He was just a fool. He would always be a fool.

"I promise you he feels remorse," Car-En said. "Otherwise your blows would not have landed. I suggest you redirect your rage. There is still an enemy to fight, if you have fight in you."

"Who?" Egil asked.

Car-En sat on the grass and gestured for the others to sit. Egil did so, as did Askr and Elika. Saga, tied to the fence, had no choice but to listen. Glancing around, Egil saw only the cows watching. No, there was Grundar, in the barn, eyeing them suspiciously from the shadows. No doubt he was mostly concerned about Elika sitting so close to Askr, but he could not have helped but notice the silver-skinned woman. The news of Car-En's strange appearance would soon spread throughout Happdal.

"Listen," Car-En said forcefully. "What I'm about to tell you may sound far-fetched, but we face a powerful enemy. I don't yet know what she wants, but I know what she's capable of. We should all fear for our lives. No one is safe."

"*She?*" said Askr. "Our enemy is a woman?"

Car-En shot Askr a look, but when she spoke her voice was calm. "Don't think of her as a woman. Think of her as a god – an angry, vengeful god."

"Like *Loki?*" Elika whispered.

"Yes, like Loki," Car-En said, "but even more like the serpent that encircles the world."

"*Jörmungandr*," Egil said. "What do you mean? Do we face a woman or a monster?"

"Maybe both. In Vandercamp, they call her the Squid Woman," said Car-En. "But you would have never seen a squid. The *kraken* woman then. You know the legend of the kraken, don't you? In addition to arms, the Squid Woman has long tentacles."

"What's a tentacle?" Elika asked.

"Where is Vandercamp?" asked Askr.

"Hold your questions – let her speak!" Egil snapped.

"Vandercamp is a settlement of ringstation people, far to the south, near the sea," Car-En said patiently. "It's where the Squid Woman is, as far as I know. Though she has a very fast ship. She could be anywhere."

"Is this woman insane?" Elika asked, befuddled. "What could she possibly have against the people of the Five Valleys? What have we ever done to her?"

"I don't know," said Car-En, "but I think it was she who created the spiders. A colleague examined one – the specimen my son captured...."

"Tem captured a spider?" Elika asked, impressed.

"A stupid stunt," said Egil, unable to help himself.

"Stupid or not," Car-En said, "the knowledge gained may be what saves our lives." She glared at Egil. He looked away, feeling ashamed. He *knew* better than to criticize a child to the mother. *Keep playing the fool, old man.* "Lydia's results, which she sent to the *Stanford*, matched another sample on file."

"The ringship has spiders too?" Egil asked.

"Not the giant spiders that attacked your village, no. But the sample was nearly identical – in terms of its structure – to the Black Tree."

"The sky people know of the tree? They've studied it?"

"Yes. Though all our field researchers were recently recalled on account of what happened in Kaldbrek" – Car-En's eyes flashed to Saga – "but not before we learned a few things. It was my son, Tem, who put the pieces together.

"The Black Tree grew from the black egg, the parasite that took over Katja ten years ago. I saw it enter her body with my own eyes. The spiders...they may be attracted to the Black Tree because they're made of the same stuff. The parasite is a Builder machine from long ago. The Squid Woman is ancient – one of the original Builders. She has lived for centuries, stealing bodies to stay alive. She treats human beings as slaves, or vessels. Bodies and minds to be used."

"Are you saying that the Squid Woman...." Egil could not bring himself to finish.

"Yes," Car-En said. "The Squid Woman is a gast."

CHAPTER TWENTY-SEVEN

Tem peered out the porthole of the *Rama*, wondering where Mongolia had been. Hundreds of kilometers below, Asia was vast and colorful. The northern third of the continent was covered in bluish-white ice, but the lower two-thirds were a complex mix of greens and beiges, with streaks of dark blue and patches of rust.

"Mongolia was right *there*," said Zin, pointing, "just below the glacial line." She was leaning over him, practically lying on top of him (which he liked), but it was annoying how she always had to *know* everything. "What?" she said, in response to his scowl. "You were talking about Mongolia earlier. I was just trying to *help*."

"Can you stop talking for five minutes?" Marcus said. He was sitting across the aisle, on the starboard side of the shuttle, next to Tirian. "Or four. No, let's make it easy – three. Do you think you could be quiet for three minutes?"

"*Sorry*," Zinthia said, throwing her hands in the air. "I'm excited, okay? I've never been on the *Liu Hui*!"

Of Tem's twenty-one classmates, only eleven had received permission to participate in the five-day exchange program. Mr. Kan, who had helped organize this year's trip and was chaperoning, had seemed disappointed but not surprised.

"Is that a whale?" said Abelton, from the row ahead of Tem.

"You can't see whales from this high!" Tirian said.

"Maybe you can. How do you know? Whales are *huge*." Little Abelton, who had lately gained some confidence, did not back down.

The whale-sighting debate continued. Tem's attention wandered. He missed Mother. She'd already been gone for a week, and now *he* would be gone for five days. Morfar Shol had insisted that Mother would be home soon, though he did not seem convinced of this himself. He *had* seemed sincere when he'd insisted that Mother missed him too.

Morfar Shol was kind to comfort him. But Morfar was old, and probably didn't remember what it was like to be a child. *Child.* It was a new idea for him. In Happdal, he had known he was young, and little, but on the *Stanford* it was as if young people had a special status. It wasn't only that they were protected and provided for; adults understood that young people wouldn't be young forever. The children would grow up and take over the world. Somehow, he had never felt that Arik and Elke or even Trond and Father understood that simple fact. It was as if they thought they would live forever, and that Tem would always be little.

"What are we doing first when we get there?" Tirian asked.

"Eating, I hope," said Zinthia. "I'm starving."

"I heard their meat comes from actual animals," Marcus said. "*Living* ones." Tirian made a face.

"I'm sure they kill them first," Abelton said.

"Either way, that's disgusting," Tirian said. "And *mean*, too."

"We hunted, and ate the meat, on Earth," Tem offered. "There were many animals in the forest who would have eaten us if they'd had the chance. Even the boar. They'll eat anything."

"Does the meat taste different?" Marcus asked.

Tem nodded. "Forest meat has a stronger flavor. I liked it, but you might not." He was trying to be diplomatic. Ringstation food wasn't exactly bland – he'd tried hundreds of new foods and flavor combinations since he'd arrived – but he missed the simple, delicious village foods: roasted boar, fresh cream, wild berries, soft cheese, oat cakes, dried deer meat, vegetable stew.

"Children, may I please have your attention?" Mr. Kan floated into the aisle, hovering a meter above everyone else. The rest of them were all strapped in their seats. His classmates' impassioned pleas to float freely in the passenger cabin for the duration of the short trip had fallen on deaf ears. Mr. Kan had insisted it wouldn't be safe. While most of the space junk had been cleared from Earth's orbit, a minor collision with debris (natural or artificial) couldn't be ruled out. It was safer to be fully secured while they were in transit, though he'd promised to give them a few minutes to float freely in zero-G once they'd docked at the *Liu Hui's* central hub.

"Let's review our vocabulary words," said Mr. Kan, once they'd settled down. "You should all know the ten politeness phrases and thirty high-frequency words by now. By the time we head home, I expect everyone to know the top one hundred high-frequency words."

Enthusiastically, Tem's class reviewed the Mandarin words and phrases Mr. Kan had selected. It was odd learning something besides math from Mr. Kan. In a way it made the lesson more fun, because it was so unusual. The whole class felt it – they were on an adventure. The trip wasn't actually dangerous, like hunting, or exploring the Blood Forest, but they were going someplace new.

"*Xièxie*," Mr. Kan said, emphasizing the descending tone of the first syllable.

"*Xièxie*," they echoed. *Shyeay-sheh.* "Thank you."

A flash of movement pulled Tem's eye to the porthole. What looked like a gargantuan black whale had materialized next to the shuttle, no farther than a stone's throw. Before he had time to blink the illusion away, the shuttle rocked violently. Tem's restraining straps bit into his shoulders and waist. The cabin twisted and lurched. Tem lost what little sense he'd had of up and down. There was only violent, silent motion. Mr. Kan sailed through the air, colliding with a porthole and leaving a smear of red.

The cabin stopped rotating. No, *something* had stopped the cabin from rotating. Tem's mind registered a booming thud that had occurred moments before. Some of the children were screaming now. Zinthia squeezed his hand with a white-knuckled grip, her face pale and serious.

"Did you see that?" he asked.

"It's still there," she said, pointing out the porthole.

The black whale was above them now. The Earth was no longer visible. They could see only the outlines of the leviathan against the blackness of space. Its great mass hid the stars.

"It's getting closer," Zinthia whispered, leaning in close. "Or *we're* getting closer – it's pulling us in."

"I think Mr. Kan is hurt," Tem said. "Should we try to help him?"

Zinthia surveyed the cabin, quickly and calmly. Little Falder was wide-eyed, mouth hanging open. Tirian had her head buried between her knees. Marcus was unbuckling his restraints.

"Marcus, check on Mr. Kan," Zinthia said. "Remember your first-aid training."

Marcus gave a quick nod.

"What should we do?" Tem asked, already unbuckling.

"Let's check the cockpit. The pilot might need help."

Zinthia led the way, floating up the length of the cabin, using the seat backs for handholds. Tem followed, not quite as deftly, but not as clumsily as when he had first tried to move in zero-G in the central hub of the *Stanford.*

"Stay calm," said Zinthia in an authoritative voice. "Stay in your seats." The other children obeyed her, relieved to have someone in charge. Maybe Zinthia had the same gift as Egil.

The cabin fell silent. Marcus hovered near Mr. Kan, who was curled up in a semi-fetal position, unconscious. Dark red droplets floated near his head. His forehead was shiny with blood.

"He's still breathing," Marcus said, "and his pulse is slow but steady."

Zinthia grabbed a folded white dishtowel from a kitchenette supply alcove. "Here. Press this against his scalp – *firmly* – right where there's the most blood. If he regains consciousness, tell him to relax and stay still."

The boarding doors opened with a violent hiss. For a moment Tem feared he would be pulled into the cold blackness of space, but after a few seconds the pressure equalized. Beyond the shuttle doors stretched a long flexible docking tube, illuminated by equidistant rows of indigo-violet lighting strips. It looked like the cavernous mouth of some deep-sea monster.

A half-dozen black-clad soldiers were the first through. They were tall and broad-shouldered. They leveled rifles at Tem and his classmates, saying nothing.

"What do you want?" Zinthia demanded. "This is a *field trip*, a peaceful academic activity. Why have you boarded us?"

Inspired by Zin's bravery, Tem tried to stand up straight and face the enemy, but only managed to slowly rotate in their general direction. Somehow, the soldiers were unaffected by the lack of gravity.

"Look," Marcus whispered, "there's…something is coming."

A long black tentacle emerged from the violet mouth, then another. A woman, or something *like* a woman, followed. In addition to the long tentacles protruding from her torso like extra arms, a squirming mass of shorter appendages grew from her chest. Her skin was pale and slick, her hairless skull smooth and mottled with beige splotches.

"You," she uttered, staring at Marcus. Her voice was terrifying; it shook Tem's insides. He clenched to prevent his bowels from voiding. "Are you Tem Ganzorig?"

For courage, Tem reached into his jacket pocket and grabbed the pouch Father had given him; he could feel the sharpness of the object within through the leather. "*I'm* Tem," he said as loudly as he could manage. Even to his own ears his voice sounded weak and tremulous. "Get off of our ship, before I kill you."

The monster smiled. "How would you do that, exactly? I invite you to try. My guards won't intervene. Give me your worst."

"Who are you?" Tem asked.

"Who I am is not import—" she started to say, but Tem was already hurtling through the air, drawing the godsteel blade from its sheath.

No one had told him not to bring it. No one had checked.

The monster lashed a tentacle forward to intercept him. He grabbed the writhing limb like a branch, swinging himself down and forward, gaining even more velocity. He thrust the blade, the longknife Farbror Trond had made for *him*, at the monster's throat.

At the last moment she twisted to the side, but not before he nicked her throat. Tem slammed into the cabin wall. A single droplet of blood welled up from the scratch on her neck and floated into the air.

She bled red, like everyone else.

One tentacle had him by the ankle. Seconds later, her second long tentacle was squeezing his wrist. He tried and failed to hold on to the blade, but managed to not cry out, despite the pain. Rage made him stronger, he realized, even as the bones in his wrist audibly cracked. He would kill her, somehow, and relish her final, painful moments.

"Young Tem Ganzorig, you remind me of your mother."

She pulled him closer. She reeked like a dead animal. He spat toward her face, but missed. "You don't know my mother."

"Not personally. Not yet. But I will. She helped me find you, and you'll help me find her."

From the front of the cabin Marcus launched himself at the monster, using a seat back to kick off. A black-clad soldier raised his rifle and pulled the trigger. There was no sound or flash, but Marcus went limp. The soldier caught the unconscious boy with one hand and hurled him to the cabin floor like a wet pillow.

"Stay in your seats, children. It's only Tem I want. You can continue your…field trip. You're visiting the *Liu Hui*? There is much to see there. You won't be disappointed!"

She pulled Tem in close. Her smaller tentacles wrapped around his chest and arms, cool and sticky. "Let's you and I have a chat, back on my ship," she whispered. "Shall we? But first let's verify that you are who you say." A slender appendage caressed his neck, then stung him, quickly and efficiently, right below the ear. He could see the long red scratch from his knife in the same place on *her* neck. "There…let's see." Clouded inner eyelids closed vertically over her bright brown eyes. "Yes, it *is* you. What a fascinating genome you have! Did you know that…no…you wouldn't know that yet."

Know what? He wanted her to finish the sentence. But she was playing with him. He wouldn't give her the satisfaction. He struggled. She tightened her grip. Pain lanced up his arm. Involuntarily, he cried out.

"Stop hurting him!" Zinthia yelled.

The shuttle doors were already sliding closed, the oversized soldiers retreating into the boarding tube. Had she issued a command? If so, he hadn't heard it.

She slowly wrapped a long tentacle around his body, loop by loop. He could feel the enormous strength in the artificial limb. She could squeeze the life out of him, if she wanted, like the python he had seen in the tropical fauna park on the *Stanford*. That had been another field trip. It had excited him at the time, being so close to a strange animal that could kill you, without walls or fences.

Now they were drifting quickly through the flexible passage, as if the wind was at their backs. No…that wasn't it. They were being *sucked* forward. Tem watched the lights pass by, helpless. He worried for Mother.

"Put! Me! Down!" he shouted.

The tentacle tightened. He should not have let so much air escape his lungs.

They entered an airlock. A door slid closed behind them. Through the viewing port, Tem caught a glimpse of the boarding tunnel collapsing and compacting. Beyond the airlock, the monster carried him along a narrow passage. Where had the soldiers gone?

She uncoiled her grip and held him up in front of her, at eye level. "Let's get a picture of you to send to your mother." She blinked. "There. Alive and well, for now."

"If you hurt me, she'll flay you."

"*Flay* me? From what I've learned, Car-En has toughened up since her days as a youngling spy. But she's not a sadist, is she? Your grandmother Elke though…*she* might flay me. That side of your family has some…spirit."

It was true, it was a threat he had only heard from Farmor Elke's lips. How did the monster know that?

"Who are you?" he asked.

"When I was your age, my name was Isabella. Would you like to call me that? It can be our secret. Everyone else who knew me by that name is dead."

"What has my mother done to cross you?"

The monster's face hardened. Behind him, he heard a metallic scraping noise, and felt a gust of cold air. Isabella's angry face receded as she pushed him into a dark, gray room. The door closed, and he was alone.

No, not alone. An old man, wrapped in a blood-stained blanket, lay in a cot box. A man or a corpse? A hand lifted weakly to greet him. A man, then.

"Good to see you again," said the old man. His face was decorated with bruises, some fresh and blue, others old and yellowing. One eye was swollen shut, caked in blood. The man lisped; there was only a black hole where one of his front teeth should be.

"I…I don't think I know you."

"You don't recognize me. It's been a rough week."

Tem's mind raced to place the voice. He *did* know the old man.

"Shane," said Tem softly. The Vandercamp soldier looked twenty years older and twenty kilos lighter than when Tem had last seen him at the mule station.

"Did she hurt you?"

Tem touched his neck. "No. I'm fine. Did she…."

"Do this to me? Not just her. Her goons helped. Though, to be fair, they were reluctant torturers. I predict a crisis of faith. She's gone mad, and they're just beginning to realize it."

"Who is she?"

"That's an excellent question. We've been calling her the Squid Woman. The crew calls her Commander Umana. Commander of what, it's not quite clear."

"She told me her name was Isabella."

"Really? That's new to my ears. You should remember that. It might prove to be useful, if we get out of this alive."

Tem gently pushed himself off from the door. He drifted toward Shane. "Is she going to kill us?"

Shane sighed. "Yesterday I was eager to die, but this morning, or whatever time it was when I woke up, I felt hopeful. And seeing you has lifted my spirits more. So – my answer – I hope not. I would like to live."

"Will you help me kill her?"

"Most definitely. At your service, Jarl Tem."

Despite their situation, Tem laughed. No one had ever called him *jarl* before, not even in jest. He liked the sound of it.

They spoke quietly for a long time, floating together in the dimly lit gray cell. Shane told Tem everything he knew about Umana: her strange origins via the Crucible program, her command position within the *Kǒngbù Wǔzéi* special forces, her uncanny powers of perception, her weaponized voice. At one point a slot in the door opened, and food bars and water cubes were pushed through. Tem asked the guard when they would be released, but Shane shook his head. He'd already tried to engage the guards. Their captors were mute, or might as well be.

Shane seemed impressed by how much Tem had learned over the course of a few months on the *Stanford*. Tem told him everything: about Mother, Shol, his unlikely audience with Repop (Shane was surprised, but believed him), and also about each and every one of his friends at school, many of whom had been aboard the *Rama*. He trusted Shane.

Tem gently touched his swollen wrist. It hurt. "Do you think they'll make it to the *Liu Hui*? Or...I'm not sure I understand...are we in the middle of a ringstation war?"

Shane shook his head. "No, I don't think so. Umana has gone rogue, as far as I can tell. If the *Liu Hui* catches wind of what happened – and I can't see how they could miss it – the diplomatic situation is going to escalate significantly. To say the least.

"But don't worry. Your friends should be fine. Umana was after *you*, and from what you've told me the shuttle wasn't badly damaged. The Squid Woman is insane but I don't think she's indiscriminately murderous. She's operating according to some plan or principle, though I have no idea what it is." *Printhiple.* Apparently it was hard to enunciate when you were missing a front tooth.

"When they tortured you, were they after information? Or were they just trying to hurt you?"

"The former. You remember Lydia, right? Lydia found a connection between the Squid Woman and those giant spiders we found by that strange black root structure. Lydia and Xenus left Vandercamp – Commander Umana wanted to know where they'd gone."

"Do you know?"

Shane grinned, revealing bloodstained teeth and bruised gums. "No idea! But it's a good sign she's asking. It means they're probably still alive."

"But why does the Squid Woman want to hurt my mother?"

"I don't know. But if I had to guess, Car-En has thrown a wrench into Umana's plans. A big, heavy, gear-grinding wrench."

"She had a battle suit," Tem confessed. "A custom one – something she commissioned from the Hair Lab."

Shane stroked his stubbled chin. "Hmm...." He put his fingers to his lips. "Let's leave it at that," he whispered.

Shane withdrew to his cot box. There was a similar cot on the other side of the room; Tem managed to drift toward it, and tucked himself into the secured sleeping bag. It would be smart to rest, to conserve his strength.

He found it impossible to relax. His wrist throbbed painfully, and the lack of gravity was distracting; there was no force pushing him *down* into the bed. He closed his eyes and tried to rest.

The door was opening. Had he fallen asleep? There were four giant guards pulling Shane from his bed. His friend went limp, but Tem caught a glimpse of his face, wide-eyed and deathly pale. A minute later Tem was alone in the quiet gray room.

Hours passed. Sleep was impossible. Tem reviewed what he could have done differently. What if his thrust had been true, and he'd sliced open the Squid Woman's neck? What would have happened then? Surely the guards would have overpowered them. The end result might have been worse, not better.

The strange thing was, when he reviewed the event in his mind, his blow *had* been true. He'd struck quickly, and with enough force to kill. But the skin of her neck had been tough, like bark. He'd done no more than scratch her, and he'd lost his blade. Was the longknife still on the *Rama*, or had the Squid Woman taken it? Either way, he now knew what to name it.

Squid Cutter.

He'd drawn blood. He'd *seen* it. If he got another chance he would drain her foul body dry as a husk.

The door was opening. The Squid Woman's tentacles preceded her body.

"Where is Shane?" he asked, pushing out of the sleeping bag and propelling himself toward the center of the room.

"Still alive, for the moment." Her voice somehow harmonized with itself, low and high. "I like him. I might keep him as a pet."

"Then why torture him?"

"The physical form is more than a shell. Mind *is* body. But if I were to keep Shane as a thrall, he could have whatever body he wanted. Ultimately, physical form is irrelevant. So are injuries. Your friend's mind is intact. But why do you care about him? I'm curious."

"I don't," said Tem, regretting that he had asked about Shane.

"Then you won't mind if I put him out of his misery? I already have too many minds living inside of me. I don't really *need* another."

"What do you want from me?"

"Would you like a tour of the *Iarudi*?" she asked, ignoring his question. "I'm sure you've seen nothing like it. When I was your age, there was nothing that boys liked more than spaceships. Is that true for you? Or is it only spiders and swords that thrill you?"

Spiders. Did she know that he had captured one?

"I'll see your ship," he said, trying to keep his own voice neutral.

"Good. Follow me."

To his surprise, she did not grab him or shackle him in any way, but simply led the way through the narrow corridors. Her long legs looked functional – powerful even – but she did not use them much; instead she gripped and pulled herself along the passageway using her two longest tentacles. Several times they changed direction: left, up, right, up again. Or was it down? Tem became disoriented. Twice they passed through doors so small he was sure the Squid Woman wouldn't fit. But somehow, like the real squids he'd seen in the *Stanford*'s aquariums, she compacted her form and squeezed through the portals. Did she have no bones?

"I know what you are," he blurted, after their fifth turn.

She twisted around in a swirl of tentacles. The white corridor was a meter wide, two meters high. "What am I?"

"A slaver, for one. Back in the jail, you didn't think I understood, but I did. Shane told me what you were. He'd never become your slave – he'd rather die."

"If I let him," she said quietly. "What *else* am I?"

"You're a gast. You should know that my family kills gasts. One captured my aunt, briefly, and that was the end of him. And my mother helped. You should stay away from our family, if you know what's good for you."

She drifted closer. She reeked of cheese that needed a good scraping. "You're *delightful*. Maybe I'll be *you* next."

What did that mean? He held her gaze. "You don't believe me, but it doesn't matter what you think. If you threaten my family, it won't end well for you."

"Then I guess I'm in mortal danger." She held his gaze, unsmiling.

"You think you're toying with me, but I'm giving you fair warning. Let me go now, and I'll pretend this never happened."

She was drifting away from him, starting to turn. "I tire of your game, little boy. You're bait to catch your mother, if you hadn't already figured that out. That's *all* you are. I thought you might have some potential, but now I see that I was wrong. You're just a little braggart, like every other boy your age."

He no longer had his longknife but he had a secret he could stab her with. Would it find its mark? He had to try.

"If you let me go, you'll be the gast that *lived*," he said. "Not like Raekae." He used the name Tante Katja had taught him, the gast's true name.

She hesitated, then slowly turned. She drifted so close that he could see her pointed teeth, and the texture of her skin, smooth and hard like boiled leather. Her breath was hot and so pungent that his eyes watered, even as he held his breath.

"What was that name? Ray K.? Little Tem, you *have* got me curious."

There – she'd bitten. Now to reel her in, slowly, like a trout. He remembered an afternoon fishing on the banks of the Upper Begna. That had been the day Pieter had helped him take revenge on Hennik. Except he *hadn't* beaten Hennik, when he'd had the chance.

"Yes, Raekae. He had thralls too, trapped inside his mind."

She drifted even closer. "What *exactly* happened to him?"

If he had a chance to kill the Squid Woman, he wouldn't hesitate. There was no goodness left inside of her. Hennik had bullied him, but Hennik might still grow into a good man. Father said that Old Lars had once been a bully, until the boar gored his leg. One-legged Lars was a good man – still brutish and rude, but also loyal and sometimes kind. Maybe Hennik would turn out the same way. But the Squid Woman's evil was old, baked in deep. "I told you, my aunt and my mother killed him. But part of him remains...."

She wrapped her two long tentacles around him and squeezed. He managed to suck in a great breath, and breathed shallowly to keep the air in his lungs. She could crush him if she wanted, but full lungs kept him from panicking.

"*Which* part?"

Should he tell her? Could his plan backfire? While you were still alive, life could *always* get worse. He worried for Shane.

"I'll tell you if—"

She cut him off with a squeeze. It was as if a heavy log was pressing down on his chest. The air whooshed from his lungs. He closed his eyes, and thought of Farbror Trond to give him strength. His lungs spasmed against his constricted rib cage, pulling in tiny spoonfuls of air. He thought again of a trout he'd caught, mouth agape as if gasping for air, black lidless eye staring. He'd given the fish to Farmor Elke to clean. She'd sliced it from tail to gills with her longknife, forced the mouth open until the cartilage cracked, and smoothly ripped off the lower jaw with guts attached.

"Tell me," the Squid Woman hissed through clenched teeth. "No *ifs*."

He opened his mouth to speak but did not have enough air to make a sound.

A question occurred to him. Why did *he* want to be powerful? For that's what he wanted, wasn't it? The real reason he'd always wanted to be strong, to become a smith. It wasn't just respect he wanted – it was *power*. But was *she* the end result of being powerful? He could think of no mightier being, in the Five Valleys or on any of the ringships. The Squid Woman was stronger than Farbror Trond, harsher than Jarl Svein, and more clever than either Father or Mother. Her voice was as seductive as Egil's, and more dangerous. She had dozens of slaves inside of her, an army of soldiers at her command, and a sleek, powerful warship. And yet she hungered for more.

The Squid Woman loosened her grip. He gulped down the stale, metallic corridor air as if it were fresh spring water.

"A black egg," he gasped. "That's what's left of Raekae. I can tell you where it is."

Her eyes widened. Would she deduce that the black egg and the Black Tree were one and the same? She must know the whereabouts of the tree; her spiders would have shown her. If she *did* know, he would have nothing left to tempt her with.

"Tell me? Why don't you *show* me?"

Still catching his breath, Tem nodded.

Her tentacles uncoiled, leaving him to drift freely. "Do you want to see the bridge?" she asked brightly.

CHAPTER TWENTY-EIGHT

Lydia took a step back, even though the leather-and-fur-clad men and women held their spears more defensively than aggressively. Who were they? There were at least a dozen of them, and twice as many children watched from the doorways and windows of the ruined palace. The place was far from deserted. They'd been spotted from afar; the residents had hidden. This was their greeting party.

One of the women shouted something in a guttural language. She was middle-aged, with smooth copper-brown skin, long black hair tied in a single thick braid, broad cheekbones, and Asiatic eyes. She looked to be a mix of Northern European and Central Asian ancestry, not unlike Car-En, but taller and heavier.

"My kit was damaged in the crash," Lydia said. "No translator – did you pick that up?"

"She asked who we were," Mèng said. "In German, but one of the words was…Nepali, I think."

A few of the spear-carriers circled behind them. Their weapons were crude: wooden shafts sharpened and fire-hardened. But one of them – a broad-shouldered, stone-faced man – wielded a rusty halberd. Others had tarnished kitchen knives lashed to their spears – makeshift glaives.

"Interesting armaments," Lydia observed.

"But deadly. Move slowly," Mèng said. She took a cautious step forward and addressed the group. "We're looking for our friend," Mèng said to the woman who had spoken. "A man. Short hair." She repeated herself in halting German. The copper-skinned woman barked something in response, and rested her spear on its butt. The others immediately relaxed their stances. The halberd carrier said something that elicited a collective chuckle.

"Zeeee-nus," said the halberd man, now smiling. Lydia's heart leapt.

★　★　★

They were led upstairs and to a small bedroom, where a pale, thin Xenus rested on a pile of crude fur blankets. Lydia gently embraced him. The spear carriers left them alone, posting no guard.

"I'm fine," Xenus said. "I could use a shower and a toothbrush, but they've treated me well."

"Who are they?" Mèng asked.

"They call themselves the *Chhaang*," said Xenus. "Descendants of Nepalese immigrants who lived in Germany."

"Your translator is working?" Mèng asked.

Xenus shook his head. "I speak some Orbital German. What they speak is a mix of...well, lots of things, but there's some overlap."

Lydia had released her embrace but still clutched Xenus's hand. "What happened to you? After the crash – what do you remember?"

"We crashed? All I have is bits and pieces. Some of their children found me. I remember being carried in a stretcher. I must have wandered and collapsed. What happened?"

"You don't remember the crash?" Lydia asked.

Xenus shook his head. "I remember flying over a forest...that's the last thing."

"Commander Umana tried to kill us," Mèng said, "with hunter drones."

"Umana?" said Xenus blankly. Lydia grimaced. Mèng looked worried. "What?" Xenus looked panicked. "Who is Umana?"

"You've lost some memory," Lydia said. "It might come back, but you need a head scan. We've got to get you to the *Stanford*, and soon."

Xenus nodded. At least he recognized the name of the ringstation. At least he recognized *her*.

★   ★   ★

They slept for a few hours, Lydia and Mèng alternating watch. The Chhaang seemed peaceful, but appearances could be deceiving. Xenus's partial amnesia was worrisome, but she hadn't found any wounds or lumps on his head. His brain had gotten a good shake during the crash: he was concussed and disoriented, probably with some minor swelling (hopefully minor – too much cranial pressure could be lethal). She needed to get him to the *Stanford*, or at least to the OETS station, quickly. Mèng had given him an anti-inflammatory and a mild sedative, but Xenus needed a full medical exam.

Mèng's nav was still working; they were roughly one hundred kilometers south of the mule station.

"Can't you put out a distress beacon?" she asked Mèng. "Or contact someone on the *Liu Hui*? Give our secure location to OETS? They could come fetch us."

"Not without signing our death warrant. Umana is…persistent. We're a threat to be eliminated."

"How many *threats* do you have on the *Liu Hui*?" asked Lydia, more bitterly than she meant to. "I thought the ringstations were at peace."

Mèng smiled tightly. "'Eternal vigilance is the price of liberty,' I believe one of your ancestors said."

They would have to walk to the mule station.

As the sky darkened, the smell of roasting meat and onions permeated the palace. Soon they were summoned for dinner by a pack of long-haired children yelling "Schweinfest!"

"Pork on the menu!" said Xenus brightly. He'd regained some color.

The Chhaang – perhaps sixty of them – were seated in the spacious dining hall at three long columns of wooden tables, what looked to be original furniture from the nineteenth century. Their hosts ushered them to their seats at one end of the central table. Lydia was seated between a woman about her own age and a younger man, both of them attractive and friendly. Looking around, Lydia noticed the seating was arranged not by family group, but by age. The little children and the elders sat together at a large table running parallel to the inner wall, the older children at the table nearest the windows, and young adults through the middle-aged at their own central table.

The children began to sing, accompanied by a heavy drum beat and the rattle of wooden percussion. With much ceremony three roast boar were carried in on spits and deposited at the center of each table. Young men and women hoisting ceramic jugs made the rounds, filling bowls with a steaming cloudy liquid. Lydia's seat mates held up their bowls to be filled as the jug-bearers passed. Across the table, a young woman leaned over Xenus, filling his bowl.

"*Chhaang*," said the handsome young man to her left, grinning. His skin was smooth except for a small goatee and a wispy mustache.

"*Chhaang!*" he repeated, pointing at the steaming bowl. He took a long draught.

She sniffed the fermented namesake, then had a sip. It was hot, earthy, and good. She made eye contact with her partner, across the table. Xenus, grinning, said something.

"What?" she yelled. The hall was reverberant with singing, talking, and clatter.

"This hits the spot!" he yelled back, lifting his bowl in a toast. She smiled and raised her own bowl. There would be no conversation over the din.

Mèng, seated at the end of the table between two men that might have been father and son, looked wary, and took only tiny sips from her bowl. Lydia tried and failed to catch her eye. Mèng was either lost in thought or accessing something in her m'eye.

A carver worked on each roast, slicing off chunks of meat and passing them along. The long carving knives were thin from corrosion, wear, and centuries of sharpening. To have survived at all the blades must have been made from enormously strong alloys – high-end Corporate Age cutlery. Whatever technologies the Chhaang possessed, metalworking wasn't one of them. They were a relic people, devolving. Since they were likely illiterate – she'd seen no sign of books or writing of any kind – that was unlikely to change. She wished Car-En were here (meeting the Chhaang was an enormous anthropological discovery) but part of her was just sad. What kind of a life was devoid of books, understanding, and discovery?

A raucous cheer interrupted her reverie. At the children's table, a little girl had just been awarded a curly boar tail. The girl waved the crispy prize in the air, laughing hysterically. Lydia reconsidered her judgmental attitude – the Chhaang didn't *look* unhappy.

Chhaang (the beverage) and boar meat were followed by roasted onion soup, dense brown bread, more chhaang, and slow-cooked greens drenched in boar fat, spicy and delicious. Lydia relaxed, sinking deeper into her well-preserved nineteenth-century chair. Xenus, across the table, chatted with the large-breasted, broad-nosed woman next to him. The woman laughed, pretending to understand, and scooted her chair closer to Xenus. Surprisingly, Lydia didn't feel jealous. The Chhaang, despite their spears and sharp knives, did not make her feel threatened. Instead she felt welcome, accepted, and well-fed.

"*Gut?*" asked the man on her left, rubbing his belly. Except that he didn't *have* a belly, he was lean and well-muscled. Oh…he meant *good*, not *gut*.

"*Ja, gut!*" she managed.

He patted her shoulder, smiling. His hand lingered for a moment, and she found she didn't mind. The Chhaang were touchy-feely. Who was she to judge? This close to the glacial line, the more shared body warmth, the better. She realized the soot she'd seen on the outside of the buildings would be from controlled wood fires – possibly even ovens. How did they not choke to death on the smoke?

"Johann," said the goateed man, pointing at himself, still grinning.

"Lydia," she answered, unable to suppress a smile.

He waved over a jug girl. "Chhaang!" Before she knew it, her bowl was full and steaming.

★   ★   ★

The children were making the rounds, saying goodnight. "*Gute Nacht*, Aama, *Gute Nacht*, Buwa, *Gute Nacht*, Aama." All the adults were addressed as Aama or Buwa – general terms of endearment. Lydia recognized the little girl who'd won the boar tail. She looked a bit like Maggie – Vandercamp's first Earth-born child. Lydia felt a pang of homesickness. The little girl was moving down the line, approaching Lydia.

"*Gute Nacht*, Buwa," the girl said to Johann.

"*Gute Nacht*, Kirsten." Johann embraced the girl and kissed the top of her head.

Kirsten looked up at Lydia, hesitating. Then she smiled and gave Lydia a peck on the cheek. "*Gute Nacht,* Aama."

"*Gute Nacht*," Lydia muttered, and was soon receiving a goodnight kiss from a long column of children. Xenus and Mèng were doing the same. Johann did not say all the children's names – some he simply called *Nanu* or *Babu* – but he embraced and kissed nearly all of them.

The young children filed from the hall, escorted to bed by the elders. Instead of decreasing, the din intensified, with the young adults at the window table – some of them openly drunk – screaming, laughing, and shouting. Across the table, the large-breasted woman was touching Xenus's head, running her fingers through his short-cropped hair.

"*Buda?*" Johann asked, pointing at Xenus. Was he asking if Xenus was a Buddhist? Beyond the statue in the gardens, she'd seen no indication that the Chhaang practiced formal religion. Lydia hesitated, not wanting to offend. "*Buda?*" Johann repeated, embracing himself with both arms.

Ah, *buda* meant something along the lines of husband/boyfriend/ lover. "Yes, *buda!*" she said, exhaling. Johann smiled and nodded, then kissed her on the lips.

What? She must have misunderstood.

Panicked, she looked for Xenus and Mèng. Xenus, eyes closed and blissfully spaced out, was getting his head rubbed by the big-breasted woman and his shoulders massaged by one of the chhaang-jug girls. Mèng was nowhere to be seen.

Johann looked at her quizzically, then grinned and moved in for another kiss.

She kissed him back, wondering if she'd been drugged. No, she was in control – tipsy but not intoxicated. She sensed that if she told Johann to stop, he would. She didn't want him to. Her skin glowed pleasantly with heat. If she stood, she would surely faint from low blood pressure. Better to fall into Johann's strong arms.

She glanced again at Xenus. Eyes still closed.

A portion of her mind worked it out, analytically. The children had called all the adults *aama* or *buwa*: this was a community where parenting was fully shared. Did the kids even *know* who their parents were? They must know their mothers, but their fathers? The Chhaang had no paternity certainty; exact familial relations were not important. Everyone was cared for.

And the feast was leading into an orgy.

The thought snapped her out of her reverie. She pulled away from Johann and stood, but immediately swayed, catching herself on his sturdy shoulder. He was still smiling, holding up strong brown arms to catch her. She looked over at Xenus. His eyes were now open, but unfocused; he was still concussed.

"Xenus!"

He snapped to attention.

"Where's Mèng?"

Xenus looked around, confused.

"Sorry," she said to Johann, "I have to find my friend."

She left through the hall's north door, closest to where Mèng had been sitting. Outside of the dining hall, the palace halls were frigid. The moon's bright light penetrated the warped, soot-gray window glass and gave her just enough light to find her way. Trying to put herself in Mèng's mind, she climbed some stairs. "Mèng!" she shouted. She heard only the quick echo of her own voice. All the Chhaang were at the feast...or whatever it was turning into. "Mèng!" she cried again.

"Over here," she heard faintly.

She found Mèng on a balcony, looking over a broad swath of moonlit hills. "I wouldn't trust the railing," said Mèng.

"Are you okay?"

"Yes. The man next to me put his hand on my leg, and I sensed where the night was heading. I...wasn't in the mood for such things, but you and Xenus were having a better time, so I slipped out."

"They seem harmless," Lydia said.

Mèng looked unconvinced. "If you mean they're not malicious, then yes, I agree. But their existence has...implications."

"What do you mean?"

Mèng said nothing, but pointed out at the forested hills.

"What? What am I looking for?"

"Turn on your heat vision."

Despite her damaged kit, most of her vision enhancements still worked – the augments were directly integrated into her optic nerves.

It took about a minute of looking, adjusting sensitivity, and zooming in and out, but Lydia eventually counted five broad patches of heat, between two and twelve kilometers distant. "Are those settlements?"

"I think so."

"More Chhaang?"

"It stands to reason."

"Why haven't we seen them before? From the ringstation observatories?"

"Because they use preexisting structures? Because they use small-scale gardening? Maybe we just weren't looking hard enough."

Lydia watched the distant heat blobs for a while, but there was nothing much to see. She turned off the augments; the hills darkened.

"So everything we know is wrong."

Mèng nodded. "It's unlikely that the Chhaang are the only undiscovered surviving human community. More terrestrial exploration will probably reveal hundreds of micro-societies like them. Or unlike them, rather. Isolated communities are more likely to be culturally distinct...."

Lydia – still feeling the alcohol – laughed. It made so much sense. All of the ringstations' ponderous, overwrought plans for a slow, orderly, cooperative repopulation of the home planet were for nothing. Repop had already begun. And it would proceed the way evolution always proceeded: quickly, chaotically, and unpredictably.

Mèng had a surprised look on her face.

"What is it?"

Mèng frowned. "I'm not sure how, but someone has located our position. I just received a message."

Lydia's heart sank. "Umana's forces?"

Mèng shook her head. "Someone named Javier. Apparently your bioskin was emitting a distress call. He says he can pick us up."

CHAPTER TWENTY-NINE

"Please, sit down," Svilsson said. Karl Turen was standing awkwardly in the doorway of his study.

"I'd feel more comfortable...."

So stand. But please get on with it. Svilsson, as was his habit, held his tongue, and waited patiently for the tall bearded man to complete his sentence.

"Can we go dark before I show you the results? Can your residence disconnect?"

Svilsson, after a moment's work on the nearest control pad, nodded.

"I mean, *completely*," Turen said. "This can't show up in the public feeds."

"Privacy is never complete, but I'm confident we're not being surveilled. The Over Council takes the Second Right very seriously."

Turen looked unconvinced. "This...potentially changes the balance of power within the Coalition."

Svilsson was intensely curious, and equally aware that his face appeared impassive, even bored. He didn't *try* to have a poker face – it was just his natural demeanor. Two weeks ago he would have dismissed Turen's caution as paranoia, but that was before his daughter's field trip shuttle had been attacked by a madwoman from the *Liu Hui*. He tapped a command into the control pad. "There...nothing's getting in or out. Decoherence field."

Turen nodded, then fished something out of his pocket. He handed Svilsson a tiny glass cylinder filled with light pink liquid: a nucleic-acid-chain archive. Whatever Turen wanted to show him was huge. Svilsson took the vial and dropped it into his desk sequencer. A few seconds later, the sequencer estimated it would take four minutes.

"It's big," said Turen, unnecessarily. "Really big."

Genta popped her head in. "Oh...sorry." Turen, who had just started to lower himself onto a simple woodish stool made by Zinthia as a school project, snapped up straight. Genta, almost universally, had that effect on men. "Didn't mean to interrupt, but either my kit is on the fritz, or—"

"Karl, this is my wife, Genta. Genta, Karl Turen is the young engineer I was telling you about."

"Delighted," Genta said, extending her hand. "Always a pleasure to meet the next generation of geniuses who keep the frisbee flying." Her dress of shimmering teals and blues complemented her dark, flawless skin. Turen shook hands and mumbled something about not being *that* kind of engineer, but Genta was already looking at Svilsson expectantly.

"It's the house," Svilsson said to his wife. "Sorry, I should have warned you. It will only be a few minutes."

"Right. Well, I *was* in the middle of several conversations."

"I'll make it up to you," said Svilsson, meaning it. She wasn't really angry – she wouldn't be talking to him if she were – but he'd been in the wrong.

Genta scowled playfully and vanished. The two men watched the timer count down. Turen was at least two decades younger than Svilsson, but already leading his own engineering team, specializing in low-level physical simulations.

"How's your daughter doing?" Turen asked.

"Fine, thank you."

"And the other children – her classmates?"

Turen was trying to be tactful, not asking about the abduction directly. "They'll all receive counseling for the next year or so, but physically, they're whole. The teacher was the only one injured."

"Taking a leave of absence, I heard. But he's okay?"

"We'll see," said Svilsson. The truth was that Abel Kan, the math teacher who had been escorting Zinthia's class to the *Liu Hui*, was wracked by guilt, a sleepless, paranoid mess, ten kilos underweight, and at least a year away from functioning as a productive human being. Just as unfortunately, Kan had not witnessed the actual attack, and was thus worthless as a source of intelligence in regards to Commander Umana. A thorough debriefing of the children had been inevitable. Svilsson had had the same reservations as the other parents, but had reluctantly supported the gentle, parentally supervised questioning of Zinthia and her classmates.

"Any word on the attackers?"

"Nothing new," said Svilsson, tiring of Turen's questions. "The *Jūnshì* still insist that Umana has gone rogue – that they'll reel her in soon. She's been relieved of any official title or command, but her crew may not know that. Or they may stay loyal, regardless."

"Is it true that—"

"Look," Svilsson interrupted. "It's ready."

The study lights dimmed as a detailed visualization appeared on Svilsson's holoprojector: a blast of white light that condensed into clouds of swirling plasma, further densification into bright energetic tendrils, then into swirling blobs of matter.

Svilsson waited for Turen to explain himself. Nothing was forthcoming.

"Is this a joke?" Svilsson asked. "I asked you to run the algorithm, not provide some theoretical visualization. If you think the algorithm is a Nascency simulator, then—"

"We did run it," Turen insisted. "It's sped up – obviously – but this is what happened when we plugged in the constants."

That's impossible. And yet, 'that's impossible' was the too-obvious thought, the habitual one.

"Which values did you use?" Svilsson asked.

"The real ones," said Turen. "The actual constants from our own universe."

Svilsson nodded. Not every universe was viable. If the algorithm were a *universal* universe simulator, it made sense to seed it with constants from a universe with properties of relative persistence and stability, such as their own. Relative to *what* was a reasonable question. Hypothetically, other universes were created all the time, new existences bubbling out of the spacetime continuum. The fact that none of those universes were directly observable was irrelevant; they could still be modeled mathematically. These 'bubble universes,' with different physical laws and constants, might exist for mere milliseconds, or might exist long enough to produce complex, evolving structures and systems.

Zoë Sach's algorithm (Svilsson had learned the scientist's name from Car-En, who had learned it from her son, Tem, who had learned it from his aunt Katja Elkesdóttir, who had learned it from the entrapped Crucible volunteer) was generative. That much they had determined just by looking at it. *What* it would generate, and on what scale, had been the question. Processing power and data storage had not been real obstacles to detailed, large-scale simulations since the ascension of quantum cores and DNA media during the Late Corporate Age. But what Turen was showing him implied a level of simulation so deep and detailed that it was essentially indistinguishable from physical reality. It shouldn't be possible to accurately simulate the creation of space and time itself, energy coalescing into subatomic particles, then into elements and molecules and their corresponding macroscopic counterparts: nebula, stars, planets. To do so would require a computer the size of the universe itself. If for some reason that *wasn't* the case, and Zoë's algorithm really *was* accurately simulating a true Nascency on the most fundamental level…that would have strange implications. For one, it would lend support to the faintly ridiculous Bostrom's Simulation Hypothesis: the idea that probabilistically they were *already* living in a….

"The algorithm appears to 'level-jump.' Or 'layerize,' as my colleague Bosch puts it," Turen was saying.

"As in NENT? What does it stand for again? Nested, evolving…."

"…network theory," finished Turen. "Yes. We've just been saying 'reality layers.' Each layer or level of reality is wholly dependent on lower, more foundational, less abstract sublayers or sublevels. Biological transactions can't exist without chemical transactions, and so on. Communication between the agents or holons on one layer creates the next layer, or evolutionary space."

"I'm familiar with the idea," said Svilsson impatiently. "A mutated agent creates a new type of information transaction, and a new level of reality springs into existence. Prokaryotes evolve tissue specialization, and thus we have bodies, and the evolutionary theater created by the interaction of bodies."

"The somatic space – exactly!" Turen enthused, not picking up on Svilsson's hint to hurry things along.

"Menthe?" said Genta perkily, waltzing into the room with three tall glasses of bright green liquid.

"Thank you, I'd love one," Turen said, mistaking Genta's curiosity for hospitality. Genta's eyes were already glued to the simulation, now displaying recognizable astronomical features.

"Can you navigate within the simulation?" Genta asked. She put down the full tray (Turen awkwardly withdrew his hand) and pointed at a particularly bright spot on the screen. "What if you go over there?"

"You can," said Turen. "But this is a recording, not the actual simulation."

"How old is this universe?" she asked.

"Have you been lurking outside my study?" Svilsson asked in return.

"You two are practically shouting at each other – it's impossible not to overhear. And what else am I supposed to do? You've cut off our house."

"Only five billion years old," Turen answered. "Quite young."

"Have you done any...planetary exploration?" Svilsson asked.

"Wait until you see this. May I?" Svilsson handed Turen the control pad. "Look at this." A still frame showed a rocky, two-mooned planet, with a sun brighter than Sol. The image smoothly shifted, the point of view following each revolution of the planet around its star. "Now we speed up." The moons became a blur, then disappeared, as did any details on the surface of the planet itself. "A million years per second, now." The blackish planet acquired shades of gray, then orange and yellow, then blue and tan, then spots of purple and green. "There... photosynthesis – or something like it. I'll slow it down now."

"Can you zoom in?" asked Genta. The green drinks stood untouched.

"Yes. But remember this is all recorded."

"Recorded...how? How do you get a camera in there?"

"Not *literally* recorded," Turen said. "The data – well, a minute portion of the data – was extrapolated to create the images you're seeing."

Genta furrowed her brow. She wasn't dim – far from it – but the idea of 'recording' the simulation was counterintuitive. No photons or sound waves were being captured and encoded onto a storage medium. Instead, the results of the algorithm, now running for at least a googol of recursive iterations, were analyzed, with various patterns of data mapped to known observable properties such as space, time, and matter. How did they know those mappings were correct? They didn't, with any certainty, but ending up with a recognizable visualization was a good sign.

The 'camera' was closing in on the lush green planet, following its rotation so that geographic features became visible: inland seas, craggy mountain ranges, sparse jungles. "More land than sea," Genta observed.

"Yes. We're calling this planet *Devonaria*," said Turen excitedly. "There are some botanical similarities to Earth's Devonian period. We've only discovered about a dozen Earth-like planets so far."

"Is there animal life?" Svilsson asked.

"See for yourself."

The image zoomed in rapidly, until it seemed they were drifting above the sandy banks of a vast lake. Various tube-like plants dotted the area, narrow green ones and squat purple ones. "Look," Genta said, with a gesticulation that nearly knocked over the drinks. "Is that a... snake?"

"More centipede-like, I think," said Turen. "It might have a name, but we've only just begun to catalog Devonarian lifeforms."

"It's the size of a child," Svilsson said, feeling more amazed than he'd anticipated. "Unless my sense of scale is completely off." The many-legged Devonarian crawled into the murky water and disappeared. Svilsson leaned back in his chair. "It's Wolfram's Grail – the ultimate generative algorithm. The creature we just saw was the result of millions of years of evolution, wasn't it? It's as real as we are."

"Billions of years," Turen corrected. "But yes, at least in terms of how this universe operates, it's as real as ours."

"Wait a minute," said Genta. "Does that mean that if you found intelligent life...would they actually be conscious? Would they have thoughts and self-awareness? Could we...*communicate* with them?"

"Yes, yes, and no," said Turen earnestly. "As far as we can tell, everything going on in the algorithmic universe is as real – right down to subatomic particles – as our own reality. So it stands to reason that if complex consciousness emerges, it would be as real as our own."

"Well, *has it* emerged?" Genta asked.

"We don't know. We haven't seen any signs of anything resembling a civilization, or even a species that looks like it might be capable of building one. But the simulation is young...only five billion years or so. And remember, it's a universe – it's *vast*! We can search the data for patterns, but we're having to build new tools to handle what we've got. We don't have anything resembling an infallible, fast search."

"So if we're gods, we're not omniscient," said Svilsson.

"Or omnipresent, or omnipotent. In fact, we can't do *anything* in regards to the simulation, except to run it and look at the results."

"A read-only universe," Genta said.

"How many linked cores are running the simulation?" Svilsson asked. "Does the passage of time speed up or slow down depending on how much you throw at it?"

"Yes. Right now it's running at a rate of about a billion years per day. It's running on Hair Lab 7, which is about fifty thousand cores."

"They gave you that much?"

"They were very curious, when I hinted at what the algorithm might do."

"But you didn't actually show it to them, right?"

"Of course not," Turen assured him. "As we agreed. Inner circle. But I can't promise they won't poke around and extract it."

Svilsson nodded. The cat was half out of the bag. And you couldn't put half a cat back in a bag.

Genta stepped back and rubbed her eyes. "Even with that many cores, the algorithm must be incredibly efficient. A universe, with billions of galaxies and trillions of stars and who knows how many individual lifeforms...."

Turen nodded. "That's the amazing thing – how efficient it is. The algorithm itself is deceptively simple. It's the results that are infinitely complex."

Something occurred to Svilsson. "But as the universe progresses, the simulation slows down, right? Not subjectively, for its residents, but for us, as external observers?"

"I'm not sure," said Turen, scratching his head. "It's hard to measure. There's no universal simulation clock we can check. All we can do is passively observe evolutionary events as they unfold. It's possible the simulation *isn't* slowing down, even though new classes of lifeforms are emerging. Maybe each and every recursion of the algorithm is the *same*, even though new evolutionary spaces and behaviors are emerging within the simulation."

"But you *would* expect the simulation to be slower if it were running on fewer cores."

Turen grunted in the affirmative.

"So theoretically, what if the simulation was running on a *single* core for ten years? How old of a universe could exist?"

"With the same starting constants?"

"Yes, assume so."

Turen's eyeballs twitched as he worked it out. He blinked a few times, consulting his m'eye. "Er...less than a hundred million years old. A very young universe."

Svilsson stood and paced. If what Car-En had told him was true, there might well be a young universe developing in the so-called 'Black Tree' in the Harz mountains near Happdal. Did the black threadlike material comprising the branches and roots of the tree itself extend the processing capability of the core, or was the exostructure simply a power-collection system, extracting energy from sunlight, microbial decay, and nutrients in the soil? If the former, the first universe created by Zoë Sach's algorithm could be ancient, potentially tens – even hundreds – of billions of years old. What could a person learn, spying on such a universe? What could a *civilization* learn, studying civilizations that had persisted for eons?

"What's the matter, darling? You've gone quite pale." Genta looked concerned.

"I'm fine, it's just, if the algorithm gets into the wrong hands...." He looked at Turen, but the young scientist, while looking politely concerned for Svilsson's health, didn't get it.

"The boy...."

The situation was much worse than he'd realized. It was bad enough that Umana was holding Tem hostage, a tragedy-in-the-making for Car-En and her family. But Tem knew the algorithm. His aunt had made him *memorize* it.

With perfectly bad timing, Zinthia arrived home from school. She came into the study immediately, with the same furrowed-brow, dead-serious expression she'd worn since the incident. Her skin was nearly as pale as her hair, which needed washing and brushing. Turen switched off the screen hurriedly, but Zinthia paid no attention, instead making a beeline to her father.

"Dad, any word on Tem?"

"Can you please bring me one of those menthes? Have a sip yourself."

Zinthia solemnly handed the bright-green beverage to Svilsson, rejecting the bribe. He wasn't off the hook.

"Nothing yet, my love."

"What's being done?"

What was being done? A whole lot of nothing. Diplomatic channels were open, and chock-full of useless talk. The *Zhōngyāng* were denying involvement. To their credit, the *Liu Hui* officials had handed over some useful (if disturbing) information. Commander Umana, along with a large contingent of her *Kǒngbù Wūzéi* 'terror squid' special forces, had gone rogue, with an experimental, lethal starship in their possession. *Star*ship was not a figure-of-speech in this case, the *Zhōngyāng* had as much as admitted that the *Iarudi* was capable of interstellar travel. Zinthia looked at him steadily. He'd not been hiding facts from her; her question meant *What are you going to do?*

"Dad, Tem is in danger. If our places were switched, he'd be trying to help me."

"I know." He didn't doubt it; Car-En's boy was brave.

"So? What are we going to *do?*"

He glanced at Genta, then at Karl Turen. Both were looking at him. An introduction, to buy time. "Karl, this is my daughter, Zinthia."

"I'm glad to hear you're all right," said Turen politely. "I'm sorry about your friend."

Zinthia glared at Turen, but now was not the moment to reprimand his daughter for rudeness.

"*Well?*" Zinthia said, switching her glare to him. He wasn't dodging this one.

"It does seem that the *Stanford's* response has been…anemic," ventured Turen. He was right. The *Stanford's* reaction had been downright sheeplike, even worse than their passive acceptance of the *Liu Hui* takeover of AFS-1. Diplomacy without military backing was just hot air.

But what did they expect him to do? Mobilize the *Stanford's* non-existent military force? Invent a negative mass drive? His official position as a member of the Repop Council did not grant him vast powers. He was an academic and a consultant, not a heroic warrior. Svilsson did not even consider himself to be much of a leader.

But a different part of him accepted the responsibility. He knew Tem and Car-En personally. Zinthia and Tem were friends – good ones. More than anything, his only child was *expecting* him to help.

"Zin, can you fetch us some pistachios?"

Zinthia smiled and sprinted to the kitchen. Pistachios were his thinking food, his getting-down-to-business snack. Eating pistachios was a promise of action, of forward movement.

"Big guns, huh?" Genta said.

"It's an emergency."

"Um...should I stay?" asked Turen, confused. "Family meeting or something? I can come back later."

"You'd better stay," Svilsson said. "I need to explain something to you...the implications of what you've discovered. If we've indeed stumbled across an efficient, realistic universe simulator, then we have a major problem, and a major opportunity. We need to flesh out the plan."

"What plan?" Genta asked.

Svilsson was feeling punchy, or maybe just desperate. "Let's call it *Operation Calamari*," he said. He was bluffing – he had only the faintest germ of an idea. But it was better than nothing. He had to act, to do *something* to help Car-En's son, even if that something turned out to be foolhardy and quixotic.

His daughter would accept nothing less.

PART THREE
THE BLACK TREE
CHAPTER THIRTY

Tem awoke with a sudden sense of 'up'. Gravity pressed him down into his cot.

"Shane, are you awake? What's happening?"

Shane groaned from across the gray cell. His friend's condition was worsening. When the guards had brought Tem back, Shane has been there, freshly bloodied and beaten. His fellow prisoner hadn't eaten since, and had only taken water when Tem had squeezed a stream into his mouth from their limited supply of cubes.

The cell itself rotated, as if on a central axis. Was the *Iarudi* decelerating?

"Shane, I think we might be landing...or at least entering the atmosphere. I might know where she's taking us."

No sound from across the room. Tem was pinned to his bunk with a force much stronger than Earth or ringstation gravity. He closed his eyes and endured the extra weight, breathing deliberately through his nose. Against his will, a recollection seeped into his mind: the Squid Woman's tentacles coiled around his chest, pressing his lungs flat.

The weight lifted. He floated up from his bunk.

"Free fall," said Shane weakly. "Are we going home?"

"Yes, we'll be home soon," Tem said, trying to sound confident. Even if delirious, Shane needed comfort.

Minutes later they landed with a soft bump. Gravity was once again normal. They were back on Earth, or somewhere like it.

Tem got up and stretched. His legs felt weak, jellylike. It was tempting to lie down, maybe go back to sleep. His right wrist was swollen and still ached, but he slapped his cheek with his left hand, trying to drive away the fatigue with more pain.

The remaining water cubes had fallen to the floor. He picked one up, brushed it off, and carefully tore off a corner tab.

"Shane, wake up. You have to drink something."

Shane complied, taking a few sips, but kept his eyes closed. Before, when Tem had helped him drink, Shane had managed a weak smile or a friendly wink. He'd been physically weak but mentally strong, in charge of the situation despite his missing teeth, fractured bones, and bloodied face. But Umana – or the guards – had broken him. Shane was near death, and if he had any hope left it was buried deep.

Tem would hope for both of them. *He* was not broken.

He reviewed in his mind what he'd said to the Squid Woman, to lure her into the trap. At least, he *hoped* it was a trap. His plan might just as well lead to a doubling of her power, and more misery for everyone.

She'd taken the bait – the mention of Raekae. *The Inventor*, she called him. As he'd feared, she'd quickly realized that the black egg had been the genesis of the Black Tree. He didn't need to lead her to it – she already knew where the Black Tree grew, on the high ridge east of Kaldbrek.

He'd feared she would immediately kill him, having no more use for him. But she hadn't.

He was bait, for Mother. That's why he was still alive. It gave him a lump in his throat. *Mother, run!* he shouted in his mind. *Don't fight her – she's too strong.* But Mother *would* come, if she could, if she knew where he was. That's what mothers did.

The cell doors slid open. A single guard beckoned to Tem, ignoring Shane.

"He needs a doctor," Tem said. "If he doesn't get help soon, he'll die. Are you trying to start a war?"

The guard, who upon closer examination looked greenish, perhaps land-sick, furrowed his brow. "Follow me," he said simply, in English.

Tem picked up the remaining water cubes and placed them on the edge of Shane's cot box. He bent over and whispered in his friend's ear, "I'm going to kill her. I'll come back for you." Speaking the words aloud made him believe the promise. He felt in his pocket for the small leather pouch Father had gifted him. It was still there. He slipped the pouch into Shane's hand, then turned to the guard. "Where are we?"

In two strides the guard closed the distance and grabbed Tem by his collar.

"Walk, or I'll drag you. Your choice."

He stumbled through the dimly lit corridors, half walking, half dragged, turn after turn. The Squid Woman's ship was *huge*. How did such a vast thing get into space? Tem squinted at a bright light ahead. Natural light. *Sunlight*. The guard pushed him down a ramp.

Blinking rapidly, Tem could make out only vague shapes in the brightness. *She* was there next to him, with her obscene chest tentacles and long, twisting hunting arms. A cold wind bit through his light ringstation clothing.

"The snow will be here soon," said the Squid Woman. "Have your people squirreled away enough food to survive the frost?"

His eyes adjusted. They were on the high ridge, surrounded by stubby, elfin-wood trees. The fall sun was midway through its low arc: high noon or close to it.

"Plenty," he said. "Happdal winters well."

Tem stepped into a patch of sunlight, escaping the *Iarudi*'s long, insectile shadow. He could see the outlines of the Black Tree, no more than forty meters ahead. To his left and right the Squid Woman's guards stood at the ready, long-rifles pointing down.

"You'll have to dig it up, if it's still there," he said. He did his best to keep his tone neutral, but his voice betrayed his eagerness. Looking up to see if she had noticed, he reeled back, tripped, and fell. She was flying through the air, toward the Black Tree. No – not flying – she had *launched* herself into the air, pushing off the ground with one of her long tentacles. The end of the extremity dug into the dirt less than two paces away. The tentacle was dark brown and shiny, like an eel, though he reasoned it must be a machine, a robotic attachment somehow fused to her torso, perhaps even directly to her spine. It had *felt* hard and machinelike when wrapped around his ribcage, crushing him. But it was also flexible, and she used the extra appendages like real limbs. Maybe the tentacles were real flesh...some kind of monstrous, mutated extra parts. The tentacle foot whipped away as she took her next great stride, spraying dirt in his face. Now she loomed over the Black Tree, hovering on both long tentacles, her legs neatly folded beneath her torso.

He glanced at the guards. Should he run for it? If he could make it to the tree line he might have a chance. He was not ten minutes from the tree where Egil had found him sleeping. He knew the way back to Happdal from here.

But what if he escaped? The *Iarudi* was a warship, Commander Umana a hunter. The Squid Woman could track him down and annihilate his village as easily as smashing a bug.

The Squid Woman now stood on her own two feet, and was waving her tentacles at Tem.

"Boy, come join me!" Her voice pierced the air; even at such distance he clutched his ears in pain. Her voice was thunder, rocks exploding in fire, the roaring Begna after melt, all at once.

He rose to his feet, dusted off his clothes, and slowly approached his nemesis. What would happen now? This was the moment.

She laughed gleefully, and began to dig. Her powerful tentacles burrowed into the soil underneath the narrower roots of the Black Tree. With tremendous force she lifted upwards. The roots splintered, cracked, shattered.

He froze, as if a chain from the ground were attached to the knot in his stomach, rooting him. Tante Katja had explained what the algorithm was, what it *did*. It made a new universe, from the very beginning. A *Nascency*, Mother had called it, when he had told her everything. Was the Squid Woman now destroying a world? Not *a* world but *worlds*, star systems, galaxies? Was she snuffing out trillions of lives before his eyes?

The Squid Woman caught him staring and read his face. Mercifully, she spoke softly. "Don't worry, little cub, I'm not hurting anyone. The Inventor and his thralls don't reside in these roots. The tendrils only collect sunlight and nutrients from the soil. It's the core I want. A little more digging now...."

She tore into the roots, tossing flurries of earth and broken black tendrils into the air. She dug with her main tentacles, bracing herself with powerful legs. Her body was well-muscled, and while not as physically impressive as Farbror Trond or Farfar Jense, her frame was absorbing a tremendous amount of force. How did she withstand it? He remembered how his blade had barely scratched her neck. She was made of strong stuff.

With both tentacles coiled around the main 'stump' of the Black Tree, the Squid Woman squatted and pulled. The earth shifted beneath

Tem's feet, but the stump barely moved. Frustrated, Umana tightened her grip and pulled harder. With muffled cracking sounds from beneath the soil, the stump perceptibly lifted.

"*Tem.*"

The projected whisper, so quiet that he almost didn't notice it, came from his left, from a copse of leafless elfin-wood. He recognized the voice. "Mother?"

His heart leapt. She was here! He couldn't see her, but she was here! She shouldn't have come. She would die. Whatever weapon she had, the Squid Woman was stronger. He ran toward Umana. Mother might be willing to sacrifice her own life, but he wasn't willing to let her die.

The Squid Woman released her tentacles and waved them menacingly above her head. Black dust filled the air. "Stay back!" she roared. Involuntarily, he froze. Her voice was irresistible.

"Once you find what you're looking for, will you let me go?" He said the first thing that came to his mind. He had to divert the monster's attention. *Run, Mother, now!*

His nemesis smiled. "I have another use for you. I think you can guess it. Farther back, now. There…that's good."

The Squid Woman coiled her tentacles around the stump and with a mighty heave ripped it from the earth. Carefully, she placed the stump upside down, examining the tangle of roots on the underside.

"Where is it?" she muttered. "Ah…hello, Mr. K."

Delicately she extracted a smooth oval object, plucking away the black tendrils connecting the core to the superstructure.

A quick movement caught Tem's eye. Was it Mother, concealed by her battle cloak?

No, something smaller. Something black, moving among the broken black tendrils.

The Squid Woman saw it too, and reached out a long tentacle.

A cat-sized spider scurried up the flexible limb until it reached her shoulder, where it perched. The black egg temporarily forgotten, the Squid Woman stroked her pet with one of her chest tentacles.

"Were you here the whole time?" she purred. "Why didn't you call for me? I would have come. You're the only one left, I think. *She* killed the others."

Then, to Tem's horror, the Squid Woman looked past him and said, "I can see you, you know."

Mother. She could see Mother.

A white line split the world in two. It terminated on the Squid Woman's throat, burning a black, smoking hole. The monster screamed, with all her voices.

He was on his hands and knees, retching. Warm liquid trickled from his left ear. His vision narrowed to a circle of ground below his face, then to a single black shard from the Black Tree.

"Shane," he croaked. "He's on the ship."

Darkness.

CHAPTER THIRTY-ONE

A few days earlier

In the field behind the dairy, Egil untied Saga. The black-haired girl stood and shook out her wrists, scowling at Car-En. Egil stepped between them as a precaution, but Saga was distracted, looking over his shoulder.

He turned to see a thin, brown-skinned man cautiously approaching them. A hundred paces behind the man, a hovershuttle – the same kind as Shane and Lydia's – was parked on the dirt road. The man waved tentatively. Car-En jogged over to greet him.

The two were fifty paces away, too far to eavesdrop. The brown man spoke quickly, gesticulating. Something was wrong. Car-En stood still, stiff.

"Wait here," he said to Saga.

"Maybe *you* should wait too, old man. That looks like sky people business." She was calmer now, but with no less venom in her voice.

"The worlds have collided," Egil said. "The sky people have landed." There was the beginning of a poem there. But no time to ponder it now.

The brown man stopped talking as Egil approached.

"Javier, this is Egil. A villager, and a friend." Car-En's voice was controlled, but tremulous. What had happened? "Egil, this is Javier, from the OETS station."

Javier extended his hand. He said something in his own tongue, then painfully repeated it in too-formal Norse: "Your reputation precedes you, and under other circumstances it would be a pleasure to meet you."

"Tem has been taken," Car-En said, before Egil could ask. "Commander Umana attacked a shuttle – *school* children on a field trip. She injured a teacher, and kidnapped Tem."

"Just him?" Egil asked.

"I can only guess it's *me* that she wants. She sent a picture – she sent it everywhere, to everyone – squeezing him with those awful tentacles...." Car-En clenched her jaw and exhaled through her nose. "I'll *kill* her if she's hurt him."

"You may need to kill her regardless," said Egil.

"I should never have given him permission to leave the *Stanford*," Car-En muttered. "*Damn it!*"

"We'll get him back," Egil said in his oration voice. It was enough to shock Car-En into a different state. She stared at him, wide-eyed. "*How?*"

"She wants *you*. So go to her. Let her taste your rage. See how she likes it."

Javier asked Car-En a question in his own tongue.

"Because I killed her spiders. I interrupted her attempted genocide. I think she wants everyone in the Five Valleys dead."

"Why?" Egil asked.

"I have no idea. She's sick in the head." Car-En paced a circle around the grounded shuttle.

"Have you seen Car-En fight?" said Egil to the brown man. "No warrior can match her speed and fury. Car-En will hunt and kill Umana."

Javier gave him a look and took a step back.

Car-En finished her lap. "Can we track her ship?"

Javier rubbed his narrow chin, then answered in English.

Car-En nodded. "Stay in touch with OETS, and with the *Stanford*. Let me know if you detect anything bigger than a soccer ball entering the atmosphere." She glanced back toward the village. "You'd better stay here...minimize contact. The children might find you anyway, but you'll be less disruptive if...."

"I'll bring food for Javier," said Egil. "I'll get some now." He'd followed Car-En's gaze, and to his dismay saw that Saga had left. Hopefully Katja had stayed with Esper, in case the Kaldbrek girl decided to have another go at him.

Car-En nodded. "Good. I'm going to check on my husband."

Egil brought Javier deer jerky, honey, butter, and brown bread, then went to Ilsa's house. Car-En and Katja were there, waiting on Esper. His injuries had swelled and colored.

"Saga gave you a good pummeling," said Egil.

"I'm fine!" Esper said perkily.

"Have you seen the mad girl?" Egil asked. "Did she come by?"

"She'd better not," said Katja. "I'll not let her off easy if she dares." There was a fierceness in the sister's voice that Egil had not heard for years. There was some fight left in her.

"If you don't need me here, I'll seek her."

"Go," Car-En said.

"Maybe you should tie her up again," Katja suggested.

"I'm sure she's calmed down by now," said Esper. From his cheerful countenance it was clear that Car-En had not yet shared the news about their son. Egil glanced at Car-En, but the sky woman avoided his gaze.

He found Saga sulkily wandering the perimeter of a fenced pasture. *Perhaps her rage has burned itself out.*

From ten paces he called out, "Forgiveness is the only path forward, Saga. The venom in your heart hurts you more than it hurts Esper."

She stopped walking but did not turn. "I can't forgive him," she said. "He killed my only kin."

"He was protecting his only son," said Egil. "Any man would have done the same."

Saga whirled around. "Should I forgive this *Squid Woman* as well? Should I forgive *everyone* who takes from me and kills my loved ones? What about *you*, old man? Have you forgiven Svein for sending you away from your own village?"

"I have," Egil said. In truth he had nursed his rage for two years. Was he pushing the girl too hard?

"Then you are weak through and through. Your bones are brittle sticks. Your balls are dried berries."

Egil laughed. Saga had a way with words. "It's natural to be angry," he said, "but Esper is a good man, deserving of your forgiveness. And if you touch him again, his sister will kill you. Or his mother, or his wife."

Saga shook her head. "I won't touch him. But not because I'm scared of his women."

"Then why?"

"The Squid Woman deserves my wrath more so than Esper." Saga lifted her gaze. Her tears had left salt-streaks on her face, but her eyes were dry.

"Good. Come with me. We'll eat, and prepare."

He took Saga to Elke's. He didn't want a confrontation, but he knew of nowhere else to go. Happdal was not his home. Elke would feed them, at least. He made Saga wait outside, taking a minute to speak to Esper's mother alone. Elke had already heard some of the day's events. He filled her in on the rest.

"The girl is not entirely of right mind," Egil said, "but I have calmed her down."

"She attacked my son," said Elke, chopping onions with a tarnished longknife. The vegetables yielded easily to Elke's casual movements, as if deciding on their own to divide into cubes.

"She can help us. Save your anger for another day."

Elke nodded her assent and Egil brought the girl in. Saga sat sullenly while Elke laid out smoked fish and pickled vegetables.

"Eat," Elke said. It was invitation enough. Egil and Saga consumed the food quickly and quietly.

The appetizers, and the smell of soup which soon filled the room, calmed their tensions. After some time Elke broke the silence. "If you bring Tem back to me I will be grateful."

"I will cut off the Squid Woman's many limbs, one by one," said Saga. "Your grandson will be free to go where he pleases then." *Half promise, half insult*, thought Egil.

"My grandson knows his place is in the smithy," Elke said. "He chose that path the day he could lift a hammer. The same path as his uncle and his grandfather."

"He is half sky person," said Saga, through a mouthful of smoked trout.

"We are all human," Egil interjected, "not that different."

Elke snorted. "You don't believe that."

"Is your grandson not proof of it?"

"A lynx and a wildcat can mate and have kittens," said Elke, "but that doesn't mean the lynx and the cat are the same."

Egil raised an eyebrow. She had a point. He would have to think on it.

Elke rapped a small red glass on the wooden table in front of Egil, then set out two more. She unstoppered a ceramic jug and filled each glass with a dark brown liquid. A sharp herbal scent arose from the bitters. Elke lifted her glass. "Promise me, bard, that you will bring my grandson home, or die trying."

Lifting his own glass, Egil looked into Elke's pale blue eyes and found himself charmed. Age had not dimmed Elke's beauty, but carved it deeper into her face. To his own surprise he felt his loins stir. He hadn't thought of Elke that way.

No, he had. He hadn't dwelled on it, because he feared her. But of course he had.

He was old. Was there a *more* worthy cause for his remaining years, than to try to rescue young Tem? Probably not. But he would make a promise only if he meant to keep it. He was a poet and a bard. He would live and die by his word.

"Well, old man?" Her eyes smiled. Did she read him so easily? "Is your old life so precious that you won't make me this promise?"

The door rattled and shook, as if a great boar were knocking against it. Saga screamed. Elke was unperturbed. The door swung open; the daylight was blocked by a treelike figure in the doorway. With steps that shook the house, Elke's firstborn entered.

Trond's red beard reached halfway down his chest. A warhammer was slung across his back. His nostrils flared as he regarded the scene before him. "What's this? Eating and drinking while my nephew is missing, and my brother convalesces? Why are we letting the hours pass?"

Egil stood. "Your sentiment is correct, Trond. But to fight the kraken woman, we can't just rush in. We need a plan."

"Then let us discuss it. We'll talk while we walk. Drink up!" Trond took a glass from the shelf and filled it from the jug. "To finding Tem!" he shouted. He drained his glass and slammed it on the table.

Egil gave Elke a nod before he drank. The promise was made.

★   ★   ★

They gathered in the clearing where Happdal's sick men had once been Burned, before the sky people had intervened, purifying the water supply and curing the ill. Now the field was used to play *fótrknöttur*, though the children were elsewhere today.

"We have a common enemy," Egil said. All eyes were on him. "The Squid Woman, the kraken, Commander Umana — whatever her real name. Her spiders killed twenty-two souls in Kaldbrek, and now she has stolen a child dear to us. In addition, she is accused of being a slaver. She is evil, crazed." He paused and looked at each in turn: Car-En in her shimmering skin, tall Askr, black-haired Saga, the mighty smith Trond, tiny brown Javier. "Tell me, how do we fight her?"

Car-En stepped forward. "You saw her spiders near the Black Tree, on the ridge. Maybe she'll go back there."

"Or to Vandercamp," said Javier in English. Egil recognized the name of the sky-person settlement.

Askr raised his hand. "The sky-person village...isn't that far to the south? By the sea?"

Javier said something to Car-En, who repeated it in Norse. "Some of us could take the flying machine," she said. "With a full load we'd have to fly low and slow, but it would be faster than walking."

"How does the kraken fight?" Saga asked. "Who has seen her?"

"It's not just her," said Car-En. "She'll have highly trained soldiers with her. Look, the Squid Woman is...she'll slaughter you if you try to fight her. Even you, Trond. The weapons she has at her disposal—"

"You think I don't know what the sky people are capable of?" Trond said, scratching his chin through his thick beard. "Your weapons are like magic to us. I fear this Squid Woman – I would be a fool not to. And I have my own child – I'm not eager to die. But there *must* be some way we can fight her."

"We know the land," said Saga. "Better than her, better than you."

"That's true," Javier said in halting Norse. Evidently he was tracking the conversation, even if not fluent in the village tongue.

"Okay," Car-En said, "but *I* will be the one to fight her, if she comes. I'm the only one equipped to do so. I'll accept your help, but I won't be able to protect you."

"Where is Katja?" Askr asked.

"Still with Esper," said Egil. It was just as well, considering that Saga was dry tinder waiting for a spark. They'd be no good to Tem if they killed each other before finding the Squid Woman.

"The shuttle was built to carry four at the most," Javier said, shooting Trond a nervous glance. "Five would be a stretch. More than that and we'd be grounded."

"If I am too heavy for your machine," said Trond, "then I will walk, and arrive late to the fight. Better my sister go in my place. Katja will bring Biter, and give the kraken a taste of godsteel."

"Biter, forged by Stian, first smith of Happdal?" Saga asked, eyes wide. "The wolf blade?"

Trond laughed. "*Now* you fear my sister."

★   ★   ★

The next morning Egil and Katja met Car-En and Javier at the shuttle, where the sky people had camped. As agreed, Trond, Saga, and Askr had left at first light, hiking northwest toward the high ridge that shadowed Kaldbrek's eastern side. By now those three would have crossed the Upper Begna once already; later they would cross a wider branch and begin a steep ascent that would bring them directly to the Black Tree. Egil, Katja, Car-En, and Javier had planned a more circuitous, less steep route; they would take the flying machine north past the Three Stones, cut west along the High Pass, then fly south along the entire length of Kaldbrek's high ridge until they met the others at the Black Tree. If anyone were spying from above, splitting into two groups would obfuscate their intentions.

Taking flight, the actual lifting off of the vehicle, brought Egil's stomach to his throat. Once they were afloat his fear subsided. It was not unlike his dreams: flying as an eagle would, soaring over treetops. If only his vision were like a hunting bird's, to see rabbits and tiny mice from such a height. The sky people could do that, he supposed, with their special eyes. He could see the extra layer covering Javier's cornea, if he looked closely. At times the brown-skinned man's gaze unfocused; Egil guessed he was watching something in his artificial eye.

Such thoughts reminded him of the spyglass, and he remembered that in his haste to run to Kaldbrek he had left the Builder artifact on the flat rock overlooking the Black Tree. Well, he would find out soon enough if it was still there.

He stole a glance at Katja. Her cheeks were ruddy from the wind. She had only some of her mother's beauty; with age her face had become more square and strong. She looked more like Arik than Elke. Her heart was more like Arik's too, fair and loyal and steady. Maybe *she* would be jarl one day. He had always thought it would be Esper (and Elke surely thought so too), but Esper might end up on the *Stanford*, with his wife and son.

"Did you sharpen Biter?" he asked.

She grinned. "No need. Godsteel holds its edge. Care to run your finger along the blade?"

"No thank you. Is it true that holding a soulsword, you can feel the rage of the trapped soul?"

Katja extended the sword to him, hilt first. The sheathed blade stretched across both their laps. Car-En, riding in front, raised an eyebrow at Javier.

He took the hilt. The soft leather grip was warm – had Katja been holding the weapon? He hadn't noticed. He closed his eyes and let his mind go blank.

Yes. He was a wolf, part of a pack padding across a snowy meadow. But he didn't feel angry. Just...wolflike: hungry, alert, protected by the pack.

"You tamed it!" he cried out, amazed.

Katja smiled. "Biter is my companion now, not my slave."

Car-En looked at them as if they were mad. He grinned at her. There were some things the sky people might never understand.

★   ★   ★

There was no sign of the others when they reached the Black Tree, well before noon. Egil found the spyglass on the rock where he had left it, knocked over by the wind but undamaged. He returned it to its case and stowed it in the hovershuttle.

"Now what?" he asked Car-En.

"Wait, and watch the sky. Javier should be able to detect her ship before we can see it. We'll have time to hide."

He nodded, watching the Black Tree. Even from fifty paces he could feel its heat.

The windblown elfin-wood provided little cover, so they hid the shuttle behind Egil's lookout rock, piling loose branches and debris atop. They waited and watched the skies, but saw only clouds, birds, and lazy flies.

Car-En asked something of Javier. They had a brief, heated exchange in their own tongue. "We don't have time," muttered Car-En in Norse, running her fingers along her forearm. "*Tem* doesn't have time."

They heard Trond and the others long before they crested the ridge. Trond and Askr were loudly debating the merits of vinegar pickling versus fermentation. For a smith, Trond had strong opinions about the correct preservation methods for carrots, cabbage, and onions.

"There's no sign of her yet," Egil said, meeting them before they got too close to the Black Tree, "but if there were, you'd be dead men. You're as noisy as bears."

"I'd not be a dead man," said Saga. The Kaldbrek girl sounded cheerful. Perhaps the vigorous climb and the company of handsome young men had lifted her spirits.

The day passed, and the night, and half the next day. Even with the heat from the Black Tree the night had been brutally cold. Egil had awoken twice, thinking he'd heard an animal scurrying nearby. Perhaps a marten, scouring for dinner scraps.

"Go for a walk, old man," Saga advised. "You look stiffer than your staff." He nodded and forced himself to his feet, too weary to devise a retort. At least he had not had to climb the ridge. Sleeping on the hard ground had given him aches enough.

"Don't leave yet," Javier said from the grounded shuttle. He'd pushed aside the branches to climb into the pilot's seat, and was watching a small screen. "I've got something."

The black ship appeared first as a dot, then as a black beetle, then as a longship, a shape Egil knew only from carvings; he'd never seen a sea with his own eyes.

"It's the *Iarudi* for sure," said Javier quietly, first in his own tongue, then in Norse. "She's descending slowly."

Egil watched Car-En: her eyes were locked on the ship as a lynx might stalk a bird. The sky woman pulled her hood over her head and her second skin dissolved, leaving a shimmer in the air. Saga did not even notice Car-En disappear.

"The rest of us should split up and hide," Javier said. "You know your roles. Don't make a move before Car-En."

As planned, Egil and Saga descended the west side of the ridge, hiding as best they could behind a stubby spruce.

"Car-En will surely die," Saga said.

"Don't underestimate a mother's fierceness when she fights to protect her child."

"Bravery is not the same as might," said the girl.

The black ship landed gently, scorching the earth with its fiery thrusters. Thin legs telescoped out from the hull and sunk into the dirt. They crept forward just enough to get a peek at the sleek black ship. Its form was like a huge insect that had emerged from a soft larval casing, then hardened and darkened. Three thick cylindrical rings encircled the main body like arm hoops. They watched until the charred grass and shrubs beneath the ship burned themselves out.

"They wait," Saga said, but just then a ramp unfurled, securing itself to the ground with pincerlike grips. Black-uniformed guards – men and women as tall as Askr and nearly as broad as Trond – streamed out, stationing themselves near each landing strut.

"They're giants!" said Saga. He pressed a finger to her lips but she swatted it away.

The Squid Woman's long limbs came first, probing the air. The eight shorter tentacles were visible next, then the woman-part. Saga gasped into her palm. Egil grabbed the girl's shoulder, both to support himself, and to restrain her in case she lost her sense. This time she did not brush him away.

A few minutes later a boy stumbled down the ramp, shielding his eyes from the bright noon sun. "It's Tem," Saga whispered, gripping the hilt of the slim knife Car-En had lent her. Among them, only Egil was unarmed: even his staff was stowed in the shuttle. If all went according to plan, he would need both hands free.

The boy was whole, not visibly injured: two arms, two legs, no visible marks. As for his mind and soul, who could say? But Tem came from hardy stock. This trauma would scar him, but if he was anything like his mother, the psychic wound would strengthen him in the long run.

Tem and the monstrosity conversed briefly. Without warning the Squid Woman leapt toward the Black Tree, launching herself from a tentacle. Tem stumbled and fell. Saga tensed.

"Be still!" Egil hissed. "Wait for Car-En."

The Squid Woman took another leaping stride toward the Black Tree and disappeared from view. "Should we move closer?" Saga whispered. Egil nodded and they crept forward, hiding behind a cracked gray snag. The Squid Woman's tentacles were lashing wildly about, spraying dirt in high arcs, like a hound unearthing a buried shank. "What's she looking for?"

"The soul of the Black Tree, I think. The black egg that Katja swallowed, and spit up, that became the tree."

"And if she finds it, what then?"

"I don't know," said Egil. Who *could* know? If he'd understood Car-En, the sky people did not fully understand the machinery behind the gast. Even to them, it was like magic.

The Squid Woman attacked the main trunk, wrapping her sinewy tentacles around the black stump and pulling. Even from their distant vantage point Egil could see the power in her limbs. Would Car-En stand a chance against this monster?

After several attempts the Black Tree yielded; with muffled cracking sounds the Squid Woman pulled the dark trunk from the earth and upended it. Busying all her tentacles at once, she dug about the roots with frenzied intensity.

Saga reached out and squeezed his arm. "Where is Car-En?"

"Close, I think. Be ready."

The Squid Woman pulled a small object from the black roots and brushed it off.

"Is that it? The egg?"

Saga said something else, but Egil didn't hear it; he was following the Squid Woman's gaze. She'd seen something. *She sees Car-En.*

Saga cried out, shielding her eyes. A beam of blinding white light had sprung from the Squid Woman's neck. No, it was *burning* her neck. Car-En was attacking.

"Now!" Egil shouted, springing to his feet. Just as quickly a deafening scream knocked him flat. The sound was the boom of thunder, metal scraping on metal, a dying animal, all at once. Egil looked up at the cold blue sky, clutching his ears.

He clambered to his feet and lurched up the hill. "Come!" he shouted to Saga, but his voice sounded faint and faraway. *Run, old man.* The boy's life depended on his tired legs.

The Squid Woman twisted around, wide-eyed, looking for something to kill. One of her shorter tentacles pressed against the hole in her neck. Trond, twenty paces behind her, shouted and swung his huge hammer. Had the Squid's great cry not felled him? Perhaps the years of hammering steel had numbed his ears; recently Trond had taken to shouting in normal conversation. The Squid lashed at the smith with a long tentacle, but he struck the limb aside with his hammer. She drew the limb back, then snapped it forward like a whip, snatching the warhammer from Trond's grasp. With a mighty swing she heaved the weapon over the ridge. Egil could not help but pause to watch the arc of the hammer, and listen as it faintly crashed through spruce branches far below. The Squid Woman stiffened the snake-arm and struck Trond in the chest with a deep thud. The big smith grunted and went down.

Egil glanced at the guards. They had their rifles leveled, sweeping the area, but held their fire. Most were focused on the Squid Woman. Several were running back up the ramp.

He found the boy. Tem lay on his back, eyes unfocused, blood trickling from one ear. Egil bent his knees and heaved, slinging Tem over his shoulder like a sack of coal. *Run. Run!* His legs moved as if pushing through sludge. He plodded toward the shuttle, cursing his age and weakness.

"Put her down!"

Egil turned. Saga was screaming at the Squid Woman, throwing stones.

The Squid Woman had both long tentacles and several shorter ones held high above her head, in coiled positions. She was holding something, some*one*. Car-En's suit flickered black as the Squid Woman squeezed.

"Let her go," Saga shouted, hurling another stone. The heavy rock struck the Squid Woman's face, snapping her head back. Enraged, the Squid Woman hurled Car-En aside. The sky woman tumbled through the air, soaring like a cloth doll until she smashed into the lookout rock and fell limp to the ground. Egil turned so the boy could not see it, and forced his aching legs forward. The guards shouted to each other in an unfamiliar tongue.

From the corner of his eye he saw something long and straight fly at the Squid Woman and lodge in her shoulder. Askr's spear! With two tentacles she dislodged the shaft and cracked it in half.

The Squid Woman pressed the ends of both long tentacles into the ground, preparing a great leap in Saga's direction. Egil feared for the Kaldbrek girl.

Katja pulled back her blade. *Where had she come from?* Trond's sister sliced the godsteel through the air, then through whatever flesh, gristle, and exotic materials comprised the Squid Woman's long tentacle. The monster tumbled down in a squirming heap, brown fluid squirting from the severed limb.

Run, Katja! Run while you still live!

He took his own advice and closed the remaining distance to the flying machine. Javier was throwing the last branches aside. The small man grabbed Tem with surprising strength and gently lowered the boy into the backseat bench of the hovershuttle.

"Quick, get in!"

Egil clambered in and placed his body over Tem as a shield.

"Go!"

The shuttle lifted off. Egil kept his head down, expecting at any second to feel a powerful tentacle wrap around his neck, yank him upwards, and smash him against the hard earth.

He hoped Saga and Katja and Askr had sense enough to flee. He hoped that Trond still lived – and that the Squid Woman thought him dead. And he hoped that Car-En had somehow survived her fall.

If they could get Tem to safety, it would all be worth it.

CHAPTER THIRTY-TWO

Shane awoke to gravity. They'd set down, lifted off some time later, and now they were grounded again. They were somewhere on Earth, unless the *Liu Hui* ship had some way to generate gravity artificially – he couldn't rule that out. Somehow, despite a culture that supposedly nourished innovation and scientific research, the *Stanford* was technologically lagging behind the other ringstations, or at least behind the *Liu Hui* – but it made him wonder what kinds of new tech the *Alhazen*, the *Hedonark*, and the other orbiting worlds might be concealing. He wondered what had enabled the *Liu Hui*'s great leap forward.

Guards entered the cell and loaded him onto a stretcher with surprising gentleness. What was *this*? Regime change? Had the *Liu Hui* reined in their rogue commander? He did not resist; he had neither the strength nor the will. Instead he practiced his Mandarin, but the guards remained stone-faced when he asked about the weather.

His new quarters were large and comfortable, even plush. The guards fed him real food: noodle soup and tangerine juice, the latter which somehow tasted fresh. Once the dried blood on his teeth rinsed away, the food tasted heavenly. He almost slipped and said *thank you*, then remembered these goons might be the same who had beaten him only days earlier. They'd worn masks; he wouldn't be able to identify his torturers. Except for Umana – she'd taken pleasure in looking him in the eye while she interrogated him, crushing the air from his lungs and cracking his ribs with her tentacles. *Where is Car-En?* she'd asked him a hundred times. Had she found Car-En, and killed her?

He wondered if this would be his last meal, a moment of grace before his execution.

Dessert was a small black egg served in a round wooden bowl.

"Swallow it whole," said one of the guards. The guard was tall and wore his black hair cropped short. He looked ethnically Chinese, except for his bright green eyes.

Tentatively Shane picked up the egg. Its surface was smooth and warm. Did some pulsing embryo live within? Or was this his method of execution? He wasn't sure if the thing in his hand was biological or artificial, or some combination.

He had little to lose at this point. His body was wrecked. He could not return to Vandercamp. He had no job, no role, no purpose. The woman he loved was...not available.

He swallowed the egg. Tem had mentioned something about a black egg, hadn't he? Or was that a figment from one of his fever dreams?

The egg slid down his throat easily, then caught.

He finished his juice. The egg was stuck in his esophagus. It refused to descend into his stomach.

He coughed and patted his chest. "It's stuck," he told the guard. The tall man stared ahead, avoiding his gaze.

This was the way they would kill him? A chunk of food in his throat? It wasn't choking him; it was just lodged halfway down his gullet. Was it some kind of mini-grenade, poised to explode on a timer?

The guards cleared his bowls and glass, and left him alone.

He crawled into the comfortable cot and slept. Maybe his last sleep. He didn't really care – it just felt good to close his eyes and surrender to a full stomach.

The fullness in his throat was already subsiding.

★   ★   ★

He awoke ravenous, to the smell of meat. The warm overhead lights brightened as he climbed out of the cot. He sensed his full, normal weight on the floor; the ship was still grounded.

A breakfast feast had been laid out for him: boiled eggs (real ones), sausage, seasoned black rice, pickled vegetables, and sticky pastry squares. He ate it all, gingerly avoiding the raw gap from his missing tooth, and drank the entire pitcher of cold water they'd left for him. He used the small bathroom attached to his room, which also included a steam cube and a supply of clean white towels. Luxurious, for a spaceship. He washed himself, and discovered that most of his wounds had healed. Even his bruises had faded. How long had he slept?

He rested and waited. His entire body felt warm and tingly, maybe from the steam bath. He felt *good*, somehow, in direct contrast to his circumstances. He couldn't have long to live, could he? Had the Squid Woman somehow been deposed? Did he dare let himself hope? He couldn't help it. He thought about Lydia. He hoped she was safe, wherever she was.

Guards cleared his breakfast dishes. An hour later they brought another meal. He ate it, and another one after that. His hunger refused to subside.

He became suspicious. What was happening to his body? It had to be the black egg. It was changing him somehow, from the inside out.

But into what?

The realization floored him, literally. He pressed his forehead against the cool carbonlattice and tried to control his breathing. *The egg was the tree, the tree was the egg.* That's what Tem had told him. It hadn't been a dream. The Black Tree was *growing* inside of him, consuming his body for fuel.

He dragged himself to the cot, feeling weak and jellylike even though he'd felt hale and hearty a minute ago. There was a parasite inside of him, consuming him.

No, there's more to it than that.

His brain was waking up, slowly. Maybe it was the food, maybe it was the black egg growing inside of him, but his mind fog had lifted. A little of the old Shane Jaecks was coming back, confident and resourceful. *Hold on to that. Think.*

The egg – the machine parasite – had come from the Black Tree. What had Tem said? The black egg had contained an entity – a gast, or ghost – that had taken over Tem's aunt's body, nearly killing her.

Another Crucible subject, still alive after hundreds of years.

But in the battle, something had happened. He closed his eyes and tried to remember Tem's words. The boy had talked on and on, while Shane drifted in and out of consciousness.

Zoë had killed the gast.

Who was Zoë? It didn't matter. What *did* matter is that he knew something that the Squid Woman didn't. Umana wanted access to the other Crucible subject…maybe to interrogate, or maybe just to have the company of another centuries-old being. But that being didn't exist anymore.

So what was growing inside of him? *Something* was. He could feel it. His nausea and jellylike fatigue had passed; now his muscles, skin, even his organs felt as though they were vibrating; his entire body pulsed with mild electric current. Except for a minor twinge here and there he wasn't in pain, but his body was *transforming* into something different.

Whatever it was, it wasn't taking over his brain. His mind, if anything, felt clearer. He felt more conscious, alert, and electrified with each passing minute. His consciousness was blazing, one hundred per cent Shane Jaecks.

And she didn't know that. She was expecting *someone else*.

When the guards came to deliver his next meal, he stood up straight, looked the taller one dead in the eye, and said, "I'm ready to see her. Tell Umana I'm here." His voice sounded louder than he expected – almost a shout. The fair-skinned guard he'd addressed – she might have been Russian – stepped back and reached for her weapon. He presented his palms and took a step back. "No need for that. Just tell her the process is complete."

The Russian gestured to the other guard, a young, ethnically Chinese woman with a shaved head, who placed a stack of steaming wooden boxes on the table, avoiding eye contact the whole time.

He felt strong, alert. He wondered if he could overpower the two women and escape. He didn't know the layout of the ship, but he was fairly sure they were on Earth. If he could just get off the ship....

Then what? They could be anywhere. It was nearly winter, or nearly summer, depending on the hemisphere. He could die of exposure, be eaten by animals.

Or they might be parked in Vandercamp. He had no way to know.

The Russian watched him suspiciously, hand on her sidearm (probably a disruptor, though he didn't recognize the make). Maybe Umana had warned her that he would be...changed.

The guards made no move to leave, but stationed themselves on either side of the sliding door. The young bald one – was she subvocalizing, or just swallowing?

Deliberately, he sat at the table and slid the lids off the boxes. If they wanted to watch him eat, fine. He wasn't going to offer to share – he was *ravenous*. The meal was simple: some kind of savory legume-flour cake on a bed of greens, seasoned with a tangy brown sauce, and green tea.

The doors slid open. A pungent smell filled the suite. The Squid Woman looked smaller than before, when she had interrogated him. It took him several seconds to realize that one of her long brown tentacles was missing. Only a stubby meter or so remained. The end was capped in moist pink flesh; it was growing back.

The Squid Woman ignored his gaze. "I read that you liked green tea. Does the flavor still appeal?" She had a bruise under her left eye.

"Yes, it's delicious. Thank you," he said. It seemed like a safe thing to say. *Shane* wanted to gloat at the sight of her injuries, but he was supposed to be someone else. He had no idea *who*, but she was already providing clues. Whoever it was liked green tea.

What else did he know? Umana was expecting a Crucible volunteer, or maybe one of the program founders. *You're a tea-drinking Corporate Age academic body thief who has been alive for five centuries. Act like it.*

"So quickly, then?" She sidled forward. The doors slid shut behind her. Her chest tentacles probed the air near his face. Were they reading him, somehow? "The soldier didn't put up much of a fight?"

The soldier – that was *him*, Shane. "He was a beaten man," he said coldly. Umana's eyes narrowed. Her inner, vertical eyelids closed, briefly masking her irises with a milky layer. Had his tone been wrong? Too warriorlike, maybe? Think scientist, or doctor. *What would Lydia say?* "You tortured him. Why?"

"To find out what he knew," Umana said flatly. One of her chest tentacles twitched close to his face. He blinked, but didn't flinch.

He wanted to say *I can just tell you*, but stopped himself. The process by which the parasite acquired memories and replicated the consciousness of the host – that had to take time. It was plausible that the parasite would be able to commandeer motor and sensory functions relatively quickly, but mirroring each axon, dendritic pathway, and microtubule would take significantly longer. He tried to feign sudden comprehension. "Ah, he knew the location of the...egg." He hoped there wasn't a more precise word for the machine parasite.

"No, he didn't. Someone else led me to the core. Were *you* aware of your previous location?"

"No. I've been host-less," he said, winging it. "No external sensation for years. But there must have been an energy source. I've been fully conscious, residing in various simulations. You should see what I've built."

She nodded: a single, brief lowering of her chin. It was the kind of imperious gesture an emperor might make to authorize an execution. Had he just blown it?

He took a sip of tea. It had cooled. "So where was I?" he asked. "Physically, where was I?"

"The core had implanted in the earth. The threads were feeding on sunlight and nitrogen decomposition."

He drank more tea before responding. "Fascinating. Is that the first case of such a thing?"

"As far as I know," she said. Her tone was still cool. She didn't trust him yet, whoever *him* was supposed to be. How could he convince her that he was really a Crucible subject? *What would he know? What would he want to know?*

"So obviously, you've figured out who *I* am," he said, "but the question remains...."

She smiled. "Who am I? I was wondering when you'd ask. So you don't recognize me?"

He widened his eyes, hoping he wasn't overdoing it. "Are you saying...but I thought I was the only one. It's been *five hundred* years."

"If you, why not another?"

"But which one? Forgive me, it's been a *long* time." Should he make up names? No...even after centuries, she might remember all the original Crucible subjects intimately.

The Squid Woman slowly shook her head. Her chest tentacles waved side-to-side, in synchrony.

"I'm making a fool out of myself. Put me out of my misery," he said, hoping she wouldn't take the statement literally.

She smiled, and whispered a name.

He leaned forward. "Sorry? I didn't catch that."

"Isabella," she said, only a little louder.

The guards looked uncomfortable, as if the Squid Woman had just unselfconsciously removed her clothes and peed on the floor.

He had no idea how to react, but it was obvious that a neutral reaction wouldn't suffice. Her tone implied there had been a *relationship* between the young Isabella and whatever Crucible subject he was meant to be. He had to *choose* a reaction, or else the jig was up.

"Isabella," he said softly. "It *can't* be."

"It is," she whispered. Surprisingly, her eyes were welling up with tears. *She believes!* He felt a moment of remorse for deceiving her, then quashed the feeling. She had tortured him. She'd wanted to kill Car-En; maybe she already had. And Tem...was he still alive? If the mother was dead, Umana might dispose of the son.

"I thought I was the only one left," he said, hoping to buy a few more seconds to think.

"You were." She moved around the table. He stood and backed away, but something was pushing him toward her. Her remaining long tentacle had snuck behind him, blocking his retreat. Her chest tentacles gently embraced him. "You *were* the last one. I ate the others."

"You *ate* them?"

"I consumed and integrated their cores. They're my thralls now. Remember Zhan? He's inside of me now. So are Iain and Natalie. You'll have plenty of time to catch up." Her tentacles tightened; it was difficult to breathe. "I'm *very* curious as to what you've been doing all these years, but I'll find out soon enough. What hosts did you find? What worlds have you built?"

"It's an *upgrade*, being part of me. I'm the most powerful being in the solar system. I *rescued* you from oblivion. You were buried in the damn *dirt*. You were a *tree*. I'm giving you a new life."

"What about this host?" he gasped. "It's not...I haven't captured its memories yet."

She squeezed tighter. "The security guard? He doesn't interest me. A boring man with an insignificant life. He played his part... as meat, for you. I wanted to verify what I suspected, that the great inventor was still alive...." His ribs pressed painfully into his lungs and liver.

"Commander Umana!" The Russian guard's voice sounded urgent, even panicked.

"Silence!" roared the Squid Woman. The sound flattened his eardrums and made his bowels rumble. So be it – if his last act were to shit on her, that would suit him. "The boy," Umana continued, whispering into his ear, "now *he* interests me. I may even use him as a host, in due time. This form has suited me for years, but soon I may need to disappear for a time. The boy could be ideal."

Something cold and smooth was slithering up the side of his neck. The tentacle curled around his cheek. He clenched his jaw and lips closed. The tip of the tentacle hardened and pressed through his tightened lips, up against his teeth. He reached for the limb, but she swiftly grabbed his wrists with her other tentacles and pressed his arms to his sides.

"Open wide," she said, smiling. She gripped his head with her hands and dug her thumbs into the hinges of his jaw. He cried out as his mouth was levered open. She jammed a tentacle into his mouth – it tasted like seawater – and against the back of his throat. Slowly, it pressed down into his esophagus. He couldn't breathe. What a strange way to die!

"Commander! The Cimtari are approaching. They're within ten kilometers and closing quickly."

"The *who*?" she shrieked. The tentacle stopped moving, still lodged in his throat. He had maybe a minute of air left in his bloodstream before he passed out. Had the guard said *Cimtari*? The Cimtari were the highly trained security branch of the *Alhazen*, specializing in martial arts and nonlethal weapons. He'd heard they were equipped with a small number of armed shuttles that patrolled the area around the compact tubelike station (structurally, the *Alhazen* was an O'Neill-cylinder). Were the *Alhazen* shuttles atmosphere capable? Was this really what he wanted to think about with his last moments of consciousness? His lungs burned; he might have thirty seconds before he blacked out.

The lights dimmed; the room shook with a dull boom. His throat spasmed as Umana extracted herself. He collapsed to the floor in a limp heap, panting for air.

The door shut behind them. He was alone. He heard shouts from the corridor.

He grinned, realizing something. *The boy could be ideal*, she'd said.

Tem was still alive.

CHAPTER THIRTY-THREE

Tem was in his own bed, in his own loft. The air chilled his face, but he was warm underneath the supple rabbit pelt blanket. He could hear Father puttering around downstairs. He heard the sizzle of fat, and soon after smelled frying meat. Bacon for breakfast – *real* bacon. He hoped there would be oatmeal too.

"Father!" he yelled, refusing to leave his warm nest. "When is Solstice?"

"Not for three weeks," Father answered cheerfully. "Now get up, if you want to eat."

"Will Farfar Arik be back by then?"

"He said he would be, so in all likelihood he will."

"Will there be a feast?"

"*I* am about to feast, on your breakfast."

He doubted Father would make good on the threat, but even a small chance of losing even a single piece of bacon gave him the will to leave his soft cocoon. He dressed quickly, shivering the whole time, and carefully climbed down the ladder using only his left arm. His right wrist was still healing.

"There, hot tea," said Father, pointing to a steaming mug. It wasn't *real* tea, like he'd had on the *Stanford*, just hot water poured over dried forest herbs. Happdal had real meat, the ringship had real tea. But the drink was hot, and Father had masked the bitterness with a chunk of honeycomb. He drank quickly to warm himself, burning his throat a little, then chewed on the waxy comb to squeeze out the last of the sweet. Father *had* made oatmeal, with more honey, and they ate with gusto.

"Wait," said Tem, wiping his mouth, "should we have saved some for Mother? Is she coming home today?" With dismay he saw there was nothing left – they'd eaten every last morsel.

"I'm sure Elika is feeding her," Father said. "Let's go see her, and she can tell us herself if she's ready to come home."

★   ★   ★

Ilsa's house, where the old woman tended to the sick, was warm, and smelled like smoke and fresh bread. Isla herself had gone to Kaldbrek with Egil and Saga, to help the injured. In Ilsa's absence, Elika, Ilsa's grandniece, had cracked some windows and lit a fire in the old hearth. Askr was helping out too, chopping wood and fetching food. The bread, a dense brown sourdough, baked in a tight-lidded iron pot near the fire.

Mother, in a bed near the hearth, was awake and in good spirits. Her left arm was in a sling, her left leg splinted and raised. "Tem, my love, come here." He did, expecting a hug, but instead she grabbed a nearby rag and wiped his mouth. "Your face is covered in grease."

"Can you come home today?" he asked. He noticed the black battleskin, neatly folded on a chair, looking like any other piece of ringstation clothing. Atop the skinsuit were slim battery packs that looked like smooth bracelets fashioned from some dull dark stone, as well as other compact components from the suit's weapon and security systems.

"It saved my life, you know," she said, following his gaze. "And possibly yours."

"I know," he said, "you told me. You would have been crushed against the rock otherwise." Still, he hated the thing, and hoped she would never wear it again. "*I* had a plan, you know. It might have worked."

"It might still," said Mother softly. "Come here." She hugged him this time, tightly. After a few seconds he pushed away (only because he was having trouble breathing) and looked at each of his parents in turn. He needed to tell them everything he'd learned about the Squid Woman, and just as importantly *ask* them a few questions. The time for secrets was over. The enemy was still alive and dangerous. If they were going to work together as a family, *everyone* needed to know *everything*.

"How are we going to fight her?" he asked, looking at Mother.

"It's enough that Car-En is alive, Tem. Let her rest," said Father.

"We need to rescue Shane! We can't rest too long. What if the Squid Woman makes more spiders, and they attack Happdal? She wants to kill everyone. She doesn't think people *belong* on Earth. She has some crazy idea that—"

"Tem!" Father's voice was hard – it almost never sounded like that, and Tem was shocked into silence. Mother was smiling, but she looked pale and tired. He wasn't sure she'd heard anything he'd just said. "Tem, let's go. We'll come back later. Your mother needs to sleep."

He ran from the room, and left Ilsa's house. The cold air outside whistled in his left ear, where the Squid Woman's scream had punctured his eardrum. For days sounds had been muffled and dull in that ear, but his hearing was beginning to return. Mother had said the eardrum would fully heal in time.

Father was right – Mother needed time to rest. He'd been wrong to push her so soon. But *somebody* needed to act right away. He found himself making his way to the smithy. Farbror Trond had fought the Squid Woman – he knew how strong she was.

Tomas was pumping the bellows. "Hello, Tem!" he yelled, still pumping. "You've finally returned to do your shift. Good thing, my arm is about to fall off."

With dismay he saw that Tomas, who was a little younger than Tem, looked both taller and stronger in the shoulder than when he'd last seen him. Dutifully, without thinking about it, Tem moved to take the bellows handle with his one good arm.

Tomas laughed. "I'm kidding! I just took over from Hennik. I'm fresh as a flower."

"*Hennik* is a bellows boy?" Tem's mouth hung open. It was hard to imagine the bully who had beaten him in the road humbly pumping at the bellows handle, hour after hour.

"Yes, soon after you left for the sky ship, he asked Trond and Jense. They were short, so they let him. He'll never make apprentice, but they're happy to have another pair of arms. Even if he is a little old."

Shaking his head, Tem pushed on the heavy oaken door. Inside the smithy, Nine-Finger Pieter was adding coal to the furnace. Trond looked up from examining an axehead. "Nephew! Have you returned to work?" Except for a few cracked ribs, Trond had survived the battle with the Squid Woman unscathed.

"I tried, but Tomas wouldn't let me. He said that Hennik is bellows boy now."

"Don't worry, Tem. I'll kick Hennik back to the dairy the second you tell me you're ready to take up the handle. You will always be welcome here."

"Thank you," said Tem, surprised to realize that he *didn't* want to return to the thankless job of pumping the bellows. Trond already had an apprentice – Nine-Finger Pieter – and though he might take on another because Tem was family, he didn't *need* one. And if Tem were to return to the bellows, that would crush any slim hope Tomas had of his own apprenticeship. Tem didn't know what his own future held, but he no longer felt it would take place in the Happdal smithy. And that was a strange feeling indeed.

"We're busy here – is there something you need? Do you have a message for me?" Trond's tone was friendly, but his uncle's mind was on his work.

"I want to talk to you about...." Even as he said the words, he realized he was in the wrong place. Trond's life was in the village. He had work here, and family. But there *was* someone in Happdal who would help him fight the Squid Woman. It should have been his first stop. "I was just looking for Tante Katja. Have you seen her?"

*   *   *

Tante Katja was at her home, where she almost always was, reading tattered Builder books. When she saw Tem she rose from her chair and stretched. "Good! I was just thinking it was time to get some exercise. Will you spar with me?"

They fought with wooden staves in the yard between Katja's tiny hut and Trond's grand house. Katja worked him hard, bruising his shins and arms, even striking him lightly in the head with controlled strikes. His fencing training helped, but still he blocked fewer than half of her blows. His aunt had always been strong and fast, but people said that after her injury she'd become unnaturally quick. She struck him hard in the stomach. He begged off, panting. "I need a rest!"

Katja laughed, not at all winded. "You've grown soft on the ringship, but your form isn't bad."

"I fence every week with Per Anders. He's not as quick as you, but he's stronger than me. Yvette, my instructor, she's very good. Fast and sneaky, like you."

"I'm not sneaky! It just seems that way because you don't think ahead. You've got to look beyond your weapon."

"Look where?"

"Into your opponent's mind. See what they're thinking. It's not that hard. It's written right there, on their face."

Katja brought out smoked fish. They sat on uncomfortable chairs she had made herself. His aunt was more warrior than woodworker. Tem asked her the question he'd first thought to ask his uncle. "How do we kill the Squid Woman?"

Katja sighed. "Not easily. The black threads – the same ones that grew inside of me when the gast took my body – they make her fast. And her skin is hard."

"I know!" said Tem. "I struck her with the knife Trond gave me. I only nicked her, but still I named the blade Squid Cutter, before I lost it. I hope it's still on the *Rama*."

"The blade was godsteel?"

"Yes."

Katja laughed. "You're a lucky boy, to wield godsteel at your age. And to draw blood with it. Mudsteel would not have pierced her skin, I think."

"But the godsteel blade Biter did."

"Yes. Biter cut off the kraken's limb. But barely. It would have been easier to lop a two-year sapling. I swung again, to finish her, but she brushed the blade aside. She opened her mouth to scream – I was already deafened from her first bloody yell. I wanted to cover my ears, but I dared not drop Biter. Instead I thrust at her face.

"She leapt back, coughing. I saw the hole in her throat, from Car-En's light lance. I chased her, but with her single long tentacle she pushed herself off and flew through the air. She went inside her ship. The ramp curled up behind her, the air itself shivered. I ran to find your uncle. He was winded and bruised, but you know how strong he is."

"And Saga?"

"I didn't see her. By the time I had returned to the village, she had left with Egil to return to Kaldbrek. Good riddance. I wish Ilsa had stayed."

"Ilsa goes where she is needed," Tem said.

"We were lucky to survive the fight," said Katja. "To kill her...I don't know. What do *you* think, nephew?"

"I hoped she would eat the black egg, and that Zoë's world would consume her."

Katja nodded. "A desperate idea, but not a bad one. I don't know what would happen if the Squid Woman ate the gast egg. I fear that somehow she could learn the pattern."

Tem's gut tightened. "She *has* the egg."

Katja tousled his hair. "There's no point in fearing what you can't see in front of you. What's done is done. You're safe here, for now, and so is your family."

Tem stood and thrust his face at Tante Katja, so that their noses nearly touched. "We *must* rescue Shane. And if we don't kill the Squid Woman, she'll kill us all."

"What do you propose, little jarl?"

Tem shrunk back, trying not to cry.

"What's the matter? What have I said?" His aunt embraced him awkwardly. It was unlike her to touch anyone, unless she was beating them with a weapon.

"That's what *he* called me," he said between sobs. "Shane. He called me *Jarl Tem.*"

His aunt held him tightly. "Your friend might still live. You said he was strong."

Tem sniffed. "He is."

"Then don't give up."

Outside, children were shouting. Katja followed Tem to the door. Raakel, Elika's niece, ran by; Tem sprinted after her. He grabbed her arm, spinning her around and nearly knocking her down.

"Ouch!" Raakel wrenched her arm away, frowning.

"Sorry. What's happening?"

"Another flying machine, in the field. Four sky people."

"Who?"

"How should *I* know?"

Tem and Katja followed Raakel; they soon caught up with the gang of children running to greet the shuttle. Tem saw that Hennik was among them, though the blond boy did not notice Tem. Unlike Tomas, Hennik had not grown significantly taller. If anything he looked less tall, and perhaps a bit fatter. Maybe Tem himself had grown during his months on the *Stanford.*

The hovershuttle had landed in the middle of the *fótrknöttur* field. Tante Katja, the only adult among the villagers, stepped forward to greet the sky people. They had climbed out of the machine and now stood in a row. Tem recognized two of them.

"I am Katja Elkesdóttir of Happdal. Who are you?" Tem had not noticed before, but Katja had slung Biter across her back. The sky people eyed his aunt nervously.

"It's okay. I know them. That one is Lydia," he said, pointing at the copper-haired woman. "Hello, Javier!" He waved to his friend. There were two others: a pale man with close-shorn hair standing next to Lydia, and a black-haired woman with Asian features standing a few paces away, as if she were not quite part of the group.

"Hello, Tem!" said Javier. Katja's posture relaxed. Javier continued in English. "It's good to see you are safe. We heard that you had been kidnapped. We were worried. Commander Umana widecasted a picture, but gave no demands. People on the *Stanford* have spoken of little else since you went missing."

"I'm fine," Tem said. "My family rescued me." He reached out and took Tante Katja's hand.

"I'm relieved. We all are. I just picked these three up from a place not far from here. We decided to stop by Happdal on our way back to the mule station to see if there was anything we could do to help. But it seems our help isn't needed. May I tell everyone on the *Stanford* that you're okay?"

Tem felt a stab of guilt. He had not thought about Morfar Shol.

"Yes…of course. Please let my grandfather know I'm fine. And Per Anders, and my classmates and teachers."

Javier's eyes and lips moved rapidly for a few seconds, though he made no sound. His eyes refocused on Tem. "There, I've sent a message. Everyone will know you're fine."

Tante Katja escorted the sky people to the village center, where they were met with curious stares and some hostile ones, for many of the villagers resented being spied upon (though to Tem's satisfaction, reports of forest 'ghosts' had diminished). Katja ushered them into the longhouse, barring the children. Tem protested, but Katja gave him a look that silenced him. As soon as she was gone, Hennik and several others snuck underneath the longhouse. Tem followed. He had a right to listen as much as anyone. In the dark beneath the floorboards, Hennik finally noticed him, but looked away. There was fear in his eyes. Had Tem grown so big? No…Hennik was scared because Farbror Trond's words had been true: his uncle would send Hennik away without a second thought if Tem wanted the bellows station back.

Tem wanted to tell Hennik, *You have nothing to fear.* Tem's life was bigger now. Hennik was a villager, and always would be. Let him have the bellows.

Heavy footsteps on the boards above: Tem heard Father's voice, and Katja's, and then Mother's. Was she well enough to be up and about? The adults exchanged formal greetings in a mixture of Norse and English. The black-haired woman and the pale man had strange names, difficult to remember. There was an exchange of news: the battle with the Squid Woman, politics among the ringstations, and something about the 'Cimtari.' Mostly Mother and Javier spoke, in English. Tem caught Hennik glaring at him. The blond boy resented Tem for understanding, but was too proud to ask for a translation.

"They speak of the fight on the ridge, and bickering among the ringships," whispered Tem, scooting closer. Hennik pursed his lips and nodded.

"Vandercamp is blacked out," Javier was saying. There were large gaps between the floorboards – it was easy to hear every word. "Vanderplotz must be freaking out with Umana on the run. We have no idea what the situation is. Just how crazy is he?"

"Is Adrian in charge, or this Foster character?" Mother asked.

"Foster," said a higher voice – Lydia's. "As far as we know, AFS-1 is still under *Liu Hui* martial law."

"I thought you said the *Liu Hui* had completely disassociated themselves from Umana, after…after the attack on the *Rama*." He could hear the rage and hurt in Mother's voice; it scared him.

"They did." A man's voice – the pale man. "That leaves AFS-1 in flux."

"The *Stanford* is still staying out of it?" This voice – a woman's – was soft and accented. It must be the black-haired woman. Was she from the *Liu Hui*?

"Oddly, yes," Javier said. "Pacifistic, or just passive, I'm not sure."

Father spoke rapidly in Norse, and Mother was agreeing with him. This time, Hennik understood, and smiled spitefully.

Father would take Tem to the *Stanford*, where it was safe, until the Squid Woman was dealt with. Mother and the others would go to the sky people settlement and assess the situation there.

Tem's gut roiled. He didn't want Mother to go. But he *did* want to return to the *Stanford*. He missed Morfar Shol and Zin, and his other friends from school, and even his teachers. But at the same time he wasn't ready to say goodbye to Farbror Trond and Tante Katja and Farfar Jense, and Farfar Arik had yet to return.

"Go to your home in the sky, little boy," Hennik whispered. "Life on the ground is too dangerous for you."

"Shut up!" Tem yelled, and punched Hennik in the nose.

CHAPTER THIRTY-FOUR

Umana smiled. The Cimtari fighters – squat and sleek, like little piglets – were heating the *Iarudi* with zetawatt laser pulses on each pass. They probably considered it an all-out assault. The hull ceramics reflected most of the energy, enough to incinerate patches of forest, if the Cimtari missed, and evenly distributing the rest. Let them warm her cocoon – it was *cold* outside.

The use of heavy weapons within the atmosphere bothered her, aesthetically. Hadn't the home planet's crust been ripped and burnt enough? *Let's take this outside.* She gave the command to Chiang just as quickly. *Outside the atmosphere, that is.* She braced herself, sparing her injured tentacle. It ached only a little. After all, she'd chosen how sensitive the additional limbs would be, and she'd never liked pain.

What would it be like to take a new thrall, and thus a new body? It had been a while. She'd have no augments, no enhanced or redundant organs. She'd be new, vulnerable, pink. She'd pick a young body. She thought about the boy, how he'd slipped away. She'd get him back. At least the mother was out of the way. She recalled, with satisfaction, hurling Car-En's limp body against the rocks. The woman had murdered Umana's children. She would be kinder to Car-En's son. She'd put his body to good use, and preserve his young mind for service. Another thrall – it was always a thrill! She wished they could see her benevolence. No one could see inside her mind, to appreciate how she cherished her thralls.

Umana was a *life giver*. She'd lovingly created the third-tiers: semi-sentients with specialized computational specialties and an overwhelming desire to serve. The first-tiers were her past lives and past bodies, those select minds to whom she'd granted immortality. They served her too, not always as willingly, but she wasn't above a censure when required: she'd stripped Zhan of his kingly feline avatar and given him a new, less glamorous one. The second-tiers were the thralls (or co-minds, for those who had not become slave-keepers) of the first-tiers. The original Crucible volunteers had spread far and wide, jumping to new bodies when the old ones wore out, accumulating minds as they went. She'd collected most of them, and learned their histories.

How many, all together? She'd lost count. There were eleven first-tiers. There'd been more, but she'd euthanized those who'd gone insane or become too troublesome. Of those eleven, five were completely loyal. She treated them well – they should *all* be loyal – but a few, like Zhan, though useful, were disrespectful, at times even disobedient.

A year or two as a bullfrog would teach Zhan a thing or two. Let him eat flies. Not even a *talking* bullfrog – just a croaking one. He'd be *eager* to serve when she returned his voice.

The second-tiers: how many? It required effort to count them; like nesting dolls they were obscured. At least a hundred. She tolerated the second-tiers. If nothing else they kept the first-tiers company. Minds within minds.

The blast shook her cocoon; the raw, regenerating tip of her tentacle banged painfully against the control desk. The *Alhazen* worms were using munitions. She hadn't known the Cimtari fighters *had* munitions. Was their reputation of 'minimum-effective-coercion' just a ruse? Clever bastards.

Who'd gotten the *Alhazen* involved? Not good that the other ringstations were paying attention. She'd counted on the *Michelangelo*, in particular, maintaining their isolationism. The mad artists were the only ones that worried her. The fools on the *Stanford* were the softest. They'd *engineered* themselves into sheep *on purpose*. Her own people on the *Liu Hui* were competent and efficient. It was unfortunate they were working against her now – the *Zhōngyāng* had issued an official disavowal. The *Alhazen* forces were competent too, and perhaps less peace-loving than they'd let on. But only the denizens of the *Michelangelo* – deeply paranoid and armed to the teeth – worried her. Were they truly insane? She supposed they might be like her: deeply principled beings who appeared amoral to lesser minds.

Yes, she *feared* what might emerge from the *Michelangelo*. The feeling, so unfamiliar, enlivened her.

What was keeping Chiang? Just as she reached for the controls (she'd learned to navigate the *Iarudi* sufficiently on her own, without the help of the crew), she heard a deep boom. The floor pressed up against her feet. She settled into her throne, deliciously anticipating the heaviness. A memory flashed from her childhood: a sunny day, an amusement park, a rocket ship. *Fly, Isabella, fly!*

Sinking into her seat, she fantasized about the blond woman who'd violated her. She'd catch her and tear her limbs off, one by one. A stimulant/coagulant cocktail would keep her conscious; she'd bleed out slowly, with complete and lucid awareness. Idly, she ran the woman's face. There was a match within the *Stanford*'s open libraries. What trusting fools they were. The woman – Katja – was Tem's aunt! The boy had told her story; she'd almost become the Inventor's thrall.

Had the replication completed? What if a copy of Katja resided within the Inventor's core? If that was the case, Umana could exact a slow, precise revenge, prolonging the thrall's pain.

Though that wouldn't be fair. Katja had injured her *after* she'd been replicated. The copy didn't deserve to be punished for the sins of the original; they were separate beings.

Still, it would be satisfying. Besides, a little torture never hurt anyone. It was good to toughen up the thralls.

The Cimtari were chasing them. She'd given the *Alhazen* forces a chance to save face, to slink back to their masters and victoriously proclaim *We drove her off!* But they'd squandered that chance. Now they would die frozen, with empty lungs, tasting the metallic tang of space.

She summoned a panorama from the Earth-facing eyes. She was truly flying now, watching the crystalline Mediterranean shrink below her. She'd gone *swimming* there – what a pleasure! When her work was done, she'd have Earth as a park – the whole planet – to herself, to explore at her leisure. If the promise of the *Iarudi*'s engineers proved true, she'd return from her galactic explorations every few decades to remove the weeds. The survivors would call it genocide, but in time they'd learn the one rule: leave Earth uninhabited. Obey, and your orbiting worlds will go unmolested. Defy, and Umana – the returning comet – will destroy you. She would be like a raging goddess: Kali, Menhit, Otrera.

Where would she go? She had only the loosest of plans. There were several dozen habitable planets within the *Iarudi*'s range, all with breathable atmospheres, survivable gravity, and clear signs of life, but no signals, no pollution, no signs of 'civilization.' They were park worlds, as Earth should be. She'd explore those. Maybe in time she'd even share her findings with the ringstations. Later she'd need to restore relations with the Coalition, or whatever the Coalition evolved into. She would need them to augment her bodies, and to provide a pool for the selection of new ones.

All in good time. In a century or two her enemies would be dead.

"Commander!" Chiang sounded tense. "The Cimtari are in pursuit."

"Put some distance between us," she said. "Thrusters only, but double our current velocity."

"I would recommend against it. Just leaving the atmosphere left two crew members unconscious."

Weaklings. The threads buttressed her own tissues against higher gravities. Her crew had no such augmentations, but their training and conditioning should count for something. She wondered how the prisoner was holding up. The threads would be laced through his tissues by now, mirroring his nervous system, but also penetrating into his organs, muscles, and circulatory system. In addition, he was suspended in oxygenated gel; she wanted him whole. She'd been interrupted when she'd first tried to extract the core, but if she waited a little longer she'd gain another second-tier. The prisoner would reside within the Inventor, a thrall-within-a-thrall. She dispatched a third-tier to check on his vitals.

Best give Chiang his orders while he was still conscious. "Let's give them a taste of our armaments. Maser pulses, to tickle their palate. Then a few rounds from the rail guns for the entree. My guess is they'll pass on dessert."

"Initiating EMPs," said Chiang, sounding calmer now that he had a job to do.

She'd miss Chiang when it came time to do the inevitable. He'd served her well. Briefly, she considered keeping him alive and in her service a while longer. But no, Chiang knew too much. Better to die an honorable death aboard the *Iarudi*.

"EMPs ineffective," Chiang said. "Targeting rail guns now."

"Leave some alive," she ordered. "How many ships are there?"

"Twelve," said Chiang.

Twelve! She hadn't known there were that many Cimtari fighters in total. The *Alhazen* builders had been busy. Dispatching that many, they must have some awareness of the *Iarudi*'s strength. Though if they truly knew what they were up against, they'd have left her alone in the first place.

She switched her view to the rear-facing eyes, and watched impassively as twelve became nine. Even as three sleek Cimtari ships wheeled chaotically out of formation, hulls breached beyond repair, spewing air, debris, and bodies into the cold black vacuum, she wished for more. She would use the new weapon, even if she didn't need to.

She took the helm without warning, delighting in the navigation room's confusion. She left weapons in her crew's control for now, but she was ready to pilot. Even secured to their seats, her crew paled as she changed direction impulsively, weaving evasive patterns as they occurred to her. A third-tier leapt forward with suggestions, and she took them, painting unpredictable geometries in the blackness. The Cimtari fighters followed her like disciplined wolfhounds, shortening her lead with tight, calculated triangulations. She didn't care. They were near their top, pitiful speeds.

She stole another peek at nav. Several of her crew lolled in their chairs, unconscious. One convulsed, puking thin bile: shiny weightless globules. There'd be some cleanup when all was said and done. She'd freeze the bodies – nutrition for the long voyage ahead. She was not wasteful.

"Commander, please modulate the intensity of the directional changes! More crew members have lost consciousness. You're operating well outside of test parameters."

"We're in a *battle* if you hadn't noticed," she snapped, using more of her voice than she'd intended. The limiters on Chiang's feed flatlined. Predictably, the line went silent.

Then, weakly, "We won't be much use to you, if—"

Enough. She was done with them. She closed the feed and seized full control of all ship systems. It took less than a minute to charge and target the weapon. She cut thrusters; the *Iarudi* cruised on inertia. Still accelerating, the Cimtari slingshotted by, looped back, and flanked her in twin crescent formations, matching her speed, four on each side. The ninth ship flew ahead, taunting her. With a brief pulse forward she matched that one, calibrating the perfect distance.

For an instant she instantiated the warp bubble. The Cimtari ship was caught half-in, half-out. The fighter's hull buckled, imploded, disintegrated into debris. The field was already deactivated, but it had been enough.

She watched the dead and dying through the *Iarudi*'s eyes. So arrogant and wasteful, to crew fighters with *people*. The *Alhazen* engineers were clever, but they had not prepared for war.

Predictably, shamefully, the surviving Cimtari ships peeled away. She could have picked them off easily, but what was the point in that? Let them spread the word. She was untouchable.

Impulsively, she reopened Chiang's feed and a few nav room eyes. She was curious.

Chiang's skin had a greenish cast, but he was conscious. Most of the other crew were passed out in their chairs.

"Commander...well done," said Chiang. "Another victory." He was struggling to regain his composure, but his voice sounded thin and tremulous. Admirable, though: brave to the end!

She wondered what had become of the youngling Mèng. The young navigator had fled, deserting ship and ringstation. Treasonous cockroach. But Umana liked her.

"Your orders?" Chiang was weakly straightening his uniform.

She could use the Natario-White drive right now. There would be no acceleration; her crew would survive. But there was no point in that. Her new life had begun. She was no longer *Kǒngbù Wǔzéi*.

"No orders," she said. "Goodbye, Chiang." She commanded the ship forward into deep space, with an acceleration rate that would finish her crew.

CHAPTER THIRTY-FIVE

They coasted into the outskirts of Vandercamp, mid-morning. The name still rankled Lydia, but she could no longer call the settlement 'AFS-1'; there was no research; there was no longer any association with the Academy or with the *Stanford*. She said as much, out loud.

"I have an idea for a new name," said Xenus. She waited, but apparently he wasn't ready to reveal it. He'd been acting strange. It was the head injury – his brain was still healing.

Car-En hopped out of the shuttle before Lydia and immediately strode off toward the Shell. The spiraling structure gleamed in the morning light. Lydia's impression of the settlement was that it was *bustling*; there were more people, new structures, and everyone was moving quickly, trying to keep warm. Even this far south they could feel winter's chill.

Most notably, the *Iarudi* was nowhere to be seen, and there was nowhere nearby to hide a ship of that size. The *Stanford* feeds were reporting that the *Iarudi* had skirmished with a squadron of *Alhazen* fighters, then catapulted into deep space with a lethal acceleration rate. Absent unknown means of attenuating inertial forces, everyone on board the *Iarudi* was dead.

Lydia did not believe that Commander Umana was dead, but she feared the worst for Shane.

"Wait!" Lydia clambered out of the hovershuttle and chased after Car-En. She wasn't going to let her old friend do something stupid. "Wait, please!" She touched Car-En's arm, then yanked her hand back. "Ow!" The battleskin had shocked her.

Car-En glared. "Please don't touch me. What do you want?"

Lydia's blood rose. She was just trying to help. She exhaled slowly, trying to calm herself. Car-En's safety was more important than her own hurt feelings. "Please tell me what you're thinking…what you're planning on doing. Are you going to confront Adrian?"

Car-En snorted. "*Confront.* I guess you could say that."

"What do you mean?"

"The *Stanford* has no jurisdiction here. Neither does the *Liu Hui* – at least not yet. Adrian has always done what he wanted to. Why shouldn't I? You can't say he doesn't deserve it. I've waited too long for someone else to bring Adrian to justice."

It took a second for Lydia to absorb Car-En's meaning.

"You don't want to do that," Lydia said quietly.

"Adrian almost killed me. He hacked into my bioskin and administered enough insulin to put me into a coma. I would have died if I'd been alone. Ilsa saved my life. If it were just that, and he'd stayed on the *Stanford*, I would have tried to forget about what he did and move on with my life. But now he's living on Earth, and somehow allied with Umana, who attacked and abducted Tem. I can't forgive him for that. And it's not just my family he's hurt. He's a dangerous, out-of-control megalomaniac, and no one on the *Stanford* is reining him in. So that task falls to me."

In a way Car-En was right – Adrian existed outside of any legal system. No one could touch him through official channels. Car-En waited patiently while Lydia thought the situation through. She didn't seem to be angry anymore, at least not at Lydia. Just determined. She was going to hear Lydia out – maybe for old time's sake – then go murder Adrian. The old Car-En would never have considered such a drastic act. Life in Happdal, among the villagers, had hardened her. Or maybe motherhood had changed her.

"They'll arrest you," Lydia pointed out. "This place is under martial law. Foster might have you executed."

Car-En didn't blink. "They can't kill me..." – she pulled up the dark hood; the battleskin shimmered and disappeared – "...if they can't see me."

"Just listen for a minute!" Lydia snapped. Car-En's floating face gained a body. "You have no idea what you're walking into. If we've learned anything about the *Liu Hui* in the past weeks, it's that we have no idea what they're capable of. Umana in particular."

"She's not here," said Car-En.

"You don't know that for sure."

"Why do you care?" Car-En asked.

The question caught her off guard. *Because I care about you!* she screamed to herself. But honestly, that wasn't the main thing. She *did* care about Car-En, but not like she once had.

"I don't want Tem to lose a mother." Lydia shuddered, saying the words. She'd held that burden for so long, knowing about Marivic's death, when Car-En didn't.

Car-En tensed. "You hardly know him."

"You lost *your* mother. Why are you so eager to endanger yourself? And to become a murderer?"

Car-En turned away. Lydia looked back at the shuttle. Javier was pretending to check the dashboard indicators. Xenus was lost in his own thoughts, oblivious of the unfolding drama.

"Fine. We'll do it your way." Car-En was angry again. A good sign, maybe.

"*Our* way. Let's talk about it."

★　★　★

Regis Foster personally came out to greet them, not ten minutes later. Tall, broad-shouldered, with craggy features and blue eyes, he could have easily blended in among Happdal folk. Foster was grinning, genuinely happy to see them, as far as Lydia could tell. "Greetings!" he boomed. A young woman with pale green eyes accompanied him. Neither was in uniform, or armed.

"Are we welcome here?" Xenus asked.

"Of course you are. Free Passage."

"Shane Jaecks was taken. Tortured, we heard." The strength of Xenus's voice, confident and authoritative, startled Lydia. Foster registered the difference; the lieutenant stood up straighter.

"I apologize for that situation," said Foster. "Umana has gone rogue. She's been stripped of rank and title."

"And brought to justice?" Xenus pressed.

"The situation is still unfolding. Please, all of you, come eat and drink with us. And it looks like some introductions are in order. We'll bring you all up to speed."

New domes had been built, in the same style as the others, but larger. All around, Lydia saw the big-bodied *Liu Hui* men and women working away, intermingled and conversing with the original inhabitants of the field station. Some recognized them, and waved from afar, but Foster quickly ushered them into one of the new structures. They sat around a low table. A young man, clearly a plainclothes *Liu Hui* soldier from his demeanor, served them tea.

"There will be time later to meet-and-greet," Foster said. "You've been missed. But let's start with some introductions, and reorientation. A lot has happened – we're at a crucial juncture here. You must have questions, and I have a few—"

"Who's in charge?" Xenus interrupted.

Foster was taken aback but maintained his composure. "I am, for the moment, but this place runs itself."

"So Vandercamp is under martial law?" said Xenus, more loudly than necessary.

"Vandercamp declared independence – that still stands," said the green-eyed woman sitting to the right of the lieutenant. A long, faded scar ran from her left eye to the corner of her mouth.

"Who are you?" Car-En asked.

"Dadre Tenner, Liaison to the *Stanford*. I'm in close communication with the Repopulation Council. You're Car-En Ganzorig. I have a message for you."

Car-En sat up straight. "You can tell me now. I have no secrets from these people." Lydia doubted very much that was true, but hearing the words still softened her feelings toward Car-En. Being trusted was more important than being liked.

"Talk to Penelope Townes," said Dadre. "Immediately. Before you…*do* anything."

Car-En bristled. "Talk to her about what?"

"That's the extent of my message." Dadre eyed Car-En steadily.

"If Vandercamp *isn't* under martial law, where is Adrian Vanderplotz?" Xenus asked.

"Adrian is unwell," said Foster, shifting in his seat.

"Unwell *how*?" Lydia asked. "Does he require medical attention? Is he receiving it?" She felt a stab of guilt for abandoning Vandercamp. She was a physician – she'd made a commitment to serve this community, then fled at the first sign of trouble. Shane hadn't run. He'd stayed and done his job, even though he'd officially been fired.

"Physically, he's fine," said Foster. "Mentally, he's…."

"Out of balance," Dadre suggested.

"That would be euphemistic," Foster said, "but honestly none of my medical crew are sophisticated enough to offer an accurate diagnosis. They're used to spraying gel on open wounds, setting broken bones, that sort of thing. Physical shock and injury. This is something different."

"Where is he?" Lydia asked.

"At his quarters, under observation," said Dadre.

"Confined?" Xenus asked.

"You're welcome to visit him." Dadre met Xenus's gaze and refused to look away.

Javier, who up until now had remained silent, introduced himself, and explained that he would be returning to the OETS station shortly. Did anyone or anything require transport to the *Stanford*? Foster answered in the affirmative; they discussed the logistics of who and what for several minutes. The tension eased, and soon the conversation turned to recent events. Foster explained, using colorful language, that what had started out as a diplomatic power play – *defensive*, from the point of view of the *Zhōngyāng* central council – had turned into a full-scale clusterfuck. Commander Umana had gone batshit crazy, morphing overnight from a competent, well-respected special forces officer into a power-mad, raging monster fueled by bloodlust, ego, and who-knows-what-else. Giving her command of the *Iarudi* – an experimental interstellar vessel – had been a fatal mistake. Perhaps gaining control of the powerful ship had been the trigger that had pushed Umana over some psychological brink.

Lydia watched Foster as he spoke. He was letting it all hang out – not just the swearing, but his frank admission that he was in over his head, with no plan. She didn't think he was hiding anything. She glanced at the others. Xenus looked suspicious, Car-En brooding, Javier thoughtful. Briefly she locked eyes with Dadre, who also appeared to be taking an emotional inventory of the table.

"My liaison position is new," said Dadre. "We're in full damage control. The *Liu Hui* is trying to contain Umana, but we need help. We don't want to start a war among the ringstations."

"I'm happy to hear that," Xenus said dryly.

"I'm just following orders," Foster said. "If I'm in command, it's only to keep the peace, to keep this place stable and running until Adrian –

or *anyone*, as far as I'm concerned – can take over. I don't want the—"

Javier interrupted. "The skirmish with the *Alhazen* Cimtari – that was you *asking for help?*"

Foster glared at Javier.

"Not exactly," Dadre interjected. "That initiative came from…well, we're not sure exactly. While we agree that Umana needs to be stopped, it was the wrong approach. The confrontation did not go as planned, and there were multiple casualties on the *Alhazen* side. We believe they underestimated the capabilities of the *Iarudi*."

"They should have fucking talked to us first," Foster grumbled. "They never had a chance. Attacking the *Iarudi* was a suicide mission."

"What weapons is the ship equipped with?" Car-En asked.

"Disruptive masers, rail guns, and the rest is classified," said Foster. "But fuck it, it's all over the feeds. The *Iarudi* possesses a functional Natario-White warp drive. The drive generates a river of Alcubierre-compressed spacetime using negative mass fields. The ship itself is safely contained in the warp bubble, but the *edge* of the bubble can be used as a weapon."

"That's what happened with the Cimtari fighters?" asked Xenus. "They were…warped?"

"Only one, apparently. Others were destroyed by more conventional means."

Lydia was confused. "A negative mass field – is that antimatter?"

Dadre smiled condescendingly, but Javier answered matter-of-factly. "The *Iarudi* uses antimatter as an energy source to generate the warp bubble, but negative mass is something different. Antimatter has mass – the particles have opposite charges, but they still have density and energy. Negative mass means the energy density is less than that of a vacuum…less than zero."

"How is that possible?" Lydia asked.

"Had the weapon been tested?" asked Xenus at the same time.

Dadre shook her head, responding to Xenus. "There was never any intention to use the Natario-White drive as a weapon. No *need* for it, either. The intended use of the drive is interstellar travel."

"So you say," said Car-En.

Foster stood and paced along the length of the table. "Look, I understand your skepticism. I won't deny that the *Liu Hui* has been developing military technology more aggressively than the *Stanford*. It would be impossible *not* to…you're fucking *pacifists*. Can we agree on that much at least? But we weren't trying to start a war."

"What do you think Umana will do?" Javier asked.

Foster and Dadre exchanged a look.

"They have no idea," said Xenus. Nobody denied it. "She's insane, and she's in possession of an insanely powerful weapon."

"Where was she heading?" Lydia asked. "Toward what system?"

"Tau Ceti," said Foster. "Twelve light years away, if that was your next question."

"I know where Tau Ceti is," Lydia said. "The question is…will she be coming back?" *Will* he *be coming back* was her thought.

"That's an impossible question to answer," Dadre replied.

"Not necessarily," said Xenus. "If the *Iarudi* can achieve superluminal speeds, we can be sure she'll be back. We'll all be dead and gone, but for Umana, the voyage will be a short walk in the park."

Lydia's throat tightened. If Shane did survive and return, it would be too late.

"Actually that's not correct," Dadre said. "Time dilation doesn't apply to warp drives. The time frame within the warp bubble will be the same as ours. Her maximum speed is equivalent to about seven times the speed of light, but that's via spacetime compression, not classical acceleration. There's absolutely no experience of acceleration with warp travel."

Xenus furrowed his brow. Lydia tried hard not to smile; he would think she was gloating at his mistake. But she didn't care what he knew or didn't know about warp drives – she was just happy that Shane might not be lost forever.

Xenus stood. "I'd like to see Adrian now. Will you take me to him?"

"*Us*," Car-En stated. "Take *us* to him."

"Let's take a short break and reconvene here in ten minutes," said Dadre. "Car-En, maybe you'd like to use that time to contact Townes? I would appreciate if you did so."

Car-En grunted noncommittally.

★   ★   ★

Lydia didn't know what to expect as they approached Adrian's quarters. No one was posted at the entrance to his dome. When Foster had said Adrian was 'under observation,' perhaps he'd meant by drones. She thought back to her conversation with Shane; he'd speculated that *Liu Hui* drone tech was a class above their own. In that case they were *all* under observation, whether they knew it or not.

Adrian was hunched over a table, making notes on a large printed map of the Po Valley and the surrounding mountains and seas. He didn't look up right away, even when all four of them crowded into the main room. (Lieutenant Foster and Javier had stayed behind, but Xenus had come, and Dadre was with them too, keeping a close eye on Car-En). It took Lydia a second to realize it was Adrian: his hair had gone from black with a few streaks of gray to solid gray with some white; his bronze skin had faded to a yellowish pallor. It had been a long time since his last rejuv, but this was something more. Something – immense stress or stimulant abuse – had accelerated his aging.

Adrian looked up and smiled, accentuating the crow's feet around his eyes. "Lydia, Xenus, welcome back. Car-En, it's good to see you." He stood and pointed at the map. "I've been working on the Fifty-Year Plan. You might think it looks like more of a *century* plan, but I'm an optimist. And why shouldn't I be? Thanks to Campi Flegrei, our humble valley has more arable land than the Fertile Crescent ever did. Is there a better place to reestablish civilization? I don't think so. New beginnings. A new age. With Vanderton at the center of things."

Vanderton. That was a new one. Did the man's ego know no bounds?

"As you can see, we'll establish rail lines here, here, and here, connecting the main settlements. Magnetic air lines – minimal environmental impact. They'll be powered from compost reactors, augmented with solar films on the trains themselves...perhaps also on the mounting poles."

Car-En was staring, wide-eyed. Xenus had a gleam in his eye. Adrian's full attention was on his map; he continued to point and speak.

"This settlement near the coast – perhaps we'll name it *Fosterton* after the fine Lieutenant. Regis has been kind enough to temporarily handle day-to-day operations while I focus on the greater picture. Fosterton will be the base of our marine research, and also a source of fresh seafood. Which I've been *missing*. Haven't you? I'll be happy if I never eat another g'nerf bar as long as I live!"

Car-En lunged. Dadre was ready, and grabbed Car-En's arm to hold her back. Just as quickly Dadre yelled and pulled her hand away, then doubled over, clutching her hand. Car-En moved swiftly. She grabbed Adrian by the neck and slammed his head against the table, pinning him, mashing his cheek against the map. A line of spittle moistened the paper near the Alps. Adrian closed his eyes, relaxing into the hold, unresisting. Car-En's fingers squeezed off the Station Director's neck arteries; in seconds he would be unconscious, strangled soon after.

"Let him go!" yelled Lydia. And then, to Xenus, "Stop her!" Xenus gave her a puzzled look. She realized the request was absurd. How could he stop her? How could *any of them* stop her? But she thought of Shane; Shane would at least *try*.

Dadre blinked rapidly, summoning help via her m'eye. Armed soldiers would come soon, and then what? Mayhem. Car-En was as dangerous as the Squid Woman.

"He tried to kill me," Car-En hissed through clenched teeth. "Admit it!" she yelled at Adrian. "You tried to kill me…because I *disobeyed* you."

Adrian gurgled.

"He's trying to talk!" Lydia shouted. She took a step forward, but dared not touch Car-En. The battleskin was shimmering with electricity. "Let him go. Let him apologize."

Car-En met Lydia's eyes for an instant. She released her grip on Adrian's neck. A moment later she was several meters away, in the far corner of the room, pulling up her hood, lifting her face mask. Lydia tracked her for a second, then Car-En was gone.

Adrian coughed, clutching his throat. "She's *insane*! I never laid a finger on her. She was my *student*. I *protected* her."

"Stop talking, if you're going to lie," Lydia said. The rage in her voice surprised her, but it felt right, and she went with it, letting the emotion sweep her along. "You're lucky she didn't kill you. Just shut up."

Adrian looked stunned. His eyes raced around the room, looking for an ally. Dadre had backed up and was trying to block the door. Lydia suspected Car-En was long gone.

"Where…where is she?" Adrian sputtered.

"Try to calm down." Xenus gently touched Adrian's shoulder and directed him back to his seat. "You're safe now. She's gone."

Adrian shook his head. "She was a *pup* before she came to Earth. I guided her. I made her *famous*." He pointed at the map. "*I'm* the one who should be famous. It was *me* who jumpstarted Repop. The councils would have debated it until the sun flared out. *I* got things moving. It was *me*!" He was shouting now, stabbing at the dot labeled *Vanderton*.

"It was you," Xenus mirrored, trying to calm him.

"It was *me* who brought us back to Earth. *I* did it!"

"You did it."

"Car-En is a fucking ungrateful *bitch*!"

The room went silent. Adrian's head snapped back, then slammed down against the table. The Station Director clutched his nose and cried out. Blood streamed through his fingers and dripped down his forearm.

Dadre rushed forward, yelling for help. A shadow briefly darkened the door of Adrian's dome.

CHAPTER THIRTY-SIX

Svilsson straightened his shirt. He'd dressed carefully; he wanted to make a good impression on the newcomers. Absurd, when he considered it: the Happdal villagers would not be impressed by his shirt. Nor would Tem. Nor would the young defector from Commander Umana's crew. He tried to relax, letting his hands hang at his sides, but that felt awkward. He folded his arms.

"*I'm* the one who should be nervous," Shol said. "I'm the one meeting my son-in-law for the first time." Shol grinned, looking relaxed and happy and not nervous at all.

"Esper is a good man," said Per Anders, grinning. "You will like him! Everyone likes Esper. Even when Esper shoots a bear in the eye at one hundred paces, the bear thanks Esper for giving him a good death."

Shol smiled, noticeably less relaxed. "But you only knew him as a boy. Was he hunting bears as a child?"

"I knew him briefly as a man," Per Anders said, "though my mushroom memories are foggy. Most of what I know of Esper is from your grandson. But who knows him better?" Per Anders blew his nose into his hand and wiped his hand on his shirt. "No one," he said, answering his own question. "No one knows him better than Tem. Tem told me the bear story, and I believe him."

They were in the spoke station, waiting for Esper, Askr, Tem, and Mèng to descend from the central hub. The room was decorated with sprawling ferns, towering succulents, and a glistening blue-black water wall. Decon was taking a long time.

The main entrance doors slid open with a soft hiss. Penelope Townes re-entered the room, looking worried. Svilsson raised an eyebrow. Townes sidled close and spoke under her breath. "I just had a disturbing conversation with Car-En. We have a problem."

Townes tended to understate things. Svilsson guessed that someone was dead or seriously injured, but he was loath to break the welcoming mood. Townes, understanding his silence, took a step away. They would discuss it later. He focused his mind, putting the trouble with Car-En – whatever it was – *aside*. It wasn't the only concern he was repressing; his worries regarding the aftermath of *Operation Calamari* formed their own black cloud. He'd been wrong to give the deadly venture a frivolous moniker. Men and women were dead, ridiculously expensive ships were destroyed, and it was his own fault as much as anyone's.

"I miss the little man!" Per Anders said.

"Me too, my friend," Shol said. "I miss him sorely. It's selfish to say, but I hope he never leaves the *Stanford* again."

"Don't count on it, grandpa," said Per Anders. "Tem has found his wander legs and he won't give them up now. Just be glad that he's moved on from his dream of working in a smoky room the rest of his life, hitting metal with a hammer."

"*Has* he given that up?"

Per Anders nodded confidently. "He will forge weapons, to be sure, but his sights have broadened. He's not the same boy who boarded the ringship months ago."

The approach light glowed green, intensifying as the elevator descended toward Main.

"They're coming!" Per Anders shouted, bouncing on his toes. Shol grinned, and Svilsson found himself smiling too. Townes stood off to the side, pensive and distracted.

Tem was out of the tube before the port was fully open. He ran to Shol and embraced him. A slight, serious Asian woman emerged next. She glanced at each of them in turn, then approached Penelope Townes, evidently deciding that Townes was the one in charge. Svilsson was not offended; he and Penelope held equal stations but he preferred not to be the face of things. Two tall, bearded men remained in the elevator, testing the ground beneath their feet. The taller one looked wide-eyed and dumbstruck. The other man, who was strikingly handsome, regarded his surroundings calmly.

"I am Mèng," the woman said, standing to attention in front of Townes. "Thank you for offering asylum."

"You're very brave," said Townes.

"I am neither brave nor cowardly," Mèng said, "but I do not believe

Commander Umana is sane. I defected to save my own life, and to escape her service."

"Well, you were right about that – the *not being sane* part," Townes said.

"You've grown!" said Shol to Tem. "Five centimeters at least. Is that possible? What do they feed you down there?"

"Cheese and boar meat," Tem said, smiling. The boy did look taller. "Where's Zin?" he asked Svilsson.

"At school. Where you'll be soon. You have some catching up to do." He'd considered allowing Zinthia to join the greeting party, and now he wished he had. He would need to reunite Tem with *all* the other children from the *Rama* soon; they needed to see that he was whole and well. The children had been traumatized by the attack. Not all of them had bounced back.

The shorter of the two Happdal men stepped tentatively into the greeting room. Per Anders grasped his forearm. "Greetings, Esper!" he said in English. "What do you think of the ringship? You've seen the rings from below for years, and now you stand in one!"

"Greetings, Per Anders, you look well. So far, the ringship amazes me. Where does the light come from? We are inside, yet there are thriving plants. The more I see, the more questions I have."

"Mirrors!" Per Anders shouted. "Mirrors!"

With some difficulty Esper pulled his arm away from Per Anders and formally extended his hand to Shol. "My son is embracing you, so you must be his morfar. I am Esper Ariksson, of Happdal. Thank you for welcoming me to your ship."

Shol grasped Esper's forearm in the same way the Happdal men had greeted each other, then pulled Esper into an embrace, squishing Tem.

"It's good to finally meet you. It makes me happy. If only my daughter were here too…but I hope she will join us soon?"

"Soon," said Esper, with more confidence than Svilsson thought was merited.

"I can't breathe!" Tem said, squeezing his way out from between his father and grandfather.

More introductions were made. The very tall man was Askr. He spoke only a few words of English, and grinned widely when Svilsson greeted him in Norse. Soon the three Happdal men formed a clique, speaking rapidly to each other in their own tongue. There would be a Happdal expat community on the *Stanford*, Svilsson realized, and it was likely to grow. A fascinating thought, but he put it aside. There were matters to be dealt with.

Someone was tugging on his sleeve – Tem. "Can we speak for a moment?" the boy asked. Svilsson allowed himself to be pulled behind a tree fern. Tem's face was pale, his brow compressed with worry. The boy spoke in low tones. "There's something you need to know. The Squid Woman has *the egg*. It's my fault! I led her right to it. I thought she would consume it and die. I thought the egg would consume *her*. But she lives, doesn't she? She's not dead?"

He wouldn't lie to the boy. "She lives."

Tem punched his palm. "I've made a terrible mistake. What can we do?" Though the boy's earnestness was charming, Svilsson did not smile. Tem was worried, and rightfully so. Svilsson was worried too. He'd known about the Crucible core – Car-En had summarized the encounter with Umana to Townes – and it was indeed terrible news that Umana might have access to the algorithm. The possibility had occurred to him the day he'd seen Karl Turen's sim: if the algorithm fell into the hands of a malevolent party with access to sufficient processing cores, the Ringstation Coalition would be in deep trouble. If, as Svilsson suspected, the algorithm was capable of simulating cultural and technological evolution as well as....

"What are we going *to do*?" Tem was poking him in the stomach.

"*We?* Nothing. Tem, you've been braver and stronger than anyone could ask. You've done your part. It's time for the grown-ups to take over."

Tem scowled. "If it's my fault the Squid Woman has the egg, I'm going to fix it."

"It's not your problem to fix." He gently touched Tem's shoulder, hoping to soothe the boy.

Tem swatted his hand away. "It *is* my problem, and you can't stop me from fighting her! I'll find a way! I'll kill her!"

Svilsson glanced at the others. As he'd feared, conversations had stopped. Everyone was staring.

"Tem!" Esper said sternly. "Respect your elders."

"He's not respecting *me*," said Tem, stomping away. Svilsson considered it – the boy was right. Tem turned. "And where's my blade? Was Squid Cutter found? If so, I want it back, immediately."

Esper shrugged, and Svilsson felt a wave of gratitude that the boy's father was even-tempered. He would have no idea what to do if one of the Happdal men lost their temper.

"Kill who?" Per Anders asked.

"The Squid Woman," said Tem.

Penelope Townes addressed the newcomers as if Tem had not spoken. "Now that you've all arrived, why don't we get you some refreshments? There's a good café right next door. Askr, have you ever tried coffee before?"

At the café, Tem avoided eye contact with Svilsson and continued to sulk, even refusing an offer of ice cream. ("There's no *cream* in it – they should call it something else!") Per Anders went to comfort the boy; soon the two were speaking in conspiratorial hushed tones. What trouble could Tem get up to now that he was safely on the *Stanford* with both his father and grandfather to look after him? The thought provided no solace; the answer was *plenty*.

Svilsson sat alone at a small table, not wanting to intrude on Shol and Esper bonding, nor on whatever topic Mèng and Townes were discussing. He was wary of the *Liu Hui* woman; could she be a spy? Unlikely, but he would recommend caution nonetheless. Diplomatically, the situation was sticky. Umana had been declared rogue by the *Zhōngyāng*; technically Mèng didn't *need* asylum. But the young navigator didn't feel comfortable returning to her home ring, and it would be helpful to debrief her on the capabilities of the *Iarudi* and whatever other new tech the *Liu Hui* might be developing in secret. They were in uncharted diplomatic territory with the *Liu Hui*, not at war but not fully at peace. He had always assumed the Ringstation Coalition was solid, a permanent institution as much as any. But what if it wasn't? This fraying might turn into a tear.

It wasn't only relations with the *Liu Hui* that were rocky. The *Alhazen* was involved too, having lost both lives and ships in the failed attack on the *Iarudi*. Their council members were furious with Svilsson in particular; it had been his idea to launch the stealth attack. The *Zhōngyāng* council had reluctantly approved the plan, and the *Alhazen* had been eager to show off the full capabilities of their newly re-engineered

Cimtari. The plan had been for the Cimtari to quickly disable the *Iarudi*, knock everyone out with neural disruptors, then turn the whole mess over to the *Liu Hui* to sort out. (The *Zhōngyáng* had been concerned about internal access to the *Iarudi*, but Svilsson had convinced them that boarding the ship would not be necessary.) Now the *Alhazen* council was accusing the *Zhōngyáng* of being stingy with intelligence regarding the *Iarudi*'s defensive capabilities, while the *Liu Hui* claimed that their warnings had been ignored and the debacle was the result of Cimtari hubris. What a mess.

And what was to be done now? Umana's current whereabouts were unknown, but she was out there, lethal and insane. There was one option in the back of Svilsson's mind. The *Michelangelo* was part of the Ringstation Coalition – very loosely – but he didn't exactly count them as allies. What had started out as an artists' colony had morphed, over the centuries, into a society of paranoid isolationists. Still, they might provide assistance, if approached carefully....

Townes was sitting down at his table, coffee in hand. "I need to tell you about Car-En," she said without preamble. He glanced at Mèng – he guessed hearing enhancement was standard issue for the *Jūnshì* – but for the moment the young woman was listening intently to Shol. "Really?" said Townes, noting Svilsson's suspicion. "You're worried about *her*? She's just relieved to be in one piece."

"Why hasn't she requested passage home?" Svilsson said. "The *Zhōngyáng* was clear that no charges would be filed against her. It's not considered desertion when your commander goes insane."

Townes shrugged. "Maybe she just needs a break. I imagine she'll face quite the debriefing when she does return."

"Maybe. So...what happened with Car-En?"

Townes leaned in close, and he became aware of her, physically. It would be easy to get lost in those green eyes. He looked away, focusing on her voice. "...resigned after the attack. I tried to stop it but the events were already in motion. It was a judgment error on my part, and I apologize."

"Resigned? Adrian Vanderplotz?"

"It was...convenient, in a way, that AFS-1 was temporarily out of our jurisdiction. Vanderplotz was a problem that wasn't going away, and Car-En...well, let's just say she didn't take much convincing, especially when she learned that Lydia was potentially in danger. I backed the development of the battleskin – probably should have checked with the council first – and arranged for Car-En to—"

"Wait, slow down."

Townes stopped talking while he struggled to catch up. Part of what was making comprehension difficult was the open, relaxed expression on her face: no guilt, no remorse. It didn't jibe with the words from her mouth.

"Did you authorize an attack? An *assassination?*"

"Nobody died! Adrian will be fine. But don't feel sorry for him – he tried to murder Car-En."

"*Allegedly.* He was never tried by any court."

"I called it off as soon as I learned he was no longer a threat. He might be – or might have been – mentally ill."

"But you *didn't* call it off. Not in time."

"Car-En wasn't thinking rationally, and she wasn't in the mood to take orders. She can run hot, you know."

"Just…let me get this straight. You told Car-En she could kill Adrian Vanderplotz, without repercussions? And you created a battleskin to help her do it?"

"I didn't *create* it. The Hair Lab whiz kids did that."

"But the authorization part…."

Townes sat up straight and sighed. "C'mon, Svilsson. Did you really think we were going to let AFS-1 go? Their 'independence declaration' provided an opportunity, and I took it."

"You manipulated Car-En."

"I did no such thing," Townes whispered fiercely. "I planted a seed, maybe, but that's all. I let nature take its course. Civilization is a construct based on an implied contract, and Vanderplotz gave up any rights to that contract long ago. I'll admit to stooping to his level, but Earth is better for it. The *Stanford* is better for it."

"You could have turned Car-En into a murderer," he said, more loudly than he meant to.

"Keep your voice down, for fuck's sake."

He glanced around. Only Tem, sullen and angry, was watching them. He hoped the boy hadn't heard.

"I need to get some air."

He left the café, and walked the park trails for an hour, hoping to clear his head. It took twice that long to calm down, but by the time the mirrored light faded from the rounded sky he knew what he had to do.

CHAPTER THIRTY-SEVEN

Shane awoke underwater, his lungs filled with liquid. Oddly, he felt no desire to breathe. He could hold his breath forever, effortlessly. What change was this? He opened his eyes to dim light and blurry shapes. A shadow loomed over him. Strong arms slipped underneath his torso and lifted him up, into the air.

He gagged silently, purging the oxygenated gel from his lungs. His gags turned to coughs as he struggled to breathe. He was weightless. Space. But where? He rubbed his eyes. He was alone in the tank room with the Squid Woman.

He was naked. She regarded him as if he were a worm. He tried to speak but only gurgled.

"You may dress," she said, gesturing with a wave of her chest tentacles to a dull gray storage crate strapped to the wall. "Your clothes."

He coughed, cleared his throat. "I...clean up," he managed to say. His skin was still slimy with thick clear gel. She left. The doors slid closed, locking him in. He spun slowly, taking in the room. There was a bathing cubby on the same wall as the tank.

Cleaning himself took a long time; he was tender and sore. Carefully he wiped his limbs and torso with a damp sponge and dried himself with a fresh towel, all the while taking an inventory of his physical state. He was emaciated, at least twenty kilos lighter than when she'd taken him. One of his teeth was missing, another was loose. But the soreness wasn't from the beatings he'd received; those injuries had healed. Despite his nudity and the cool ship air he felt warm. The egg was heating him from the inside.

He could feel its presence within him. The warmth was centered near his heart and emanated throughout his body along his major arteries and nerves. What was it doing inside of him? It wasn't taking over his mind; he was still himself.

He considered his predicament as he donned his clothes. Umana still thought he was someone else, but that was no longer relevant. She intended to remove the egg from his body, then throw away the meat. In the Squid Woman's mind Shane Jaecks was already dead. She'd used his body as an incubator, a test subject. She'd eject him into space as soon as she'd extracted the Crucible core.

In a sudden panic he patted his chest. The item was still there, in the inner shirt pocket where he'd tucked it away. He removed the small leather pouch he'd found in his hand: a gift from Tem. He twisted his body so that his back faced the door. He opened the pouch. Inside was a sharp, stained tooth, curved and as long as his index finger. It had obviously belonged to a carnivore, maybe a hunting cat or a wolf. He closed his hand and squeezed until the sharp point bit into his palm.

The doors hissed. He spun to face her, tucking the pouch away. A long tentacle entered first, probing ahead as if it had eyes of its own. He wondered what would happen when the Squid Woman ripped the egg from his body and consumed it herself. Probably nothing. The Crucible core had become a benevolent parasite, as far as he could tell. Not only was he still in control of his own faculties, but he felt *good*. He was warm and alert, and now that he was moving the soreness was fading. The egg was life-giving, a source of biological renewal.

She floated into the room, drifting closer, reaching out with a long tentacle. She wrapped it around his waist and drew him in to her anemone-like nest of chest tentacles. Her injured tentacle she held back; he could see that it was still healing. Could her entire body regenerate, or only her artificial limbs? Was there any part of her that was *not* artificial?

The latest host might have once been pretty, but now her visage was monstrous. She was bald with no stubble. Her pale skin was aged and blotchy, her face bloated from the weightlessness. He looked into her eyes as she tightened her grip. She made another coil around his torso and pushed the air from his lungs. Her dark eyes were small, deeply set in her skull, with almost no whites visible: animal eyes. Her opaque inner lenses slid closed, maybe to protect against the ensuing splatter of his bodily fluids.

She didn't offer him last words. Unceremoniously she forced the tip of a chest tentacle into his mouth and down his throat. He tried to bite down, to hurt her a little before he died, but his jaw had lost all strength. He began to suffocate. His vision blurred. She was ripping out his throat, or his heart. His chest would soon burst, coating the walls in blood. Screaming soundlessly, he jammed the wolf fang into her left eye. It stuck deep. Her grip clutched tighter; he felt several of his ribs crack. The room darkened. He heard a deep, furious roar. The tentacle was emerging from his throat, pulling something with it. Something hard scraped across his teeth. The dark egg glistened with blood. She was still screaming, plucking at what remained of her eye with two of her chest tentacles. He gasped, sucking in a huge breath. As she flung him away her writhing body shrunk. How could she be so small? Had she somehow flung him into space? He grinned, feeling gratitude toward Tem for leaving him a weapon. There was some pride to his death. The wall slammed into his back.

★ ★ ★

He came to as his head gently bumped into the wall. He was in the same room. The doors were closed and he was alone. He shivered. His entire body ached; his throat and chest were painfully raw. He wiped his mouth and the back of his hand came away red and wet.

All the warmth had left him. His mind was slow and fuzzy. Tenderly he traced the lump on the back of his head. At least three of his ribs were broken. He was dehydrated, emaciated, concussed, and in shock, but also *alive*.

What now?

He pulled himself along the wall to the wash cubby. Thankfully there was no mirror, but there was water. He rinsed his mouth, drank at least two liters, then wiped the blood from his face. His teeth were chattering so violently he was afraid they would chip.

"Ship. Can you increase the temperature of this room to twenty-five degrees Celsius?"

No response. A silly idea, but it was better than giving up. *Hang in there, Shane Jaecks. Keep trying things.*

The room contained his suspension chamber, still filled with clear gel. Why had she put him in there? Had he been in an induced hibernation, perhaps for years? No, there'd been no feeding tubes. The gel had provided oxygen, but no sustenance, not even water as far as he could tell. He'd been there for days – perhaps weeks if his temperature had been lowered and his metabolism slowed – but definitely not years.

The storage crate affixed to the wall that had contained his clothes was now empty. There was nothing else in the room. The walls were smooth carbonlattice, interrupted only by a ceiling grid of dim lighting strips and narrow circulation vents. Another prison cell, this one without even a cot.

So…he would die in here, bored and alone. He wished she'd just killed him and got it over with. At least he was warming up.

He'd stopped shivering completely, in fact. For an instant he wondered if the Crucible core was still inside of him, heating him from within.

No, the heat was coming from *outside*. The room was getting warmer.

"Ship, open the doors to this room."

The doors immediately slid open, revealing an empty hallway. He laughed, not quite believing his eyes. Was he really free? Tentatively he pushed himself off from the back wall and floated out of the room, into the hall.

His death might not be so boring after all.

"Ship, direct me to navigation." Umana's ship wasn't talkative, but so far it had done what he'd asked. Sure enough, the indigo lighting strips flashed to the left. He pulled himself along, listening carefully. Except for the low hum of the air circulators, the ship was quiet.

The hallway curved gently to the left. Was the ship stationary, drifting in space, or hurtling toward some destination at tremendous speed? The corridor took a sharp left. He peeked around the corner before proceeding. A guard in a black uniform floated toward him.

He raised his hands. "Sorry, I'm lost. My cell doors opened—"

The dead guard's eyes were solid red. Blood at the corner of his mouth had dried into a crust. His skin looked desiccated; he was partially mummified. Shane flashed back to his medical training; the injuries were consistent with massive internal trauma, or sheer force.

G-force. The ship had accelerated at a rate beyond what a human body could survive. The gel suspension had kept Shane alive, kept his lungs from collapsing, kept his brain from slamming into the side of his skull.

He nudged the guard aside with his boot and continued down the passage. For ten minutes he made slow progress, guided by the indigo lighting strips, passing through airlocks (each opened on request), and pushing the dead aside.

He found the Squid Woman in the navigation room, floating motionless. One of her chest tentacles was lodged deep in her throat. Dried blood surrounded her empty left eye socket. He watched her drift for a long time. Finally he pushed himself toward her. Tentatively he reached out and touched her pale, bluish skin. *Warm.* He yanked his hand away, sending himself into an awkward spin. He twisted desperately, trying to face her before the long tentacles captured him again and crushed him for good.

He recovered, catching himself on a control panel, and turned to watch her. She *was* dead. The egg must be inside of her, feeding off her corpse, keeping the flesh warm. She'd tried to remove it. *But why?*

What had she said? That she'd consumed other cores – other eggs – as a way to capture and enslave the virtualized personalities contained within them. And those multiple eggs, lodged in her body, each growing threadlike tendrils laced throughout her tissues, must have somehow kept her alive. Maybe the new egg, somehow different, had taken over and disrupted the thread network and other cores.

Several other uniformed corpses floated around the room. The ship had malfunctioned, accelerating at a lethal rate. He was alone in deep space, the lone passenger on a rogue ship full of dead bodies. What was the archaic phrase? *Out of the frying pan, into the fire.*

"Ship, where are we?"

Instantly a display panel lit up: a star map. He stared at it for minutes, trying to understand. There was Sol, clearly indicated. And there was bright Sirius. Closer: Barnard's Star, Alpha Centauri, Wolf. The display plotted a course toward a star approximately twelve light years from Sol: Tau Ceti. According to the display, the *Iarudi* had already traveled a third of a light year.

"Ship, what is our current velocity in relation to Earth?"

The display changed to a number: 5.26327c. The fifth decimal place wavered; apparently their speed was not perfectly constant. *Five times the speed of light.* How was that possible? He tried to recall what he'd learned about faster-than-light travel in his Academy physics classes. It had all been theoretical at the time: high energy X-rays and gamma rays, time dilation, even time travel. To travel faster than light would mean going backward in time, an impossibility. The details were lost.

The *Iarudi* would know. "Ship, how long, ship time, have we been traveling away from Sol? And how much time has passed on Earth during the voyage?"

The ship *did* know. He stared at the display, not quite believing what the *Iarudi* was showing him.

CHAPTER THIRTY-EIGHT

It was weird being back in school. At first Tem hadn't wanted to go; he'd asked Father if he'd had to. Father had shrugged (he was a newcomer here and didn't know the customs) and deferred to Shol. Morfar had told Tem he should go back when he was ready, and not before.

In the end Tem had only taken a week off. He'd fenced with Per Anders; he'd shown Father around; he'd hung around the apartment with Shol, cooking and eating and watching zero-G lacrosse games. Finally he'd gotten bored and gone back to class midday, without telling anyone. His teachers and classmates welcomed him back casually, without making a fuss. He guessed his classmates had been coached, but he was still relieved. He didn't want a welcome-back party.

"You missed a *lot* of geometry," said Marcus, during math workshop. "I can help you catch up, if you want."

"Marcus is actually decent at geometry," Zinthia admitted, in a rare show of graciousness. "I can help you too, if you want."

"How's Mr. Kan?" Tem asked.

"Doing better," said Zin. "He's still on sabbatical. I heard he was working in the greenhouses."

"Is he coming back?"

Zinthia shrugged.

"Have they...found her?" Marcus asked. "The Squid Woman?"

"No," Zinthia said. "Her ship just disappeared. The *Iarudi* can bend space – it's the fastest ship in the solar system. My dad thinks that it went too fast – that everyone on it is dead."

"She's not dead," Tem said. "She won't die until someone cuts off her head."

"That reminds me," said Zinthia. "My father has your knife. You can come over and get it whenever you want."

It would be awkward to see Zinthia's father, but he was no longer angry with Svilsson. Zin's father just wanted to keep him safe, the same way Mother and Father did. "Good. Can I come get it tonight?" "Sure. I think so. I'll ask Genta. But probably yes. Just come over and then we'll ask. Marcus, do you want to come too? We can help Tem catch up on geometry before dinner."

"Thanks, but I can't tonight," said Marcus. Then, quietly, he asked, "Tem, any word from your mom?"

Tem shook his head. "I'm not too worried though. I think she's probably all right. My mom is a lot stronger than I thought."

Father didn't mind that Tem would be eating with Zinthia and Svilsson. He said he might have dinner with Askr and Per Anders, and they would invite Shol too, as Morfar was learning Norse and was eager to practice.

When Tem arrived at Zinthia's spacious home, Genta already had appetizers laid out. "How is your father finding life on the *Stanford*?" Genta asked. Her dark brown dress was only a little darker than her skin, and if not for the vibrating orange stripes she would look nude. They sat at a table too large for the four of them. Svilsson was still in the kitchen, putting the finishing touches on what Tem suspected was a meal of only vegetables.

"He likes it. He misses Mother and he misses hunting, but he's impressed by the ringstation. He's seen it in the sky his whole life."

"Which does he miss more?" Zinthia asked.

"That's not a polite question," said Svilsson, entering with a large platter of roasted leeks and asparagus. Tem tried not to make a face.

"Mother, definitely. But he thinks the food is better on Earth."

"And what about you, Tem?" Svilsson asked. "Do you prefer ringstation life or roughing it in the mountains?"

"The mountains, I think. Ringstation life is too soft. But it's easier to make things here. That part I like."

"The fab labs you mean?" Zinthia asked. "It was fun building the arbalest."

Tem nodded.

"But I thought you were a budding smith," said Genta. "Will you be able to make a sword on the *Stanford*?"

"I have Squid Cutter now," Tem said, patting his hip. "It will be years before I can best Farbror Trond's work. In time I'll make my own sword."

After dinner Svilsson took Tem and Zinthia to his study and showed them the simulation based on Zoë's algorithm.

"What's wrong with it?" Zinthia asked, zooming in on a star orbited by two gas giants and a handful of rocky worlds. "That sun looks... frozen. Not *cold* frozen, but frozen like a still picture. What happened?"

"Complex brains happened, equivalent to Earth mammals, more or less," Svilsson said. "The higher intelligence level only exists on one planet, as far as we can tell, but that was enough to slow the entire simulation to a crawl, even with all the cores we've got running it."

"Can't you just add more cores?" asked Tem.

"It wouldn't make a significant difference, even if we used every core on the *Stanford*."

"That's too bad," Zinthia said. "I was curious about what might happen if you ran it long enough. Now we'll never know."

"It's actually a huge relief," said Svilsson. "Think what might have happened if the simulation hadn't slowed down."

"It might have been *amazing*," Zinthia protested. "It could have been like looking into the distant future."

"That's what scared me," Svilsson said. "What if Commander Umana was able to run the simulation, and see into the future herself?"

"Oh, that might be bad," said Zinthia.

Tem still didn't understand. Zinthia saw as much in his expression. "Weapons, Tem. Or other powerful technologies. She might have been able to steal them from the simulation, and use them against us."

"But she can't, right?" His heart was beating faster.

"Even if she was somehow able to extract the algorithm from the core, she wouldn't be able to evolve a universe beyond the most rudimentary of lifeforms."

"Like squid?" Zinthia quipped.

"Squid are complex, intelligent creatures," said Svilsson, "and I fear her moniker has done them a disservice."

"You're sure she can't look into the future?" Tem asked.

"I'm sure," said Svilsson, but he didn't meet Tem's eyes when he said it.

He watched the screen. The star slowly undulated. "It *is* moving!"

"What if *we're* in a simulation?" Zinthia asked. "How would we know?"

"We're not," Tem said. "We'd be frozen. Time would slow to a crawl, just like that star."

"Not necessarily," said Svilsson. "Even if we appeared to be living at a snail's pace to an external observer of the simulation, we would experience time normally."

"Time dilation," Genta said. She was holding a platter. "Who wants a chocolate-chip peanut-butter cookie?"

They ate cookies and talked until bedtime. Tem still didn't believe there was any way they could be living in their own simulation, but Svilsson stubbornly argued that it *might* be possible, and that there was really no way to know for sure. At the end of the evening Svilsson offered to walk Tem home. Tem politely declined. He wanted to be alone, to think.

He took a quickslide to Sub-1, a tram to Elon, then walked the rest of the way to Morfar Shol's apartment. Father was still out with Askr and Per Anders, but Shol had come home early. He looked tired but happy.

"Your father is a remarkable man," said Shol.

"What did you talk about?" Tem asked, plopping down on the couch next to his morfar.

"Your grandmother, mostly. He was curious about Marivic." Tem was silent. "Are *you* curious?" Shol eventually said. "You've never asked about her."

"I didn't want to upset Mother."

"Yes. I can see that. Would you like to see some pictures of your mormor?"

Tem nodded. Shol blinked a few times; the apartment screen lit up with a picture of a short, pretty, brown-skinned woman in a black dress. "That's what she looked like when I met her," said Shol. "Beautiful, isn't she?"

"She looks like Mother," Tem said.

"You think?" Morfar Shol was grinning ear to ear, and Tem was suddenly glad he'd come home to the ringship.

CHAPTER THIRTY-NINE

Once again they were gathered in the Shell. Only last night they'd met to accept Adrian's resignation and pay respects to the ex-Station Director. All of Vandercamp had been invited, but only a few dozen had shown up, and the event had been subdued. Few had known Adrian well. Lydia wondered if *anyone* had. Maybe Car-En had known him, once; as a student she'd idolized him. Lydia remembered more than one conversation from their Academy years when Adrian's opinion had been interjected into the conversation, unsolicited, as if Car-En were a proxy representing her advisor's 'big ideas' out in the world. *Adrian thinks….* Lydia had heard enough of that phrase for a lifetime.

So had Car-En, in the end.

Xenus had spoken eloquently and at length, calling Adrian bold, brilliant, forward-thinking: a visionary. Adrian Vanderplotz, gray-haired and ashen-skinned, accepted the praise quietly, unsmiling.

Last night no one had referenced the *Liu Hui* coup and occupation. It was as if those events had never happened, weren't *happening*. Everything was in flux, but the soldiers were still there. They weren't acting like soldiers; they were gardening and turning compost and shoveling shit into the bioreactors like everyone else – but they hadn't left.

She suspected tonight's meeting might concern that very fact. Despite the Shell's muted warm lighting, the atmosphere was tense. Xenus and Regis Foster had called the meeting jointly. She didn't know what was on the agenda; she'd asked that morning but Xenus had just offered her coffee and changed the subject. She was in the dark as much as anyone else.

Xenus had changed. She suspected hypomania, an overstimulated state falling short of a full manic episode. He was alert and energetic despite sleeping only a few hours each night. He'd been emotionally distant, unwilling to share his feelings or to listen to hers, insisting he was fine (no – not fine, *great*), and walking everywhere at half-again his usual pace. He had zero patience, snapping at her more than once for speaking unclearly or understanding something too slowly. It was as if he existed in a different timeframe entirely. She'd tried to broach the topic with him; would he submit to a neurological scan? She suspected lingering brain trauma from the hovershuttle crash and ensuing concussion. He'd rejected the idea out of hand. It felt like he was rejecting *her*. Despite her own ambivalence about the relationship (she thought about Shane constantly), the change in his behavior was jarring and disturbing.

Xenus approached the podium at a half jog. He exchanged a look with Regis Foster, who was sitting in the front row, but didn't look at her. Lydia had seated herself a few rows back, near people she didn't know well. The room was crowded but she didn't feel like socializing. She just wanted to learn what was going on and then return to the clinic. *When will things be normal again?* she caught herself thinking. Never. They were making it up as they went along. There was no normal anymore.

"Friends and associates," Xenus began. There was an intensity in his eyes and posture, though he spoke carefully, containing his fervor. "Thank you for joining me here. Tonight we will begin to decide our future, to choose our own course for this settlement."

Settlement. Not *research station.*

"As a community, we are at a pivot point. Recent events, whatever political machinations might have preceded them, have left us independent. We are our *own* governors. We're no longer part of the Ringstation Coalition. We no longer answer to the Academy, or Repop Council, or to any entity or individual on the *Stanford*. Nor, despite the presence of our new friends, are we in any way beholden to the *Liu Hui*."

He let the words sink in. There was some seat shifting and murmuring.

"Despite our independence, we have no constitution, no rights charter, no development plan. It's time to decide for ourselves what kind of community we will be. I have some ideas…."

Again, he waited. The Shell was silent. People wanted to hear what Xenus Troy had to say. His long pause was a question; the rapt attention was the response. *Yes, we trust you, we will follow you.*

"First of all, we need to decide what this place is called. 'AFS-1' was never a name, just a label. As for 'Vandercamp,' we could keep it in memory of Adrian, but I know many of you disliked that name. I'd like to ask for suggestions. You can call them out right now if you have ideas."

Regis Foster stood and faced the crowd. "I suggest *Troy*," he said in a booming voice. Xenus feigned surprise. They'd planned this. "It's an appropriate name," Regis continued. "Troy was a real city, not far from here, and withstood a decade-long siege by the world's most powerful army. Why not Troy? A vote of confidence in Xenus, if nothing else."

At the podium, Xenus was ready. "No, not Troy. Our settlement can't be named after a person...it's one of the reasons people found *Vandercamp* distasteful. But I like the idea of a nod to the region. Maybe another Mediterranean city."

"*Ilium*, then, if not Troy," said Foster, even louder.

"Ilium," Xenus repeated. "I like the sound of that."

The crowd murmured appreciatively. Other suggestions were called out, but none received such a warm response. There would be a vote. Lydia smiled ruefully; Xenus was a skillful manipulator. He was not well; she shouldn't judge him for his current behaviors. He would recover, in time. The egotism was a symptom of the mania; the mania a compensatory biological reaction to the brain trauma. *It's not really him.* But where did you draw the line? People *did* change, with age, trauma, experience... and sometimes they just *decided* to change. Maybe this was the real Xenus now, and she was pining for a past version that would never return.

The thought depressed her.

"Great, now we have some ideas," Xenus was saying. "Let's move on to another topic. Effectively, we've added nearly a hundred new members – our *Liu Hui* guests – to our community. But it's time to make their status official. Regis, you wanted to say something?"

Regis Foster approached the podium, grinning. Whatever he had to say, he couldn't wait to say it. Xenus stepped aside.

"Friends," Foster began, "I've thought about this decision for some time. The researchers at AFS-1 – Vandercamp if you prefer – greeted us and welcomed us when they could have fought us instead. We came to provide security and ensure independence, but we were perfectly aware that our presence might have been seen as an occupation...even an *invasion*.

"We were relieved it didn't turn out that way. No blood was shed. We put away our weapons and picked up farming tools. We exchanged our uniforms for work clothes. While the ringstations debated our fates, we dug in and helped this community grow and thrive. Some of us have formed relationships. I've heard rumors of a pregnancy. Whatever our role here, it's more than security. In fact, I'm ready to leave the military behind....

"I've decided to resign from the *Jūnshì*. If necessary, I'll relinquish my *Liu Hui* citizenship. I'm staying here, in Ilium – or whatever we decide to call ourselves – as a citizen of Earth. Soldiers, you are no longer under my command. Consider your next move carefully."

Foster returned to his seat, grin gone. Now he was pale, eyes downcast, shaken, as if he had only understood the weight of his decision by saying the words aloud. The Shell was again silent.

"I join Foster!" called a voice from the crowd. Lydia turned to see a tall brown-skinned Asian man standing tall, fist raised.

"I'll stay too! I resign from the *Jūnshì!*"

"I quit! To Ilium!"

The Shell erupted into yelling, fist-pumping, and cheering. Some were ecstatic, others stunned. Xenus watched impassively from the podium. When he next spoke his voice was amplified and reverberant. *Godlike.* It reminded her of the Squid Woman.

"Welcome!" he shouted. "Welcome to our community! We will need to put it to a vote, to make it official once we have a system for deciding such things, but for now can I see a rough show of hands? Who approves of welcoming any *Liu Hui* citizen into our community provided that they resign from the *Jūnshì?*"

Tentatively, a few hands went up. Then two dozen more. More followed, until a clear majority of the original research community had a hand raised. Lydia kept her own hand down. It was happening too fast. But *what* was happening, exactly? A reverse military coup? Xenus was grabbing the reins, but he was clearly proposing a democratic government. He'd be elected on the strength of his charisma and manic optimism; he wasn't coercing anyone.

It was too much. She left the Shell, pushing her way through the crowd.

Outside the night was cool and clear and smelled like damp mushrooms. She walked past the gardens and greenhouses and domes until she neared the landing platform. *What had brought her here?* Did she expect Shane to miraculously descend from the skies, piloting the Squid Woman's captured ship?

But there *was* a ship on the platform. Not the *Iarudi*, but a short, squat rocket – a mule. Someone was approaching her in the dark.

"Greetings!" A familiar voice, a man's voice, but whose? She couldn't yet place it, but her body relaxed; whoever it was, her subconscious mind did not consider a threat. "I'm here on shuttle duty."

Javier, from the mule station. He smiled and embraced her. She was surprised by the affectionate gesture, but hugged him back. It was a good, simple feeling, to trust someone – a feeling she missed.

"Have you seen Car-En?" she asked. She didn't mean for those to be the first words out of her mouth, but suddenly she needed to know.

Javier's creased brow was answer enough. "I heard about what happened," he said, "but no, I haven't seen her. I'm not sure if she'll return to the *Stanford*."

"She has to," said Lydia. "Her son is there, and her husband."

Javier sighed. "Do you know why she attacked Vanderplotz?"

Revenge, she thought. But was there more to it? What if Car-En's motive had been to protect? "I don't know," she said, which felt true. Car-En was fiercely protective of her son, of the people of Happdal, maybe even of Lydia. At some point Car-En had decided that taking matters into her own hands was the best course of action. Was it vigilantism? Vigilantism implied defying and overriding an existing justice system. Adrian had been operating in his own moral universe, outside of any official jurisdiction.

"What's done is done," said Javier. "If she returns to the *Stanford* I don't think she'll be prosecuted. This place – whatever it's called now – has declared independence, and the Over Council has acknowledged it."

"But *why?*"

Javier shrugged. "Maybe they didn't want to tangle with the *Jünshi*. Maybe they figured everything would sort itself out. Anything to avoid bloodshed…at least that's how I imagine the conversation went."

"I hope Car-En is okay," Lydia said.

"You know she's okay," said Javier, grinning. "Car-En can take care of herself."

Javier was probably right. Car-En was a survivor. But even if Car-En was physically fine, Lydia was still worried about her heart, her mind, her place in the world.

CHAPTER FORTY

"Tem, you're a man now!" Farmor Elke hugged him fiercely, then held him at arm's length. She looked the same; her face was weathered but still smooth. Somehow his grandmother resisted aging, even without rejuvs. Maybe her fierceness kept her young.

"I'm only ten," said Tem. "Just a few months older than when you last saw me."

"You look like a man," Farmor said. "A pale, soft man, but a man nonetheless. We'll feed you well while you're here…get some color in your skin."

"The food isn't bad on the *Stanford*."

"They don't have food on the ringship, from what I hear. Not real food."

"Where's Farfar?" Tem asked.

"In the longhouse, meeting with Esper and the others. He has much to report from his travels."

"Will Silfrdal and Vaggabœr be invited to Summer Trade?"

"We'll see, when the snow melts. Now go fetch your father so I can give him a squeeze. I don't like having him away."

Tem put on his coat and trundled out into the snow. It was strange to be…*home*? He wasn't sure if the word applied anymore. But he was happy. Tonight he would eat boar meat with his entire family and as many villagers who could cram into the longhouse. Almost everyone he loved was here in Happdal: his parents, all his grandparents (even Shol), and his aunt and uncle. Askr had returned for good, and Per Anders was here too, though Tem guessed he would return to the *Stanford* when Javier came with the hovershuttle.

He hadn't seen Farfar Arik yet. His grandfather had just recently returned to Happdal after months of trekking and visiting villages throughout the Five Valleys. Like everyone, Tem was curious as to what Arik had seen and heard on his travels. But mostly he just missed the old man.

Tem trudged through the dirty snow. The winter had been mild and easy. None had starved; the villagers had stored plenty and did not even look thin. But what if there was a hard winter, next year? Would the ringstations help the villages? Now there were connections between the Earth people and the sky people. Tem himself was a thread that held the two worlds together, as were Mother, Father, and Per Anders. Even Morfar Shol was family now, making himself at home in the village as if he had lived there all his life. No longer were the two worlds entirely separate.

Smoke rose from the twin chimneys of the longhouse. Tem walked faster in anticipation of the warmth of the open fires. A short man stood guard at the longhouse door. As he neared Tem saw that it was no man, but a tall boy: Hennik.

"They asked me to keep the children out," Hennik said. His tone was defensive, but not malicious.

"Then move aside," said Tem. "I'm a man now, Messenger of the Jarls from the ringship the *Stanford*."

Hennik held his gaze for a three count, then stepped aside. Tem had not lied; the Repop Council had assigned him the honorary title. He was of both worlds – who better? The council had honored one of Tem's demands: the *Stanford* now recognized the Five Valleys as a sovereign territory, and would not trespass without permission. As for the *Liu Hui*, the *Alhazen*, and the other members of the Ringstation Coalition, Repop could make no guarantees. But they had made their own position public. It was a start.

As Tem passed by, Hennik rubbed his nose.

The longhouse was warm and only a little smoky; the fires were burning bright and clean. Farfar Arik's voice filled the room. Hearing his grandfather speak swelled his heart; for minutes he listened only to the deep melodious tones of the jarl's voice. Eventually he began to pay attention, and listen to Arik's actual words.

"Hulda, the smith, is jarl of Vaggaboer. The village is not so far beyond Kaldbrek, only a day's march farther west."

"Hulda," said Gustav the cobbler. "That's a woman's name."

"Because she *is* a woman," Arik said, laughing. "And she would smite you down if you challenged her, Gustav. She is a good jarl, and will trade with us this summer. Vaggaboer is rich in furs and food – especially acorns – but will pay dearly for our cheese. They have no cows."

"Is it true that her sister killed a lion?" a man asked.

"Some sort of hunting cat, yes, but Jarl Heidrun lost her life."

"So their jarl is *always* a woman?" Gustav asked, shaking his head.

"Try to wrap your mind around it," Arik answered. "There are stranger things even in the Five Valleys."

"And what of Silfrdal?" asked someone else.

"Rich in silver, as their name suggests," Arik said, "but also a town of skilled glassblowers. They'll also bring their wares to Summer Trade. We'll see relics too – the children of Silfrdal scavenge Builder ruins with enthusiasm."

Tem jostled his way to the front. "And what of the *Stanford*?" he asked loudly. "Will you invite the sky people to Summer Trade? They have knives as light as air but stronger than steel, and a food called chocolate that will make your mouth water."

"Tem, son of my son!" Arik grinned. "I hear you have a new title. Does it come with any power? Come forward and say your piece."

Tem strode forward and briefly locked eyes with his aunt; Tante Katja leaned against a post on the far side of the room. "Not power," Tem said, "but responsibility. Should any jarl of the Five Valleys wish to relay a message to the ringship, I will help. I will visit Happdal twice a year."

"More than that, according to my wife," said Arik.

"At *least* twice a year, and always for Summer Trade."

"And can you name the jarls you wish to serve?" his grandfather asked.

"Yourself, Jarl Arik, of Happdal," Tem answered. "Jarl Hulda of Vaggabœr, Jarl Loke of Silfrdal, Jarl Jakob of Skrova, and Jarl Svein of Kaldbrek." The last name was bitter on his tongue.

"Wrong," said Arik, grinning with hoarded knowledge. "Svein is no longer jarl of Kaldbrek."

"He is dead?" Tem asked. He was not surprised.

"No, he lives," Arik said, "but he is no longer jarl. Young Saga challenged him and won."

"Saga, the black-haired *girl*?" asked Gustav, horrified.

"Yes, *two* women jarls," Katja snapped. "Say no more of it, cobbler." Gustav scowled but shut his mouth.

"I thought...." Tem faltered, not wanting to raise his aunt's ire. "Saga did not seem to have the temperament to be jarl. She is hot-headed." He glanced at Tante Katja but his aunt was still glaring at Gustav.

"She has *me* to guide her." The deep voice came from the corner.

Egil stood, stroking the forks of his beard with one hand, gripping his staff with the other. "Kaldbrek will join Summer Trade, and eat better next winter. We survived this season only because so many were slaughtered by the Squid Woman's spawn."

"You'll *feast* next winter," Arik said, "on Happdal cheese, and dried fish, and my wife's pickles, and fresh cold apples, and acorns from Vaggabœr, and—"

"Like we offered so long ago!" yelled Farbror Trond, leaping to his feet. "There is plenty of food in the Five Valleys. None need go hungry."

"Yes, Trond," Egil said, lowering himself with his staff, his piece said. Trond, face reddened, looked down.

Arik had many tales. He had seen giants from afar, and had discovered unfamiliar Builder ruins south of the Long Lake. Arik stopped numerous times to answer questions or to listen to the unsolicited opinions and proffered expertise of the other villagers, many of whom had never traveled more than a day's march from Happdal. When it was clear there would be no more talk of the giants, but instead a ceaseless discussion of which goods would be exchanged at Summer Trade, Tem retreated to a far corner of the longhouse, found a spot under a table near one of the fires, and – despite the din – fell asleep.

He awoke to silence and darkness. At least it was still warm. Everyone had gone home. Perhaps they were looking for him. He strained his ears but heard nothing; if his family was shouting his name their voices were lost in the snow. Tem lay in the dark under the table, enjoying the warmth and the silence and thinking about nothing in particular. Absently he wondered where his parents were. He wasn't worried. This was village life; they were close. He was safe here, with his kin nearby, under the table in the warm longhouse. For the first time in his life Kaldbrek was not a threat – Saga was hot-headed but not bloodthirsty like Svein, nor a cold-blooded murderer like Svein's father Haakon had been. And the Squid Woman was gone – Zin's father, Svilsson, had told him as much. Commander Umana might one day return in her sleek insectile ship, but the *Stanford* would see her coming. Maybe Shane had somehow killed her. He would hope...no, he would *believe* that Shane had slain the monster, at least until he knew otherwise. Maybe believing would make it so.

A loud scrape broke the silence; a great claw raked across the floor planks.

Tem rolled, stood, and drew Squid Cutter in less than two heartbeats. "Relax, boy, it's just me. The fire lulled me to sleep. As it did you." It was Egil, the Kaldbrek bard. The old poet planted his staff, which had scraped against the floor, and hoisted himself to his feet. "I'm not the same man since I ran down the mountain. My hips and knees ache all the time."

"See Ilsa for a salve," said Tem. "Better yet, come to the ringship and visit *Stanford* Medical. They can replace your bones and joints one by one if you like, and give you new blood that will make you young again."

"An old man with a young man's blood would be a dangerous thing," Egil said. "Old men are more cruel and selfish than the young. Only fatigue and forgetfulness keep us in check. Otherwise we would destroy the world."

Tem did not know what to make of this, and said nothing.

"Besides, if they replaced my parts one by one, would I still be me?"

"I think so," Tem said, "unless they replaced your brain. But I don't think they can do that."

"Why not?"

"They don't have any wood on the ringships. There are a few trees, but they're for decoration, not lumber."

Egil stared at him angrily, and Tem feared he had gone too far. But the fork-bearded man laughed, loud and long, and beckoned to Tem. "Come here, bellows boy, and tell me something. Are the ringship jarls to be trusted?"

He thought of Svilsson, and Penelope Townes, and the crafty old man Kardosh. "Some can be trusted. With others we should be cautious."

"Just like on Earth then."

Tem nodded.

"And you'll tell us which is which, I suppose?"

"Yes," Tem answered.

"They could destroy us with a single stroke, couldn't they?"

Tem shrugged. "The *Stanford* has little interest in war. The *Liu Hui* is better armed, but mostly peaceful, I think. I don't think we need to fear the Ringstation Coalition."

"Then what should we fear? Are there other monstrosities in the sky, like that tentacled beast?"

"If there are, I haven't seen them."

Egil grunted. "No solace."

"Life isn't safe," said Tem. That much he knew. In the last year he'd been kidnapped twice, come close to death three times. And he was only ten.

Egil raised a bushy eyebrow. "Wise words, for a boy."

"A man now. Farmor Elke said so."

Egil nodded, unsmiling, and in that moment Tem loved him for the respect he offered, even if Tem had not fully earned it. "A young *man* then," said Egil. "But still with a few things to learn from an old goat like me. Listen well...."

"You are the son of a man and a woman: Esper and Car-En. And they were each the child of parents, and so on, for hundreds of generations. That much you know. What you may not yet realize is that the hopes and fears and passions of your ancestors flow in your blood. The souls of men and women you never met push you this way and that. Their terrors are your terrors. Their strengths are your strengths. Their war and famine, their victory and ecstasy – that is the stuff of which you are made. You will pay debts you never incurred. You will reap the bounty of seeds you never planted. That is life, the inheritance of flesh and soul.

"I see that my words fly over your head like sparrows, but listen well and think back in twenty or forty years. Then maybe you will understand.

"What I've already said is just part of it. There is more to the mystery of the hidden will, the push and pull you feel from within but cannot attribute to any corner of your *own* mind. There are cycles, long and short, that make this world, and I think *all* worlds. Your friends in the sky see time as a line, do they not? Events occurring one after the other, in a neat row. But time is also a circle. Time goes around. Now there is snow, but it will melt, and things will grow. Then it will snow again. Earth was once full of people. Now it is nearly empty. But it will be full again, and then empty again. Time goes round and round. It is a line, yes, but the line curls around and eats its own tail."

"Like *Jörmungandr*," Tem said. "The world serpent."

"Yes," said Egil, "maybe you do understand." The old man smoothed one fork of his beard, then the other. "Let's get you back to your kin, before they worry. I'll not risk Elke's ire, even if you are a man now."

CHAPTER FORTY-ONE

Svilsson felt familiar hands on his shoulders. He tried to relax into Genta's touch, but winced when her thumbs dug into the muscle tissue behind his shoulder blades.

"Sorry. Wow, you're tense." She stepped away.

"I can't believe...." he said, turning.

Genta gracefully lowered herself into the woodish recliner on the other side of his study. "That she's getting away with it? She was three steps ahead of you. At least."

"You don't seem sympathetic."

"Quit whining. You were outwitted."

"Should we move to the settlement?" he asked, half-serious. "To Ilium?"

"Why? So you don't have to live in disgrace as an *ex*-council member?"

"Well sure, male pride is part of it. But wouldn't it be nice to live on Earth? Big skies?"

Genta laughed. "*Nice*. That's one way of putting it. Wild animals. Making your own fertilizer. Insects that suck your blood...."

Svilsson persisted. "Direct sunlight? No fear of decompression? *Real* gravity."

"Don't even get me started on pathogens. Viruses we've lost all immunity to. Parasites. Tem's friend, what's his name?"

"Per Anders."

"Look what happened to *him*. Brain riddled with mushroom spores. Poor fellow."

"The food must be wonderful," said Svilsson, palming his stomach. "So much more variety. And we could kill something and eat it — real meat."

He'd gone too far; she looked genuinely disgusted. "Sorry."

"You're not serious, are you?" she said softly. "Zin...her friends. Her *mother*, for heaven's sake."

"Zin might like it." He avoided her gaze. "Others might go too. It's the home planet – that has a pull for some people."

"For you."

"You're right though, it's not practical." He looked at her, saw that he'd scared her, apologized again.

"It's okay, you're working through some stuff. I'll make us some drinks. Zin will be home soon." She rose and kissed his forehead and left him to stew in his own thoughts.

Penelope Townes had skillfully played the backlash from the ill-fated *Operation Calamari*. Svilsson had been forced to resign from Repop. Relations within the Ringstation Coalition were at a nadir; even if agreements could be made regarding reparations to the *Alhazen*, trust had been shattered.

He'd planned to expose Townes, but she'd struck first. Any accusation he made now would come across as a petty, impotent smear attempt. Maybe in time, if he could ever persuade Car-En to corroborate, he could expose Townes's plan to use Car-En against Adrian, possibly even to murder him. But for the moment Car-En had made herself scarce. He assumed Tem's mother was in Happdal, but the department had pulled the Harz field researchers. He had no way of knowing.

Svilsson smiled, thinking of Tem. The boy's audacious approach had nearly gotten him kicked out of the council meeting. But Repop would honor one of Tem's requests nonetheless, simply because it made sense from a diplomatic standpoint. No more spying. It was a first step toward offering the Five Valleys full membership in the Coalition and a place on the new Repop Council. The new format would include all the ringstations as well as all the Earth settlements. The Sardinians would also be invited, as would the kibbutzniks and the Chhaang. The new communities would be expected to conform to the core ringstation values, especially the Human Rights Charter, but would also shape the Coalition, bringing their own histories and perspectives. Change was coming.

With or without the expanded council, Earth would repopulate with human beings. It was already happening – *had* been happening for decades, right under their noses. The Coalition would try to control human repopulation. They'd fail, but maybe they could provide a guiding nudge here and there. But toward what? Compassion, progress, the avoidance of strife and slaughter – the sky people's idealistic fantasies. Svilsson sighed heavily.

"What's the matter, Dad?" Zinthia stood in the doorway of his study, backpack straps cycling though a neon spectrum.

"Nothing, my love. Things aren't so bad. There's still air in the ring, right?"

"Last I checked."

"How was school?"

"Good. We built a radio transmitter. I miss Tem though."

"I know. I hope he returns soon."

"Will he? He might stay in Happdal."

"He'll be back. I've never seen a boy happier to receive a title. To be Messenger to the Jarls he'll need to spend time both here and on Earth. And his mother wants him here, I think."

Car-En was free to return. No one had actually *seen* her attack Adrian. More importantly, no one cared. Even if that changed, Ilium was its own separate jurisdiction now, with its own laws. He took satisfaction in that last point; Townes had been wrong to think that the settlement would return to being a research station under the department's thumb.

"Would you ever want to live on Earth?" he asked his daughter.

She shrugged. "Maybe for a while. Not for*ever*. Maybe for a summer?"

"You think we could get Genta to come?"

Zinthia pursed her lips and shook her head slowly.

"Maybe just you and I then? Would your mother mind?"

"Maybe she'd like to come too."

Svilsson raised an eyebrow.

"I don't mean it like that – I'm not trying to get you and Mom back together. It's just that she might like to see Earth. Most people would, I think, now that it's opening up."

"Opening up? Who told you that?"

"Nobody. It's just my impression of things."

He didn't press. People chattered; it made sense that impressions were already changing. There weren't many secrets on the *Stanford*. Mèng was making friends, accepting interviews; she'd spoken publicly about her encounter with the Chhaang. The consensual view that the repopulation of Earth would be orderly, and directed by the ringstations, already seemed quaint and naïve.

A message blinked in his m'eye: Petra from the OETS station. He opened it immediately.

Friends of yours? They'll rest the night and mule up in the morning.

The attached picture showed Tem, his parents, Car-En's father, and Per Anders, all looking rough around the edges.

"What is it?" Zinthia asked. "Why are you smiling?"

He sent the picture to his screen and showed her. "I haven't been weightless in a while. Want to greet them in the hub tomorrow morning?"

Her grin made him forget, for a minute, his ruined career. He'd find something to do. Maybe he'd assemble a team to develop Zoë's algorithm, combine resources among the ringstations. It would open things up for him politically, and more importantly, it could help repair relationships within the Coalition.

It wouldn't be dangerous with the right team, the right security precautions. The *Liu Hui* had some brilliant dev teams that might be able to speed up the later simulation stages. His earlier concerns now seemed paranoid.

"Can Marcus come too? He misses Tem as much as I do."

"Of course," he said, not really listening. Running Zoë's algorithm was an *opportunity*. More than that, it was a scientific obligation. He opened a feed to Karl Turen.

They would keep things under control.

CHAPTER FORTY-TWO

Lydia helped her last patient, an ex-*Liu Hui* soldier with an inflamed rotator cuff, and closed up the clinic. It was good to get back into the flow of work: doing what she knew how to do, making simple decisions, helping people. The past months had contained far too much excitement. Her optimistic side wanted to chalk it up to *adventure,* but her inner skeptic scoffed at the term. *Trauma* was more accurate. AFS-1 had defected from the *Stanford,* or had been invaded and occupied, depending on your perspective. She'd been attacked by giant mutant dogs. A centuries-old, prosthetic-tentacled psychopath had tried to kill her with guided missiles. She'd leapt out of a speeding vehicle. She'd narrowly dodged a communal orgy with the descendants of Nepalese refugees. She'd tried and failed to reconnect with an old friend. And all that added up to only half the pain of falling in love and losing Shane, feeling her hope fade day by day.

She applied a low-dose sedative patch – she allowed herself one a day – and wished for something stronger.

Of all the recent dangers and hardships, her thoughts lingered most on her relationships. She had finally come to some kind of acceptance around Car-En. For a long time she had held out hope that Car-En would reach out and apologize for being cold and distant. Lydia would forgive her. It was understandable, with all the strife and upheaval in Car-En's life, that her old friend would remain guarded, and be slow to trust. Maybe some of Car-En's anger was misplaced pain or blame in reaction to Marivic's death. They would reconcile, become close again. Car-En would thank Lydia for staying friends with Marivic and Shol, and for rescuing her from Svein. Maybe Car-En would even apologize for leaving the *Stanford* in the first place, for abandoning their friendship.

But that hadn't happened. Lydia was left to wonder what Car-En was thinking and feeling. She chose to forgive her anyway, and accept the relationship for what it was, or wasn't. Maybe their paths would cross again. Or maybe Car-En was now just part of her past.

She thought about Shane too, and Xenus. It was hard to think of one without thinking about the other.

★   ★   ★

Ilium was bustling. New domes were being built for the new citizens. They had a constitution and city charter now – citizenship in Ilium was a real thing – and efforts were underway to double food production. The *Liu Hui* folks attacked their chores with tremendous energy and purpose; even with so much to do it was hard to keep everyone busy. A few of Umana's soldiers had returned to their ringstation, but most had stayed in Ilium. Lydia suspected they'd had the same experience as the original AFS-1 researchers: despite a lifetime of living in space, life on Earth felt comfortable and familiar.

"May I walk with you?" It was Mèng. After weeks on the *Stanford,* giving interviews and watching the skies for the Squid Woman, Mèng had returned to the settlement. Mèng had not been welcomed warmly on the *Stanford.* Anyone associated with Umana was seen as responsible for the attack on the *Rama* and the abductions of both Tem and Shane. Her welcome in Ilium had been equally cool. The ex-soldiers resented her for speaking out to the ringstation media, selecting herself as *Kǒngbù Wúzéi* spokeswoman before checking with anyone. But who had they expected her to check with? Mèng had simply told the truth that needed telling.

"Of course," Lydia answered, looping her arm around Mèng's. They'd become close. Mèng helped out in the clinic some mornings. She had a nice touch around children; her quiet, reserved nature inspired trust and talkativeness. What Lydia had initially perceived as coolness in Mèng's character had actually been coolness under pressure. Mèng, rightfully, had been terrified of Umana. Now that her life was no longer in immediate danger, she had relaxed and opened up.

They walked in silence past the greenhouses, the Shell, fields of vegetables: carrots, beets, parsnips, spinach, and cress. Mèng broke the silence. "Avoiding home?"

"It's that obvious?"

"You and Xenus seem to live in different worlds."

"He's getting better, you know." Xenus's mania had faded as soon as Ilium's constitution and city charter were in place. His high mood had been replaced by melancholy and self-pity. Weeks later, glimpses of the old Xenus, cheerful and confident, were starting to reemerge, but she was still walking on eggshells.

"Good," said Mèng. "I'm glad the injury wasn't more serious. We were all lucky that day."

Lydia stopped, let go of Mèng's arm. "Lucky? We were almost killed."

"But we survived." Mèng stared. "Do you…do you *blame* me?"

Mèng's face was inscrutable. Was it a straight question? And *did* she blame Mèng? If Mèng hadn't defected, Umana would not have sent the lances. Xenus would never have been injured. "Maybe," she admitted, "but I should forgive you. I *do* forgive you. You did the right thing."

Mèng smiled thinly. "I'm not sure my ex-comrades agree. But I accept your forgiveness, and I apologize for putting you in danger when I asked you and Xenus for asylum."

They continued walking, Mèng a few paces ahead. They were approaching the eucalyptus grove where Shane and Lydia had met to discuss their escape plan. She should have insisted he come with them, denied him the martyr role. Responsibilities be damned – he would still be alive if he'd come. She kicked at a loose rock, sent it skittering dangerously close to Mèng's calf.

"Sorry."

They stopped and sat to watch the sunset, leaning against the smooth trunks of towering eucalyptus. The trees, bark peeling like paper, filled the air with a sharp clean scent.

"What do you think Johann is doing right now?" Mèng asked.

"Who?"

"Johann, the handsome Chhaang with the little beard." Mèng rubbed her chin.

Lydia laughed. The sound startled her. Had it really been so long since she'd laughed? "I'd forgotten his name."

"*Gut, ya?*" Mèng rubbed her belly and pretended to lift a bowl.

The absurdity of that encounter caught up with them. A minute later they were still laughing, cheeks hurting.

"That *was* a good meal." Lydia breathed through her nose, tried to catch her breath. "I think Xenus wanted to stay and see what happened."

"Didn't he?" said Mèng. Xenus had joined them that night on the balcony, but it had been later. She couldn't remember how much later; the details of that night were foggy; maybe she'd been slightly concussed as well. She'd been so excited to tell Xenus what she'd learned about the Chhaang – that there were multiple settlements, that there were probably hundreds of undetected human settlements on Earth in addition to the ones they knew about – that she'd forgotten to ask him what happened in the dining hall after she'd left. Maybe he'd had his own fun that night, just as she'd enjoyed kissing Johann. Maybe he'd taken things further. She felt a flash of jealousy.

"I'm in love with someone else," she said abruptly.

Mèng was silent until Lydia spoke again.

"But he's not here," she added. "I'm not even sure he's alive." She supposed Mèng knew who she was talking about, but she felt reluctant to say his name. It was better if everything was foggy, undetermined. Right now Shane's death was a probability, not a reality. She wanted to keep it that way.

"Do you still love Xenus?"

"Yes." She did. And not just because she'd felt jealous a moment ago – that meant nothing. She loved him because he was brilliant and kind and brave. She wasn't the kind of person to run away because of minor brain trauma. Xenus would heal – was *already* healing – and even if he didn't, she'd stick around. The awkwardness between them was temporary. She felt sure of it.

"It's okay to love more than one person," said Mèng.

Of course it was. But it felt good to hear it in a voice outside of her own head.

"I'm getting hungry." Lydia stood and stretched. "Ready to head back?"

Mèng was staring up at something. A black dot, moving slowly. Lydia's heart leapt.

"A falcon. No...." Mèng squinted. "A bearded vulture, I think. It must be nearly a kilometer up."

"Amazing," said Lydia, meaning it, her heart as full as it ever had been.

CHAPTER FORTY-THREE

The mule trips had become routine for Tem. Being weightless felt familiar, and it no longer shocked him to see the colorful planet (oceanic blues, lush greens, icy whites) against the vast blackness of space. He knew and anticipated each step of the docking sequence, the trip down the spoke, the sense of weight returning to his bones and muscles.

He was the first one out of the elevator as the port slid open. Zinthia was there to greet him. Svilsson stood a few paces behind his daughter, staring at a tree fern with such fierce concentration that Tem himself could not help but stare as well.

"Ignore him, he's been in deep space all day." Zinthia hugged him tightly. "I missed you so much!" Her affection caught Tem off-guard, but he hugged her back; he'd missed her too. "How is Happdal? How are your Earth grandparents?" She glanced over his shoulder at the rest of the party (his parents, Morfar Shol, and Per Anders) and looked disappointed. "When is your uncle Trond coming to visit?"

Never, he thought. Farbror Trond had cheerfully said as much. "He likes to keep his feet on the ground."

"I hope he changes his mind. I feel like I already know him. But I can't believe he's as big and strong as you say he is."

"He is!" Tem protested, but he had no way to prove it. He'd asked Mother if he could have a m'eye – just so that he could take pictures – but she'd forbidden it as severely as if he'd asked for a greatsword, or a battleskin. "Maybe you'll come visit Happdal someday."

"I'd love to," Zinthia said.

"You'd be whining about the food and the cold in two days," said Per Anders, tousling Zinthia's hair and nearly knocking her down. Svilsson, still staring at the fern, did not notice his daughter's distress.

"Let go of me!" she shouted. "I *wouldn't* whine! Not if I came in the summer."

"Any friend of my son is welcome to visit, any season," Father said, gently pulling Per Anders back.

"Don't I need permission from the jarls first?" said Zinthia, smoothing her hair.

"As Messenger of the Jarls, I grant you permission to visit Happdal," Tem said proudly.

"Shouldn't you check with Farfar Arik?" Mother asked.

Tem shook his head. "Farmor Elke wants me to visit as much as possible, so if Zinthia wants to visit – of course I'll come too – Farmor would make Farfar allow it even if he didn't want to."

Father stuck out his lower lip and nodded, finding no flaw in the logic.

"Already savvy in your duties, I see," said Svilsson, coming out of his reverie. "Welcome back to the *Stanford*, Tem. And all of you."

"Will you come to school right now?" Zinthia asked. "Classes will be ending soon, and everyone wants to see you. Especially Marcus and Tirian and Falder."

"How's Falder? Has he grown any?" asked Tem.

"He has, in fact. And last time we played soccer he was picked third."

This time around it was easier to get back into the rhythm of school and ringstation life. They all moved to a larger apartment, one with four bedrooms. Mother and Father shared one, Tem and Shol each had their own, and the smallest bedroom became an armory of sorts. Squid Cutter lived there, as did Father's sword, and Mother's battleskin, and Father's bow. (He would teach Tem to shoot properly this year, with both eyes open, the arrow on the pulling side of the limb.) The room was kept locked, coded only to Mother and Father.

"War is behind us," said Father, explaining the locked room to Tem as they walked home from the Academy one day. "And even if it weren't, you can't carry Squid Cutter to school."

"I'm glad I had it with me on the *Rama*. The day it earned its name, I drew her blood."

"And for that I'm proud. But weapons are for sport now, not killing. You have your fencing, and we'll start archery soon."

Tem shook his head. "I don't believe you. Otherwise you wouldn't insist on teaching me the proper way to shoot, fast and while running. The archers here shoot slowly, while standing still, with one eye closed.

That's good for hitting a still target, but useless for war. You want to teach me how to truly fight."

Father sighed, not denying it. He switched to Norse. "Your mother needs time to recover. Let us not speak of fighting and killing. She's had enough of that for many lifetimes."

Tem understood. For the first weeks home, Mother had spent most of her time alone in the apartment, reading or sleeping. She cried easily, yelled easily. Morfar Shol had suggested she get treatment. She'd said no, then maybe, then no again, but had finally relented. Now, some days, she was less fragile.

"What do they do to Mother at the clinic?" he asked.

Father shrugged. "Machines, drugs, talking, who knows what else. Such things are beyond me. But she's better, don't you think?"

"A little," Tem admitted. He thought back to the day on the ridge, Mother appearing from nowhere, scorching the Squid Woman's throat with her beam weapon. Had that day somehow hurt her? He didn't understand. She was a hero. Had it been him, he would bask in the glory and tell the story to whoever would listen.

"It wasn't the fighting, you know," said Father, seeming to read his mind. "It was losing you."

"But I'm back. I'm fine. I was always fine. I wasn't even gone that long."

Father nodded and patted his back. "Yes, you were. To us, it was a very long time."

★   ★   ★

Two months later there was a modest memorial service for Shane. The warp trail of the *Iarudi* had been analyzed to no avail; there was no sign of the ship, no visual or signal of any sort. The *Iarudi* and the Squid Woman (and Shane with them) were simply gone. The memorial was timed to coincide with the one in Ilium; there were shared feeds. Tem dressed in new, uncomfortable clothes. Mother said he looked handsome. Father wore new clothes in a similar style, and looked equally uncomfortable. Mother cried during the service, as did several others. Tem sat respectfully but didn't cry.

He did not think Shane was dead.

After the service there was a party at McLaren Park. From their field they could clearly see the gentle upward slope of the ring in both directions. As usual, the weather was comfortable, the air warm and slightly humid with only a slight breeze. The white-yellow 'sky' looked wrong to Tem. He missed the sharpness of Earth: the biting wind, the brilliant blue sky, the blinding white of winter snow. There was no shortage of color and green life on the *Stanford*, but everything had a warmth to it, and blended together softly. He tried to articulate his thoughts to Father.

"I know what you mean. Life is softer here, in every way. Yet more dangerous I think. Outside the hull it's cold, with no air, from what I understand. What if the ring cracked in two? We'd all die in moments." Father sat cross-legged on the grass, staring at the upper Earthside slopes.

Tem hadn't considered such a thing; the idea unsettled him. "We're safe, I think. The engineers are careful, as careful as smiths."

"And yet even Jense has a few crushed toes," said Father.

Tem wondered if he would ever work as a smith. His world was bigger now, but his original plan for his life seemed as good as any. It wouldn't be a bad existence, making tools and knives, stepping outside to breathe cold air and look at a blue sky. Farbror Trond was as happy as any man, with his chubby wife and growing family. Though he sensed he was different in some fundamental way from his uncle, and not just that he was smaller. Tem was *hungrier* for life.

"Look," Father said. "Your mother and Shol."

"What about them?" asked Tem. Mother and Morfar Shol were sitting on grass not ten paces away, talking about something. Mother leaned back on her elbows, legs stretched out. His Morfar, old but still flexible, sat squat like a child.

"Something has changed between them."

Tem looked but noticed nothing unusual. "What do you mean?"

"They act like father and daughter now." Father was grinning.

"Didn't they always?" Tem asked, but even as he said it he realized that Mother was different, less angry, less suspicious.

"What's that green drink called?" asked Father.

"Limeade?"

"Yes, Zinthia's mother – the black-skinned woman – I saw her put some on the table. Let's go get some."

Tem stood and led the way, not bothering to correct Father about Genta not actually being Zinthia's mother. He'd work it out for himself soon enough.

★   ★   ★

A year passed. Tem was now eleven. None of the jarls – not even Arik – had asked him to deliver a message to the sky people, and not once had the Repop Council called on him. He began to wonder if his title meant anything. One day at Zinthia's house he asked Svilsson as much.

"I'm not on the council anymore," Svilsson said, "but I think Kardosh meant to put you to good use."

"Then why haven't they called on me?"

"There's been no need."

"There are no more spies? What Car-En used to do?" He was trying to use his mother's name now, instead of just calling her *Mother*. It still felt strange on his tongue.

Svilsson frowned. "Field researchers, not spies. But no, or yes rather, we've honored our agreement, as far as I know. None have trespassed in the Harz mountains. Should there be a need for a delegation, the council will go through the official channels."

"Me."

"Including you, yes. But not only you. You're still a child."

He believed Svilsson, though he did not fully trust all the members of the Repopulation Council. Kardosh was cunning but honest. Penelope Townes was just as cunning, though she pretended not to be, and honest when it suited her. As Svilsson had learned, Townes could switch easily from friend to foe.

"Perhaps I should attend a meeting, to remind them that I exist."

Svilsson nodded. "They haven't forgotten, but that's not a bad idea. Would you like help with the attendance petition?"

"Yes."

"Tem, come here!" Zinthia yelled from her room. "I've got it working!"

"I have to go," said Tem, but Svilsson's attention had already returned to his screen.

*   *   *

A few weeks later, in fencing class, Tem beat Per Anders fair and square, with no tricks. Per Anders was still faster and had a longer reach, but Tem had memorized all of his opponent's habits. Per Anders overextended when he lunged and was vulnerable as he recovered his stance. Tem scored two points that way. His quick attacks were predictable, and could almost always be blocked with simple circular sweeps. Yvette disapproved of such clumsy, all-purpose defenses, but they worked against Per Anders, and for the moment that was what counted. The next two points Tem scored with a double disengage, used twice in immediate sequence, much to Per Anders's frustration. He won the bout with a deft stop-thrust as Per Anders charged wildly.

His opponent took off his mask. "Well done."

"You lost your cool," said Tem. Per Anders ignored him, flexing his foil against the floor. "Thanks," he added, remembering his manners.

"You're welcome. How is archery coming along?"

"Poorly. It's much harder than fencing. Father says I couldn't hit the side of a barn."

Per Anders scowled. "There aren't any barns on the ringship."

Tem explained the phrase. Even with the nanodrone therapy, Per Anders's brain had not fully recovered from the mushroom spore infection. He would always be dim. People were only capable of so much change. Still, Per Anders had made a good life for himself. He was happy. Tem was not sure if the same was true for himself.

"What's the matter, my young friend? A shadow crossed your face."

Tem shrugged. They showered, changed, and went to the gym lounge for a beverage. Only then was Tem able to articulate his thoughts.

"I don't know where I should be. Where do I belong? In the village, or on the *Stanford*? You've made your choice – you seem happy with it."

Per Anders grinned. "To me it's obvious, life is better here. Easier, for sure."

"I have responsibilities," said Tem, frowning. "Life isn't only about ease."

"Yes, you're *Messenger of the Jarls*."

"*Someone* should be, if not me," Tem protested. "Why do you mock me?"

Per Anders hit his shoulder. "Ease up. Don't take yourself so seriously. Yes, your role is important – I'll admit it. Perhaps I'm just jealous. I'm not destined for greatness, as you are."

"Greatness?"

"Hm-hmmm." Per Anders sucked his drink through a long straw. "You are a living bridge between worlds. You've been born into an important role. It's your choice what to do with it, but whatever you do will bend history this way or that." He slurped up the last of his drink. "The same isn't true for me. My own life is a story off to the side – not the main tale. Don't pity me though. You're right, I'm a happy man. I've made peace with my lot."

His friend's words didn't ring true. There was more to it than that. History was the past, but the story of the future was still being told. Anyone could choose to insert themselves into the telling with their actions and decisions. But Tem was tired from the bout, and had no energy to explain his view to Per Anders.

* * *

The week before he turned twelve, Tem met Zinthia at a park on Earthside Slope-2. A fifty-meter-wide rectangular port provided one of the most stunning views of Earth on all the ringstation. In the past months the *Stanford* had gradually relocated its geosynchronous position, and now overlooked the pale beiges and deep greens of the Americas. The glacial wall covered half the northern continent. The bottom half of the same continent looked bloated, bigger than the old maps Tante Katja had shown him. The ice sheets had sucked up much of the seawater, turning bays and shallow ocean basins into broad valleys.

They sat together on a garden bench and ate their picnic. They were in different classes now, and Tem found himself at Zin's house less and less in the afternoons. When he was there, Svilsson was often closed away in his study.

"Does your dad still like me?" he asked.

"Don't be stupid. Of course he does."

"He seems a little...."

"I know what you mean, but don't worry, it's not you. He's like that all the time."

"Are things okay with Genta?" he asked tentatively.

"Yeah, I think so. It's work stuff."

"What kind of stuff?"

Zinthia got up and wandered toward the willow tunnel. He followed her into the living tube of twisted branches. Even though Tem had grown five centimeters in the past six months, he could still stand upright. By next year he would be stooping.

"It has something to do with the search for other groups, I think," Zinthia finally answered. "That's why we've moved, you know, to look for signs."

"I know," Tem lied. He'd noticed their changing position – it was impossible not to – but hadn't guessed there'd been a reason for the relocation beyond changing the view.

"He's still in the anthropology department, you know. Even though he's not on Repop."

Tem's council petition had been granted. Repop had seen him, heard his questions politely, and answered while saying nothing, revealing nothing. He'd left the meeting frustrated and angry. Kardosh, Townes, Balasubramanian – they'd treated him like a child. Svilsson had been his only true ally on the council. For weeks he fumed. He'd remembered the hunger from years back, the need for power, the need to force others to respect him. Back in the village, when he'd still been a child, he'd felt that same hunger when Hennik had beaten him. Pieter had given him that power, until he'd earned the ability to stand up to Hennik himself.

Who would help him now? Father didn't care about the council, or even acknowledge their power. Mother was learning to relax; she didn't deserve to be pulled back into politics. Per Anders was dim. Svilsson was lost in his work, whatever that was now. Zinthia was a child.

Zinthia looked at him curiously. "You went somewhere. Where?"

"I was thinking about the council."

"Repop? My dad says they don't matter anymore. 'That ship has sailed,' he says."

"What do you think?"

She pursed her lips, narrowed her eyes. "I think ringstations are like the ancient gods...like the Norse gods of your own ancestors. They don't control fate, but they meddle in the affairs of humans."

"But we are humans," Tem said.

"Yes and no," said Zinthia. "We're a little different."

Tem, insulted, hid his feelings. He was of both worlds, and understood both village and ringstation ways. People were mostly the same. Still, he knew what she meant. From what he knew, people on Earth were wilder, and also more varied. There were exceptions – like the Squid Woman – but the generalization was true more often than not. Some, like himself, could live comfortably in either world. Others, like Farbror Trond, clearly belonged in one place and not the other.

"Maybe what it means to be human is changing, gradually," he said. "Maybe we're slowly becoming different species, like wolves and dogs." He'd learned about the domestication of dogs and cats in biology class.

Zinthia nodded absentmindedly, refusing to be drawn into his speculations. They sat in silence for a while, until she sprang to her feet. "Let's race!" Before he could answer, she spun on one foot and sprinted away.

"Zin, wait!" he yelled. "No fair!"

He ran after her, slowly gaining ground, feeling like a wolf.